Bone Appétit

**Center Point
Large Print**

**This Large Print Book carries the
Seal of Approval of N.A.V.H.**

Bone Appétit

CAROLYN HAINES

CENTER POINT LARGE PRINT
THORNDIKE, MAINE

This Center Point Large Print edition is published in the year 2011 by arrangement with St. Martin's Press.

This is a work of fiction. All of the characters, organizations, and events portrayed in this novel are either products of the author's imagination or are used fictitiously.

The text of this Large Print edition is unabridged. In other aspects, this book may vary from the original edition. Printed in the United States of America. Set in 16-point Times New Roman type.

ISBN: 978-1-60285-944-9

Library of Congress Cataloging-in-Publication Data

Haines, Carolyn.
Bone appetit / Carolyn Haines.
    p. cm.
ISBN 978-1-60285-944-9 (library binding : alk. paper)
1. Delaney, Sarah Booth (Fictitious character)—Fiction.
    2. Women private investigators—Fiction.
    3. Cooking schools—Fiction. 4. Beauty contests—Fiction.
    5. Cookery—Competitions—Fiction.
    6. Murder—Investigation—Fiction. 7. Mississippi—Fiction.
    8. Large type books. I. Title.
PS3558.A329B65 2010b
813'.54—dc22
                                                          2010029547

Bone Appétit

For Suzann Ledbetter Ellingsworth—
may your keyboard never stop clicking
and your pencil never grow dull.

Acknowledgments

First of all, I want to thank Rhonda Zion for the fabulous title. It's so perfect for this story. I am always amazed—and flattered—by the time and energy my friends and readers put into my characters and books. When I'm frustrated by my errant characters or a plot that constantly tangles on itself, I only have to remember the many people who care about Sarah Booth, Tinkie, and the Zinnia gang.

While writing is done alone, the final read-through is best done by someone with distance from the work. Suzann L. Ellingsworth has been invaluable. A woman of many talents.

Kelley Ragland and the entire team at Minotaur Books put the final polish on this book with their sharp eyes, great editing, and attention to detail. A good book is always a reflection of great editors.

My experiences at Minotaur Books have been wonderful, and part of this is working with Matt Martz in editorial and Anne Gardner and Sarah Melnyk in publicity and the entire marketing department. Professionals in every sense of the word.

And I love this cover! Hiro Kimura—what a fun and wonderful creation.

With each of my books, the sales staff has worked harder and harder. Talk about unsung heroes, the men and women in sales have gone above and beyond to bring the Mississippi Delta mysteries to the attention of booksellers across the board. Thank you.

My agent Marian Young has served as professional representative and so much more over the years. Therapist, friend, shoulder to whine on, and motivational speaker when necessary. Thank you.

I'd like to thank the booksellers who carry my books. Many stores have staffers who hand-sell books they love. How wonderful that my books are on some of those lists.

One of those booksellers (and a former student) is my assistant, Priya Bhakta. She has made my life easier with her great attitude, fun ideas, and smart actions. If you ever want to know what I'm up to, check out my Facebook page, where Priya keeps everything up-to-date and posted.

You can also sign up for my newsletter at my Web Site www.carolynhaines.com.

And because I love animals, please look at the Web Site www.goodfortunefarmrefuge.org. My friends and I are trying to find homes for stray cats, dogs, horses, and other creatures. If you have space in your home, please adopt. And be sure to spay and neuter.

1

Spring smote the Delta and fled before the onslaught of May heat. A thick haze of warmth hangs over the fields and the rivers, blanketing the land and the cotton bursting from the ground, green and vibrant. Hope is alive here, where farming is still a way of life.

To my shame, hope has died in me. The loss of my child, my potential son or daughter, has done something to me, and I'm afraid it can't be repaired. While the cotton is growing and my partner's husband, Oscar, and Deputy Gordon Walters have both fully recovered from the "plague" that nearly killed them, I have not fared so well. At least not emotionally. Doc says my body is healing fine. No permanent internal injuries, and my broken arm is all but mended. There should be no ill effects.

So what's wrong with my heart?

Dahlia House, my family home, echoes with loneliness. The familiar rooms are too big and empty in a way I never noticed. Perhaps this malaise of melancholy is hormone induced, as Cece Dee Falcon, my transgender friend who is an authority on the tricky role of endocrine chemistry, tells me. She assures me that my body will balance itself and that time will buffer this loss.

I wish I could trust her words. There are no known Delaney genes for moping, yet I can't seem to stop. Songwriter Jesse Winchester says it best, it takes "nothing to pity yourself—but it's dangerous fun."

Unable to endure the shadows of Dahlia House, I've taken myself outdoors into the heat laden with the smell of summer. The scent of this sun-warmed land—the taste of it—is imprinted on my DNA. These fields have been my solace through so many losses, but I find no comfort here now. I walk to the oak grove behind the Delaney Family Cemetery—the place I saw my dead mother in a dream or vision or visit from the spirit world. She assured me I would recover from this miscarriage. I hope she'll return today to guide me to that path, but I know she won't. She's warned me about lingering in the past, and she won't facilitate my melancholy.

"You're damn right, she won't!"

Jitty, the resident haint of Dahlia House, has found me. Jitty has the tracking abilities of a Parchman prison bloodhound and the fashion sense of Jackie Kennedy or, on some days, Carrie Bradshaw. Therefore I'm stunned by her white apron and chef's hat. Jitty does not "do" domestic, despite the fact she was my great-great-grandmother Alice's nanny and best friend. What she does do is tap into my private thoughts—a habit I find more than annoying.

"Don't badger me, Jitty, I'm not in the mood," I warned her.

"Pull it together, Sarah Booth. Tinkie will be here any minute to pick you up. You're packed and ready, so quit waffling. This trip will be good for you, and the Richmonds have spared no expense. Tinkie and Oscar are tryin' to bust you loose from the tar baby of grief. 'Course, instead of lettin' go, you keep pokin' in another appendage. Soon enough you won't be able to let loose."

"I'm not going to Greenwood."

"Says who?"

"Says me." My fingers brushed against the rough bark of an oak tree, igniting a tickle of childhood sensation, just a split second of the past. I don't want a vacation or a stay in a luxury boutique hotel. What I want is to time travel, to go back to a place where my parents are alive and I'm the protected and beloved child.

Jitty is having none of that. "Wrong. Tinkie has gone to a lot of trouble to plan this trip for you. From what I've seen, you can sure benefit from some cookin' classes. Girl, that handsome Graf Milieu is gonna wanna eat sometimes. Even movie stars got to feed the gullet on occasion."

"Then he can cook." My tone was reasonable,

cloaking the deep sense of loneliness brought on by the mention of Graf's name. He was my man, and I needed him beside me even though my logical brain knew he could not walk out on a movie. "At the moment, Graf is building his film career, and he doesn't care if I cook or not. Eating at Millie's Café makes me happy. She's a better cook than I'll ever be."

Jitty eyed me. "*I* would be happy—if you'd eat. You go up there and stir the food around on your plate. You look like an abused greyhound."

"Nothing like a compliment to make a girl feel better." That she was right only made me more morose. I did look unhealthy. My skin was waxen, and I'd given up shirts that showed my protruding collarbone. I didn't wear grief well.

"You want some compliments? Then go down to Greenwood and relax with Tinkie. Take your mind off things here. Have some laughs." Her expression became sly. "You can kill two birds with one stone."

"What two birds?"

"One, get away from here and start to heal your heart, and two, let your business partner take care of you. She wants to do that, Sarah Booth. It's selfish not to let her." Tinkie and I co-owned Delaney Detective Agency, but she was so much more than half owner. She was my closest friend.

She'd planned a vacation getaway for us to the

14

nearby town of Greenwood and the famous Viking Cooking School. While it was a ruse to pull me away from Dahlia House and my depression, it was also, as Jitty pointed out, a chance for Tinkie to care for me. Jitty was right, but the lethargy that tugged at my heart left me unable to move.

"Sarah Booth, only time can help you get by this, and pinin' away here, alone, is only prolongin' it."

Another point on Jitty's scorecard. I pushed away from the old oak. I had to fight this depression. I couldn't give in to it. The Delaneys were fighters, not quitters. "Okay."

The smile that spread across her face carried enough wattage to light up Dahlia House. "That's my girl." She fell into step beside me as we walked past the old cemetery shaded by cedars and toward the house. "Now focus your cookin' lessons on manly foods. None a' that froufrou stuff that don't satisfy. And remember, don't ever eat nothin' pink and foamy. Those are words to live by."

I stopped in my tracks. "Pink and foamy? Like what?"

"Like cherries or strawberries mixed with cottage cheese. Or none a' that pink mousse stuff." She shuddered. "Nothing crème-filled that's pink. Just take my advice and stay away from it."

I'd never known Jitty to have an anti-pink obsession. "There's more to this story."

"And I'd tell it, but your ride to vacationland is here."

Sure enough, I heard the crunch of tires on the shell drive. Though the house blocked my view, I knew my coach and driver had arrived in the form of a brand-new Cadillac with Tinkie behind the wheel.

"Have fun." Jitty swept off the chef's hat as she faded into oblivion—a trick I was determined to learn if I ever got stuck between Earth and the Great Beyond.

"Sarah Booth! Sarah Booth!" Tinkie's little fists beat at the front door as she called my name.

"I'm in the backyard," I yelled. I put my ass into gear and trotted around the corner of the house to meet my friend.

"Your chariot awaits," she said, waving at the brand-new tomato red Caddy Oscar had given her as a gift.

"Let me grab my bags."

A silver bowl of green apples centered the marble registration desk of the Alluvian Hotel. I sampled some iced peach tea in the lobby as Tinkie checked us in. Although I wasn't P.I.-ing, I did deduce that the Alluvian had a great dental plan—the hotel staff all smiled, displaying handsome teeth.

The lobby was quiet, a reflection of the noon hour, and cool, a tribute to man's ability to air-condition. A bar and restaurant branched off one side of the lobby, and a series of lounging areas were on the other side. Peeking into a room, I could imagine folks gathered around the grand piano in a far corner.

Across the street was the famed Viking Cooking School. Delta ladies entered and exited with shopping bags full of kitchen spices and the latest in equipment and gadgets. Tinkie and I were scheduled to take classes at the school in a matter of hours.

"Ready?" she asked. A bellman loaded our bags on a cart.

"Absolutely."

Tinkie offered separate rooms, but I'd opted to share one. After all, the point was to battle the loneliness, not give in to the desire to hide in the dark. The bellman took our luggage to the top floor, where a chilled bottle of champagne and a pitcher of orange juice awaited us in a room that gave a view of downtown Greenwood.

"The hotel staff thinks of everything, don't they?" Tinkie said, popping the cork with proficiency.

She mixed mimosas in crystal champagne flutes. Indeed, the hotel supplied a polished touch. She kicked off her shoes and climbed into one of the double beds. "So, we have our first class this afternoon. It's party appetizers. When we get home, Sarah Booth, let's have a party. We can show off our new entertaining skills."

"You assume I'll acquire some." The mimosa was delicious, and I settled onto my bed. The tension in my shoulders lessened.

"Oh, we'll both be prepared to dazzle guests when we finish this course."

From the hallway came a loud thumping and banging. Tinkie and I both started to our feet. What sounded like a scuffle ensued, and someone pounded on the door of our room. Before we could react, the door flew open and two beautiful young women tumbled in. They were almost buried in luggage, which they unceremoniously dumped to the floor.

"Who put us in the same room?" the brunette growled.

"I'm going straight to the desk." The blonde picked up a huge suitcase and tossed it into the hall where it slammed against something—or someone.

Tinkie calmly put down her drink and picked up the telephone. She punched in the number for the front desk. "Yes, this is Mrs. Oscar Richmond. We have intruders in our room. Please come immediately." She hung up with a smile.

Both young women finally realized they had

an audience. They stood, luggage up to their thighs, and stared at us.

"Who the hell are you?" the brunette asked.

"Tinkie Bellcase Richmond." She hoisted her drink as if in a toast. "Don't bother with your name. You won't be staying long enough for me to give a damn." She settled back onto the bed. Tinkie had taken an instant dislike to the women, which was unusual for her.

The brunette rose to the challenge. "Wanna bet? We'll have those beds stripped and you out on your ass before the flies can settle on you."

The blonde, petite and wide-eyed, put a restraining hand on the brunette. "Calm down, Karrie."

Karrie shook her off. "Don't touch me, you country-fried hick. If this old bat wants a fight, I'll give it to her." Karrie, whoever she was, had seriously misjudged Tinkie. While my partner was short, she could kick ass like a Spartan.

Tinkie slid to her feet. She was a good ten inches shorter than Karrie, but she was undaunted. Tinkie and her eight-ounce dustmop dog, Chablis, had more courage and spunk than a busload of gang members. "Who, exactly, are you calling an old bat?" she asked, advancing.

I snapped to, aware that for the last three minutes I hadn't been depressed at all. "Hold on,

Tink," I said. I fell in beside her. If there was going to be a hair-pulling, Tinkie and I were going in together.

The blonde stepped between Karrie and Tinkie. "Stop it. We obviously have the wrong room." She pushed Karrie's bags toward the door. "Let's go to the desk and get this straight. I want another roommate, anyway."

Karrie wasn't ready to back down. She glared at Tinkie. "Do you have a daughter in the contest? You're too old to cut the competition."

"I may have a few years on you, honey, but genetics tell all," Tinkie said. "Your bone structure gives it away—some combination of Snopes and Wicked Witch of the West."

"What contest?" I couldn't help myself. I felt like my earlier wish had been partially answered and I'd fallen backward in time to high school. I'd actually been aiming for grammar school, but time travel is hard to predict.

"The Miss Viking beauty contest and spokesperson competition," the blonde answered with a world-weary roll of her eyes. "The finalists are here this week for the cook-off and the runway talent contests. The winner gets a $200,000 contract to serve as Viking spokesperson and travel the world, not to mention scholarships and potential endorsements of food products worth millions."

"Fascinating," Tinkie said.

"I'm Crystal Belle Wadell." The blonde made it clear the rhyming of her name caused her much grief. "That's Karrie Kompton." She pointed at the brunette. "She's already way ahead in the Bitch on Wheels category and she's about to win the Most PMS-ing title."

"I see," Tinkie said in a droll tone that told me Crystal Belle had amused her.

"Ladies, you obviously have the wrong room. Best to take this up with the desk." I'd enjoyed the fireworks, but now I was done with it.

And just in time, two hotel staffers appeared in the doorway. In a matter of moments, Karrie and Crystal were assisted down the hallway. A door slammed and loud complaints blasted from both women as the hotel staff did their best to resolve the roommate issue. From what I overheard, the lodging decisions had specifically been made at the request of the contest manager —someone with a wide streak of sadism or who'd perhaps grown weary of the spectacular bitchiness of Karrie Kompton. I felt a brief second of pity for Crystal Belle.

"Surely all the contestants can't be that awful," Tinkie said, somewhat echoing my thoughts.

"Might be worth catching the talent competition if it's being held locally."

Tinkie's face lit up. "Excellent idea. I'll check at the desk for tickets or information. For now, let's have a facial. The spa across the street has

21

this to-die-for facial. Then we're on to appetizer school at four o'clock."

She babbled happily about beauty products I'd never heard of as we refilled our glasses with mimosas and ambled across the street for a full beauty treatment.

2

Even I, a non-cook, was dazzled by the Viking Cooking School. I donned my apron and stood surrounded by state-of-the-art appliances that actually had me thinking of whipping up a batch of . . . well, nothing specific came to mind, but I wanted to create some magnificent edible concoction. Such is the power of fancy tools. I couldn't help but wonder if the same would apply if someone put a really nice drill into my hands. Would the urge to "do" carpentry come with the tool?

"Earth to Sarah Booth! Earth to Sarah Booth!" Tinkie tugged at my sleeve. "What in the world are you thinking?"

"About carpentry," I admitted.

She shook her head. "Don't even try to explain." Her smile told me that whatever my mental deficiencies, I looked more relaxed. She gave me a big hug. "Let's make those appetizers."

I'd never considered appetizers had a history, so it was interesting to learn the Athenians introduced the first hors d'oeuvre buffet. Even more fascinating was the concept that appetizers are meant to *whet* the appetite. I'd always assumed they were designed to keep guests from chowing down like porkers at the main course.

Tinkie, of course, was a scholar in this field. We chopped, blended, whirred, and designed our Bouche Cream Cheese Prosciutto into elegant scoops nestled in crystal star-shaped holders and garnished with cross-cut cherry tomatoes. We then turned our hands to Miniature Quiches as light and delicate as the flowers they resembled. During the process I watched Tinkie with pleasure. She loved to cook—as long as it wasn't part of her job description. She cooked for pleasure, not necessity, and her parents and Oscar provided her a life that allowed such an attitude. Tinkie had married well.

To my surprise, the class was a total delight. When we finished, Tinkie and I headed back to the Alluvian and a revitalizing cocktail. The hotel bar was jammed with beautiful young women, and we found a table in the corner and sat back to watch the interaction.

Karrie held court at the bar, surrounded by a half dozen well-dressed men who did everything except chew her martini olive for her.

Beauty is a powerful weapon, and those men had been mortally gaffed. They hung on Karrie's looks, flirtations, and expressed whims.

A dark-haired woman, half in shadows, sitting alone in the farthest corner of the bar, caught my attention. Black eyebrows over china blue eyes, delicate cheekbones, and full lips—she looked like a movie star.

"Who's that?" Tinkie asked.

I shook my head. "Never saw her before, but she is striking."

"She's got a burn on for Karrie Kompton." Tinkie, too, had observed the way the dark stranger's gaze drilled holes in Karrie's back.

"Somehow, I can understand that." We clinked our glasses in a toast.

"Think she's part of the beauty pageant thing?" Tinkie asked.

"Yeah, I'd say so. The other women seem to know her, but I wonder why no one is sitting with her."

"Maybe she has cooties," Tinkie said.

"And I thought we'd been time-warped back to high school. Now I see we've regressed all the way to second grade, where classmates are infested with that legendary parasite."

"Seriously," Tinkie said. "I've been watching the interaction. The other girls act like they're afraid of our Dark Stranger."

I signaled the barkeep for another round of

cosmopolitans. Despite Jitty's admonitions, we were drinking pink in honor of Cece Dee Falcon, who would join us as soon as she finished a deadline at the *Zinnia Dispatch*, where she was society editor and chief investigative reporter. It was an unusual combination of journalistic work, but then all the best crimes in the Mississippi Delta involved high society. She had the background knowledge on debutants and debuts, soirées, socials, engagements (broken and otherwise), marriages (those that held and those that didn't), and other information crucial to a good juicy story when a crime spree broke out amongst the landed gentry.

Cece had also been a part of the landed gentry until she went to Sweden and had the part of her that bore the name Cecil permanently excised. Her family had disowned her, but Cece carved out a new life for herself from the ruins of her old one. She had strength I could only envy.

The bartender brought our drinks, and Tinkie motioned him closer. "Who's that woman in the corner?" she asked.

"Hedy," he said without hesitation. "Really nice gal, unlike some of the other contestants." He glared at Karrie's back. "Some of these girls think the whole world spins in an orbit around them."

Before he could collect our empties, a bouquet

of white roses as wide as the doorway waddled into the room on two human legs.

"Karrie Kompton?" a rough, low voice said from the midst of the flowers.

"For me?" Karrie squealed with the best sorority girl abandon I'd heard in years. "Oh, look, everybody, someone sent me flowers."

While the bartender rushed over to help the deliveryman put the flowers in a safe place, Karrie snatched the card and ripped it open. Her face flushed with pleasure, and she tapped her glass with a cigarette lighter to make everyone hush.

"Everyone! Shut! Up! I want to read my card." She cleared her throat. " 'A gift for the fairest princess in the land. Knock 'em dead.' " She fluttered the note and squealed again. "It's signed, 'Your secret admirer.' Isn't that just the best? A secret admirer. It's so . . . romantic."

The deliveryman produced a giant box and handed it to Karrie. "This is also for you." He stood a moment and when it became clear she had no intention of tipping him, he gave her a disgusted look and left.

One thing about Karrie Kompton: She knew how to play a moment to the hilt. She held out the box, shook it lightly, and then very carefully untied the pink organdy ribbon that adorned an ornate, foil-stamped, fuchsia box. Chocolates were my guess.

26

When she lifted the lid, instead of a squeal, she sighed with pleasure. "Look at this. I've never seen chocolates like this before. They're so big and dark and expensive looking."

The girls and male admirers all leaned in to examine the box. Even after eating a dozen or more appetizers, I couldn't stop my mouth from watering. Chocolate was definitely my weakness, and Karrie had the ability to make others want what she had, even a box of candies. I waited for her to pass them around to her friends. Instead, she picked one out and held it up for all to see.

"It's like a chocolate shell," she declared, turning it this way and that. "And stamped onto the top is an exact replica of the crown I'm going to win. These had to have been handmade just for me."

"Eat the damn thing or put it down," Crystal Belle Wadell finally said. "You aren't going to share, so just eat it and shut up about it. Brook, Janet, Gretchen—let's go find out about our schedules."

The four young women stood.

"Jealous because I have a secret admirer?" Karrie taunted. Her laughter danced around the room. "I'll bet this is a gift from one of the judges."

The audacity of her statement made Tinkie's eyes widen. "What an instigator she is," Tinkie whispered. "I'm surprised one of the other contestants hasn't whipped her ass."

"The night is still young." I sipped my drink as Karrie teased the other contestants with her flowers and candy. She had a genuine talent for torment, and everybody in the bar, including Tinkie and me, couldn't stop watching. Whatever Karrie lacked in kindness, or even basic human decency, she made up in spades with the ability to mesmerize an audience.

Two women stepped into the bar, one a bit older than me and the other obviously one of the contestants. Pale and elfin, she had an ethereal quality. When she turned around, I checked to see if she sported fairy wings. Whoever she was, she was lovely. And the older woman was attractive, too. The possibility that they were sisters crossed my mind.

"Amanda, let's order something in the room," the older one said.

"I want to stay here, Mother."

My relationship questions were answered. Mother and daughter. If I were a beauty contestant, I'd want my mother with me for moral support. Hey, given my druthers, I'd have my mom around for all occasions.

Karrie reclaimed the floor as she eased the candy to her mouth. She did it slowly, playing to her audience. She placed her perfect white teeth on the delicacy, and then she slowly bit the candy in half.

To my utter horror, the half she still held in her

hand began to move. Hairy legs protruded, and the back half of a giant cockroach fell onto the bar and began crawling crazily around. Headless, it had no sense of direction.

Karrie froze. She stared at the half-a-roach, which wouldn't accept its own death. The most intriguing expression passed across her face, and then she spat chocolate and roach all over the bar.

Shouts, shrieks, and screams of laughter erupted. Pandemonium ruled. Tinkie and I stood on our chairs for a better view of a fistfight between several of the contestants. Women shoved and trampled one another to get away from Karrie. Ingeniously, Tinkie clicked photos of the mayhem with her cell phone.

Someone pushed the candy to the floor, and in the melee, people stepped on the chocolates, freeing more roaches that had survived being dipped in chocolate and were understandably pissed off. The area around Karrie was an expanding disaster.

"Holy Christmas." Tinkie was having a blast. "Can you believe that? Someone sent her chocolate-covered roaches. That is too creepy." And then she burst out laughing. Karrie didn't generate a lot of sympathy. At least not from Tinkie. Or me. I was enjoying the spectacle as much as she was.

I looked over to see Hedy's reaction. She was

gone. As were the mother-daughter duo. The roaches sent a lot of people scurrying, but a team of Alluvian staff arrived to work damage control.

"How hard would it be to chocolate-coat a roach?" I asked. "Maybe just heat a little chocolate—"

"You wouldn't even have to do that. There's a product that hardens instantly on cold surfaces. Someone froze those roaches—like fishermen do catalpa worms—then coated them in chocolate and got them over here before they thawed enough to eat their way out of the shells."

"Someone really doesn't like Karrie Kompton." My smile was painfully wide.

"We'll have to remember this. The day might come when we want to make our own chocolate delivery." Tinkie loved mischief.

We raised our glasses and drained them. "Thank you, Tinkie. This was exactly what I needed."

We'd just ordered another round when Tinkie's cell phone rang. Cece had been delayed at the newspaper and would come the next evening for sure. When Tinkie relayed the roach episode, Cece wanted Tinkie's photos for the newspaper.

Tinkie held the phone so we could share it. "Cece wants to hire us to cover the beauty contest until she gets here."

For some reason, that appealed to me. "Sure."
"We're on," Tinkie agreed into the phone. "I'll get someone to help me send the photos from my phone. And, yes, we'll buy a better camera."

My aunt Loulane, my father's sister, cared for me after my parents died in a car wreck when I was twelve. She was a Southern cook who could make a table groan under the weight of ham and sweet potatoes or cheese grits and homemade biscuits. There was not a day when I came in from school that a hot dewberry cobbler or a fresh apple pie wasn't cooling in the kitchen window. She fed me like a prize steer headed for the state fair.

She mentored me in table manners, but she never taught me the basics of cooking. In my second class at the Viking Cooking School, I did my best to strain a lumpy mass of butter and flour through cheesecloth. I conceded that just because I could sometimes make Sawmill or Redeye Gravy, I had not mastered the French "sauce." In my own defense, my stiff arm impeded my work. The break I'd suffered in my last case had healed at warp speed. Nonetheless, the arm was weak.

The "saucier" directing the morning lesson was a kind woman, but I could read my failure in her eyes. I managed to retain some facts: A famous French chef had categorized sauces into four families, each based on a mother sauce—béchamel, espagnole, velouté, or allemande. I hadn't mastered the art of creating any of them, but I was learning. There were white roux, blond roux—some based on milk or brown stock, some requiring egg yolks and heavy cream as a binding agent. By lunchtime, my head was spinning with the many aspects of sauce.

"Taste mine," Tinkie said.

I glared at her simmering pan of béchamel. It was neither lumpy nor watery. It was perfect. And it tasted good, too.

Covered in splotches of food, my apron askew, and my chef's hat sunk low to my eyebrows, I was relieved when the class was done.

Tinkie's cell phone rang. "Cece, darling," she said, talking as we left the cooking school behind and stepped onto the downtown Greenwood street. She grabbed my uninjured arm. "The photos made the front page of the paper! Cece said everyone is calling in to say how great the story is."

I gave her a thumbs-up. This vacation was something Tinkie and I both needed. My depression was still with me, but it had receded due to the frontal assault of fun and good cheer Tinkie aimed at it. I'd fallen out of my life and I didn't know how to get back in, but the distance no longer seemed insurmountable. I was finally starting to heal emotionally, as Jitty predicted.

While Tinkie chatted away, giving Cece a blow-by-blow of her successful sauce morning, I took in the scenery. Greenwood had once been the heart of cotton production in the landlocked portion of the Delta. The cotton was ginned and baled here and then taken by rail to Greenville on the Mississippi River, where it was shipped far and wide.

Greenwood's streets were paved with bricks, and railroad tracks crisscrossed the town. Both the Yazoo and Sunflower rivers swirled around the city, which boasted some of the finest antebellum "town" houses—in contrast to the working plantations—in the South. But Greenwood had fallen on hard times in recent years, like much of the Delta. The twenty-first century hadn't been kind to agrarian cultures.

The Delta city was rebudding, though. The Viking Range headquarters, the Alluvian, the blossoming of Turnrow Books were all signs of downtown revitalization. Life had touched this Delta town, as it had Dahlia House. And me.

Tinkie took off to find a digital camera with a telephoto lens, and I went back to the hotel room and placed a call to Graf. They were wrapping the Western he was shooting in Northern California, and I hoped to catch him on lunch break.

In the four weeks since I'd been so savagely attacked during my last case, Graf had been back to Zinnia twice and called every day. He was worried about me. All of my friends were concerned—Graf more than anyone else.

"Hey, baby," he said. "How's cooking school?"

"I'm hell on appetizers, but sauces have whipped me."

"Ah, a pun. A bad one, but an attempt at humor is welcomed. This sounds hopeful." His voice, filled with relief, was supersexy.

I related the chocolate-roach incident and had him howling with laughter. I promised to get Tink to e-mail the photos to him.

"Your friend is a genius," he said. "This is exactly what you needed, Sarah Booth. You sound like your old self."

"I'm better." A lump formed in my throat. "It's difficult. But I'm getting better."

"Whenever you feel up to coming out here, there's work waiting."

Panic squeezed my chest. "Not yet." I wasn't ready to try acting again. While my movie career wasn't responsible for all that had happened, it had been the initiating factor. Or so it seemed.

"There's all the time in the world," Graf said softly. "I don't care if you never make another film. I want you to be with me, working or not. I love you."

"And I love you." I turned the diamond ring on my left hand. "I miss you." His absence was like a toothache, a low-key, throbbing pain. But sometimes, especially when I woke up in the middle of the night alone and scared, it was a sharp and angry sensation.

"They're calling us back to the set. Another few weeks and I'll be done. Maybe we could take a trip to Europe. Didn't your friend Lee tell you about a horseback ride up the western coast of Ireland? That would be incredible."

"You have an excellent memory."

"Check it out and see if it would interest you. I want to spend some time alone with you in a beautiful place."

"I'll hold you to that." When I hung up, I caught my reflection in the mirror. I was smiling, and it felt good.

3

"Quit wiggling!" Tinkie tucked in the straps of the new dress she'd bought me while she was supposed to be shopping for a camera. The apple green dress fit me like a glove. Both Tinkie and Cece had the shopping gene. Alas, I did not. But then I didn't need it because my friends were happy to make sure my wardrobe met their high standards.

A knock on the hotel room door drew an exclamation of pleasure from Tinkie. "Cece is here!" She threw open the door to reveal our journalistic friend, already dressed for the occasion. We were attending the "Poise and Confidence" segment of the beauty pageant. Evening dress was de rigueur. Since I wasn't in the habit of traveling with a formal gown, Tinkie had provided one. She'd packed six large suitcases with everything she'd need for a summer season with the Royal Family.

"You look marvelous, Sarah Booth, dahling." Cece air-kissed both my cheeks and then Tinkie's. "And you, Tinkie Richmond, are stunning."

Tinkie wore a midnight blue velvet gown that plunged low in front and laced down the back. With her glitzed blond hair she was glam.

"You don't look too shabby yourself," I told Cece, whose russet gown showed her slender hips to advantage. "Are the dogs behaving?" Oscar was keeping my hound, Sweetie Pie, along with Chablis. Cece had promised to check on them every day.

"Living the life of pampered pooches. Oscar has been riding them to get ice cream. I see them parked in the drive-thru window of the Sweetheart Café. He gets two cones, one to share between the dogs, and one for himself."

Oscar had once had me convinced that he

didn't give a damn about Chablis. Either his heart had changed or he'd deliberately covered up his affection for the little Yorkie that masqueraded as Tinkie's dog/child. Sweetie Pie was a red tic hound I'd acquired on my first case. I would never have had a second case had it not been for Sweetie's intervention. Likewise, Chablis had saved my bacon more than once.

"Are we ready, ladies?" Tinkie clutched her sequined bag.

"Let's do it."

As we rode to the auditorium, we filled Cece in on what we knew about the contestants. The driver tried not to laugh when Tinkie gave her rendition of Karrie biting into the chocolate roach. Apparently, Karrie's personality had been inflicted on almost all of the service staff of the hotel.

"And this Hedy woman is a mystery," Cece said. "I went through the list of contestants and did a little research."

"Spill!" Tinkie said.

"That's the problem," Cece said. "There's nothing. She's twenty-two, graduated high school in a tiny town on the Pearl River near the Louisiana line, and just . . . nothing."

"She's only twenty-two," Tinkie pointed out.

"All the other girls list modeling jobs, dramatic roles in community theater, job titles and positions, even if they're made up."

I saw Cece's point. A young woman vying for a job as spokesperson would want any and all experience dealing with public situations front and center on a résumé.

"She did appear to be a loner," I said.

"Anything else?" Tinkie asked.

"There's a young woman named Amanda Payne. She always travels with her mother, Voncil Payne, who was a runner-up in the late 1970s for the Miss America title. Voncil and Amanda have worked the beauty pageant circuit since Amanda was old enough to sit up and have her photo taken."

"That's a hard life for a kid," Tinkie said.

"Thank goodness our parents didn't push us into that," I said.

Cece and Tinkie burst out laughing.

"And what's so funny about that?" I demanded.

"Sarah Booth, your mother couldn't make you wear a slip, much less a pageant dress. Don't you remember how you'd tear your petticoat off behind the church and stuff it in that old pecan tree? You were the scandal of the entire Methodist congregation."

"I was only six! The slip scratched."

Cece leaned across the van seat and whispered in my ear, "One has to suffer for fashion, dahling."

They both thought that was a lot funnier than I did. Even the driver was grinning as he pulled in front of the auditorium. We entered and found our seats with plenty of time to peruse the audience. The Delta had turned out in tux and gown.

This part of the competition involved a runway walk, where poise was evaluated, and had drawn a large crowd of locals who wanted to watch. Cece and Tinkie's story about the roach incident had put the competition on the map. Like at a NASCAR event, some of the audience hoped for blood.

"There's Johnny Durant! And he's with Melonie Mason!" Cece was making notes. Tinkie pulled out her new camera with a telephoto lens and snapped the socialites. Johnny had been dating June Petra for the last two years, dangling the promise of a ring but never putting it on her finger. Now he was miles from home with another woman on his arm. Cece had some juicy tidbits for the *Dispatch*'s next edition.

We recognized dozens of Delta society members. "This is an event," Cece said. "Thanks to Tinkie's quick thinking, half the Delta has turned out for this. Until I got Tinkie's fabulous photos, no one had even heard of the competition."

"My pleasure," Tinkie said. "Now, shush! The lights are dimming."

I settled into my seat, prepared for a couple of hours of boredom watching glue-sprayed butts in tight swimsuits strut down the runway. Even worse would be the Q&A. The contestants would, no doubt, be interested in bringing about world peace.

The field had already been narrowed to ten contestants. Lined up on stage, they almost blinded the audience with pearly teeth and naked ambition.

The panel of judges wasn't too shabby, either. Former Miss America Dawn Gonzalez had traded her crown for motherhood, but she still had presence. TV chef Harley Pitts, thanks to a bad temper that looked good on camera, had worked his way into a major cooking empire and led the cooking segments with his expertise. Belinda Buck, a Mississippi native, had starred in her own TV show, *La Femme Noir*, in the 1990s. I'd actually enjoyed the show, and time —or a plastic surgeon—had been kind to her. Ms. Buck sizzled with vitality. The fourth judge was Clive Gladstone, a handsome Delta bachelor with an eye for athletic horses and a reputation as one of the finest riders in the Southeast. Clive's horses were his life, a fact that had drawn more than a bit of gossip.

The contestants wore traditional one-piece swimwear and stiletto heels. Anyone who could actually walk in those shoes deserved to win something.

They paraded down the runway with the

confidence of ships at full sail. I couldn't begrudge them the soft glow of youth that clung to their skin. No one escaped hardship or time. Misfortune, in the shape of either illness, accident, or consequence, knocked at everyone's door eventually. Time stood still for no one, a difficult concept for the young to grasp. Which was probably a good thing.

"Hedy is striking." Tinkie lasered in on the raven-haired beauty who'd chosen a black swimsuit. The other women wore red, blue, or green. Hedy stood out like a dark priestess.

"She is that."

"Karrie Kompton seems supremely confident," Cece pointed out.

"She gives the impression she doesn't consider the other girls real competition." I fanned myself with the program. The auditorium was a little stuffy.

One by one, each girl came forward and answered a series of questions from the judges. To my amazement, the questions weren't mere fluff. Some involved basic current events, and others covered complicated etiquette issues. Tinkie and Cece were both stirred by the answers. Social graces mattered.

When Karrie Kompton walked to the microphone, I couldn't help but lean forward.

"Karrie, you have a long list of pageant wins," Dawn Gonzalez began. "Which one means the

41

most to you, and what's been your hardest lesson?"

"When I was nine, I won the Little Miss Rankin County Sunshine Pageant," Karrie said. "It was one of the few times my father was able to attend a pageant and it meant more to me than any other, because he was there."

An audible sigh of approval wafted across the entire auditorium.

I hated to admit how smart she was. She knew exactly how to play on the heartstrings of the judges and the audience.

"And as to the second part of your question" —Karrie cleared her throat—"I've always been very competitive . . ."

"Cutthroat is more like it," Tinkie whispered.

". . . and I've had to learn to control that. A competitive spirit is good, but too much, or one that isn't checked, can hurt the feelings of the other girls, and I'd never want to do that."

When "the other girls" didn't pull off their shoes and throw them at her, I stood up and applauded their self-restraint. Both Tinkie and Cece yanked me down in my seat.

"And finally," judge Belinda Buck asked in a soft drawl, "if you were given a chance to star in a television show, would you take it?"

"It would depend on the content, Ms. Buck. If the show was as good as *La Femme Noir*, I'd be on it like a heart attack on a deep-fried moon pie."

The audience erupted in applause. Karrie had managed to work in the line of dialogue Belinda used in almost every single one of her shows.

"Damn," Cece said. "Karrie is good."

"She's clever," Tinkie agreed.

"She's doesn't have it sewn up yet," Cece said. There were several girls who had come across with more thoughtful answers.

"There's still the talent competition," Tinkie said. "Maybe she'll suck at that."

I laughed. Somehow, all three of us had become vested in the outcome of a competition we hadn't even known about two days previous. And we didn't have a favorite in the running, we had an anti-favorite. Life was strange indeed.

The girls finished the Q&A and strolled the catwalk with the grace of young felines, then assembled to hear the judges' verdict. Tinkie, Cece, and I eased to the edge of our seats.

Dawn Gonzalez accepted the microphone from the emcee. "The judges have tallied their votes," she said. Her smile revealed either genetic superiority or expensive orthodontic measures. "What we've decided is to keep the scores secret until the last event. We want every girl to give this competition her all, and the title truly is up for grabs until the final evening. So pick your favorites, keep a tally of your scores, and see if you can best the judges."

The young women on the stage maintained

bright smiles, but dismay crossed the faces of several. I could only imagine that some, feeling they didn't have a chance, were eager to call it quits and go home. Now they were fated to carry on until the bitter end.

Dawn wasn't finished, though. She held up a hand to calm the growing buzz in the audience. "We do have one award to give tonight. The girls voted among themselves for 'Best-Humored Contestant.' " A drumroll came from backstage. "And the winner is Babs Lafitte."

Babs was tall, nearly six feet, with long red hair that captured the stage lighting in a dazzling halo. She wasn't a squealer, thank goodness, and she seemed genuinely surprised and pleased.

"Babs, would you like to say a few words?" Dawn signaled her to the microphone and held out the trophy.

As Babs stepped forward, her knees buckled. She went down like she'd been bolt shot. Once her body hit the floor, it didn't stop. She began bucking, screaming, and what appeared to be convulsing. Her long fingernails dug into her scalp, and she tore out tufts of hair.

The smile faded from Dawn's face. A startled "What the hell is wrong with her?" echoed over the silent auditorium. The other contestants froze for what seemed like an eon before Brook Oniada and Janet Menton dropped to their knees beside Babs and tried to control the convulsions.

44

"Is there a doctor in the house?" Dawn asked into the microphone.

Several stagehands rushed from behind the curtains and restrained Babs while an ambulance was called. Evangeline Phelps, the pageant organizer, took control of the stage, urging Brook and Janet away from the stricken girl. She removed the microphone from Dawn's hand.

"Ladies and gentlemen, please move on to the reception. I'm sure we'll have this situation righted in no time and our lovely contestants will join you." She shooed the remaining young women stage left. They cast looks of horror over their shoulders at Babs, who was being held to the floor by the two stagehands. Karrie Kompton pointed at the writhing girl.

"This is just an act," Karrie said loudly. "She knew she wasn't going to win, and she pulled this crap."

Before she could continue, Mrs. Phelps grasped Karrie's arm in what appeared to be a death grip and hustled her toward the wings.

"She isn't sick. It's an act!" Karrie threw over her shoulder as she was dragged away.

Mrs. Phelps was unshaken. "A doctor has been called, and if the audience would please continue to the reception." There was a steely order in her tone. I gathered my purse and made to leave, but Tinkie pinched my arm.

"I need a photo," she said.

"Mrs. Phelps will have you drawn and quartered." The pageant organizer reminded me of a particularly stern grammar school teacher who'd always been able to bully me. "I'm not up to hand-to-hand combat with an old guerrilla fighter. My arm is still weak."

"Have the car running," Cece said as Tinkie tossed me the keys to the Cadillac. "We'll be with you in two minutes."

While I was tempted to watch, I went to get the car. I would be able to see the results of their investigative, or some would call it tabloid, journalism in the newspaper tomorrow, and likely on the faces of the contestants when the story broke. The rest of the week in Greenwood was going to be an interesting ride.

The after-competition party was held in the private home of Drew and Bethann Madison. The Madison estate was one of the largest contiguous plantations that spread across five thousand acres. Bethann had also been a beauty contestant at one point in her life, and I chatted with her about a woman who'd figured into my last case, Lana Entrekin Carlisle.

Bethann and Lana had competed against each other frequently in state beauty pageants, and Bethann held her old rival in high regard. She told me a few humorous tales of pranks the girls played on each other before, during, and after some of the pageants they'd participated in. While I listened to Bethann's reminiscences, Tinkie cornered and photographed the pageant contenders while Cece grilled them. My partner had taken to the role of paparazzi like a duck to water. I watched in amusement as they double-teamed girl after girl. The only one who evaded them was Hedy Lamarr Blackledge. Which was strange, because the more publicity a girl got, the higher her profile; therefore, most of the girls sought TV and print interviews. Trained in the art of public presentation, the smart ones turned any moment into an opportunity for publicity.

Not Hedy. She drifted around the edges of the party, slipping up to speak with a judge here or there but avoiding Cece and Tinkie like the plague. Intrigued, I followed her out into one of the most incredible gardens I'd ever stepped into. Cross vines climbed Greek columns to create a shady pergola. In the center a fountain gurgled softly, sending water cascading over glass blocks lit to resemble giant ice cubes. Flowers of all descriptions were abloom, and the sweet singing of night birds wafted on the balmy breeze.

Money could buy everything. Well, maybe not happiness. The jury was still out on that one.

"Ms. Blackledge," I called as I jogged after her. Drat Tinkie and her fashion slavery. My heels were good looking but not worth a hoot for pursuit.

Hedy stopped at a bench beneath an arbor covered in Virginia creeper. "Miss Delaney," she said, "what can I do for you?"

"You know my name?" I was surprised.

"All of the girls know who you are. They're wondering why a private investigator is at our pageant."

"Vacation." I wanted to put her at ease. "Tinkie and I are taking cooking lessons. It just happened that the pageant was going on, too."

"Is that the truth?" She was deadly earnest.

"Why else would we be here?"

A smile passed across her face, and in that flash I saw a beauty far greater than anything Karrie Kompton could summon. "I thought maybe Karrie had hired you to sabotage the contest. I mean, what's wrong with Babs? She was fine an hour ago, then suddenly she's on the floor like someone suffering from a heroin overdose."

Her choice of descriptions gave me a second's pause, but I addressed her concern. "Karrie hasn't hired me or my partner." I wanted to make that clear before I asked any other questions. Hedy struck me as someone who watched others. She paid attention.

"Then you aren't . . . investigating any of us?"

The question begged another. "Is there something that needs investigating?"

"Only how Karrie has bribed the judges with special presents and gifts. That's not supposed to be allowed, but she gets around it."

"I'm sure she has her ways." Girls like Karrie always broke the rules and got away with it.

Hedy looked beyond me, as if someone in the shadows beckoned her. "It's been a pleasure, Ms. Delaney, but I have to get back to . . . uh, I'm tired."

"You're not going to the hotel, are you?" Somewhere in the pageant material I thought I'd read that the girls were required to stay in the Alluvian.

"No," she admitted. "Please, I have to leave." The fraction of hesitation signaled a half-truth if not an outright lie. "I'm visiting relatives tonight." Her lips curved tentatively. "I don't see them often. They'll be worried about me if I'm any later."

She had her purse in one hand and car keys in the other. "So you're leaving now?" The party had only been in swing for an hour. It behooved her to work the crowd—and the judges—like the rest of the girls were doing.

"Yes. It's a school night for my . . . niece. If I want to see her before bedtime, I need to leave now. I was headed out to my car when you called my name."

"How well do you know Babs Lafitte?" I couldn't let this opportunity pass.

"If you aren't investigating something, why do you care?"

"Out-of-the-ordinary events stir my curiosity. The thing you said about Babs, about a heroin overdose. Does she use drugs?"

Hedy glanced behind me to the lights and soft sounds of the party. "I don't think so. I've never seen Babs use any drugs. It was a figure of speech. From television shows. I shouldn't have said it."

"Thanks, Hedy. Have a safe trip. Tomorrow is another cook-off event for you contestants, isn't it?"

"Yes."

"What are you preparing?"

"I'm not certain. Sometimes I can't always get the ingredients I need for my special dishes." She shrugged. "I guess I can always make something chocolate. That's popular with the judges."

"Interesting choice."

4

When I got up, an issue of the *Zinnia Dispatch*, special delivery arranged by Cece, had been slid under our hotel room door. Rather than party last night, Cece had bustled back to Zinnia to lay out the newspaper. Tinkie's front-page photo—Babs clawing at her head—was centered at the top of the page. Inside, Cece had also done a spread in the society section with numerous party pix from the Madison plantation reception.

Looking over the photos, I was proud to acknowledge Tinkie had a knack for capturing action and a flare for composition. Cece had chosen the shots wisely, and the photos were supported with great copy.

As it turned out, Babs's condition wasn't life threatening, or even severe. Someone had combined red pepper and a caustic irritant in her pump hair spray bottle. Though the reaction had struck at a truly inappropriate time, there was no permanent damage. Babs had lost a great deal of her hair, but it would grow back. The paramedics had treated her on the spot and released her to go straight to The Split End for a thorough shampoo and oatmeal scalp treatment.

A smaller front-page photo showed Babs exiting the EMT vehicle. Her head looked like she'd walked into a stump grinder, but the caption contained her vow to be at all remaining pageant events. "Someone desperately wants me to drop out of the competition, but that's not going to happen," she was quoted as saying. "I've been assured this incident won't be held against me, and according to the pageant rules, I'm still very much in the running."

One contestant had plenty to say about that.

"While it's obvious I won the 'Poise and Confidence' category, I don't mind that the other girls will have another chance. Even if it is, technically, unfair. But the judges have ruled," Karrie Kompton was fool enough to say. "Bring on the talent competition. But just a helpful hint: The others should spare themselves humiliation, pack up and go home. I'm taking this crown." The photo of Karrie made her look like she'd bitten into a green persimmon.

Karrie might have swayed the judges with gifts and fake niceness, but she hadn't fooled Cece or Tinkie. Karrie was going to be hot when she saw the *Dispatch*, and somehow I knew Tinkie was going to enjoy jerking her chain.

I put the newspaper on the foot of Tinkie's bed. She snoozed away, and I decided to take a quick elevator ride to the fourth floor for some caffeine. A big urn of steaming coffee, as well as a laden buffet, waited in the dining area, and I could almost smell the delicious brew. My morning couldn't start without a cup of java.

After my jeans and shoes were on, I eased out of the room and down the hall to the elevators, pondering whether I should bring Tinkie a cup. We'd stayed up late, gabbing and laughing about the contestants, Tinkie's newfound talent as a photographer, and the dynamics of the strange world of pageants.

In high school, Tinkie had been selected a freshman, sophomore, and junior maid, crowning those glories with the title of Sunflower County Homecoming Queen her senior year. She was a finalist in the statewide Junior Miss contest and voted Miss Cotton, representing the entire Delta as the fairest of the bolls in the state.

I gently teased her about those high school tiaras, but I also respected her insight into the mindset of the pageant contestants.

"There's a lot at stake here, Sarah Booth," she told me. "Think how people talk about professional athletes and how short their careers are. They're over the hill at thirty-five, or that's what a lot of people say. It's so much worse for beauty contestants. They're done at twenty-four or -five. And these girls here—for some of them, this is the final shot at a title that offers real money. This is deadly serious."

I thought about that as I ambled down the hall

to the dining area. I caught a whiff of strong coffee and I sighed in anticipation. Six steps outside the dining room, I heard Karrie Kompton's crisp enunciation.

"That bitch got what she deserved. I hope to God someone videotaped her wallowing around on the floor screaming like she was possessed. I've never seen anything that funny in my life."

Karrie and Voncil Payne stood at the breakfast buffet. Karrie had a plate of fruit. Voncil, who'd hung up her crown years before, had loaded up with eggs, bacon, grits, and biscuits. She had to have one helluva metabolism to eat like that at her age.

Voncil, rumpled and blowsy in the morning light, followed behind Karrie, talking to her back. Karrie's sundress, sandals, and makeup defined perfection, as usual. By talking with the girls and pageant staff, I'd learned that Voncil was a sort of housemother to all the girls, though she made it clear Amanda was her priority. Mothering Karrie would be tantamount to nurturing a pit viper.

"Amanda was really upset," Voncil said. "She likes Babs, and she was distraught that someone would play such a dreadful prank on her."

Karrie rolled her eyes. "Like Amanda wouldn't take out Babs if it moved her closer to winning. Amanda can pretend to be nice, but every girl

54

here is cutthroat when it comes to this title. There's too much money on the line."

Voncil popped a bite of bacon into her mouth. "When I was younger I was like you, Karrie. Ambitious. Amanda is . . . softer." She lifted one shoulder. "But we need this title. Financially we're up against a wall. So it's up to Amanda to take this crown. When she gets the scholarship, she wants to go to medical school and study childhood diseases."

"Hold the 'save the little children' speech for the judges. It doesn't fly with me." Karrie stepped closer. "Just remember, Backstage Mother of the Year, I'm going to win, and anyone who stands between me and that title will get crushed."

Voncil looked as if she'd been slapped. Karrie executed an about-face but stopped when she saw me. "Well, if it isn't the Over-the-Hill Eavesdropper." She made a show of peering behind me. "Where's your Wealthy Sidekick, the one who foots all the bills for you?"

"Desperation isn't your color, Karrie, but green with envy suits you well. I guess you've worn it enough." I sashayed to the stack of cups and grabbed one.

A giggle erupted from Voncil, and she fled in the opposite direction.

"That old bag," Karrie said with a sneer. "If she doesn't stop clogging her arteries with fat, she won't live long enough to see me crowned."

"How charming of you to care." I walked past her to the coffee urn. The aromatic black liquid filled my cup. No sugar, no cream—just coffee. I lifted the cup and inhaled.

"I don't care if she drops dead this second," Karrie said. "Amanda doesn't stand a chance. She's too mousey and always trying to be friends with all the girls." Her smile was feral. "She doesn't understand this isn't about bonding and friendships like some teenage church group. It's about money and who'll make the best spokesperson."

"What do you know about Babs Lafitte's bad luck?"

Karrie put down her fruit plate and looked around before she spoke. "Hedy made a Cajun dish yesterday that required a special red pepper, one she dried and ground herself. The dish was so hot, the judges broke into a sweat."

She aimed the smoking gun of pepper at Hedy without hesitation. Which made it mighty convenient. Besides, Karrie didn't strike me as someone who would do me a good turn out of the kindness of her heart. *If* her information was accurate—and that was a big if—she'd done it only to promote herself. By knocking Hedy out of the competition, she bettered the odds.

"Thanks," I said.

"Will you look into Hedy?"

"No, I'm going to look into why you'd point me at Hedy. She must be a top contender."

"Bite me." Karrie abandoned her fruit plate and stalked off toward the elevators.

When I got back to the room, Tinkie was in the shower warbling "Old Man River." I sipped my coffee and enjoyed the entertainment. The newspaper was scattered around the room, indicating she'd already perused her latest journalistic coup.

My cell phone rang. Graf was calling. Eager to hear his voice, I answered.

"How's my fiancée?" The baritone timbre of his voice made me close my eyes in pleasure. I could see his eyes, his thick dark hair, the way his top lip gently dipped beneath his nose. He was classically handsome, and his voice conveyed it all.

"I'm better," I said, realizing it was true. "Tinkie's master plan is proving effective."

"Is that her caterwauling in the background?"

"She's showering."

"Maybe you could ask to have the water pressure increased, drown her out a little."

"I'm actually enjoying it," I said. "I adore show tunes."

"You always loved them." There was a pause. "Do you want to go back to Broadway, Sarah Booth?"

"Heavens no," I said in all sincerity. "I want to head out to Hollywood with you. Film is where your career is, Graf. That's where I want to be." I meant every word. I just wasn't ready. "Maybe in a few weeks."

Silence filled the line and I knew he was wondering if my delay was real or some unspoken message he should be trying to read.

"I'm healing," I said softly. "It's taking longer than I thought, but it is happening. Doc says the arm will be one hundred percent in a week."

"You take your time, Sarah Booth. Everyone here understands, and most of all, I do. This film will wrap soon. Then, if you aren't ready to come out here, I'll return to Zinnia. We'll work it out."

His calm reassurances were exactly the balm my wounded heart needed. No pressure, no guilt. He knew how to make me want him even more.

I filled him in on my progress—or lack of—at the cooking school, and also about the Miss Viking beauty contest and spokesperson competition. He found the red pepper prank amusing. "That probably ate her scalp up," he said. "It's terrible, I know, but the way you describe it is funny."

"Tinkie got some great photos." When I told him about her newfound profession, he was strangely silent. "What's wrong?" I asked.

"I'm glad Tinkie has found something else to do."

On the surface, the remark was harmless, but on a deeper level it concerned me. "This photography thing is just temporary. We're here and can help Cece out, but this isn't a career move."

"Oscar would be happy if Tinkie became a society photographer."

"When did Oscar decide this?" The question flew out of my mouth and down the phone line, and I knew my tone was all wrong. But the idea that Oscar and Graf had discussed Tinkie and her future as if she were a child struck me as peculiar.

"He hasn't decided anything. When I spoke with him this morning, I could tell he was pleased at the photographs. That's all I'm saying."

But it wasn't. He was saying a whole lot more. I started to ask him why he was calling Oscar, but such a question would put me firmly in the camp of the churlish. "How's the weather?" I asked.

"What's wrong, Sarah Booth?"

"Nothing, Graf. I just think we should leave Tinkie alone to decide what her career might be."

"And I agree with that. She's an adult and deserves to make her own choices."

The bathroom door opened, and Tinkie came

59

out in a towel. She took one look at my face. "What's wrong?"

I pinned on a smile. "Graf was just saying he spoke with Oscar. It's good the two of them are becoming friends." I said it into the phone.

"That terrific." Tinkie grabbed some clothes. "Tell Graf you have to shake the lead out and get ready for our cooking class."

"I heard her," Graf said. "Have fun, Sarah Booth. I love you."

"And I love you." I flipped the phone shut. "What's on the agenda today?"

Tinkie gave me a quizzical look, but she didn't press the matter. "I think it's salad day, but it might be soup. We'll find out when we get there."

The engineers who designed the Viking equipment had to be female, because things worked the way a woman wants them to. Even with my weak arm, I could manage. When help was needed, a chef's assistant magically appeared to hold my bowl or help me. A girl could get used to such attention.

It was indeed salad-preparation day, and while I'd torn many a head of romaine or iceberg lettuce into bite-size pieces and thrown in a handful of other traditional salad components, I didn't know salad played a long role in history.

Chef Alana, our specialist for the day, told us that the word "salad" comes from the Latin *sal*, meaning "salt," because the dressings often included brine or salt.

Using the *Encyclopedia of Food and Culture*, Alana clarified the long debate from the idea that salad should be the opening of the meal (harkening back to Hippocrates and Galen, who believed raw vegetables eased through the digestive tract and so should be served first) to other opinions that the vinegar in the dressing destroyed the taste of the wine served at the meal, and so therefore the salad should be served last.

As I prepared a basic "backyard salad," Tinkie took on a more ambitious and exotic selection. I was charmed to learn that at one point in history, tossed plates of mixed greens were considered messy and disorderly. This concept of an "out-of-order" salad really appealed to me, and perhaps explained my dislike of molded gelatin salads—which Chef Alana noted offered "maximum control." I loved it. Maximum control of salad greens!

Alana taught from *Perfection Salad: Women and Cooking at the Turn of the Century*, by Laura Shapiro. " 'The object of scientific salad making was to subdue the raw greens until they bore as little resemblance as possible to their natural state. If a plain green salad was called for, the experts tried to avoid simply letting a disorganized pile of leaves drop messily onto the plate. . . . This arduous approach to salad making became an identifying feature of cooking school cookery and the signature of a refined household.' " This approach to salad contrasted the "natural" against the constructed and designed. Messy, as in natural, was unacceptable in "refined" households. I connected the dots quickly: Salads, like women, should be rigorously bound and controlled. Women's clothing of that era reflected the same mentality.

Well, "refined" was never a word that applied to me, and I had a sudden overwhelming attachment for the raw leaves and vegetables of a messy green salad.

"I'm going to pen an ode to the green salad," I told Tinkie. "Maybe one of the contestants could recite it as part of her talent."

"Save me from salad poets and SaladShooters," Tinkie said, making the sign of the cross.

I feared Alana would lose her patience and exile me from the school, but it didn't happen. Tinkie and I sampled each other's dishes before we hit the street just after noon. We were too full to think about eating lunch, so we strolled along Howard Street, finally stopping at Turnrow Books.

A reading was in progress, and we listened to Jack Pendarvis share his dark and hilarious visions before I bought his book, eased out of the store, and went back to the hotel. The concierge allowed me computer access, and I did a bit of basic research on the pageant.

The title of Miss Viking was brand spanking new, so there was no history or scuttlebutt to find on the Internet. To fill the time until the talent competition, I started a search of the various contestants, beginning with Karrie Kompton.

She was a professional pageant contestant who'd started as a toddler. Her mother had once been her manager, but they'd split when Karrie was seventeen. Since then, Karrie had charted her own career. She was a professional dancer, a passable singer, and had some acting credits in regional TV ads. She'd also done a stint as a weather girl on a Memphis TV station. Her tenure there was short-lived, due to an altercation with the news anchor.

There was little or nothing on Hedy Lamarr Blackledge. Her "official" Web site was one page and simply contained a photograph—albeit a striking one—and the personal comment that she'd been named for the famous movie star because Hedy Lamarr had been her grand-mother's favorite.

Janet Menton had professional representation and a list of acting credits that covered regional stage and TV ads as well as a nine-week guest appearance on a daytime soap opera as a femme fatale. She was a beautiful girl with mocha skin, hazel eyes, and a dazzling smile. Whether she won Miss Viking or not, this girl had a career in film. The camera loved her.

Crystal Belle Wadell had numerous regional titles to her credits, as did Gretchen Teatree. Both were accomplished chefs. Regina Jones was clearly the academic star. Brook Oniada, a resident of Hawaii, had plenty of credits in dance, acrobatics, and performance. Rita Tierce was a former child-figure-skating star.

To my surprise, Amanda Payne had the most impressive string of accomplishments. She'd played supporting roles in two independent Florida films, earning good reviews and a high level of respectability. She'd also composed and sold several country songs, two of which I recognized. Big-name stars had cut them.

And Babs Lafitte was the darling of Jackson, Mississippi. She was a featured singer at Bessie's House of Blues and linked herself to the pirate Jean Lafitte. All in all, she was a colorful character who now owned half interest in a French Quarter cabaret club, where she performed on a regular basis. Duly noted was her turn on a number of cooking and fashion shows, including the run-up to the Oscars the previous year, where she dished the dirt on red-carpet dresses and shoes with Joan Rivers. At twenty-five, she was the oldest of the finalists, so this was truly a desperation year for her.

I exited out of the computer. Poking around in the pageant was fun, but it wasn't a paying case, nor was anyone in trouble. Tomorrow, if I was still curious, I'd continue with my research.

5

I ran into Tinkie in the lobby and helped haul the load of books she'd purchased on the history of cooking back to our hotel room. At last, massage time. As the strong hands of the masseuse worked out the kinks in my back muscles, I drifted between reality and dream.

I was in the kitchen at Dahlia House, and a slender woman wearing a long dress stood near the kitchen counter whipping a bowl of something with a wooden spoon. When she turned around, I saw it was Jitty. Instead of her usual coif, her hair was bound in a calico cloth, but the smile was unmistakable. Behind Jitty, the oven had disappeared and in its stead was a wood-burning stove.

"Nothin' says lovin' like something from the oven," she sang.

"You're out of era," I told her. "That's a slogan song from the 1960s for Pillsbury."

She shrugged. "How can you expect me to keep all that minutia straight? And who cares?" She put down the bowl of yellow batter, and I slipped a finger into it for a taste. She tried to whack my hand with the wooden spoon, but I was faster. "What's cooking?" My cleverness knew no bounds.

"Coker loves pound cake, and since you've set me loose in the land of dreamy dreams, I thought I'd take the opportunity to make him one."

Coker was Jitty's husband, who'd died in the War Between the States with Great-Great-Grandmother Alice's husband. But one thing I'd learned from Jitty: The rules of the Great Beyond were even more confusing in a dream state. "You're both dead. Can't you see him whenever you'd like?"

She turned away and looked out the window. "It's complicated."

I could see it wasn't a happy subject, so I let it drop. "I'm healing," I told Jitty.

"I can see that." She rinsed her hands at the sink and dried them on a cloth.

"So this is what the kitchen looked like when Great-Great-Grandma Alice was alive." The room had been modernized at least twice. Electricity had been added, running water, stainless-steel sinks. But even without modern conveniences, the room had a big, airy charm.

"It was Alice's favorite room." Jitty opened a

cabinet to reveal neatly lined jars, each labeled corn or tomatoes or pickles. "We put up our own food."

Imagining the work that had gone into simple food preparation made me tired. That generation of women worked.

"Why are you visiting me?" I asked.

"If I have to put a reason to it, your brain won't get any exercise at all."

"Great, a cryptic ghost. Just this once, can't you just tell me?" Soon, the dream would fade and she would vanish. If I didn't get an answer now, I likely never would.

"The key to being a great cook is to know what you wish to prepare," she said. "Like any other endeavor, cookin' requires clarity."

"Gee, thanks." But she was already fading and I was back under the pummeling hands of the masseuse and the annoying ring of my cell phone. Without a word the masseuse handed me a towel and stepped from the room while I took the phone call from Cece.

"I've had the most brilliant idea, dahling," Cece drawled.

"What?" I was excited just by her tone.

"I'm bringing Madame Tomeeka with me tonight. She's going to *predict* the winner of the pageant! I included a notice of her pending forecast in this morning's paper."

"Brilliance!" Cece was a genius. That would

boost readership of the paper by at least 20 percent. "Have you told Tinkie?" I asked.

"You tell her, dahling. We'll be there at seven for the talent competition."

Cece's press credentials garnered us front-row seats. I noticed reluctance on the part of Madame Tomeeka, Zinnia's resident psychic and my school chum, whom I knew as Tammy Odom. Tammy had a true gift, and more than once she'd shared her prophetic dreams with me, warning me of impending danger. Or heartbreak. Or both. Living with Jitty, I had no reason to doubt that messages from the other side could be sent to us. Tammy was the perfect conduit, but the drawback was she couldn't force the spirit world to comply with my need for information. Like Jitty, the visions of Madame Tomeeka came at their own whim.

I sat between Tinkie and Tammy, and we had a clear view of the judges, seated right in front of us. Sun-kissed and blessed by the gods with good looks, abundant hair, and a body that would inspire a sculptor, Clive whispered with Belinda and Dawn. The female judges were obviously charmed. Harley sat it out alone.

"I'm sorry for those girls," Madame Tomeeka said. "Dawn Gonzalez and Belinda Buck are old enough to take care of themselves, but those girls . . . Clive is irresistible, and trying to get his attention is one more way for them to short sell their value. A number of them will give away another little piece of themselves."

Tammy spoke from bitter experience. Maybe bringing her to this event was not Cece's best idea, though it had certainly appealed to me, too. Nothing like handicapping a pageant with help from a psychic.

"Hush!" Cece ordered. "We have to concentrate."

While I'm no advocate of pageants, I had to admit the energy generated onstage as the girls pranced out was exciting. As they performed a musical number from *Hello, Dolly!* they all managed to act like this was the best moment of their lives. Whatever the truth, the girls appeared to be having fun and reveling in their shared moment. Such is the illusion good theater is able to create. I had no doubt that behind the black velvet curtain, ruthlessness ruled.

They finished the number and rushed backstage for a costume change. Mrs. Phelps took the microphone and enumerated the rules of the talent segment. Any talent or combination was acceptable as long as it was suited for a general audience. The girls had been allowed to bring their coaches, makeup artists, and backup musical accompaniment, whether recorded or live.

Finally, the first competitor was called. Regina

Jones, first in the lineup, was an accomplished pianist. But as soon as Karrie Kompton walked onto the stage, I forgot the first contestant. Karrie had presence, and when the music started and she gave a bump-and-grind medley of Broadway numbers, I was wowed.

She had no real competition until Brook Oniada came out dressed in a grass skirt to the beat of Hawaiian drums. Before she started her number, ten waiters clad in bright island shirts rushed through the auditorium distributing grilled chicken and fruit kebabs and trays of pineapple daiquiris.

"I made the appetizers myself," Brook said, "honoring my father's island heritage. My act is a tribute to him and my people."

She carried three fire batons—and she hulaed, twirled, and juggled simultaneously. Though she was slender, the vigorous motion of her hips could churn butter. Her act brought down the house, and I watched the judges nod and beam, marking on their pads. Brook had propelled herself into a top slot. The refreshments were not only delicious but a stroke of brilliance for someone who wanted to represent a company that specialized in cooking.

The audience finally settled down, and Hedy walked out with a stool and a violin. She sat without fanfare or introduction and began to play. The haunting music swelled over the audience. I saw Tammy wipe a tear from her eye. Hedy demonstrated a talent worthy of a concert tour. She drew a standing ovation at the conclusion. She was definitely in the running.

To my surprise, Amanda Payne belted out a Dolly Parton song that had the audience on its feet stomping and whistling. Who would have thought such a big voice would come from such a tiny and timid young woman. Whatever self-confidence issues Amanda had, once she hit the stage, they evaporated and she was 100 percent dazzle.

Babs Lafitte, wearing a wig, had recovered enough to participate, and the audience welcomed her with thunderous applause. Everyone in town knew what had happened, and her "the show must go on" attitude made her a favorite. Not to mention that she could play the piano with real talent. Her medley of raucous blues tunes had the audience whistling and begging for more.

The last of the girls I'd placed in my top five, Janet Menton, did a dramatic monologue from a play I adored, called *'night, Mother*. I couldn't fault her performance, which was Broadway worthy. The level of talent made me feel sorry for the judges. How would they possibly pick?

Cece made copious notes, and Tinkie rushed up and down the stage taking photographs. As the competition drew to a close, all of the girls came out on stage in a lineup that made me realize that each one deserved to win.

"What did you think?" I asked Tammy. I meant it as casual conversation.

"I think there's bad energy in the group. I smell tragedy in the air. Someone is about to get hurt."

While Tammy had the gift of second sight, she wasn't in the habit of predicting doom and gloom, at least not for people other than me. Her words stopped me short. "What did you see?"

Tammy stood up. She moved slowly, her attention focused on the stage.

"Tammy?" I tried to grab her hand, but she shook free. "Everyone! Get out!"

For a moment no one paid her any attention. The judges slowly turned to frown at her.

"Hush up," Harley Pitts hissed.

Tammy ignored him. She eased past my knees and stepped into the aisle. "Get those girls off the stage!"

I scrabbled out after her. "Hey," I said, grabbing her elbow. "What is it?"

"We have to get out." She started toward the exit, visibly upset. Halfway down the aisle she paused, obviously torn between leaving the auditorium and breaking up the last of the pageant. "Get off that stage!" She tried one more time.

Two big men with scowls headed our way.

"Tammy, what is it?" I asked.

"I have to get out of here. Stay away from

those girls, Sarah Booth. You and Tinkie both."
She pointed up at the stage. All of the contestants—except Brook Oniada—were staring at Madame Tomeeka as if she'd cursed in church.

Something else was going on with Brook. She faltered, slowly spinning in a circle as if she'd lost her vision. She staggered, almost dropping to her knees, but she caught herself. The fire batons sputtered as her arms jerked. There was nothing I could do to help Brook. I had my hands full with Tammy.

"Sit back down," I whispered harshly to her.

"Get me outside. Stay away from them." Tammy was terrified, and her fingers dug into my arm.

"Other than Tinkie taking photographs, we don't have anything to do with them." I stepped in front of her and the approaching bouncers, effectively blocking the bum's rush she was about to get. "What did you see?"

"I saw flames—"

Screams erupted from the stage. Brook Oniada was on fire. The flame from her batons had ignited her clothes and hair, and she was a human torch. Instead of screaming and running, though, she stood perfectly still. She raised one hand and pointed at Hedy. "Help me."

Pageant contestants fled the stage, pushing, shoving, and stumbling over one another. Only Hedy remained. She held her violin in one hand and the bow in the other, and she didn't move, mesmerized by the sight of her burning competitor.

At last she dropped the bow and reached out her hand. So help me, it was like a moment from a nightmare. Hedy said something, but in the pandemonium I couldn't hear.

Clive Gladstone leaped onto the stage and wrapped his coat around Brook, effectively smothering the flames that had danced along her arms and head. Several men joined him, doing their best to help Brook and drag Hedy off the stage. The audience beat a hasty retreat. Cece and Tinkie were all over it, a journalistic double-team.

Paramedics and police officers arrived and loaded Brook onto a stretcher. They whisked her away, leaving Mrs. Phelps to urge what remained of the audience to leave the auditorium in an orderly manner. Tammy and I filed out with the noisy crowd that hummed with whispers and sobs. Tammy was shaken, but no more than I.

We arrived at the Cadillac, and Tammy leaned against it.

"Tell me exactly what you saw," I said softly. "You saw the flames before it happened."

She didn't face me, but stared into the dark night. "I saw someone burning. And I heard screaming. I didn't know who it was, but I knew it involved those girls." Her breath was ragged as she inhaled. "If I were you, I'd find me another hotel to stay in. There's someone truly evil around those girls, someone who will stop at nothing to attain the goal."

I mulled over the warning as Tinkie and Cece approached. They both looked shell-shocked, and I felt a rush of anger that we hadn't been able to escape suffering and cruelty for even a week at a damn cooking school. Private investigators are often forced to confront hard things. And Cece, even though she was technically the society editor, was always in the thick of the news. But enough was enough. I'd come to Greenwood to heal, not watch a lovely young girl become a human torch. And Tammy had made it clear she thought the incident was no accident.

"Are you okay?" Tinkie asked us. She was ashen.

"What happened?"

"No one knows for certain. The speculation is that the flames from the fire baton jumped and caught in her hair." Cece tucked her notebook into her purse. "I've never seen anything like that before in my life."

"What are the police doing?" Tammy asked. "This didn't just happen. Someone made that girl burn."

Cece, Tinkie, and I exchanged looks at Tammy's tone. "His name is Franz Jansen, and he's investigating," Cece said. "Let's hope this was just an awful accident."

Tammy snorted and opened the car door and sat down.

"Tammy, this may be bad form, coming on the heels of that . . . event. But I promoed your pageant prediction in tomorrow's paper. It's too late to pull the story. Would you hazard a guess who's going to win?" Cece asked.

"I can't be certain." Tammy swung her legs into the car so she faced straight ahead.

"Not even a guess?" Cece obviously didn't relish pressing her friend, but she had readers who hung on her society column. She'd promised them something, and she had to deliver.

"It won't be the hula dancer," Tammy said. "Would you mind taking me home? I've got a splitting headache." She closed the door, shutting us out.

"She saw something bad," I told Cece and Tinkie. "She saw the fire and was about to tell me her vision when Brook ignited. She's upset, and she thinks someone evil is behind all of this."

"And she may well be right," Cece said. "Would you take us to my car at the hotel lot? I need to get Tammy home. Tinkie, e-mail me your photos, if you don't mind."

As we washed the makeup off our faces and prepared for bed, Tinkie was unnaturally quiet.

Cece telephoned and told us Brook died en route to the hospital. Police Chief Jansen wasn't labeling it a homicide, Cece said, nor was he calling it an accident. In the quiet luxury of the hotel room, Tinkie and I prepared for bed in a state of shock. The horror of Brook Oniada's death made it impossible to relax.

"How did such an awful thing happen?" Tinkie plopped on her bed, her posture slumped. "Did you see her? She just stood there—all covered in flames. Like she couldn't move or didn't know enough to drop and roll." She put a hand over her eyes. "I've never seen anything so awful."

"Maybe it was an accident." I didn't believe it for a minute. Tammy had sensed malevolence and doom, and she'd been right.

"Let's try to get some sleep." Tinkie peeled back the covers and slid into the bed.

"Good idea." I was reaching up to turn off the bedside light when the hotel phone rang. Tempted to ignore it, I finally grabbed it when Tinkie started to climb out of the covers to answer. She was so short she had to use steps to get in her bed, so it was easier for me. "Hello."

"Miss Delaney, this is Hedy Blackledge." Her voice shook, and I could tell she'd been crying.

The image of her standing on the stage while Brook burned would stay with me for a long time. "What can I do for you, Hedy?"

"I need your help."

Now this was a strange turn of events.

"How?"

"I want to hire you and your partner."

"For what?" I asked automatically.

"To prove I didn't kill Brook. The police just finished questioning me, and they let me go, but I overheard the police chief say he was going to keep an eye on me. He's acting like Brook was murdered."

"But you haven't been charged, right?" Hedy didn't understand that everyone connected to the pageant would be questioned, even if the death was determined to be an accident. Hedy's strange behavior, the way she'd stood reaching out to a burning woman, had likely put her at the top of the list.

"Not yet. But I can't be charged. I can't have the cops poking into my past."

Hedy was the candidate without a Facebook page or an Internet presence. She'd listed no performance credits, not even where she'd learned to play the violin. What was she cloaking? "My advice is to calm down and see what happens. There were hundreds of witnesses who saw Brook set herself on fire. As awful as that is, I don't think anyone is to blame."

"I can't calm down. I can't afford to wait. Will you help me or not?"

"Hold on a minute." I covered the phone and

met Tinkie's curious gaze. I filled her in on Hedy's request.

"Let's take the case," she said. "We can write off this whole vacation as a business expense." She caught a glimpse of my face, though I'd tried to control my expression. "What's wrong?"

"I'm not certain I want to continue as a private investigator." I sure hadn't meant to tell her this way. I hadn't even thought it through myself.

If I'd slapped her, I couldn't have stunned her more. She bit her bottom lip. It popped free of her teeth in a way that weakened the most well-armored men. "What are you saying?" she finally asked. "You're quitting the agency?"

"Now isn't the time for this discussion." My hand still covered the phone. I'd greatly upset my friend. Tears glittered in her eyes.

"This can't wait." She got up and took the phone from my hand. "Hedy, we're going to discuss this and call you back tomorrow." She took down the phone number. When she finished, she replaced the receiver and climbed on the bed across from me. "Tell me what you're thinking."

The truth was, I *hadn't* thought. At all. I'd simply spoken, a habit that had gotten me into hot water more than once. Now, I didn't know what I felt but I'd pried the lid off a can of worms and they were out and crawling. "I don't know what I want to do," I said.

"But you've thought about quitting and you never mentioned it to me?"

"Tinkie, I don't know." Frustration—at myself, not her—laced my voice. These two days in Greenwood were the first time I'd felt alive in weeks. It was like my body was awakening, little by little. Along with the tinglings of joy came jolts of pain.

"I'm not angry," Tinkie said softly. "But I need to know where you are, Sarah Booth. I know you'll be spending a lot of time in Hollywood and on location with Graf and with your career, but I always thought we'd continue with the P.I. agency when you were home. I don't want to let it go."

"If I hadn't been working on a case, my baby would be alive." There it was. The guilt gnawing at me in the darkness of my subconscious had finally strode into the light of day.

I thought Tinkie would deny it, but she didn't. Her hand gently rubbed my back. "What can I say to make it better?"

How like her to do the perfect thing. Rationalization of guilt never works. Nor did she try to coddle me out of my feelings. My wise friend simply wanted to help and she was asking how.

"Maybe this feeling will fade," I said, helpless to control the depression that so easily slipped around me.

"It probably will," she said, kneading the tight spot between my shoulder blades. "Until it does, though, I'm here for you. No one judges you as harshly as you judge yourself, Sarah Booth. I could play psychologist and ask you, 'If Coleman were injured in the line of duty, would you blame him?' But that won't help you now, will it?"

"No, because I probably would blame him." Coleman Peters, Sunflower County Sheriff and a man who held a special place in my heart, was often in the path of danger.

Tinkie gave me a hug. "You're a tough nut, but you're my nut."

"What about Hedy?" I asked.

Tinkie shrugged. "She probably won't be charged with anything, but it makes me wonder why she's jumping the gun like that. Hiring us would make her look guilty whether she is or not. Maybe it's best if we don't take the case, and as time passes, you'll want to investigate again."

"Then you'll tell her no?" Not only was I confused, but I'd also developed a huge yellow streak. I didn't even want to turn down a potential client face-to-face.

"In the morning," Tinkie said. She assisted me under the covers. "Now get some sleep. Tomorrow our class is in main courses."

I feigned interest. "I've always wanted to

learn to make cheeseburgers and fries. Or, better yet, chips and salsa."

"Ha. Ha. Very funny. One day, when you've got a couple of little rug rats clutching your ankles and you're trying to cook dinner for Graf, you'll appreciate all of this."

Her words were like an old wound. The pain of my loss flashed. "Right."

"It will happen, Sarah Booth. Nothing will replace what you lost, but you will have children and be happy. I have to believe that, and so do you."

She did her best to hide her worry, but I could see it. "I'll be okay, Tinkie. It's just going to take more time than I thought. Funny that my arm is almost healed and Doc says I won't even know it was broken after a bit of therapy. But my heart . . ."

"They say the heart is just a muscle, Sarah Booth, and everyone knows that muscle heals more slowly than bone."

"You're the best friend ever." I snuggled into the bed, suddenly exhausted, as if I'd run uphill for a long, long time. Whatever Tinkie replied, I never heard it. I was asleep before she finished talking.

6

I'd been asleep no more than six seconds when a loud pounding at the door startled me awake. Tinkie and I sat bolt upright like some 1940s choreographed comedy. The pounding came again, followed by a muffled plea.

"Miss Delaney! Miss Richmond! Let me in, please."

"Hedy Lamarr Blackledge," we said in unison. Startled awake and angry, I jettisoned myself from the bed.

"It's three in the morning," Tinkie said, indignation growing in her voice. She flung back the covers and padded after me.

"This had better be an emergency," I said as I swung the door open. Hedy stood there in sweats and tennis shoes. Her hair was wild and her makeup was smeared. She looked like hell.

"Janet Menton is dead."

"What?" Tinkie and I were perfectly synchronized. If we gave up P.I. work, maybe we could take up swimming.

"I found her. She's dead in our room."

I glanced at my partner. She gave a tiny frown that told me she didn't completely believe Hedy. "Come inside." Tinkie drew the young woman into the room and closed the door.

"After everything that happened . . . so horrible . . . Brook catching on fire, I mean." She actually flinched. "You've got to help me. There's more at stake here than just a title or money or what happens to me." Despite my doubts about my P.I. future, I felt sorry for her.

"Tell us what happened. Slowly." I steered her into a chair.

She nodded, composing herself. "I left the auditorium and I was in a state. I didn't trust myself to drive to Panther Holler, so I decided to stay in the hotel instead of going to my . . . relatives'. Janet is . . . was . . . my roommate." Her voice got shakier, and she seemed to study the plush carpet. "We were both upset, but we went to bed. I couldn't sleep. I knew that once the cops started investigating Brook . . . I called you, and then I went to the auditorium to play my violin. I do that sometimes when I'm having an anxiety attack. Janet couldn't sleep, either. She said she was hungry." Hedy took a deep breath. "Finally I calmed down, and I thought I could rest, so I went back to the room." Her voice broke, but she drew a deep breath. "I found Janet on the floor." She couldn't hold it together any longer and started crying.

Tinkie was beside her, always kinder and

gentler than I could be. "It's okay, Hedy," she said. "What did the police say?"

Hedy's head snapped up. "I didn't call them. I came here, to you. They're going to think I killed Janet, too. You can tell them I wasn't in the room. You can say I was with you, can't you?"

Tinkie slowly eased away. "We can't do that, Hedy."

"You have to. Otherwise, I don't have an alibi. They'll assume I'm the killer."

"Not necessarily. Give us just a minute, Hedy." Tinkie motioned me toward the bathroom. Once inside, she shut the door. "We have to call the police."

"We do." I concurred wholeheartedly. Was Hedy playing me and Tinkie? Had she come to our room to get us to collude with her on a murder? Or was she naïve and simply afraid? I didn't have the answer, and I could tell from Tinkie's expression that she was as flummoxed as I was. But none of that mattered. Chief Jansen would have to be notified.

"Do you think Hedy is killing the other contestants?"

My gut reaction was no. Hedy simply didn't strike me as a serial murderer. Not even for the title of Miss Viking. "We don't have enough information. You talk Hedy into calling the cops. It'll be much better for her if she does it herself." Tinkie was far more persuasive than I.

85

"I'm going to get dressed and go inspect Hedy's room. Once the cops arrive, we won't have a chance to examine the crime scene."

"Do you want me to help you?"

"No." Tinkie would hold more sway with Hedy. "I'll do it."

"Be careful and don't touch anything."

I nodded as I stepped back into the room, where Hedy continued to sob. I grabbed some jeans and shoes. "I need your room key," I told her.

She gave it over without even a question. She was either very trusting or very good at acting. As I closed the room door behind me, I heard Tinkie talking with her in a calm, reasonable tone. In ten minutes Tinkie would convince Hedy to call the police.

That meant I had about twenty minutes to examine the scene. Greenwood was a small town. Once the law was called, it wouldn't take them long to arrive.

Perhaps it was only my imagination, but the smell of carnations—funeral flowers—lingered in the hotel room where Janet Menton lay on the floor beside the bed. Her face, partially smushed into the carpet, was drawn into a rictus of suffering. Whatever killed her had hurt like hell.

Judging from the body position, she'd been trying to crawl to the bathroom when she died. I didn't touch her, but she was scantily clad and there were no bullet holes, stab wounds, or blood. It was possible—highly unlikely, but possible—she'd died of natural causes. Heart attack, aneurysm, seizure. Healthy young people spontaneously die. On rare occasion they could even combust. Millie, my friend who ran a café in Zinnia, had hundreds of back copies of the tabloids that discussed such cases.

But in this instance, "natural causes" was a far reach. If I had to guess, I'd say Janet Menton died from some type of poison. That wasn't good for Hedy, who had more opportunity than most to poison her roommate.

The police chief would expect to find Hedy's fingerprints in her room, but the same could not be said of mine. Unless I wanted to become a suspect—and thank you very much, I'd already done that once and didn't enjoy it—I had to be careful to leave no trace of my visit to the room. Pulling down my shirtsleeve to cover my hand, I opened the bathroom door.

Holy cow. Beauty products were everywhere. The place looked as if a Clinique counter had exploded. Scrubs, brushes, pots of color, cakes of glittery stuff, jars, jugs, bars—the assortment was mind boggling. The crime lab in Leflore County would be a busy, busy place. If Janet was poisoned, and if she didn't ingest the substance, it could have been placed in any of the hundreds of cosmetics. Contact poisons were tricky, but just as deadly. I'd learned this from bitter personal experience.

With one ear listening for the wail of the police cars, I walked the scene. Hedy's small overnight bag was against one wall, her violin beside it. The bed I took to be hers was barely mussed, supporting her story she'd tried to sleep and then left to play her fiddle.

The room was cluttered with discarded clothes, some bearing designer labels. When I opened a dresser drawer I found vials of what I took to be ground spices. None were labeled, and they could have contained anything from basil to tobacco.

I eased closer to the body. Bingo! Under the dowdy dress Janet wore for her monologue were several smushed pastries in a plain white bakery box.

Without the benefits of someone who could truly analyze a crime scene, I couldn't come to any solid conclusions, but at least I had an idea of the physical layout of the room and the body. Now it was time to skedaddle before Police Chief Jansen caught me and locked me up.

On the way back to our room, I struggled with my own demons. It was clear Tinkie wanted to take this case. Was my reluctance borne of guilt or fear of being injured? Was dissolving the P.I. agency just one more way to punish myself? I didn't know, and that was the most frustrating part.

When I slipped inside the room, I found Hedy in a comfortable chair with a strong bourbon in her hand. Tinkie perched on the arm of the chair. "Chief Jansen is on the way. He asked me to keep Hedy here," she said.

"There's no place else for me to go," Hedy said morosely. "I knew this whole pageant thing was a foolish idea. I never wanted to do it to begin with."

"Then why did you?" I asked.

She put her glass on the table beside the chair. "It's a long story."

"You've got about five minutes." I sounded cold and heartless, but I was a pussycat compared to what she'd face at the hands of the law. "Chief Jansen will be here, and my guess is that you're right. He's going to take you in for questioning. So if there's a story here, spill it while you have the chance."

"I'm trying to get custody of my daughter."

Both Tinkie and I converged on Hedy. "Your daughter?" Tinkie said. Had Hedy revealed she was growing a second head, I wouldn't have been more stunned.

"Yes." Hedy was grim.

"Where is she?"

"Here. In the Delta. Her father has her. That's where I go after the pageant events. I park outside his home, so I can maybe catch a glimpse of her."

"Wait a minute." I had to have misunderstood. "You have a child and you're lurking around outside someone's home trying to 'catch a glimpse of her.' This doesn't make sense."

Hedy swallowed. "I gave away my rights to Vivian. I thought I was doing the best thing for her, but I made a big mistake. I want to be part of her life. I'm her mother, and she needs me." Her throat worked again. "And I need her."

"How old is your daughter?" Tinkie asked.

"Two." She spoke so softly, I had to strain to hear.

"When did you give her up?" I asked.

"Just after she was born," Hedy said in a whisper.

"You haven't seen your daughter for two years? Have you tried?" I asked. Tinkie cut me a hard look at my tone, but she didn't say anything.

"Oh, I've tried. But I don't have a weapon to fight the Wellington money. He convinced me to sign the papers giving him total parental rights, and now he won't even let me spend an hour with Vivian."

"The Wellingtons of Panther Holler?" Tinkie and I spoke as one.

Hedy nodded. "You know the family, so you know what I'm talking about."

And I did. The Wellingtons were perhaps the wealthiest family in the state. They had money, power, political influence—everything to convince a judge to see a custody battle their way. Of course I didn't know Hedy or her background, and she'd voluntarily signed away her rights.

"Marcus is the child's father?" Tinkie asked.

There were several generations of Wellingtons to pick from. The fertilizer of wealth had grown an extended family tree. I figured the father to be Marcus or maybe his father, Gilliard. There were uncles and cousins, too. The Wellingtons were known for the Midas touch and heroic sperm.

"Yes, Marcus," Hedy said. "I met him at the Gulf one summer. He was so charming. And he seemed so nice."

"And he was filthy rich," I threw in. "Money is the most potent aphrodisiac, isn't it?"

"That's not the way it was." Hedy wasn't combative; she was defeated. "He pursued me. I was working at the Dauphin Island Sea Lab, planning a career in botany and marine science. I was a good student and graduated high school early. I was in my sophomore year of college and had a full scholarship to finish my degree. I had no intention of falling in love with anyone. I was only nineteen."

She was, for all practical purposes, a child at

the time. I knew Marcus and I traveled in some circles where he was a regular. He was a handsome man with polished manners and an easy self-deprecation about his family status. While Marcus seemed pleasant enough on the surface, his family was known to be ruthless in the pursuit of what they wanted. There had been talk about Marcus, too. He was one of the most eligible bachelors in the Delta, and he'd broken the hearts of more than a dozen Delta belles. Hedy, a naïve young woman of nineteen, might easily have been swept off her feet by Marcus.

"But you fell in love," Tinkie said, "and you got pregnant."

"I never planned on having a child. My dream was to work to save marine life and vegetation, to make a difference for the planet. When I found out I was pregnant, I was upset, of course. My family . . . my mother was young when she had me. She raised me alone. I was determined to break the cur . . ." She took a breath and looked at the floor. "The curse of repetitive mistakes. Anyway, Marcus offered to marry me. He even took me to his home in Panther Holler to meet his family."

A red flush climbed her cheeks, and I could imagine how the Wellingtons had treated this pregnant girl who'd tagged onto the family fortune by "trapping" Marcus. "And did he follow through on the marriage?"

She shook her head. "As I got bigger and bigger, he came up with one excuse after another. Finally, Marcus wouldn't take my calls. I couldn't go home. I just couldn't. For the sake of my daughter, I—" She swallowed and regained her composure. "I was on my own. That's the simplest way to put it."

My cold, cold heart was melting, even though I fought it. Hedy's story certainly wasn't original, but it was heart-wrenching. Young girl seduced by wealthy, experienced man, impregnated, and dumped. Where this got interesting was that Marcus had returned for the child.

Her mouth worked as she struggled to contain her emotion. "Marcus showed up just after she was born. I was working at one of the casinos. Dealing blackjack was the only job I could get." She looked at Tinkie and then me. "I was so stupid. I thought he wanted to do right by his daughter."

"And?"

"He'd hired this fabulous nanny. She stayed with me a week, and I could see she was competent and attentive to Vivian's needs. Then Marcus started working on me. He forced me to see how much better Vivian's life would be with him and his family than what I could provide for her." She wiped a tear from her cheek. "Marcus has had her ever since."

"Couldn't you hire a lawyer?" Tinkie asked.

"With what money? I did talk to ten firms. They weren't interested in taking my case because I didn't have money to fight with and I'd voluntarily signed away my rights. They told me that realistically the Wellingtons had the resources to keep me in court until Vivian was eighteen, and that the whole time they would be poisoning my daughter against me. They were correct. Marcus won't even let me see Vivian. I haven't held my own baby in two years."

Fury sparked in her eyes for a split second. "I heard about this contest, and I knew if I could win, I could use the money to hire a lawyer. A good one. I have to get Vivian back before they turn her completely against me. Before they turn her into one of them."

"Do the pageant officials know you've had a child?" Somewhere in the back of my head I felt certain there was a rule against beauty contestants also being mothers. Maybe not a rule, but definitely a prejudice. I'd never heard of a contestant who balanced a tiara and a child.

"No one knows. They'd kick me out."

"But if they discover the truth about Vivian, they'll strip you of the title and likely file suit against you to return the money."

"Maybe I can convince them that a spokeswoman who manages a career and a child can only make their product more appealing. That is their market: young mothers who demand the finest equipment. Besides, if I can get Vivian away from those people, I'll risk jail."

"And who would care for Vivian?" To take her from the Wellingtons only to put her in the foster care system didn't seem wise.

"I've come to an understanding with my mother. She would take Vivian and raise her. I don't want my little girl growing up to believe she can get away with anything because she's a Wellington. I don't want her to think using people is part of doing business. I don't want her *corrupted* by that way of living. My family is poor, and we live in a rural area, but Vivian would have love." Hedy sensed the weak link and she focused on Tinkie. "Will you help me? There's no one else I can turn to. I swear, I'll find a way to pay you. I swear it."

A loud knock saved us from committing to a case I saw clearly would be for charity and that already involved two dead women.

"I'll get the door," I said. "I'm sure it's Police Chief Jansen." I didn't have to have Madame Tomeeka's abilities to figure that one out.

Jansen was a burly man with a deep voice and an impressive mustache. He allowed Hedy to remain in our room—with a police officer posted outside the door—while he scoped out the crime scene.

Tinkie distracted Hedy by encouraging her to

95

talk about Vivian. When I could stand it no longer, I told Tinkie I was going to investigate and then left. No worries on being stealthy—the entire second-floor hallway around Hedy's room was filled with cops, curious hotel guests, and management. I eased closer and closer, hoping to overhear some scuttlebutt. I made it almost to the door before Jansen spied me and beckoned one of the officers to halt me.

"Was she poisoned?" I realized a moment too late I'd revealed too much.

"Won't know until the coroner examines her." Jansen gave me the once-over. "What makes you think she was poisoned?"

"I didn't hear a gunshot. This whole place would've been like an ant bed."

"Yet you didn't assume she'd been stabbed," he pondered aloud.

It was time to turn the focus of the conversation. "Any idea what happened to Brook? Is there an explanation why she caught on fire and never lifted a finger to help herself?"

"Are you working this case, Ms. Delaney?" he asked.

"Not officially. How'd you know I was a private investigator?"

"Let's just say your reputation precedes you, and while Sheriff Peters may put up with your meddling in his cases, I won't. Do you understand?"

"Perfectly," I said with a huge crocodile smile. Tinkie had taught me to "emote pleasantness" when I wanted to plant a boot up someone's butt. It took all of my willpower to restrain my foot, but I needed something from Jansen. "You never answered my question about Brook."

"We're looking at Miss Oniada's death as a potential murder," he said. "It appears we have a double homicide here in Leflore County."

"How was Brook killed?" I'd watched the stage the whole time. She'd been standing with her fire batons, but no one had gone near her. She'd staggered and turned in a circle like she was suddenly lost or blind. Then she'd burst into flames, all unassisted.

"A highly combustible substance in her skin lotion wasn't listed on the bottle's ingredients. When the lit baton got too close to her—whoosh!"

"You think someone tampered with her skin lotion?"

"I do," he said.

"How do you know Brook didn't change the ingredients of the lotion herself?"

"No fingerprints on the bottle." He nodded sagely. "She wouldn't wear gloves to put on lotion, but a murderer would if he or she tampered with the lotion. That girl was set on fire and burned alive by someone who meant to harm her."

The very idea was appalling. "You believe someone intended for her to catch fire?"

"No doubt about it." He leaned closer to me. "And I have a pretty good suspect."

"Who might that be?"

"Miss Blackledge." He watched my reaction.

"Why would Hedy set Brook on fire?"

"Are you trying to play me or are you just plain stupid?"

"Not the latter," I answered. "It might be the former, but could a mere private dick from Zinnia pull the wool over your eyes?" Jansen was short on manners, but I'd had lessons in charm from Tinkie. "What would you say is Hedy's motive? Killing Brook—or Janet, for that matter—wouldn't guarantee her the title."

"It might move her two steps closer."

"Or it might not. No one knows how the girls are ranked by the judges. And why would she kill her roommate, of all the contestants? That points the finger of blame right at her. It doesn't make sense."

I thought I'd worked him around to my way of thinking, until he smiled. "You're slippery as an eel," he said, "and I don't like eels."

"What kind of accelerant was used in Brook's lotion?"

The look he gave me was crafty. "Ask Miss Blackledge."

"I would if she had the answer." He was

maneuvering me into defensive mode for a young woman who wasn't even my client. "Why don't you just tell me and make it easy on both of us?"

"We're still looking into that, but I do know Miss Blackledge was experimenting with volatile liquids that had the capacity to ignite. She was in the Viking kitchen and several of the girls saw her."

"There are a lot of recipes calling for flaming foods. I'm sure Hedy wasn't the only contestant who went for the spectacle of Bananas Foster or whatever she cooked," I said.

"Maybe not. And I'll get to the bottom of that, I assure you." He almost growled the words. "Now I have work to do."

"Thank you, Chief Jansen." I smiled sweetly.

"Thank me by staying out of this case. This killer means business and deserves to pay for the terrible crimes that have been committed."

"I couldn't agree more. The *guilty* party needs to pay. I just want to be sure you arrest the person who actually is guilty."

7

Sleep evaded me, so I took my cell phone out to the Alluvian's small courtyard. A fountain tinkled soothingly, and I debated whether to call Graf or not. Dawn was breaking in the Delta, which meant it was way early in Los Angeles, but I calculated that I'd been a trouper so far and hadn't asked for much in the way of babying or consolation. I dialed his number.

Groggy at first, Graf came instantly awake when he realized it was me. "Are you okay?" he asked.

I was both pleased and appalled by his reaction. Delighted that he cared about me, but sorry my early-morning call generated alarm rather than simple pleasure. "I'm fine. I miss you."

"Are we going to have phone sex?" he asked.

"If I weren't sitting outside in a public court-yard we might."

His warm chuckle made me tingle. Phone sex wasn't what I wanted. I needed a dose of the real thing.

"Why are you calling from some courtyard in the predawn hours?" he asked, curiosity plain in his tone.

"Tinkie and I are still at the Alluvian. Graf, two of the beauty contestants have been murdered, and the most likely suspect is asleep in the room with Tinkie."

Perhaps I'd phrased the situation indelicately, but I wasn't prepared for the blast of anger from the West Coast. "Are you insane?" Graf asked. "You left Tinkie asleep with a potential murderer in the room? And what is he doing in your room? What's wrong with you?"

Stunned didn't begin to capture my reaction. "Wait a minute," I said, but he was having none of that.

"After everything you and Tinkie have been through, I can't believe you let a possible killer into your room. What, is he an accused rapist, too?"

"It's not a man, it's a woman." My diction was perfect, and my drawl had evaporated. "Hedy Lamarr Blackledge, one of the contestants."

"I don't care if it's Julia Roberts. Haven't you been hurt enough, Sarah Booth? You're supposed to be healing so you can return to your life, the one we're planning together. I'd hoped you'd voluntarily give up this private-eye business. You and Tinkie are going to get hurt. Oscar and I agree, it would be best if you closed the detective agency."

My fingers gripping the cell phone refused to obey my mental command to release. Surely this was a dream. Graf would never insert himself into my life in such a bullying way.

"Sarah Booth, are you there?"

"Yes."

"We need to talk."

"Yes."

There was a pause. "I'm sorry. I didn't mean to go off like that, but I've been worried sick about you."

No one would ever give me credit for beating back the impulse to let the shit fly, but I managed to remain silent. To open my mouth would invite catastrophe into the conversation.

"Aren't you going to respond?" he asked.

"Maybe later." Oh, the cost of those four syllables.

"I'm awake now, and I think we need to talk about this. Neither Oscar nor I wanted to push you to close the agency. But you and Tinkie are right smack in the middle of another case, and you haven't even recovered from the last one."

I inhaled, letting the breath fill my lungs. I would have given a lot for a cigarette. For a pack. Maybe for a carton and a bottle of Jack Daniel's. My entire body was trembling.

"Graf, I don't think I can talk about this now."

If he heard the tremor in my voice, he didn't understand what it meant. After the death of my parents, few things in life ever made me cry.

Graf's unexpected assault had startled me and then angered me until I was close to tears. A very, very bad sign. If I produced tears of anger, it would take a cleaning crew to pick up the debris.

"We need to talk, Sarah Booth. Have you taken this case?"

"No."

"Thank goodness."

"Let's discuss this later, please." I had to get off the phone before I said something I would regret.

"You promise we'll talk before you sign a new client?"

"Graf, I'm going to hang up now. I don't want to end this conversation abruptly. I don't like that. But I am ending it. We'll talk later." I closed the phone and as I brought my hand down, the interior hotel lights caught in the facets of my beautiful diamond engagement ring.

Sitting in the courtyard, I could almost make myself believe the conversation had never happened. Graf had always been so supportive of my private investigative efforts. More than that, he'd been proud of me. And now, he and Oscar had plotted behind mine and Tinkie's backs to get us to quit. My body was still numb from the betrayal.

The hours just before dawn are the quietest of the night. Greenwood slept all around me.

Somewhere in the distance the lonesome wail of a train carried over the cotton fields. A few robins, cardinals, wrens, and mockingbirds fluttered into the courtyard to keep me company. Soon, the hotel's day staff would arrive. My solitude couldn't last much longer—I'd have to face my partner.

Before I spoke to Tinkie, I needed to assess how much I was to blame for the way the conversation with Graf had gone. I'd startled him awake and ignited his fear factor, then blithely dumped the information that a potential murderess was asleep in my hotel room with my best friend.

Graf was a continent away and he couldn't protect me. Yet I'd callously painted a dangerous picture in his head. That was no justification for him and Oscar meddling in the business of Delaney Detective Agency, but I had to assume some responsibility for the train wreck of the conversation. It hadn't occurred to me that Graf would be so upset about my work. He knew I was a P.I. when we got together. Sure, he wanted me to be an actress, but he'd indicated he would support me in bi-professional careers—one strongly rooted in the Mississippi Delta and the other in Los Angeles.

Another sound mingled with the murmur of the fountain. Silver bangles jounced and tinkled together, and I turned to find Jitty standing behind me. The predawn breeze caught the hem of a jewel blue dress that hugged every one of Jitty's luscious curves—a welcome relief after her most recent tenure in the thirties Depression era. She'd gone from starving waif to cupcake. Her makeup was flawless, and her hair was a straight bob curved in along her jawline. She looked vaguely familiar, but I couldn't place it exactly.

"Wanna know what's cookin'?" she asked. Before I could answer, she held up a hand. "Delicious home-cooked meals in thirty minutes or less. Sorry, I'm not doing Southern right now. Would you like to know the menu I'm planning?"

Even as far down in the dumps as I was, Jitty could amuse me. "Why are you copycatting Rachael Ray?"

"Imitation is the sincerest form of flattery. Want to hear my menu?"

Because I'd rather do anything than confront Tinkie—even listen to Jitty's concept of a thirty-minute meal—I said, "I'm all ears."

She took a seat at the table. "Not yet," she said. "There's something else to consider. Did you know your ears continue to grow as long as you live? Your nose, too. Not so bad on the nose front, but I have to say, your ears could use a good bobbing. Say you live to be eighty, they'll probably be touching your shoulders.

Your boobs will be down to your waist. Your—"

"Stop it!" I couldn't decide if I wanted to laugh or punch her. "Can't you see I'm depressed already?"

"A blind man couldn't miss that."

"Then quit picking on me." I sounded petulant, but I didn't care.

"Okay. Let's talk cookin'. I've run across the best recipes ever. Only takes half an hour, and they are yum-o."

"Rachael Ray is going to sue you for impersonating her. Not all celebrities are tolerant of such things."

"She's too busy making lots of money to worry about someone in the Great Beyond," Jitty said matter-of-factly. "Normal folks don't care what us noncorporeals get into. Besides, who's going to tell her? You? 'Ms. Ray, I'm haunted by the ghost of a black woman who impersonates you.' I can see how well that would work."

"What's your point?" I was tired and depressed and hurt. "And what are you doing in Greenwood, anyway? I didn't call for you."

"Like I'm your fairy godmother or something and have to wait for a call?" She puffed up like an adder. "That'll be the day. I come and go as I please."

"Then go." I turned away from her.

"That man got to you, didn't he?"

Tears burned behind my eyes, but I was determined not to cry. "He was a jackass, but part of it was my doing."

"He only wants to protect you, Sarah Booth."

"When does protection flip and become suffocation?"

"What are you going to do?"

I knew what she meant. I could give up my P.I. agency or risk losing Graf. I'd already lost everyone else I loved. Though he hadn't given me an ultimatum, I knew the drill. He didn't want to be hurt, either, and he considered my work dangerous. "I don't know."

"Not the right answer," she said.

"I have to talk with Tinkie. Oscar's in this up to his eyeballs." Anger swept over me. "You'd think that Oscar would be a little grateful after I saved his poxied ass only a few weeks ago."

"At the risk of your own," Jitty reminded me.

"I know that. But had I not gone through everything I did, Oscar would be dead. No one wants to look at it that way, but it's true. Without my loss and suffering, Oscar would be counting his money in the Great Beyond with you."

Jitty reached into the front of her dress and pulled out what appeared to be index cards.

"What are those?" I asked, hoping she'd found some Delaney family notes on how to deal with this situation.

"Chicken Picante recipe." She scanned it with

interest, then flipped to the next one. "What about Hamburger Delight?"

I wanted to snatch the cards and throw them all over the courtyard, but I couldn't. They were no more solid than Jitty. "Why are you here?"

"What's your special talent, Sarah Booth?"

"Is this a trick question?"

"I have better things to do in the Great Beyond than come and play tricks on a depressed person. Your mama would stomp my ass."

Despite myself, I smiled. "She would, wouldn't she?"

"So answer the question."

"I'm a good actress. I think I could be great if I tried."

"Uh-huh. Now what else?"

Jitty had lowered the cards, and she watched me intently, as if my body language would reveal far more than my words. There were times when she could read my mind, but so far, she was waiting to see what I would say.

"I'm a respectable private investigator. And Tinkie is, too. We've done some good in the world. We've made sure innocent people didn't go to jail, and we've put some bad guys behind bars. Despite the fact that Tinkie and I have both been injured—"

"And don't forget Chablis and Sweetie Pie. They've been wounded in the line of duty."

She was right. Both dogs had suffered traumas due to their allegiance to us.

"What else would you claim as a talent?" she asked.

"I'm tenacious."

"That's such a nice way to say you're pig-headed."

"I'm making this list, so leave me be. I don't need editing from a haint who refuses to move on. Talk about mulish, take a look in the mirror."

"Okay, what else?"

"I'm a good friend."

"You are indeed." She pushed a card toward me on the table. I didn't touch it, but I read it. "What gives you the most satisfaction?"

I hadn't anticipated that question. "You got a thirty-minute recipe to help me with this answer?"

She stood up. "You don't need thirty minutes. You know. You just don't want to say it." The first rays of dawn pierced her and filtered onto the table.

"Don't you dare leave." Jitty had the most aggravating habit of starting something and then fading away when the going got sticky. "You can't say something like that and leave."

Her only answer was a soft chuckle. A gust of wind whipped across the table where we'd been sitting, and the index card swirled into the air and vaporized. Jitty had learned a new and impressive stunt.

There was nothing to do now but go inside and talk with Tinkie. I didn't relish the idea of starting trouble between her and Oscar. They were my heroes, a married couple who shared and cared in the manner my own parents had loved. But my father, James Franklin Delaney, would never have attempted to govern my mother the way Oscar—and Graf—had stepped into mine and Tinkie's lives. While I regretted the idea of talking with Tinkie, I loved her too much to hide this from her.

When Tinkie woke up, it was nearly nine o'clock. I sent Hedy to find Starbucks coffee and a *New York Times*, two items I hoped would be in scarce supply in Greenwood. Meanwhile, I retrieved two cups of the hotel's aromatic brew and locked our room door.

"We need to talk," I told Tinkie.

She sipped her coffee and listened, and for the first time since we'd become partners, I was unable to read her. Whatever she was thinking, she kept her face neutral.

When I finished, she put her coffee down and got out of bed. "What are you going to do?" she asked.

"It isn't just me," I reminded her. "This involves you, too. What are you going to do?"

She stretched and trotted into the bathroom. I heard the water running, then she came out with

110

a towel, dabbing at her face. Her expression remained unfathomable as she climbed up on the edge of my bed. "Oscar and I have been married nearly fifteen years, Sarah Booth. I married him ten seconds after I graduated from Ole Miss, and I only waited that long because Daddy said he'd paid for a degree and it would bear the name I was born with."

"But your father wanted you to marry Oscar." Avery Bellcase as much as admitted he arranged Tinkie's marriage, in the way of royalty creating alliances through legal contracts.

"He did. He picked Oscar for me and pushed me hard. I wasn't certain it was the right choice, but I'd been born and bred to marry. Life with a man like Oscar was the proscribed pattern of my life, and I was eager to get on with it. You never had that pressure on you, Sarah Booth. It didn't matter that you left college unmarried and were considered a failure and an old maid." She bit her bottom lip lightly, and it popped free of her teeth, making her look young and vulnerable. "I would never in my entire life dream of disappointing my daddy."

The point she was making came to me. In the past two years she'd grown immensely. She'd shed the cocoon that society had spun around her. Day by day, week by week she'd emerged from those expectations and built a life of her own design. Oscar was initially opposed to Tinkie

111

working with me, but he'd come around. Or so I'd thought. But what she was saying involved a skill I'd never learned.

"I can't just pretend that it's okay with me for Graf to discuss my future with Oscar as if I were a child incapable of making a decision for myself."

"You said yourself you upset Graf. Honey, if you'd told me you'd left a potential murderer in the room with Cece, I would have been shocked and might have reacted badly." She ran her hand down my arm, lightly touching the place where the bone had broken. "When someone loves you, he wants to protect you."

"I can't be suffocated."

"You don't get everything exactly like you want it, Sarah Booth. I'm telling you. Let this go. Don't chew it 'til it bleeds."

"What will you say to Oscar?"

"There's nothing to tell him. I got the impression you didn't want to take this case, anyway. So why start a fight over a nonexistent case?"

"What about Hedy?"

"There are other investigators, I'm sure. None as good as we are, but competent ones." She went to the closet and selected her wardrobe for the day. "Our cooking class today is main courses. This should be fun."

She acted as if the issue were resolved. Fat chance of that. Maybe she could brush off

Oscar's chauvinistic attitude, but I couldn't say the same about Graf. I'd always pitied women who said things like "I have to ask my husband" or "if my husband says it's okay." Perhaps it was part of a workable relationship, but to me it smacked of subservience. "I'm not okay with this."

She smiled, and something akin to sadness flickered across her face. "I didn't think you would be. You weren't raised in the tradition." She came to stand at the bedside holding several coat hangers and clothes. "Most of the time I admire the fact you fly in the face of the conventional way of doing things, but it hurts you in relationships with men, Sarah Booth."

"So you're going to let Oscar bully you and make your decisions?"

She put a pair of black slacks and a white pin-tucked shirt on the bed. "No. I won't let him bully me, but I also won't ram him head-to-head. There's no point when I know I'll do exactly as I please in the long run. Graf can't control you, but men need the illusion they have control."

Tinkie was wise, and I was headstrong. "I can't pretend and I won't manipulate my life partner."

She took a deep breath. "I'm sorry to hear that."

There was a knock on the bedroom door, and

Tinkie went to open it. Hedy stood with a tray of coffee and a newspaper. "Best I could do," she said, extending both to me.

"Thanks," I said. "Tinkie and I will take your case."

I saw Tinkie's smile shift from ear to ear.

I had been played by a master.

8

We'd barely pried the lids off our coffees when the door burst open. Police Chief Jansen and five policemen rushed into the room. The officers carried weapons, all pointed at three women, one of whom still wore baby-doll pajamas. The guns shifted from Tinkie and me to Hedy.

A bit of overkill for a young woman who weighed no more than 115 pounds.

"Hedy Lamarr Blackledge, you're under arrest for the murder of Janet Menton." Jansen grabbed Hedy's wrist and spun her around to cuff her.

"Do something!" Hedy wailed over her shoulder at Tinkie.

"We will," Tinkie assured her. "I'll get you a good lawyer and make your bail."

"Tinkie, be careful what you commit to," I whispered to my partner. Even with the plush salary I'd made as a movie star, I still owed on Dahlia House. I'd refused attempts by Tinkie's father, Avery Bellcase, to cover my debt because I'd stayed in Zinnia to help solve Oscar's mysterious illness. "Hedy doesn't have any money."

"But I do," Tinkie said, and her blue eyes danced with mischief. I could see her game. Not only was she going to do what she damn well pleased, she'd stick it to Oscar in a way he couldn't ignore: spend his money providing legal defense for her client. Tinkie, as I had ascertained, was nobody to mess with.

Jansen led Hedy from the room, the police officers withdrawing in a backward crawl as if they expected Tinkie and me to storm them, maybe beat them to death with one of my fuzzy meerkat slippers.

When the door closed, Tinkie hopped into action. "First a shower and then we need to get busy. Surely there's a good lawyer here in Greenwood. Since you're already dressed, would you mind checking the hotel's computer for legal counsel?"

"Even better, I'll ask the concierge."

Betty was an impressive source of information, and within the hour I'd provided Tinkie with the name of the best defense lawyer in Greenwood. Tinkie hired Russell Dean over the phone and sent him to talk to Hedy.

"We have to find out what evidence Jansen has against Hedy," Tinkie said, reasonably enough. "It must only be circumstantial, because she's innocent."

"Somehow I don't think Jansen is in a sharing mood." It wasn't my imagination that the police chief didn't like us—he'd stated it.

"It's so much more pleasant to work with Coleman." Tinkie slipped on a pair of killer heels. Amazingly she was able to sleuth *and* style. "But we'll manage to bend Jansen to our will." Tinkie had taken Jansen on as a personal challenge. He'd just waded into very deep water with a clever shark.

"He's arrested her for murder, so he must have something on her other than the fact that she shared a room with one woman and was in a contest with both victims."

"There have been other incidents," Tinkie pointed out. "The hot pepper in Babs Lafitte's hair spray. The chocolate roaches for Karrie Kompton."

We looked at each other. "Karrie Kompton," we said simultaneously, perfecting the stereo rendition of our brilliant and parallel thoughts.

"She's bitch enough to send herself chocolate roaches," Tinkie said.

"Too true. But would she actually bite one in half?" I shuddered at the thought.

I could deal with spiders and snakes, albeit

116

reluctantly, but roaches terrified me. The bastards had a habit of flying at me and clamping down on my skin with their scratchy, filthy little legs. When I was ten I'd accompanied my father to a fancy party in town for a visiting politician. I'd been forced to wear a frilly dress with a starched petticoat. My father and I were walking downtown singing one of his favorite Western songs about a faithful horse when a big ol' cockroach flew from the roots of an oak tree onto my leg and crawled under my petticoat. Needless to say, neither the dress nor petticoat survived.

The scandal that ensued came mostly from the fact that the First Baptist Church had just let out their evening service and the congregation burst out the front doors to find me on their steps tearing my clothes off and screeching like a wild thing.

The minister thought I was possessed and rushed over with a Bible to drive the devil out of me.

All in all, it was a hallmark event that scarred me for life when it comes to roaches. "I hate roaches," I said.

Tinkie poked me in the arm. "You're remembering the day you tore your clothes off in front of Reverend Johnny Finch and the entire Baptist church, aren't you?" She laughed. "Two of the choir ladies fainted and gave themselves concussions when they hit the cement steps. It was a helluva sight."

"Daddy gave me his shirt to cover my 'nekked-ness' as everyone was screaming." I laughed, too. It was an awful but funny memory.

"Little tatters of your dress and petticoat blew around town for at least a week. People found them in shrubbery. Mrs. Hedgepeth was going to file a complaint against you."

I hadn't thought of Mrs. Hedgepeth, the town grump, since she'd had Sweetie Pie arrested for trespassing. "Mama took care of her. She paid her a visit and whatever was said, Mrs. Hedgepeth quit yapping about my 'littering up the whole town.'"

"If anyone tried to hurt you, Sarah Booth, they had Libby Delaney to deal with."

"Yeah. Mama had my back, even when I was in the wrong." The memory was bittersweet.

"About the roaches. The answer is a big yes. Karrie Kompton would do almost anything to win this contest. If she's the one behind the murders, she's perfectly capable of eating a roach to shift the finger of blame away from herself."

"You really think Karrie could do these terrible things?" I asked.

"Perhaps my reasoning is colored by my dislike of her." Tinkie was nothing if not honest. "Nonetheless, until we have another lead to follow, let's go at this as if Karrie is behind it."

"Coleman wouldn't approve of selecting a suspect before the evidence is viewed."

"Oh, grow up. Coleman does it all the time. How else do you explain how he arrested *you* for murder?"

I zipped my lip on that one. I had volleyed with Tinkie and lost. Now it was time for action.

The Delta Correctional Facility was on Baldwin Road. Hedy was hotter than a hornet who'd been swatted with a stick, but based on lack of evidence, Russell Dean had convinced the prosecuting attorney not to file murder charges. Still, Jansen made it clear that Hedy was his number-one suspect. As she walked out of the facility with me and Tinkie, Jansen called out, "Enjoy the free air. No one commits murder in Greenwood and gets away with it."

Hedy turned and started back, but Tinkie restrained her. Judging from the hot pink of Hedy's cheeks, a physical assault on the police chief was not beyond her.

At the hotel, Hedy had been assigned a new room, which she had all to herself. The other girls refused to share space with her.

We left her there to prepare for another night of the competition. Hedy needed the title for financial reasons, and now she was more determined than ever to win. Her secrets would come out one way or another, and she was like me: She'd spit in the devil's eye just to spite him.

Tinkie made a quick trip to see the lawyer,

while I decided to find the county coroner, one Marlboro Tanner, also a preacher. In most Mississippi counties, coroners are elected and require no medical training. In cases of homicide, the state crime lab performs autopsies, and that's where Janet's body had been sent. Brook's too, I supposed. But Marlboro Tanner would be a good place to get an idea of what evidence, if any, Janet's body had revealed.

Marlboro's appearance was in direct contrast to the image of the tough cowboy his name brought to mind. The clean-cut young man with kind eyes was in the Church of Redemption office working on a sermon. He appeared to be no older than fifteen. When I told him my business, he waved me to a chair.

"This coroner's position isn't the job for me," he said. "Those poor girls. What awful ways to die. Burning and then poison. I'll never get that out of my head. The last coroner served four years and never sent a body to the crime lab."

"You're certain it was poison?" There's no denying Brook's fate, but it could have been accidental. That was a thought I intended to plant deeply in the young coroner's subconscious.

"Chief Jansen says he can't be certain about Miss Oniada. The autopsy isn't back yet on her. Probably a couple of days, and more time for Miss Menton. The state lab is backlogged, from what I hear. Bodies are stacked on top of each other."

Not exactly the kind of image one wanted floating about in one's head. But it gave Tinkie and me time to find out what was really happening with the beauty contestants.

"Prior to Janet's . . . death and Brook's . . . accident, there was an incident with Babs Lafitte."

"The pepper thing." Marlboro leaned back in his chair and steepled his fingers, an appropriate gesture for a minister. "Chief Jansen said something about sending samples off to the lab. He did take some cooking things from the school for testing. But I have to say, what appears to be a practical joke, while unpleasant for Miss Lafitte, isn't the chief's highest priority right now."

Good to know. I felt an obligation to tell the coroner, who appeared to be an open book, that Jansen wouldn't appreciate his candidness with me. But why mess up a good source? "What do you think happened?"

"That young woman this morning . . ." He went to the window to look out over the churchyard, a vista of carefully clipped centipede grass highlighted with flowering shrubs. "I thought at first it was a heart attack. My mind doesn't normally run to murder. But I do think poison killed her."

"Could she have taken something? Not on purpose, but . . ."

He arched an eyebrow. "I guess that depends on what type of poison was used."

"I mean, could she have been taking a prescription drug and had a negative reaction to it? There are a lot of ways to unintentionally kill oneself." Doubt was the crop I was trying to harvest. The coroner in rural counties relied on the findings of the state crime lab, but he might raise some questions.

"Anything is possible," he agreed. "But not likely. What's interesting is the absence of her roommate, Miss Blackledge. Had she been in the room, she might have been able to get help for Janet in time to save her."

That was an angle I hadn't thought about. Had someone lured Hedy out of the room . . . but she'd left because she couldn't sleep and wanted to play her violin? "It's possible Hedy is alive only because she wasn't in the room." I gave it ten seconds to sink in. "Did Miss Menton eat anything before she died?"

"She ordered from room service around ten o'clock. And there were some pastries on the floor. I'm guessing she died shortly after midnight, but the state lab will be able to tell me more."

"When you get the test results back on Brook and Janet, would you let me see them?"

He considered. "The fact you're asking tells me Chief Jansen won't want me to do that."

While I can fudge the truth in almost all situations, I'm not great at direct lies to a minister, especially one as decent as Marlboro. "Probably not. Jansen has already said Hedy is his primary suspect, and my partner and I are working on Hedy's behalf. But the important thing here is the truth, don't you think?"

He didn't hesitate. "That's true. The reports are factual. I don't see the harm in giving you a copy, so I'm happy to do that."

"Thank you, Reverend." I simply couldn't stop myself. "Were you named after the Marlboro man on the billboards?"

His response was a smile. "Everyone asks. The answer is yes, but the irony is neither of my parents smoked. They liked cowboys. I wish they'd named me Wyatt or Bat or even Marshal. But they liked the mountains, and every time they saw the billboard, the dream came to life for a little while. They said I was part of that dream, so they named me Marlboro."

The story touched me more than I wanted to show.

He extended his hand. "I hope you and the chief get to the bottom of this. And soon."

The logical next step was to look into the past of each girl. Both deaths had been extreme and awful. That implied a personal touch—someone who'd constructed painful deaths deliberately. Had Brook and Janet shared some place or person or event? Babs, who was still alive and kicking, might be my best source.

I turned Tinkie's Caddy back toward the hotel. Perhaps I could catch Babs before she got all involved with preparing for the next leg of competition.

After checking at the desk, I went straight to Babs's room. After the pepper incident, she'd opted for a private room, and she answered my knock on her door. The tallest of the contestants at nearly six feet, Babs was a striking redhead— or she had been. Now her hair clumped in dull tufts that brought to mind Bozo the Clown.

"Welcome to Bedlam." She waved me into the room.

Clothes, shoes, at least twenty bald Styrofoam wig heads, suitcases, and what appeared to be small dead, red creatures littered the room. Babs took a seat at a specially lit vanity and picked up a wig styled in a long shag. A half-empty bottle of Jack Daniel's rested beside her elbow, along with more small vials filled with crushed herbs and spices.

"The judges voted unanimously to allow me to wear a hairpiece," she said, watching my reaction in the mirror.

I wanted to say, "Thank god for that because your head looks like a Chernobyl site," but I only nodded. "That's good."

"What do you think of this one? It's called Candy." She fluffed out the long, red tresses.

"Too . . . whorish." I couldn't think of another way to say it.

She pulled off the wig and tossed it on the floor by the other rejected styles. "You're right. I just wanted to see if you'd tell the truth or not." She batted the empty wig head with the back of her hand and it sailed across the room, crashing against the wall and then into a heap on top of two dozen others.

"Mostly I do. Tell the truth. Sometimes I don't." I picked up a short black wig and handed it to her. "As fascinating as hair choices are, I need to talk to you about the two dead women."

"Brook was nice but naïve. Janet"—she pulled the dark wig on—"I don't really have a read on her. She stayed to herself and she was rooming with that creepy goth Blackledge gal. Speaking of goth, this hair color doesn't work for me at all. I look like a vampire."

She was correct. The black wig with her fair coloring made her look dead. It even changed the contours of her face.

"Yuck!" she said, flinging it into the reject pile.

"Why do you believe Hedy Blackledge is goth?"

She waved me toward a chair. "Let's see, could it be that she never wears anything but black, she plays funeral dirges on her violin, she wears red lipstick, and her skin hasn't seen sunlight in the last twenty years. Her family has

125

some weird voodoo connection, and she plays to that. She enjoys being dark. That pretty much puts her in the goth category for me."

Everything she said about Hedy was true, up to a point. She had translucent pale skin, wore red lipstick and black clothes, and the violin pieces I'd heard were hauntingly sad. But that didn't make her a goth. "How did you know about Hedy's family?" I was sure Hedy hadn't told her.

She thought a moment. "One of the other girls was talking about her."

"Which one?"

She hesitated. "I can't be sure."

"Karrie?"

Amusement crossed her face. "Good guess, but I think it was Crystal Belle. I don't think she meant any harm by it, just a bit of gossip."

Motives were seldom that pure, but I let it go. "Of all the contestants, why do you think someone would go after Brook and Janet?"

Babs swung her legs around to face me. "Rumor has it that Brook, Janet, Karrie, Hedy, Amanda, and *moi* are the front-runners. Most of the girls thought Brook and Janet went into the talent competition as the top two contenders based on academics and originality in cooking."

She poured herself a straight shot of Jack. "Now that they're out of the way . . ." She remembered her manners and poured a drink

126

for me without even asking. "I'm dying to have a cigarette," she said, glancing around the hotel room. "Do you think they'll be able to tell if I smoke in here?"

"There's a courtyard outside." If she lit up, I might have to join her. I'd quit smoking, but the temptation was on me hard.

"And if we go into the courtyard, it'll be just my luck a judge will walk by and catch me smoking. I hate this eighth-grade shit. You know, it would be better to have leprosy than to be a smoker these days."

I couldn't argue that, so I didn't try. "I wouldn't smoke in the room."

She sighed and took a big swallow of her Jack. "I can't wait until they start fining people for eating potato chips. They'll call it a health penalty. Soon only elegant people wearing the right designer labels will be allowed out in the daylight."

I pulled her attention back to the task at hand. "If you had to name someone who might want to harm Brook and Janet, who would it be?"

"None of the contestants really like each other. We all want to win, so we haven't bothered pretending to be perky and impressed with each other like we did back in our younger days."

Babs was twenty-five. It was peculiar to hear her talk about her "younger days."

"Was there anything about Brook or Janet that

would make someone personally dislike them? Enough to harm them?"

She'd picked up a short, auburn wig and adjusted it on her head. Staring at herself in the mirror, she answered, "To me, they were two of the least objectionable contestants. If I were going to take anyone out, it would be that bitch Karrie Kompton."

Karrie had no dearth of folks who didn't like her, but acting like a horrible human being didn't make her a killer. "Do you know who sent the chocolate-covered roaches to Karrie?"

She shifted so that our gazes didn't meet in the mirror. She knew.

"Was it you?" I asked.

She busied herself putting on shoes.

"I'm not going to tell anyone, Babs. There've been a lot of strange incidents at this competition. I need to know who's behind what."

"I sent Karrie the flowers and the roaches." Her chin lifted in defiance. "She deserved a whole lot worse. And she got even by peppering my hair spray. At least my prank didn't do any permanent damage." She pointed at her hair. "This will take months to grow out."

"How do you know Karrie was behind the pepper incident?"

"She saw a chance to ruin me and frame Hedy, and let me say she hates Hedy even more than she hates the rest of us."

"Go on."

"Hedy prepared a delicious dish using spices, specifically habanero peppers. Some of the peppers were left over, and the next morning, they'd disappeared from the countertop. Hedy assumed the cleanup crew had thrown them away, but I'd seen Karrie hovering around them. They were there, and then they were gone."

"But would Karrie call such attention to herself if she planned to use the peppers to harm you?" Karrie was egocentric, but she was also smart.

Babs tapped her long, elegant fingers on the vanity top. "Karrie is capable of anything." She shrugged.

"How did she get the peppers into your hair spray?"

"I use a pump bottle and the top unscrews. You know, environmental issues and all. Every little thing counts, and if a judge is eco-friendly and sees that in my dressing room . . ."

"So you leave your makeup and stuff in the dressing room?"

She nodded. "We all do."

"Even Brook?"

"Her too. That was awful. She practiced her fire baton routine every day. Who would have thought her costume would catch on fire like it had been doused in kerosene? And the way she just stood there, rooted to the spot, and didn't even run or scream or try to save herself." She tried on another wig.

"The last one looked better," I said.

"Ah, the Cassandra, as it's called. I agree." She switched wigs again. As she pulled a few curls to frame her face, she said, "Do you really believe Brook and Janet were murdered?"

"The autopsy reports aren't in yet. It won't officially be murder until a cause of death is established."

Babs took one last look at herself in the mirror. The Cassandra was a good choice. "I'm sorry to rush you out, but I really have to prepare for the cooking event. Tonight is family barbecue. We're demonstrating the versatility of the different cooking ranges and our personal recipes for sauce. I'm going to take top honors on this."

She showed me to the door, and I was halfway down the hall when she called out, "I heard Hedy was arrested. Is she out of the competition?"

"She wasn't charged. She'll be there tonight."

"Too bad." Babs laughed. "Killing the competition is rather extreme, but it wouldn't hurt my feelings if several of the contestants ended up in jail until the winner is declared."

9

Walking the quiet corridor of the hotel, I almost jumped when my cell phone rang—Tinkie summoning me. "Yes, ma'am," I said as I punched the elevator button to go down to the lobby.

"Don't dawdle. Hurry," she said.

I pushed the up button. Tinkie was not bossy. Far from it. But when she issued an edict, she expected obedience. I wondered what tricks Oscar performed, and the thought put a smile on my face.

Inside our room I discovered Tinkie had wrangled the use of a laptop computer from somewhere—I didn't even ask. Tinkie had her ways, and I'd find some poor fool wandering the hotel lobby, still enchanted with her flirtatious gambits.

"Look at this." She turned the computer screen so I had a better view. "That's the talent competition." I recognized the picture and realized Tinkie was reviewing the photos she'd taken for the newspaper the night before.

"Nice work, Tink. You're the Ansel Adams of pageant butts. That's a striking derriere hanging on the back of Crystal Belle Wadell's backbone."

"Look!" Her index finger pointed at the blurred image of a man lurking in the far corner of the building. "Lurk" was the only verb to describe his stance. Hat pulled low, shoulders hunched, he wore an expensive suit.

"Who wears a hat this time of year?" I asked, proud that I'd recognized the fashion faux pas right off the bat. Normally, Tinkie had to coach me in such matters.

"I'm not making a fashion comment," Tinkie said. "Don't you recognize him?"

I hadn't, but I inspected more closely. "It's Marcus Wellington, isn't it?"

"I'm positive it's him."

"Now that opens a can of worms," we said together. Tinkie held out her pinkie, and I hooked mine with hers.

"This trip to Greenwood has a *Twilight Zone* element," I warned her. "We're regressing, and it isn't going to be pretty if you ask to borrow my training bra."

She rolled her eyes. "Sometimes, Sarah Booth, you act as if you were never a young girl." For a moment, she looked stricken, remembering that a large chunk of my childhood had been stolen by the tragic death of my parents.

"It's okay." I gave her a hug. "So what do you make of Marcus Wellington attending the beauty pageant?"

"Two possibilities." She was all business. "He might have been there to watch Hedy. Maybe he still carries a torch for her."

"Maybe, but the Wellingtons aren't the kind of people to set aside their desires. If he wanted Hedy, don't you think he'd demand her? Make her an offer she couldn't refuse, so to speak."

"She thwarted him once."

"To hear her tell it," I reminded Tink. "The second possibility is that he's behind all of this to frame Hedy. No matter what papers she signed, she's still Vivian's natural mother and she stands a good shot at partial custody. Marcus may be cutting her off at the knees."

Now that sounded more like the Wellingtons I knew and loathed.

"That family has a lot of pull in this county," Tinkie continued.

"In this state. Actually, they have national juice."

"Jansen could be in their pocket."

When I'd first come home to Sunflower County, I'd wondered about Coleman's integrity as a lawman. The good ole boy, pork barrel political system was by no means exclusive to Mississippi—corruption was everywhere, from the top to the bottom of every ballot. With that in mind, I'd sniffed around trying to catch a whiff of stink on Coleman, but he'd come out clean. He was the Matt Dillon of the Delta.

Professional law enforcement was not always the rule in other counties and states. People kowtowed to wealth, because riches equated to power. I had no proof Police Chief Jansen was anything other than an upright lawman, but the Wellingtons were strongly tied to a company supplying outrageously expensive goods—some of them so inferior as to be worthless—to our overseas troops. I was merely keeping in mind that Jansen might not be a city officer version of Coleman.

"If Jansen is in their pocket, things won't go well for Hedy," I said. "A conviction . . . she'll never see her kid again."

Truer words were never spoken. Was I cynical enough to believe Marcus would have two innocent girls murdered to frame Hedy? You bet. I relayed to Tinkie what I'd discovered from Babs.

"So she was behind the roaches." Amusement glinted in her eyes. "I'm not surprised, but I really thought Karrie had done it to herself."

"And Babs feels pretty certain Karrie retaliated by putting the pepper in her hair spray. It would appear these incidents are not related to the murders."

"Two wrinkles ironed out." Tinkie went to the closet and sorted through the many items hanging there. She'd brought an outfit change for every occasion. "I've wrangled us tickets to the barbecue tonight." She hung a frilly outfit on the back of the closet door.

"I won't ask how." The tickets to any of the beauty pageant/cook-off events had become hot items. Murder brought an increased level of celebrity to the events. "Is Cece coming?"

Tinkie looked like the cat who'd swallowed the canary. "*And* Millie. We've arranged for Zinnia's famous restaurateur to be one of the local expert judges for the barbecue."

I could only nod. Tinkie had her ways, and with Cece's power as a newspaper reporter thrown in, the two were potentially lethal. "Perfect."

"The only fly in the gravy is Madame Tomeeka. Cece tried to get her to join us tonight, but she wouldn't consider it."

"Did Madame Tomeeka ever make her predictions about who would win the pageant title?" I'd almost forgotten all about Tammy's promise to handicap the competition, and I hadn't had a chance to thoroughly read the newspaper.

"Cece was annoyed, but Tammy wouldn't say anything specific."

"She wouldn't even guess?" That didn't sound like Tammy. I'd never known her to tout her abilities with claims to predict specific events, but once she told Cece she'd do it, she wasn't the kind of friend to fudge on a promise. Especially since Cece had promised her readers. "What did Tammy say?"

Tinkie tossed several pairs of shoes over her head. They thunked on the plush carpet beside the bed. "Only that a black shadow hung over the whole competition, and red seeped around the edges. She said she couldn't see the end of the pageant because a bad energy obscured the view. It was all very vague and unsatisfying. Tammy advised all of us to leave this pageant alone and 'let the forces of darkness battle each other.' "

"Did she say there would be more murders?" The thought made me sit upright.

"No, she didn't. She only said she couldn't predict anything and she wasn't pretending she could. She sort of hurt Cece's feelings, but not deliberately." Tinkie closed the closet door and faced me, suddenly serious. "Speaking of hurt feelings, Graf called me, Sarah Booth."

Anger was my first reaction. Not at Tinkie, but at Graf. "Why did he call you? To report me for some infraction of the"—I made quote marks in the air—" 'serious relationship rules.' "

"He said you wouldn't answer your phone."

"Not true." It hadn't rung, because I turned it off whenever he called.

"Call him."

"I will."

"Sooner rather than later." She gave me a look. "Learn from my mistakes and don't let something like this fester. No good will come of punishing him by not speaking to him."

She was right. I knew it even as she spoke, but Taureans are immovable at times. Graf had hurt me, and when I was wounded I had only two modes of conduct, and neither involved rational thought. I attacked like a wild shrew or I withdrew. Talking reasonably was too adult for me.

"Take off your astrological bullhorns and call the man. He made a mistake. He wants to apologize. Let him."

I nodded. "Give me a little while to let my feelings calm down."

"May I tell him that?"

She was damn persistent. Like Chablis, once she had hold of something she didn't let it go come hell or high water. "By all means, call him. Tell him we'll talk later tonight after he's done shooting and *I've* finished the barbecue competition. But Tinkie, don't hedge. If he asks if we took the case, tell him the truth. I won't sugarcoat things to salve his ego."

"Heaven forbid you sprinkle a little sugar on bitter truth." She flipped her fingers in the air. "Now that I've salvaged your love life, let's get back to the case. Why don't we track down Karrie and see what she has to allow."

Tinkie's plan was to aggravate the remaining Miss Viking contestants until they talked to us. We found Karrie in her room, sans Crystal Belle, who'd gone across the street to the hotel spa for a facial and some relaxation. Had Karrie been my suite mate, I would have spent my time buying garlic to hang around the room.

"What do Tweedle Dumb and Tweedle Dumber want?" Karrie asked through a ten-inch crack in the door.

"A few moments." Tinkie spoke in her sweetest tone.

"Nope." Karrie tried to push the door closed, but I blocked her. "I don't have time for this," she said through gritted teeth.

She was hiding something. I could tell by the way she kept looking over her shoulder into the room. Without further ado, I hit the door with my full weight and forced it open. As I stumbled into the room, Tinkie right on my heels, I came face-to-face with Marcus Wellington.

"Hello, Sarah Booth, Tinkie." He picked up a cocktail and sipped it.

"Marcus," I responded. "I didn't realize you were working your way through all the beauty contestants. You'd better hurry, only a few nights left. Surely there's one or two who haven't yet yielded to your charms. Unlike present company, some of them must have some morals, or at least a healthy self-image." My barb hit home because Karrie blushed a furious red.

"Since it's none of your business who I sleep with, I'll ignore that remark." Marcus led with amusement rather than anger.

I started to tell him that Hedy had hired us and therefore it was our business, but Tinkie indelicately stomped my toes with her stiletto heel. "Marcus," she said, "are you one of Karrie's supporters?"

"He's my number-one fan," Karrie said. "Now how about removing yourself before I throw you out."

"Hold on a moment." Marcus stepped between them. "Word is out that Hedy hired you two to prove her innocence in these murders. Take it from me, there are things about Hedy you should know."

"Like what?" I asked.

"Blackledge is her father's name, a father who disappeared when she was a small child. Some say the gators got him. Some say he drowned. Other say a dark phantom snatched him out of his motorboat, which was discovered running in circles in the Pearl River swamps. No trace of him was every found."

"And this would be Hedy's fault, how? You said she was a child, if I heard correctly. Are you saying a prekindergarten girl had something to do with the disappearance of a grown man?"

Marcus stumbled, but only for a moment. "Her mother is a conjure woman. Saulnier is her mother's maiden name, a family that goes back to old New Orleans." His lips pulled up into

139

what might be a smile. "Back to Marie Laveau."

"The voodoo priestess?" I sounded like I was about eight and had just been told the bogeyman was in the closet.

"Correct," Marcus said. "Those devil-worshipping swamp people will never raise my daughter. If you have good sense, you'll get away from Hedy as fast as you can. She's trouble. Whatever she's told you is a lie. That's the only thing you can count on. And let me make myself clear. Try to interfere with my paternal rights over Vivian, and I'll prove I'm a match in meanness for your voodoo friend. Now get out."

Grasping Tinkie's arm to keep her from slapping Marcus's smug face, I smiled. "Sure thing, Marcus, Karrie. Tell Crystal we came by to see her."

Half-dragging Tink, I got us into the hall.

"Why didn't you let me whip his ass?" she fumed.

"We came away with a lot of information, and that's what we went for. What a nugget. Karrie and Marcus know each other. The roux thickens." I deliberately ignored the accusations he'd made, but I intended to find out Hedy's background, and soon.

"You think Marcus and Karrie are working together in this?"

"I don't know," I said as I led her down the hall. "But they both gain if Hedy is charged and jailed.

Let's stop at the desk and see if Hedy got any calls last night at the room."

"What are you thinking?"

"That someone lured her out of the hotel room so he or she could murder Janet and frame Hedy."

Tinkie's eyebrows lifted almost to her scalp. "But why wouldn't Hedy tell us?"

"Because she's not a trusting young woman."

The call center operator at the hotel, once she realized we were private investigators working for Hedy, gave us the list of calls to Room 212. It was a virtual hotline—until about eight o'clock. Then, after eight, only one call. A 662 area code, which was local. There was no way to prove which girl, Hedy or Janet, received the call, but I wrote down the number. Tinkie whipped out her cell phone, dialed, and then held it so we could both hear.

"Hello," a male voice said. Marcus Wellington.

"You are so busted," Tinkie said. "You called Hedy, probably offering for her to see her child, and got her out of the room so you could murder Janet. You're going to fry for this one." She hung up.

"Mississippi doesn't fry people," I told her. "That's Alabama. We have the gas chamber or lethal injection."

"You say tomato, I say tomahto. He got the point."

"Hard to miss it when you threaten to fry him. And let me just point out that I'm sure Marcus recognized your voice, too. But the real issue here is Hedy. She lied to us. And we can't represent her if she isn't going to tell us the truth." I was dead serious. A lying client was the quickest road to trouble I'd ever found.

"I'll have a talk with her and find out the truth," Tinkie said. "I'm sure she has a reasonable explanation." She knew I was pissed. "Why don't you check out the Saulnier background?"

"My pleasure." Back in those halcyon high school days, when I had free afternoons and a library card, I'd read several novels about Marie Laveau. She was portrayed as both a misunderstood spiritualist and the devil incarnate. I was curious, to put it mildly. The idea of a conjure woman was exciting. Delaney Detective Agency once represented a faith healer, but voodoo had a different tonal quality that brought up all sorts of interesting images.

Tink and I parted ways, and I went to the room to see what I could find on the laptop Tinkie had appropriated. Soon it would be time for our cooking lesson, and then the barbecue cook-off. Life was never dull.

The official word on Marie Laveau, according to a number of Web sites devoted to her, was . . . vague and confusing. Apparently, there was a

Marie Laveau I and II, a mother and daughter, and both were thought to be voodoo priestesses. Legends about the women and their powers abounded. But one story contradicted another, making me wonder if perhaps Marie I and II deliberately obscured their backgrounds. And talents. I mean, if you were really the Mistress of Satanic Darkness, would you advertise it?

As I read the sites devoted to the New Orleans women, I searched for the Saulnier name. At last it came up, a mention of Rubella Saulnier, a devotee of Marie Laveau II in New Orleans in the late 1850s. Rubella Saulnier was also considered a spy—she collected information at the behest of a Confederate officer, a man she'd fallen in love with.

Despite my cynicism, I found myself captivated by the story of desperate love. In the 1850s, New Orleans was a rich blend of cultures and an active port city. According to the Web site, Rubella was a beautiful young woman who ran a flower and fruit shop in the French Quarter. She met and fell in love with James Gramacy, a New Orleans merchant. Their love, of course, was not acceptable to the Gramacy family, who viewed marriage as a tool to bind power to power. Rubella's Creole background was considered unsavory.

One version of the story was dark—the love shared by Rubella and James was not born of free will. Rubella used a love potion concocted by Marie Laveau to win the young man's heart through voodoo. Her love for James was obsessive and consuming, a love that drained the young man of his health and wisdom.

When the War Between the States erupted, Gramacy joined the Confederacy, as all young men of his social rank were expected to do. Fearing for her lover's life, Rubella, who had become one of Marie Laveau's most successful students, employed her skills to extract information from the families of Union sympathizers to keep James and his fellow soldiers one step ahead of the Yankee troops.

In a second version, it was James who visited Marie Laveau to win the hand of the haughty Rubella. The potion worked so well, Rubella devoted her life to serving Marie Laveau for the promise that Marie would insure James's safety.

In several variations of the tale, James and Rubella never married, but she did bear him a child, a daughter.

The most chilling aspect in all of the stories was the condition placed upon Rubella by Marie Laveau: Each generation of Saulnier women would produce a female child who would serve the voodoo priestess's spirit. It wasn't exactly the type of information I'd hoped to find regarding our newest client. Even though it was impossible to check the legends for accuracy, the Web sites ignited my anxiety.

I looked up the Pearl River County, Mississippi, Web site for Hedy Lamarr Blackledge. Nada. But the name Saulnier came up with a list of three names. All female. And one was Hedy Lamarr Saulnier. The Blackledge name was not used.

I wrote down the phone number and physical address and turned off the computer. I had just enough time to prepare for my next cooking lesson. If I didn't grab the shower first, Tinkie would soon be in the room taking over the bath, hair dryer, and other gadgets necessary for personal grooming.

10

Still wet from the shower, I bent over to rub one of the thick white towels over my hair.

"BAM!" The vocal explosion at my right ear startled me. I inhaled a gulp of air—and a whiff of pepper.

Before I could do anything else, I sneezed so hard I almost fell over. Tears flooded my eyes and I sneezed four more times, stumbling forward and backward. Someone mimicking television's Batman was in the bathroom with me and I was blinded. Had the intruder squirted me with pepper spray?

"BAM!"

More pepper. Even with my eyes shut tight against the pepper and the overwhelming need to sneeze, I knew who'd infiltrated the sanctity of my bath.

Jitty had returned to Greenwood.

"You like my spicy thang, you? Maybe we could stir up some gumbo, yes?" she asked in an almost indecipherable dialect.

"It's a good thing you're dead already, because I would do my best to kill you again if I could," I said, just before another sneeze nearly exploded my head. "Get that pepper out of this bathroom."

"It's the finest green, white, and black blend, yes?" she continued with her strange stilted accent.

Opening my eyes, I found that she'd put on a good bit of weight around the middle. Her hair was coal black, and her chocolate eyes twinkled beneath a tall white chef hat. Once again, Jitty was impersonating someone I knew. "Emeril Lagasse?" I hazarded a guess.

"The spices of Louisiana put zip in any meal, yes? You? *Oui*?"

I glared at her. "Drop the phony accent. Emeril doesn't sound like that. In fact, he sounds like he has good sense and knows how to cook. You sound like Gary Coleman trying to play Peter Sellers playing Inspector Clouseau."

"BAM!" She tossed more pepper under my nose.

After another round of sneezes, I had no energy left to battle her. "Where did you get pepper in the Great Beyond?" Jitty couldn't manipulate corporeal things. Like pepper. Which meant . . . I was more delusional than I imagined.

"Don't be so hard on yourself," she said. "Ask something useful, like why I'm here."

"I was thinking about you in the shower," I said. "I conjured you, didn't I?"

"Get a grip, Sarah Booth. If you could conjure me, that would imply I'm not real and you're losing your mind. Or already lost it. Or, maybe, have never been sound of mind." She let that sink in. "I came on my own to tell you something."

I put some mousse in my hair and fluffed it up. A Daddy's Girl would apply hair dryer, curling iron, and hair spray. Good hair was an element of good ancestry and a selling point on the marriage market. In the refined bloodlines of the Buddy Clubbers, those men born to the manor, breeding a woman with bad hair was tantamount to asking for genetic flaws in the children. At least flat feet could be covered up in shoes.

No DG worth her salt would have unruly, untamed, or un-touched-up hair. The slight natural curl in my tresses flared into rebellion during the humid summer months, which made California look good from a hair perspective. Too bad. I was done with hair preparation. A little blush, some mascara. Heck, I was going to cook, not strut the runway.

"You so busy primpin' you forgot you had a question to ask me." Jitty leaned against the bathroom wall.

"It won't do me a bit of good to ask anything. You'll tell me what you want to when you want to spill it. But I'll ask. Because it gives you such pleasure to withhold from me. What did you come to tell me?"

"Not really *tell* you," she hedged. "It's about Marie Laveau."

"How appropriate to disguise yourself as a Louisiana master chef to discuss a Louisiana voodoo priestess. I love the parallelism of your presentation."

"You aren't taking me seriously," she said with a frown.

"You think? You show up here tossing pepper in my face, wearing a hat that looks like you stole it from the Pillsbury Doughboy, and speaking in a ridiculous accent. Now you want me to take you seriously. That's a tall order."

"Folks didn't take Marie Laveau seriously. Some of them died."

It wasn't her words as much as her tone that arrested my attention. Jitty had inside knowledge of the Great Beyond, where voodoo might be a somber issue. "Why are you here?"

Satisfied I was now taking her message to heart,

she sat down on the closed toilet. "Remember when your mama came to talk with you when you were in the hospital?"

"Yes." This was no laughing matter. Some folks would insist I'd dreamed the rare moments with my dead mother, or hallucinated them, but I knew for a fact my mother's spirit had come to comfort me. There was no dark art involved, only love.

"There are things no one understands, Sarah Booth. I'm not trying to scare you, but you need to be careful."

Her words swept over me like a cold, damp wind. "Is Hedy or her family connected to voodoo or Santeria?"

"I don't know. I've poked around, but I can't be certain."

Jitty never helped me on a case. Heaven forbid she do something really useful, but it never stopped me from asking. "Brook's and Janet's deaths were terrible. Did the same person murder them? Was it a pageant contestant?"

Jitty pushed back her chef hat to fully reveal her face. "I don't know, but I wouldn't eat anything prepared by any of those girls. At the barbecue tonight, avoid all the food."

Once she pointed it out, it was an obvious action. "I'll warn Tinkie, too." A sudden realization stopped me. "But what about Millie? She's judging. She'll have to taste everything."

"Killing off the judges would disrupt the contest. Maybe cancel it. You be careful, though —you or Tinkie aren't necessary to finish the pageant."

I heard the room door open.

Jitty gave one last very low "BAM" before she faded away with a wink.

The door closed and Tinkie came to the bathroom door. "Who were you talking to?" she asked, glancing around. "I heard you in here while I was trying to find my room key."

"Just myself." One day I might explain about Jitty, but not now.

"You talk to yourself in some kind of weird Cajun accent?" Tinkie gave me a strange look.

"I was singing. Sometimes I sing in an accent."

"Does Graf know about this tendency?" she asked.

I had to deflect this conversation. "It's almost time for our date with a chef. Are you wearing that?" I let my gaze rove down her, assuming an expression of disapproval. She looked perfectly fine, of course.

"I'll grab a shower and we'll head over for the cooking class. But first I have to tell you what Hedy said."

"I'm listening." I wasn't fond of a client who lied.

"She couldn't tell us Marcus had called her, because we didn't know about Vivian then. If she'd said Marcus called, that would have opened the door to a whole new line of questions. We would have asked why, and then she would really have had to come up with a reason for his call and why she agreed to meet him."

"A reasonable enough explanation, but it doesn't mitigate the fact she lied."

Tinkie faced me. "You'd do the same thing to protect your daughter. Don't even try to deny it. Hedy was out of the room when Janet Menton was killed. That's what matters. And she did go and play her violin. So she didn't really lie."

Staring into Tinkie's determined eyes, I saw she believed Hedy. The sad truth was, so did I. "Okay. Fine. It was a lie of omission to protect her kid. Have your shower and then we'll suss out the judges."

"I was thinking the same thing." She dropped a trail of clothes as she made her way into the bathroom. Two seconds later, I heard the shower turn on. Tinkie began to hum the haunting melody Hedy had played during the talent competition. I couldn't help but wonder if perhaps there wasn't a gypsy strain as well as voodoo woven in Hedy's complicated background.

We were late for our date with epicurean destiny, so we hurried across the street and skidded to a halt just as the master chef, Godfrey Maynard, began his comments on the purpose and design of main courses.

We were to work as teams—naturally Tink and I partnered up. We drew up our menu, which Chef Maynard approved, and then we set to work preparing a feast fit for a king, or at least important dinner guests. Tinkie and I chose to go Southern. She prepared a pork roast, and I peeled and cut up sweet potatoes and put them on to boil. My ambition was to create a whipped potato and cinnamon-apricot paste to stuff in the pork.

My mind stewed on the case while my potatoes boiled. When they were done, I moved on to stage two of my recipe. Whipping the taters into a puree.

"Sarah Booth, where is your mind?" Tinkie elbowed me in the ribs as hard as she could.

Mashed sweet potatoes spewed across the room as I accidentally pulled the electric beaters from the bowl of potatoes I'd begun to fluff. Two ladies who were the recipient of my yammish generosity gave me a glare that would curdle yogurt.

"Sorry," I said, wiping a glop of orange from one of their noses.

"Do it again and I'll plant that beater where the sun don't shine," the woman growled too low for Chef Maynard to hear.

I started to reply, but Tinkie pinched my arm. "Behave!" she commanded. "What is wrong with you? You haven't paid a lick of attention to what you're doing. You've only made a huge mess here."

"Guilty as charged." I couldn't concentrate. My mind was on Hedy, voodoo, and a barbecue competition due to begin soon. "Tinkie, would you be upset if I took off now to find the pageant judges?"

She looked around our workspace. It was clear that rather than helping Tinkie, I'd only held her back. Without me, she'd stand a chance of winning Chef Maynard's approval and at least a friendly greeting from the other participants in the class, who by this time were ready to string me up.

"Go on," she said, and sighed. "No point staying here if you aren't going to listen and learn."

"Thanks!" I couldn't even pretend remorse. The idea of sweet potato stuffed pork made my mouth water, but the process of getting from raw meat to dinner on the table didn't interest me at all. Not today. Jitty had put a bee in my bonnet to talk to the judges, and I couldn't wait to find them.

A million scenarios floated through my head as I hurried back to the hotel to change from my potato-stained clothes into another pair of jeans and a blouse. At the front desk, the clerk said Dawn Gonzalez and Harley Pitts were staying at the Alluvian. Belinda Buck was not. The hotel staffer either couldn't or wouldn't say where she might be sleeping over.

Clive Gladstone, the fourth judge, lived in Cleveland, Mississippi. He wasn't registered at the hotel, so I figured he was home. Since I only had a couple of hours until the barbecue cook-off, I decided to concentrate on the judges close by. I used the house phone to call Dawn Gonzalez's room. She invited me up without hesitation.

She opened her door and signaled me in. Though her pageant years were two decades behind her, Dawn was a beautiful woman who took excellent care of herself.

"I'm in the middle of my yoga session. You don't mind, do you?"

"Not at all." I sat at the desk while she returned to a blue mat spread on the floor. In less than three seconds, she assumed a position that no normal human could attain. "Are you double-jointed?" I couldn't stop myself from asking.

"No, but I've practiced a lot." She moved slowly and with agility and strength into another contorted pose. "I've heard you and your partner were hired by one of the contestants. Hedy is a strange girl. Beautiful, but strange."

That answered my first question—if the judges were aware Hedy had been questioned by the police. News traveled fast.

Dawn stood, then leaned backward until her hands touched the floor.

"Karrie Kompton made it a point to tell me all about Hedy's encounter with Police Chief Jansen."

I started to say something catty about Karrie, but bit it back. Dogging her to a judge might only reflect poorly on Hedy. "No charges were filed," I said. "There wasn't enough evidence. Hedy was only picked up because she was Janet's roommate. The police always question people with access."

"And motive," Dawn said. She wrapped her right leg around her neck and balanced on her left.

"Hedy doesn't have any more motive than the other girls."

She slowly unwound and stood. "True. But Hedy is highly ranked." She made a surprised face and put a hand over her mouth. "Oops! I shouldn't have said that. The rankings are confidential. The other judges would be furious if they knew I'd let that out. Of course Clive reports everything to his friend, so I'm not the only gum flapper. Clive couldn't keep a secret from Marcus Wellington if you sewed his lips shut."

"Clive and Marcus are that close?" This was a gold nugget.

"Honey, I've only been in town a few days, but I've already heard the talk. Clive loves his horses and he loves Marcus Wellington. Not sexually, but as in deep loyalty and friendship."

I pressed on. "Tell me about Brook Oniada."

"What's to tell? She was so talented. The fire baton routine would have been such an asset for

Viking Range at outdoor events. Every eye in the crowd would have been on her. Her scores on cooking weren't the highest, but I have to say she moved into the top position with her unexpected refreshment service to the audience. It was a brilliant move displaying exactly the kind of innovation and creativity I want to see in Miss Viking."

"Chief Jansen hasn't been forthcoming with a lot of details, but I believe Brook's body lotion had been tampered with."

She balanced on one foot and extended her arms and leg in opposite directions. "That's what I heard, too." When she had both feet on the floor, she picked up a towel hanging on the back of a chair and rubbed her face. "Is there something else you wanted to ask? Surely you didn't stop by to confirm what you already know."

Clearly, now that her yoga was finished, so was I. She had other fish to fry, as we like to say in Mississippi. "You've helped a lot. What about Janet? Was she highly ranked, too?"

Dawn frowned. "Harley Pitts favored her. He'd offered her guest appearances on his television food show, *if* she got the title." She pushed her blond hair back from her face. "He's such a moron, he suggested that in front of the other contestants. Frankly, I hold him responsible for her death. I mean, he might as well have handed out filet knives. These girls are pure piranha when it comes to this title."

"You believe a contestant is the killer?"

"Who else would it be?" she asked. "No one in Greenwood knows these girls. It's not like some kind of local grudge. Unless a whacked serial killer has a thing for beauty contestants, it has to be one of the other girls." She grabbed bottled water from an ice chest and held it to her neck to cool off.

Competitiveness was one thing. Murder was something else, even for a lucrative title. "If it is one of the girls, aren't you afraid she'll go after the judges if she doesn't win?"

Dawn's laughter was rich and musical. "Nonsense. And if that were the case, it wouldn't be me. Unlike that fool Harley Pitts, who can't keep his mouth shut, and Clive Gladstone, who doesn't seem to have an original thought unless his school chum Marcus Wellington plants it in his head, I haven't bandied my opinions of the contestants around." She caught herself. "But I have been too verbose to you."

"No harm done."

"I need to get ready for the judging tonight. You'll have to excuse me," she said.

"Certainly." I didn't have time for a drive to Cleveland, so Clive was out of the question. Harley Pitts was my next target, and since I already had his hotel room number, I decided not to alert him with a call.

He'd taken one of the master suites on the

second floor, and I was about to knock when I heard voices inside. The thick door muffled the words, but it was clearly a male and female in a loud exchange.

The door opened and Voncil Payne almost walked into me. She carried a tray of the most beautiful petit fours I'd ever seen. Those small cakes, normally served in the South for weddings and bridal showers, are a weakness of mine. My mouth filled with saliva at the sight of them.

"It would be wrong of me to sample your daughter's baking skills," Harley said gravely. "It wouldn't be fair to the other contestants, but I appreciate the thought."

Voncil's face was a mask. "I understand, Mr. Pitts. I wouldn't want to do anything that might appear to put your *fair and balanced* judging into question."

Harley's eyebrows drew together as he tried to ascertain the level of her sarcasm, which was about chin deep, in my opinion. He turned his displeasure on me. "Who are you, and what are you doing lurking outside my room?" His expression grew stormier. "You're the one hanging around with that photographer from the Zinnia newspaper. Get away from my door before I call hotel security."

"I'm not a reporter," I said. "I'm Sarah Booth Delaney."

"She's a private investigator," Voncil threw in

sweetly. "Hedy Lamarr Blackledge hired the Delaney Detective Agency to prove she isn't a murderess."

"Ah, Hedy. Plays the violin like an angel, but there's something sad—" He broke off. "Reporter, detective, no matter to me, I have nothing to say to you. Find another place to loiter."

I tore my gaze off the petit fours. Even if Voncil offered me one, I couldn't eat it. Death by petit four sounded too ridiculous to risk. Aware of my lust for the plate of confections, Voncil picked one up, bit it in half, and gave me a Cheshire cat grin. "Mmm, mmm. Delicious, if I do say so myself."

"They're beautiful," I said. "If I were a judge, I could be bribed by them." Now it was my turn for a toothy display. Harley blanched.

"Perhaps you should come in for a moment. So I can explain," he said.

"My pleasure." I stepped past Voncil. "Will Amanda serve her petit fours tonight at the barbecue, or was this a special treat just for Judge Pitts?" What was Voncil up to? She'd already compromised Belinda Buck, now Harley Pitts. I doubted the two incidents were coincidental.

Voncil didn't say a word. She walked down the hallway, the tray balanced on her hand like a professional waitress. As I followed Harley into his room, I closed the door behind me.

11

Harley Pitts had the ruddy nose of a chronic drinker and the dapper dress of a dandy, but his disposition was more tyrant than friendly drunk. Part of his TV popularity was his willingness to make guests cry. He was an interesting combination of Simon Cowell and 80s-era TV sitcom news commentator Ted Baxter.

"Don't bother finding a seat," he said. "You won't be staying long enough to heat a chair cushion."

"Is there a chair here?" I asked innocently. The place was a pigsty. Discarded clothes covered every surface.

"What do you want?" he asked. "Other than to annoy people."

"As you know, Hedy has hired me and my partner, Tinkie Bellcase Richmond," I gave him Tinkie's entire pedigree, "to make sure Hedy isn't charged with a murder she didn't commit."

"That would be multiple murders," he noted. He went to the TV armoire and pulled a bottle of single-malt Scotch from the back. He poured a drink straight up and belted it back. "That's better. Now ask your questions. I have to get ready for tonight."

He wanted me to get to the point; I was happy to oblige. "Is it true you offered Janet Menton a spot on your television cooking show?"

"Who told you that?" He whirled around, furious. "That bitch Dawn Gonzalez has been running her mouth. She's just upset because I wouldn't let her do a cooking segment. Hell, I wouldn't let her spin-dry lettuce, much less appear on my number-one-rated Food Channel cooking show."

Talk about shameless promotion, Harley was a master at putting himself forward. "Why would Dawn Gonzalez want to be on a cooking show? She's not a chef. That was never her claim to fame."

"You are so right there. She can't boil an egg." He waved a hand in the air dismissively. "She's invented some cockamamie steaming device she wants to get on QVC. If she debuted it on my show, it would give her some creds to sell it nationally. *That* is not what my show is about." He paced the room. "I am not going to participate in hucksterism and cheap merchandising."

As I watched him huff and puff, it occurred to me he was a master of cheap theatrics if not merchandise. His show, appropriately titled *Pitt Boss*, was famous for Harley's rudeness and insults, yet he acted hurt when someone wanted to use him for a leg up.

"What was it about Janet that made you want

161

to showcase her talent?" I hoped a politely phrased question might yield better results.

"She was an excellent cook," he said. "I sampled several of her dishes, and she had a knack for spices and presentation. She loved food and cooking, the same way I do." What appeared to be real remorse crossed his face. "And she was . . . nice to me. Not ooey, like those girls who think they can work me, but genuinely nice."

So the troll had a point of vulnerability. "How so?"

He pointed a finger in my face. "Don't you dare imply she did a single inappropriate thing. She did not. She was not that kind of girl."

"And I thought chivalry was dead," I said dryly.

He stopped as if I'd smacked him in the forehead. "You are a vile woman," he said crisply. "I want you to leave."

Since I'd never sat down, I didn't have to stand up. But I also didn't move toward the door as he indicated with a sweeping gesture. "Mr. Pitts, two young women are dead. Don't you want to find out who killed them?"

I thought I saw the sheen of tears in his eyes, but he turned away so abruptly, I couldn't be sure. "I want to know who poisoned Janet. Yes, I do. And that poor girl who burned to death. What a horrible way to die. Who would do such awful things?"

"Someone very desperate to win this competition, or someone insane." The full impact of the instability of the killer hit me. Cold sweat formed along my hairline. I didn't want to be hurt. Again. Up until that moment, I'd worked the case as if I weren't involved, as if this were an exercise in mental agility or a pastime to placate Tinkie. I'd sauntered along, asking questions, poking my nose into things, acting as if graphic violence hadn't been committed and might happen again, possibly directed at me or my partner.

I leaned against the back of a chair, recoiling against the true horror of Brook's fiery death and Janet's senseless murder.

Harley retrieved the Scotch bottle and poured himself another drink, but he also poured an inch in a clean glass for me. "I have to tell you something." He sat on the bed and hung his head. "I was drinking when I offered for Janet to come on the show. I did it to show the other girls I'd chosen to help Janet, to give her a professional boost in an arena where there's money and fame for the picking. I wanted all of them to know I had power and could use it at my whim. They were such snotty little bitches, except for Janet, and they needed to see that someone had noticed Janet was a nice person. Sometimes being kind and decent really does matter." He wiped his mouth with the back of his hand. "Still, I shouldn't have made her a target. She's dead because of me."

He was as deflated as an old tire. I didn't have the heart to beat up on him. "Did Janet say anything about the other contestants? Or about anyone? A member of the audience? Someone who'd threatened or intimidated her or who acted strange?"

Tears slipped down his cheeks, and he brushed them away. "She was afraid. She said someone had been messing with her things."

"What things?" This was the best lead I'd gotten, so far.

"Her spices, in particular. She had ground herbs she'd made up for one of her special dishes. She'd grown these herbs herself in organic soil, tended them, harvested them. She was truly a chef at heart."

"Did she say who tampered with her herbs?" I tried not to appear too eager.

His expression was unreadable. "She said she caught Hedy going through her spices. Opening them and . . . sort of sniffing them."

My stomach dropped. This was not the kind of lead I was hoping for. Somewhere along the way, like Tinkie, I'd become one of Hedy's champions. "Did Janet say if Hedy said what she was doing?"

He rose and went to the Scotch bottle. I hadn't touched my drink, so when he tipped the bottle toward my glass, I shook my head. Instead of pouring another for himself, he put the bottle down. "Janet confronted Hedy, who said she was smelling them to see if she could tell what ingredients were included. The girls all have their secrets, which are basically unusual combinations of traditional spices and plants. The art of original cooking is often *how* ingredients are combined more than anything rare or exotic. Anyway, that's what Hedy said, but Janet thought Hedy might be trying to sabotage her. I thought Janet was being paranoid." Bitterness hardened his gaze. "I didn't take Janet seriously. Now she's dead."

"Harley, it's one thing to investigate a competitor's spices, but it's another to kill her. You can't blame yourself for this. How would you know to consider such an act?"

"There were other incidents."

"Could you be more specific?"

"Janet found this little bag under her bed. Brown leather and tied with a yellow ribbon. She opened it up and there was a nasty curled-up chicken foot in the bag, along with some other stuff. Janet thought Hedy was laying a curse on her." He shook his head. "A pageant like this is a perfect atmosphere for gossip, rumor, cruelty, and nastiness. The other girls said Hedy was . . . that her family practiced voodoo. It upset Janet." He shrugged. "Maybe Hedy put the gris-gris bag under Janet's bed as a joke, or just to be mean. I don't know."

"What did she do with the bag?"

"I don't know," Harley said. "I told her to get

rid of it. She was so upset, I told her it was foolishness. I meant to calm her fears."

One thing I hadn't expected from Harley Pitts was compassion. It was also interesting to note how close he'd grown with Janet. She'd confided her fears to him. Perhaps it was a ploy on her part to take advantage of his obvious fondness for her. Or maybe she was really scared. "Did you tell anyone else?"

"No. I should have, but I didn't. I thought it was a prank and I didn't want to fan the flames of silliness. Now, though, I can't help but think I made a serious mistake by not taking action."

"Did you ever talk to Hedy?"

"Not about the voodoo. I confined my talks with her to official questions. She was reserved. She answered the questions very politely, and she has an amazing talent with the violin, but she does the bare minimum at social events. I have to say, that's counted against her, especially with the other judges. This title includes a public job. The winner needs to be comfortable at functions. It isn't the right fit for someone who is shy or lacks self-confidence."

I could almost agree with him that Hedy didn't fit the job description for Miss Viking Range. She had way too many secrets. None that affected her cooking or ability to be a spokesperson, unless a secret baby fathered by one of the Delta's wealthiest men qualified as a distraction from her duties.

"If you had to pick someone as a killer, who would it be?"

He thought about it. "Hedy wouldn't be my top pick," he admitted, "but it's a woman. Maybe a male-female team."

"That's an interesting conclusion to draw."

Harley shook his head like an old, tired dog. "Burning someone alive strikes me as a male activity. And poison, well, it's a woman's specialty, isn't it? Lucrezia Borgia comes to mind."

"Another woman smeared by unproven rumors," I pointed out, proud to have hung on to at least one moment of my history classes. While Lucrezia was instantly associated with poison, there was no solid evidence to prove she'd committed any crimes. The same thing could easily happen to Hedy if Tinkie and I didn't stop it.

"If I had to pick a suspect, I'd say Karrie Kompton. There is nothing that woman wouldn't do to win."

"I agree. But she's so obvious." In my last case, I'd gone for the obvious villain, and I'd been wrong. Way wrong.

" 'Brazen' is the word I'd choose," Harley said. "Perhaps that's what she's counting on—that no one will take her seriously because she's such an obvious choice. Now you'll really have to excuse me. I must prepare for the evening competition."

"Thanks, Mr. Pitts." I put my glass on the desk. "My friend Millie, who runs a café in Zinnia, will be one of the guest judges tonight. She's one of your biggest fans. Please don't be rude to her. It would hurt her feelings."

One corner of his mouth twitched. "For you, Miss Delaney, I'll curb my tongue. Just don't ask a second time."

Harley and I had zeroed in on the same suspect, but the problem was that I no longer trusted my instincts. This pageant killer was brutal, ruthless, and cruel beyond anything I'd ever been involved with. As I took the elevator down to my room, I tried to erase the images of Brook Oniada bursting into flames.

Who could do that to a beautiful young girl who merely wanted to win a title?

As I stepped onto my floor, my cell phone rang. I checked the number, feeling an instant remorse when I thought it might be Graf and almost turned it off again. The guilt quickly shifted into anger that he could make me feel culpable. And all to no avail. The caller was Tinkie's husband, Oscar. I was a bit annoyed with him, too.

"Sarah Booth," Oscar said without bothering to identify himself.

"Yes."

"Tell me Sweetie Pie has been spayed."

Once again, Oscar had thrown me a curve. I'd been expecting a frontal assault and a demand that I accompany his wife back to Zinnia and the safety of his protection. Why was he asking about my hound? "I'm a responsible pet owner. Of course she's spayed. Why?"

"Chablis is beside herself. And so am I."

Dread crept into the pit of my stomach and punched hard. "What's wrong?"

"I'm at the Sweetheart Café. I brought Sweetie and Chablis by for an ice cream."

"And?" I prompted.

"We were waiting in line at the drive-thru and Sweetie saw this extraordinary hound come down the sidewalk dragging a leash. He took one look at her and let out this mournful, chilling howl and that was it. She leaped from the car and took off with him. Before I could even get out of the car and chase after her, she and the hound disappeared."

I blew out a long sigh. When I'd first gotten Sweetie, she'd had some unusual hormonal issues. The dog had a regenerating ovary and though she'd been spayed—twice—it seemed her body might be up to its old tricks. She'd found a suitor. While she couldn't get pregnant, she could still get into a whole lot of trouble running loose with a baying boyfriend.

"She couldn't have gotten far," I said. "Who does the hound belong to?"

"There's a visiting librarian in town, Bobbie Ann Caswell, from Jamestown, New York, who's helping Mrs. Kepler reorganize. It's her harrier hound named Danny. He's neutered, too. He broke free of her during a walk about ten minutes before he met up with Sweetie. Now they're on the lam together."

Zinnia was a small town, and Sweetie Pie was a local personality. Everyone knew she was my dog. Someone would eventually grab her and call the number embroidered on her collar, or else take her to the veterinarian. The new lady vet, Lynne Leonard, would kennel her for me. Sweetie was also microchipped, just to be on the safe side. Though all precautions had been taken, I was still worried. Sweetie and Reveler, my horse, were my family.

"I'm heartsick, Sarah Booth. And Chablis is inconsolable. She would have gone, too, but I grabbed her just as she was perched in the window to make a break for freedom. What should I do?"

"If she isn't home by ten, Oscar, call me. I'll come home."

"And Tinkie, too?"

I heard the hope in his voice and accepted that he was genuinely worried for his wife and not merely trying to control her. "I can't speak for her. She's fine, Oscar. We're attending a barbecue tonight. I'm sure she's photographing the event for Cece. Graf has told me how proud of her you are."

"Yes, Tinkie keeps discovering new talents." He hesitated, and I wondered what he was really thinking. "Rest assured Coleman and Gordon both are on the lookout for the dogs, as are the librarians. Last I heard, Ms. Kessler and Ms. Caswell had the whole eighth grade lined up to do a massive search of the town. I just don't know where those dogs could have gotten off to."

"Check behind Millie's Café. Sweetie loves Millie's cooking, and food is always the bait for hounds."

"Will do. I'll let you know what happens."

Sweetie Pie would normally never leave Chablis. This harrier must be one handsome fellow. Either that or Sweetie was on Oscar's payroll to bring me and Tinkie home.

I called the library and spoke with Danny's owner. Bobbie was concerned, but had a great trust in her hound's ability to take care of himself.

"Danny never does anything like this. He's perfectly behaved. So much so that Mrs. Kepler allowed me to bring him in the library while I was working. He saw Mr. Richmond driving by with that beautiful red tic in the front seat and that was it. He snatched the leash out of my hand and he was gone."

The fact that Mrs. Kepler allowed Danny in the library spoke volumes about Danny's winning personality. Mrs. Kepler was a "by the rules" librarian. She occasionally bent them for me, out of deference to my mother, whom she'd loved. But a dog in the stacks! Danny had to be loaded with charm.

"Sweetie knows Zinnia and Sunflower County," I assured Bobbie. "Try not to worry. Oscar will find them."

"I'm returning to New York in two days," Bobbie said. "I can't leave without Danny. He's part of our family. Fiona Ramona McFee, my thirteen-year-old Chihuahua, will be heartbroken if anything happens to him. He's her man, and he's doing her wrong."

"If he isn't back by tomorrow, I'll come home." Not that I was any better at searching than anyone else. Truth of the matter was, Sweetie would more likely come out of her love nest for Millie before anyone else. Millie equaled chicken and dumplings, chicken potpie, roast—the things Sweetie loved. "Try not to worry," I repeated.

"Danny's had a hard life. He and his sister were chained to a doghouse so tightly they could barely get out to use the bathroom. A neighbor lady rescued the two of them, and I adopted Danny. He's just so . . . innocent."

"And Sweetie is a woman of the world." She had traveled more than your average hound. "But she'll be gentle with him, and then I'm sure she'll bring him home."

As I closed my phone, I couldn't help but think

172

that now that I was trying to straighten out my romantic life, Sweetie had taken up the banner of sexual misconduct and rowdy living that my aunt Cilla had exemplified. Sweetie might *look* like a red tic hound, but when it came to wayward ovaries, she was a Delaney woman through and through.

12

Tinkie was concerned for Sweetie and her new man-dog-friend and offered to head back to Zinnia instantly, but she also believed my yodeling hound wouldn't stray too far. Sweetie might yield to a regenerating ovary stump and the charms of a traveling harrier, but she wouldn't put herself in danger. Tinkie recounted the times Sweetie had saved either my life or hers, or both. In most instances, had she stayed home like a good hound, Tinkie and I would be dead.

"Let her have a few hours of bliss," Tinkie said. "It's not every hound that turns Sweetie's head. Actually, she makes better choices in the romance department than you do, Sarah Booth."

Wisely, I ignored that jab and dressed for the barbecue. I wore my jeans and a snap-button shirt, and Tinkie shimmied into what looked to be a square dance outfit. Fitted bodice, skirt that stood out perpendicular to her shapely legs on layers and layers of petticoats, the costume brought back nightmare memories of starch and itch. I figured if Tinkie got a chance to do-si-do, she'd do it at the drop of a hat. That was one of the joys of Tinkie: She was willing to experience everything with a glad heart.

The fete was held at Rocking River Ranch, a spread where Morgan horses were bred and trained. I instantly fell in love with the sweep of the land and the miles of white fences corralling elegant horses. To my disappointment, the "guest" judges were sequestered, so Millie was out of my reach. Plates of food would be delivered, and they would judge blind—without knowing who had cooked what. Cece had chosen to accompany Millie in exile, so Tink and I were on our own.

The tangy smell of barbecue was everywhere. Kitchen equipment had been installed in a wonderful screened gazebo, and the remaining pageant contestants were cooking their little hearts out as folks strolled by, examining the chicken, pork, shrimp, beef, and vegetables the girls prepared, all while preening and posing for photos with spectators.

Over the din of laughter and talk, I heard Karrie say, "I can't believe the police released Hedy.

And here she is, just waiting to poison someone else. I wonder how many of the folks here will drop dead from her efforts."

Hedy was at the far end of the line, working over a bubbling pot of something. But she clearly heard Karrie's remarks.

The crowd parted for me like I was Cecil B. DeMille commanding the Red Sea, and I walked to stand not four inches from Karrie's perfectly made-up face. Not even a mist of perspiration touched her flawless brow, though almost everyone else was sweating in the heat.

"Hedy wasn't charged with anything because she didn't do anything," I said loudly. "Be careful or she'll slap a slander suit on you that'll make you look like you've been pulled through a keyhole." The rumors about Hedy had to be stopped immediately or she could end up charged with murder, which would necessitate losing the title of Miss Viking Range *and* her freedom *and* her child.

"How much does Hedy pay you for that kind of defense?" Karrie asked. "If you don't think she's capable of poisoning someone, ask Marcus Wellington. She tried to kill him." Marcus stepped out of the crowd, ready to relay details of his alleged near poisoning.

I saw too late the grand plan Karrie and Marcus had concocted. They would publicly paint Hedy as a dangerous psychopath who killed to get her way. Even if it didn't succeed in getting Hedy put in jail and charged with murder, it would destroy her chances at the title. This was a setup designed to accomplish one thing: the ruination of my client.

The crowd stilled and folks drew closer, eager to hear whatever insults passed between Karrie and me. As much as I wanted to shove the flat of my palm into her nose, I couldn't. Like it or not, I was Hedy's employee, and whatever I did reflected on her.

I pulled my cell phone from my pocket and pretended to dial the number for Russell Dean, the attorney Tinkie had hired to represent Hedy.

"Mr. Dean," I said loudly, "I'm calling in behalf of Hedy Blackledge. I believe we'll be filing a slander suit against . . ." I zeroed in on Karrie and Marcus in turn. My smile widened. "Marcus Wellington. Yes, of the Wellington family, from Panther Holler. He's here at the cook-off now, attempting to ruin Miss Blackledge's reputation with unsubstantiated rumors just as the judging is about to begin. Should this impact Miss Blackledge's ratings . . ."

It was a calculated risk, and perhaps such a lawsuit would never stand up in court, but my theory was to fight a lie with a lie.

"I didn't say a word," Marcus huffed. "You can't name me in a slander suit when I didn't speak."

176

"Yes," I said into the phone. "I think three million is a little low. The damages here are Ms. Blackledge's ability to make a living. I'm thinking more along the lines of ten million, which are potential earnings for a good spokesperson. Yes, we'll be at your office tomorrow morning. Have the paperwork ready."

The crowd sucked in an audible breath. Whispers snaked around the gathering.

"You can't sue me, I didn't say anything about Hedy," Marcus insisted. He reached for the telephone in my hand, but I eluded him.

"She's bluffing." Karrie pulled at his jacket. "Ignore her."

"When this is said and done"—I was still playing to the crowd—"Hedy may or may not have the title, but she will have a nice chunk of the Wellington inheritance. I can't wait to talk to Gilliard about this. Does your daddy know what you're up to, Marcus? Somehow I think he'll be very disappointed in you." I checked my watch. "I do believe I can make it to Panther Holler before the cocktail hour ends."

Marcus blanched. His father's wrath would be swift and brutal. We both knew that. The only sin unforgivable in the Wellington family was to do something stupid enough to lose money.

Marcus leaned close to my ear. "If Hedy pursues this, she'll never see Vivian again." Out of the corner of my eye, I saw Hedy approach. She'd heard the hubbub and come over. She stood not ten feet away, her fists clenched at her sides, her pale eyes boring a hole into Marcus's back. He turned away, unsettled by her malevolence.

"What else is new?" I countered. "It's not like Hedy's being treated fairly now. But that will change, Marcus. One way or the other. Hedy has rights, and not even the Wellingtons can take them away."

Hedy started forward, but Tinkie caught her arm, restraining her. Hedy tried to shake Tink off, but my partner prevailed. I'd played a dangerous hand, but I'd forestalled Karrie's attempt to ruin Hedy via the public rumor mill. Neither Marcus nor Karrie would reveal Hedy's maternity, because to do so in such a public way would give Hedy legal traction in trying to regain partial custody of her baby. My position—for this round of the battle, at least—was pretty damn good.

"This isn't over," Marcus said. "Hedy is going to pay, and so are you."

"I've already paid, Marcus," Hedy said. "For being naïve and for being young. But I'm done paying. Now it's your turn, and you will suffer for the things you've done."

"I will have you in court so fast—"

"Try it," I dared him. "You'd better have a really long reach, Marcus. Neither Hedy nor I have anything you want. You can't get blood from a turnip, as my aunt Loulane used to say. But that's about to change. If you keep mistreating Hedy and trying to damage her, you'll lose a lot. You have my word on that."

"You have no idea who you're dealing with," he said.

"Oh, I do, Marcus. You're a powerful, wealthy man accustomed to his way in every situation. You're a man with no morals or ethics, whose answer to everything is to take what he wants and to hell with the consequences. And much to my horror, I've broken one of my dear aunt Loulane's ten commandments—I've just gotten into a mud-flinging contest with an ass," I said. "My only concern is that your stink might rub off on me."

Pissing off rich and powerful people is one of my truest talents. Marcus Wellington's aquiline features contorted. Murder shone in his eyes. I held my ground, even though I had the uncomfortable sensation that someone was walking across my grave. Marcus was a caricature of a spoiled, rich brat, but he was more than that. He was smart, too. And judging by his recent conduct, he was dangerous when he was angry. It didn't seem so far-fetched that he'd kill bystanders to have his way.

He spun around and strode off. Karrie raced after him, abandoning the pot of pulled pork she'd been cooking for her entrée.

"Ladies and gentlemen," Evangeline Phelps said into a microphone, unaware of my personal little drama, "the judging is about to begin. Our panel of esteemed judges will head up a line. Once they've been served by our contestants they'll withdraw to the dining room of the main house to eat and discuss the dishes. Our guest judges, who have been confined in the main house, will be served blind. Everyone else will sample the fabulous barbecue cuisine prepared by our beautiful contestants. And as a special delight, Miss Amanda Payne will sing some of her original songs for us while we dine."

As the crowd applauded, Dawn, Clive, Harley, and Belinda Buck stepped front and center. They stopped and chatted with each of the eight contestants as they lifted pot lids, sniffed dishes, and served their plates. My mouth watered as I watched. I'm a sucker for good barbecue, and the aromas wafting through the air told me this competition was going to be close, but Jitty's warning still echoed in my brain.

Karrie returned, face flushed, just as the judges arrived at her station. Dawn held out her plate, and Karrie hefted a heaping spoonful of her shredded pork. A large round object came up with the spoon, tottered on the edge for a moment, then splatted on the floor.

"What the he . . . ck?" Karrie grabbed a paper towel and picked it up.

"That isn't pulled pork," Belinda Buck said. "That's a . . . oh, my goodness. It's a road apple!"

Several members of the audience started to laugh. Others uttered sounds of horror and disgust. Karrie's eyes blazed, and she pointed a finger at me. "You put a horse turd in my barbecue."

At the word "turd," the area erupted into gales of laughter and pandemonium broke out. Several people gave me the evil eye, but my gaze followed Tinkie across the room. She was short and moved through the crowd unnoticed, but her petticoats demanded at least a three-foot-wide clearance.

I yelled her name, but she kept walking. When I turned around, Karrie stood in front of me. She drew back her fist, but self-preservation kicked in. I ducked. She swung, lost her balance, and fell.

"I'm going to get you," she said, struggling to hold back tears I thought for one foolish moment were sincere.

"I didn't touch your barbecue," I told her. "I couldn't have, you nitwit. I was talking to you the whole time." Not waiting for her reply, I stepped over her and went after my partner, who might as well have been wearing a sign that said, "I'm a turd roller."

Tinkie would never admit it. Not even to me. Ladies didn't traffic in such pranks. And if they did, they never, ever said so. For a Daddy's Girl, discretion was the word to live by. Yet again, I found myself admiring a set of rules that I could never obey but on occasion had reason to appreciate.

It took me fifteen minutes to track Tinkie to her lair, which happened to be a big camellia bush outside the open window of the Rocking River Ranch dining room. Snuggled in the bushes, Tinkie eavesdropped on the judges' conversation. When I pushed my way through thick limbs and leaves to stand beside her, she gave me a wide grin and a "shush."

"I think Karrie Kompton should be disqualified," Dawn Gonzalez said. "I mean, I'm not going to taste her barbecue, so I can't judge it. Do you agree?"

A rumble of negative comments came from the other judges. "But it wasn't her fault," Belinda Buck pointed out. "She certainly didn't put the road apple in her pulled pork. That would be stupid."

"Or very, very clever," Harley said. "What if she knew her barbecue wasn't up to par with the others', so she did something to get hers disqualified?"

I could have kissed Harley. The best thing for Hedy would be if Karrie were tossed out of the contest and left town. Hedy wouldn't have a clear road to the winner's circle, but it would make the remainder of the race a lot more pleasant.

"I don't believe that," Clive said. "Karrie wants this title. She's worked too hard to risk a move like that. I believe we have to assume someone else put the . . . objectionable object into her dish. I don't think we can throw her out. We have to give her another chance."

It figured Clive would support Marcus's newest girlfriend, because ultimately it was a show of support for Marcus's interests.

"If Karrie were running a restaurant and someone found a . . . disgusting item in his food, what do you think would happen?" Dawn asked. "In the restaurant business, there isn't a second chance to recover from contaminated food. Where was Karrie when the turd was put in her food? Part of her job is to make sure she serves healthy and safe dishes. I say we boot her out and be done with it."

Yes! Tinkie and I silently high-fived each other.

"I object," Clive said in his resounding baritone.

"Maybe we should vote?" Belinda suggested.

Tinkie and I grasped the window ledge. If it was a show of hands, we wanted to see the result. As I peeped over the sill, I felt cold fingers dig into my neck. Tinkie let out a tiny squeak. Before I could say Jack Sprat, I found myself flying backward through the camellia bush, the thick leaves sawing at my arms.

When I finally hit the ground, I looked up into the angry gaze of Police Chief Franz Jansen. "What, exactly, do you and Mrs. Richmond think you're doing?" he asked.

"Eavesdropping on the judges." Tinkie smoothed down the hundreds of layers of petticoat. While I was bleeding from a few scratches, she didn't suffer a single injury. The petticoat had acted like chain mail. No shrub worth its salt would take on that paragon of starch.

"That's illeg—" He faded to a stop.

"It's unethical, but it isn't illegal," Tinkie corrected him.

"Hedy Blackledge put you up to it?" he asked.

"You jump to conclusions like a frog on a rolling log," I told him. "Hedy doesn't know anything about what we're doing."

Jansen waved a hand, tired of the conversation. "You'd better hope nothing untoward happens here today or your client will go to lockup and stay there until this competition is over. No matter what Russell Dean says, I think Ms. Blackledge played a role in the murders of both those young women." He straightened his posture. "And you should rethink the lawsuit I heard you were filing against Marcus Wellington."

"Why should a civil suit concern you?" Tinkie did a masterful job of hiding her surprise at how fast the news of my feigned phone call to Russell Dean traveled around the county and came back to the place where I'd woven it out of thin air. I was equally surprised. But I wasn't about to admit that to Jansen.

"I'm not worried about a proposed slander suit, Mrs. Richmond. Far from it. The Wellingtons are targets for all kinds of grifters, thieves, con artists, and lawsuit-happy women. Miss Blackledge is one in a long line of Marcus's conquests who thinks she can barter a bit of pleasure into a permanent stipend. I know all about her blackmail schemes to get Marcus to support her."

"Are you the police chief or Marcus Wellington's attack dog?" Tinkie asked.

Red moved from Jansen's neck into his face. "I don't answer to the Wellington family, but I've seen this action plenty of times. Just because the Wellingtons are wealthy doesn't mean they deserve less protection from grifters and crooks."

"Hedy deserves protection, too. She may not be a resident of Greenwood, but technically, neither is Marcus Wellington." Hedy deserved the same protection offered to the son of a rich man. "Marcus is setting Hedy up to take the fall for Janet's murder. I'm not saying he killed Janet, but he's capable of it. He'll do whatever is necessary to have his way."

"A mighty interesting theory, Miss Delaney. Trouble is, your client doesn't need any help in looking guilty." He turned toward the gazebo where folks were chowing down on barbecue. "Smells delicious," he said as he strolled away.

"There's more to that police chief than meets the eye," I said.

"What angle is he playing?" Tinkie asked.

"I wish I knew."

The front door opened and the judges came out. Dawn exited first while the other three hung back. We didn't need to eavesdrop to read the body language. Karrie was still in the running. Clive had prevailed.

The twang of an electric slide vibrated, and Amanda Payne's clear voice swung over the chatter. "You can't get no lovin' if your grits are cold." She sang the first line a cappella, then broke into a raucous, rockin' song. Feet began to stomp, and several folks jumped up to dance. Even Tinkie was tapping her tiny little slipper-clad feet. True to her responsibilities, she went to work with her camera, documenting all that transpired.

Everyone was having a good time, and I had to hand it to Amanda. She knew how to throw down at a barbecue. Her voice was spectacular, and her songs were original and complex, a blend of 70s folk, rock, and country narrative. While she was mousey in one-on-one situations, when she took the stage she was a high-wattage show.

I noticed Voncil moving around behind the scenes, adjusting wires and doing the work of a roadie. She was a typical manipulative stage mother, but in some ways Amanda was lucky. None of the other girls had such support— unconditional love that comes only from a parent.

"Is that the coroner?" I pointed across the crowd to a young man deep in conversation with Chief Jansen.

"He looks like he's twelve," Tinkie said.

I'd forgotten she hadn't met Marlboro. He did look young. "Let's go see what the powwow is about."

"My thoughts exactly." Tinkie used her petticoats like the blade of a road grader to clear a path for me.

Marlboro saw us coming. His expression made Jansen turn around to confront us. "You two skedaddle," he drawled, wiping his impressive mustache with a napkin. "I've got business here with the coroner."

"I promised Ms. Delaney I'd give her the state autopsy report," Marlboro said. He didn't squirm, but he came close.

"You did what?" Jansen wasn't really outraged, but he was good at acting the part. In fact, I was getting the sense Jansen was very good at playing a certain role, one that folks around town expected of him. The problem was that I wasn't certain who or what the real Franz Jansen might be.

"Ms. Delaney and her client have a right to know what the state lab found," Marlboro said. He reached into his coat and brought out several sheets of paper. "I made copies for her." He held them just out of reach. "But first you have to promise to keep this strictly to yourselves," he said to us. "This is not for the newspaper."

We both nodded. "We promise," we said in unison.

"Well, Marby, why don't you just jump in her lap like a good little doggie?" Jansen was disgusted.

"Thanks, Reverend Tanner," I said. "Good to know someone in Leflore County keeps his word and knows how to behave like a professional."

Jansen only rolled his eyes as I unfolded the paper. Tinkie pulled at my elbow, and I adjusted the pages so she could read along with me.

The first report was on Janet Menton. I'd seen enough autopsy reports to get the gist in a hurry, but what I read stopped me cold. "Ricin?" I asked.

Marlboro and Jansen nodded.

"That's incredibly dangerous." I didn't know much about poison, but I knew the U.S. government had worked on an antidote in case of biological warfare. "A tiny amount could kill hundreds of people. Thousands."

"And it isn't hard to get hold of," the coroner said. "Fact is, those castor plants grow wild, especially in the warmer regions of the state, like around the Gulf Coast area."

"The area where Miss Blackledge is from," Jansen said.

"Oh, for heaven's sake, I'm sure you can log

on to the Internet and buy this stuff," Tinkie threw in. "It isn't exactly like only one person here could find it."

"True," Jansen said. "Almost anyone who wanted to kill could get it, if they had enough money."

"That rules Hedy out," I said. "She's broke."

Jansen gave me a long look. "Folks sometimes acquire money when they want it bad enough."

I shuffled the papers and located the time of death. From what Hedy had told me, it appeared Janet had died within an hour of her departure from the room. The ricin could easily have been in room service food or the pastries I'd noticed on the floor.

"I've questioned the kitchen staff and the waiter who delivered food to Miss Menton," Jansen said. "Hedy was in the room when the food arrived. She had every opportunity."

"And so did anyone in the kitchen. Or the tray could have been left for a moment. Or Janet could have had someone stop by her room." Someone like Marcus Wellington. He'd gotten Hedy out of the room, I was sure. Why? Maybe to poison Janet. "If you had the evidence on Hedy, she'd be under arrest."

"The poison was in the pastries," Jansen said.

He'd deliberately riled me, but I'd learned something valuable. "Where did the pastries come from?" I asked.

"They were apparently homemade," Jansen said. "According to Miss Kompton, those cream cheese pastries were known to be Janet Menton's favorites."

"So who made them?" I asked.

"I intend to find out," Jansen said.

I flipped to the autopsy report on Brook Oniada. Sure enough, there was something strange on her skin. Ambergris.

"Isn't ambergris somehow connected to whales?" I asked. Visions of *Moby-Dick*, a book I'd hated, flashed through my mind.

"Yes." Marlboro looked pleased, like I'd answered a trivia question correctly. "It's produced in the hindgut of sperm whale and was used in perfume, but not anymore. It's been banned because folks were killing whales to harvest it. Actually, the whales expel it naturally."

"What's it used for?" Jansen asked.

"It was a fixative in perfumes. It's a cholesterol-type substance . . . and it was once considered a culinary delicacy. It's highly flammable." Marlboro swallowed.

"Where would you go about getting ambergris?" Tinkie asked.

"Like anything else, folks can get it on the Internet," the coroner said. He looked away, as if something troubled him. When he faced us again, he seemed to have aged at least a decade.

"Ambergris is sometimes used in witchcraft or voodoo ceremonies."

"How did you find out about that?" I asked.

His smile was wry. "The Internet. Like everyone else, I recognize it as a great resource."

"And if you found it, so could anyone else." I made my point clearly. "The question is, who knew ambergris was both flammable and used in voodoo? Someone is making it look like Hedy is to blame."

"That's a million-dollar question, Ms. Delaney," Jansen said. "I'm sure if you find the answer, you'll be in touch with my office."

"Count on it, Chief."

By the time Tinkie and I returned to the cooking gazebo, almost everyone had gone. Crews were there to clean up. The barbecue was over —and no one else had died.

13

It was ten when we finally met up with Cece and Millie at the bar in the Alluvian. They were staying the night, though they both had to get up early the next morning to return to Zinnia.

While my friends chatted and discussed the barbecue cook-off, I heaved a sigh of relief. The body count had not risen. But it could. It might swell to huge proportions. The illness Oscar had just recovered from could be child's play when contrasted with a minuscule release of ricin.

I wanted to tell Cece, but both Tinkie and I had promised the coroner, and we couldn't break our word. Cece was the ultimate professional and would never print such a thing, but still, we couldn't tell. Ricin was so toxic, if a hint of someone using it slipped out, a panic would be easy to start and hard to stop.

"You look worried, Sarah Booth," Millie said.

Since I couldn't reveal the information about ricin, I gave them another of my concerns. "I'm a little tired. And Sweetie Pie is running wild."

"That hound could find her way home if she got dropped down in California," Millie reassured me. "Remember, she did that once."

"She speaks the truth, dahling," Cece said. "If she hasn't come home by tomorrow, I'll talk Mr. Truesdale into doing a front-page story with a photo of her. We'll find her."

I nodded. My friends were doing everything they could to help me.

"I got some great photos at the barbecue," Tinkie said. She offered her camera so Cece and Millie could check them over.

"These are wonderful," Cece agreed. "The newspaper is certainly livelier since you started sending us photographs, Tinkie."

"Any hint of who's ahead in the competition? It was a tough call determining the best barbecue." Millie smoothed back a curl from her cheek. "I finally settled on the honey-basted pork roast. As you know, the scores were tallied, but won't be revealed until the last night of the contest. We weren't even told who'd gotten the highest score." Her eyes twinkled. "So who cooked the pork roast I liked so much? Since the judging was blind, I never found out."

Tinkie and I looked at each other. We hadn't eaten any barbecue. "I don't remember," I finally said.

"Just as well," Millie said. "From all you've told me about Karrie Kompton, if I'd voted for her dish, I might have had to be rushed to the hospital to have my stomach pumped. She makes me sick."

"If you knew what was in her dish, you'd really be sick." Tinkie recounted the awful episode, and she had Cece and Millie in horrified stitches. As much as they didn't want to laugh, they couldn't help themselves. Tinkie's descriptions even had me smiling.

"On that note, we need another round of martinis." Cece signaled the waiter. "That Kompton girl is cursed. First, chocolate-covered roaches, and now, horse by-product in her barbecue. Someone really doesn't like her."

"No one ate a bite of it," I said. "The pot of

barbecue was removed before anyone was served. Still, it was a moment to remember when she fished that lump out of the sauce."

"So how will they judge her in that event?" Millie asked.

"I have no idea, but you can bet she won't be disqualified. I'd hoped she might be cut from the contest. She's such a troublemaker."

"In all fairness, it really wasn't her fault that her dish was . . . contaminated," Millie said. "It would be wrong to disqualify her from the title because someone played a practical joke on her."

"That was a bit more than a practical joke," Cece said. "That was a spot of genius, dahling. Spill it. Which of you girls dropped in the road apple?"

Tinkie and I refrained from any response. I couldn't even look at my partner, because I was afraid I'd blow her cover.

My cell phone rang, and my heart sank when Oscar's name and number appeared on the screen. "It's about Sweetie Pie," I said to the girls before I answered. "Oscar must not have found her." The worry I'd worked so hard to bury resurrected. Sweetie could navigate her way with an uncanny sixth sense—she should have gone home by now.

"We'll all go back to Zinnia and help hunt," Tinkie said as I answered the phone.

"Sarah Booth," Oscar began. "I want to reassure you. We've had several Sweetie Pie sightings. Mr. Truesdale saw her behind the Piggly Wiggly carousing with that other hound. He said they were barking at paper sacks blowing around, and I got a report that they were down at the creek beside the high school, swimming and cavorting later this afternoon."

This all sounded good. Sweetie enjoyed the water, and she loved to play. But had she thrown over her friendship with Chablis for a man-dog? That didn't sound like my feminist hound. "I thought for sure she'd return by now. Fun's fun, but this is ridiculous." I sounded like the mother of a wayward teen, but I couldn't help it. "Have you checked at Dahlia House? She may be in the barn."

"Already checked."

There was something in his voice. "What is it, Oscar?"

"I don't know how to say this, exactly . . ."

"Spit it out." He was scaring me.

"It seems Danny the hound has a shoe fetish. Sweetie has fallen in with him on a crime spree."

It took several seconds to process this. My friends were staring at me, and I tried to control my expression. "All dogs chew shoes. What are you saying?"

"This is a serious fixation. A number of cleats from the high school football team went missing. And the cheerleaders' performance shoes, too."

"And they're blaming Sweetie and Danny? Two dogs? For what, forty pairs of shoes?"

"Fourteen, to be exact. There's not much doubt the dogs did it, Sarah Booth. Mrs. Hedgepeth saw them running behind her house. Each dog had a pair of football cleats."

I couldn't believe it. Mrs. Hedgepeth was like the old witch in *The Wizard of Oz*. She'd had it in for Sweetie from day one. "You know that old bat would lie for the fun of making trouble. She hates Sweetie."

"If it were just her word . . ."

I sensed big trouble here. "What kind of evidence does she have?"

"She got a picture of both dogs with her cell phone. There's no doubt Sweetie and Danny are guilty."

I was outraged. "Mrs. Hedgepeth knows how to use a cell phone camera?" How was that possible? Though Tinkie was up to speed on technology, I hadn't mastered the art yet. "Did she bring you the photo?"

"She showed it to Coleman, and when he only laughed, she took it to the high school football coach. He's up in arms and wants a manhunt for the dogs and the shoes. It's sounding more and more like a lynch mob."

"Look, it's possible the dogs took a couple of

pairs of shoes, but there's no point in getting all overwrought about this. When we find the dogs, we'll return the shoes." I knew the high school football coach and winning was everything to him. He would be furious about the cleats. Sweetie had shoenapped from the wrong person. "How did the dogs get the cleats?"

"The coach said they finished practice and the team was in the showers. The dogs must have moved in and nabbed the cleats. Then they moved on to the girls' gym and snared the cheerleaders' shoes. They did it all in under an hour."

As much as I wanted to defend my hound, I couldn't. Sweetie had never displayed a fondness for stinky athletic shoes, but she was under the influence of Eros. Love can generate strange behavior. "Those dogs have to be right in the neighborhood, Oscar. They've hidden the shoes somewhere nearby."

"Let me talk to Tinkie a moment," Oscar said.

I passed her the phone and watched her face. She was amused, which made me feel a little better.

"Shall Sarah Booth and I head home?" she finally asked. She listened a moment. "No, no more problems. Hedy hasn't been formally charged with anything. We can head home tonight, if necessary."

Her tone was so reasonable, so conciliatory. She was masterful at the role she'd taken on.

"Thank you, Oscar." She shut the phone and handed it to me. "He's worried about Sweetie, Sarah Booth. And he feels responsible. She got loose on his watch."

"That's nonsense. Sweetie is her own woman, but I'll run back to Zinnia while you stay here." If anyone could find Sweetie, it would be me. And I had to get those shoes returned before Sweetie and Danny became the footgear Bonnie and Clyde of Zinnia.

"Are you going to call Graf and tell him about this?" Tinkie asked.

Beneath her innocent question was the real one. "Would you take care of that for me?" Both Cece and Millie looked at me hard. I picked up my phone and her keys. "Thanks, Tinkie. And you girls be good. I'll let you know when I round up my hound."

Driving through the early-summer night home to Zinnia, I felt the Delta rise up around me like the walls of a familiar room. I knew this land the way a devotee knows the contours of her beloved. The taste and smell of the cotton fields were a huge part of my tactile memory. Riding through the night with the stars pulsing in the sky, I had such a sense of home. It was true I'd never made my living farming, but it was the basis of everything in the Delta. The land was interwoven through every facet.

I'd borrowed Tinkie's Caddy, and the head-lights illuminated the rows of cotton on either side of the two-lane. Where the light faded, I knew the cotton extended in all directions as far as the eye could see. I'd learned to gauge the seasons, both climate and financial, by those endless rows. The hard thing about farming is that a bumper crop can mean financial troubles as much as a poor crop. Too much cotton and the bottom drops out of the price.

The cotton gave way to another crop. Soybeans. As my aunt Loulane would say, it's never smart to put all of your eggs in one basket. Savvy farmers planted plenty of cotton, but they also put in soybeans and other crops. Rotating was good for the soil, cut down on the spread of insects and disease, and had other benefits.

I rolled the window down and let the night scents blow into the car. Someone had just mown grass nearby. The clean smell made me think of watermelons, cold, crisp, and juicy.

Drawing near a small creek, I caught the fresh scent of the water and heard the rustle of the trees that lined the bank and also served as a windbreak. With the land so flat and open, strong winds moved too much topsoil, and farmers planted a row of trees to block the wind.

The night cry of a hoot owl came from the trees, but other than the thrum of roadside crickets, the darkness was still and quiet. The scene through the windshield was so familiar, so much a part of who I was that I wondered had I been born in another place, would I have found my way here, to this land and these people? Was the Delta my destiny? It was a curious thought.

I'd lived in New York City, and I'd worked briefly in the movie industry, yet here I was back in the Delta, headed to the old plantation that had been my family's home since before the War Between the States. I was on a mission to find my hound, who was as much a part of my family as if she'd been carried in a Delaney womb.

I glanced at the passenger seat, half-expecting Jitty to put in an appearance. The space remained vacant, though. Good for her. Maybe she was at a spiritual retreat. I smiled at my own humor.

The miles slipped beneath the wheels, and before I realized the passage of time, I found myself in Zinnia. Millie's was closed, as was the Sweetheart Café and every other business. Like so many rural towns, Zinnia's shops closed at 5:00, the end of the workday. Millie's was normally open later, and the Sweetheart, a drive-in where the high school kids hung out, stayed open even later, but the latest of the late-night hangouts closed at 10:00 p.m., which worked for me. The silent streets allowed me to hunt for Sweetie more easily.

I pulled into the Sweetheart and got out, whistling for my hound. "Sweetie Pie Delaney, you'd better get up here," I called. "They're printing up wanted posters with your picture on them."

If she was within earshot, she'd at least give a howl. One of the things I loved about Sweetie in particular and hounds in general was they didn't play hard to get. If Sweetie heard me, she'd let me know.

Nothing. Only the sounds of a small town sleeping.

I drove around, calling her name, and growing more worried with each passing moment. I'd assumed—wrongly, it seemed—that once I got back to Zinnia and called her, she would come out of hiding. But what if she was injured? Or someone had caught her and—

I couldn't allow my thoughts to go there. First things first. On the way to Dahlia House, I called Oscar to make sure he hadn't found her in the hour since I left Greenwood.

No luck. Oscar had been hunting with Bobbie Caswell and several others. No one had seen the dogs lately.

At Dahlia House, I expected Sweetie to run out to greet me. She had a doggie door and she could come and go at her whim. Perhaps she'd grown tired of Hilltop where Oscar led a far more structured life than was our wont at Dahlia House. But no matter how long I sat in the Caddy with the motor running, moving slowly forward and back, easing the headlights over the front of the house and surrounding yard, there was no Sweetie Pie.

I knew then that finding my hound was not going to be a simple matter. Calling in reinforcements was my only option, so I recruited the best.

The kitchen, without my hound in residence, was a lonely place. Even with Coleman Peters and Deputy Gordon Walters sitting across the table from me.

"No one has reported seeing her lately," Coleman admitted. "But that doesn't mean anything bad, Sarah Booth. There are thousands of acres of fields and woods, a paradise for a hound —especially one with romance on the brain. Sweetie and that new hound have likely holed up somewhere."

"With twenty-eight pungent athletic shoes. Perfect. As soon as I get my hands on her, she's going straight to the vet. If that ovary stump has regenerated . . ." I didn't have the heart to threaten dire action for my wayward pup. I was too worried for empty threats. Sweetie Pie, since she'd come into my life, had never displayed this kind of wanton lust. Something must have happened.

Coleman and Gordon listed the locations they'd searched, all logically thought out. "Is there a special place?" Coleman asked. "Where does Sweetie Pie's heart lie?"

The question stopped me cold. I pondered that exact question on the drive from Greenwood, but I'd been thinking only of myself. Now, I needed to reframe it with Sweetie in mind. Where *did* her heart lie?

"She loves the woods behind the cemetery." Sweetie was as partial to the old grove of oak trees as I was. Some might say the Druid spirits lingered there, amongst those old trees. Or maybe Sweetie liked the possibility of snaring one of the many squirrels. Whatever her doggie reasons, she was drawn there as surely as I was.

"Let's check it out," Coleman said. "How are you holding up, Sarah Booth?" He put his hand on my shoulder and gave a gentle squeeze. The kindness almost broke me. We'd been star-crossed in our affections for each other, but such feelings don't die. We'd walked away from them, but Coleman still had a piece of my heart and always would.

"I'm okay." I fought hard for control and clung to it. "And you, Coleman?" He'd lost a young woman he'd begun to show feelings for in our last case. We'd both thought she was guilty of serious crimes, but she'd only been a victim. Misjudgment had cost us both. A lot.

"As your aunt Loulane would say, 'Time heals all wounds.' "

"That's because you die eventually. Enough time passes and you're dead. If you aren't healed, at least you can't talk about it."

Coleman pulled me close and held me as laughter rumbled in his chest. "Gordon, whatever you do, don't give this woman a gun. She's a danger to others," he said. "Now let's find that hound."

We left out the back door, flashlights in hand. "Sweetie! Sweetie Pie!" I called, and Coleman and Gordon took it up as well. As we walked past the Delaney Family Cemetery, I let my fingers run over the wrought iron surrounding the graves. Scrolled and ornate, the fence was not much good at keeping the dead in or the living out. Jitty visited me whenever she took a notion.

If I didn't find Sweetie Pie in the next half hour, I'd find an excuse to go up to my bedroom and see if I could get Jitty to help. She wasn't the most tractable ghost. She appeared when she had something to say, not when I wanted to hear from her. But I was desperate enough to seek help from the Great Beyond.

We continued to the oak grove. Coleman slowed, swinging the flashlight beam around the area. "This is like a cathedral," he said. "I'll bet it's something else in the daylight."

There was a reason our connection ran so deep. Coleman understood the land the same way I did. We would not have romance, but we had something almost greater, a love of the land. "It was my mother's favorite place," I said.

Gordon, discreet as ever, walked slightly ahead, calling for my dog.

"Listen." Coleman moved the beam along the ground until he picked up two gleaming red eyes.

"Sweetie!" I cried.

A low and mournful howl answered.

"That's her." I ran forward while Coleman held the light. I heard his gun clear the holster. I knew what he was thinking—Sweetie was so close to home. She'd heard us calling, but she hadn't responded. Something was wrong, and it could mean danger.

Though I was cautious, I was also fast. I gathered Sweetie in my arms. She was too big to carry, and for some reason she didn't want to move. "Bring a light," I yelled.

Coleman and Gordon hurried to me. In the beam of their flashlights I discovered what ailed my hound. One very sick harrier hound lay on his side, the remains of at least two dozen shoes all around him.

"Sarah Booth, can you drive a vehicle back here?" Coleman asked. "I'll get the veterinarian on the phone. I have a feeling this poor guy needs professional help."

"Come on, Sweetie." I headed for Dahlia House. I was not in danger, but Danny was.

Sweetie had listened to far too many Tammy Wynette songs. She intended to stand by her man.

I didn't waste time trying to persuade her. I sprinted through the velvety warmth of the night, hoping we could get Danny to help in time.

14

"Danny should be just fine," Dr. Lynne Leonard assured Coleman, Oscar, Bobbie Caswell, and me. "Surgery wasn't necessary. Thank goodness the blockage moved through his system, but he's still one very sick dog."

"Thank you," Bobbie said. "What a great community this is. Zinnia is a special town for everyone to help find these dogs."

Sweetie gave up her vigil at the door of the examination room and flopped at my feet. She was asleep before she hit the floor, exhausted by her crime rampage.

"I'd like to keep Danny for the rest of the night, but we can release him tomorrow," Dr. Leonard said.

"We're due to return home to New York," Bobbie said. "Will that be a problem?"

"Not at all. Danny will be fine to travel. Just

be sure your shoes are out of his reach. Obviously, he can't control himself." She patted Bobbie's arm. "Sarah Booth, I'm glad you found Sweetie Pie."

"Me too." Relief had taken the starch out of my spine. I was ready to get horizontal.

Coleman's radio barked, and he excused himself for a moment. When he returned, he was grinning. "Gordon says most of the shoes are undamaged. Danny only ate four."

"I'll replace those gladly," Bobbie said.

"And I'll kick in, too. Sweetie might not have eaten a shoe, but she was in this up to her canines." For all the times Sweetie had saved me, I couldn't fail to support her in one small criminal act.

"Then the case is solved," Coleman said. "It's after midnight. I suggest we get some sleep."

"Thank you all," I said as I nudged Sweetie gently with my foot. She got up, stretched, and followed me out the door. When she was in the front seat of the Caddy, she went back to sleep. No guilty conscience there, not even a twinge at all the worry and heartache, not to mention leather damage, she'd been the source of.

Back at Dahlia House, Sweetie perked up enough to make a quick patrol of the house and barn before she hurried up the porch steps behind me. I was dragging, so tired not even a libation held appeal. I doubted I could stay awake long enough to swallow. I opened the front door and stopped in my tracks.

Music played softly. Something old and nostalgic. At last I recognized Nat King Cole, a voice like a lover's touch. What was Jitty up to now?

I closed the door and locked it. When I turned around, Graf stood in front of me. Whatever anger I'd held against him evaporated. I flung myself into his arms. After a long, delicious kiss, I asked, "Why didn't you tell me you were coming home?"

"It would have ruined the surprise. Tinkie knew. And Oscar is the one who told me Sweetie was missing." He eased from my arms and bent down to Sweetie. "I'm glad to see the prodigal hound returns. You know, there are therapists in California who can help her overcome this shoe fetish."

I had to laugh. "Danny needs the help. Sweetie was just a willing accomplice. She isn't into stinky leather and painful cleats, but she sure can be swayed by a baritone howl."

"She just likes the bad boys, eh?"

"Indeed. She has a taste for the fast and loose. I'm just glad she's home." Sweetie walked a circle at our feet and then slumped into another coma. "She's worn out. Me too."

Graf pulled me into his arms. "Too tired to give your fiancé a proper welcome?"

"Not too tired for that," I said as I led him up the stairs to the bedroom.

We sat at the kitchen table sipping coffee and listening to the pop and sizzle of bacon in the pan. I cooked while Graf filled me in on his movie. It sounded fabulous. Action, but not overblown with special effects.

"We finish shooting in two weeks, if everything goes as planned," he said.

"And then?"

He took my hand. "What about Ireland? A real vacation. Maybe we could find an old stone country church, a priest, a couple of witnesses, and tie the knot."

It was an attractive offer. "Tinkie and Cece would kill me if I got married in Ireland and didn't let them plan the wedding."

His fingers teased my palm. "I never figured you for the type who'd want a big wedding."

"Not a big one, but one here, in my family home." I didn't tell him I wanted to have it outside, close enough to the cemetery to give those there a chance to witness the event.

"Whatever makes you happy." He leaned across the table and kissed me before he got up and turned the bacon. Good thing someone was paying attention to the food. Obviously, the cooking lessons had not penetrated my brain.

"What would make you happy, Graf?"

He didn't rush his answer. "That you're safe." He focused on the bacon and shifted so I couldn't see his face.

"Is that it? I know acting makes you happy—it shows in how wonderful you look. But isn't there anything else?"

"Being with you. Planning a life. Knowing at last I've given my heart to someone and there's a real chance to build a future together. That's . . . a big deal for me."

I related to everything he said. "We share those things in common."

He lifted the bacon from the pan and finally put the spatula down. "I want to have a child, Sarah Booth. I don't think I'd ever given it much thought until . . . well, I realize now I'd like a child. A son or daughter, it doesn't matter. But someone who is a part of each of us. Someone to carry on the Delaney traditions and to develop new Milieu traditions."

I poured us both more coffee to hide the tears, which had come unbidden. "Me too."

"We can't make that happen if you're here and I'm in Los Angeles."

"I know." But I didn't have a solution.

"We can work this out, Sarah Booth. Plenty of couples live between New York and Los Angeles. Mississippi is just a little harder to get to, plane-wise, but it's doable."

This was the spirit that made me love him. "How about French toast?" I asked.

"It's the dish you cook best. And Sweetie Pie has joined us. I'm sure she'd enjoy a piece, too."

I finished making our breakfast and we talked about everything except Hedy Lamarr Blackledge. When my cell phone rang and he saw Tinkie's number, he handed me the phone without comment.

"What's shaking, Tinkie?" I asked.

"Can you come back to Greenwood, Sarah Booth?" Worry gave her voice a brittle edge. "I know this is a bad time. I wouldn't ask if it wasn't an emergency."

"What's wrong?"

"It's Babs Lafitte."

"What about Babs?" I had a strong mental image of her flinging wigs and mannequin heads all around her hotel room.

"She's in a coma."

"What happened?"

"She was poisoned last night. And the last person she was with was Hedy. After the barbecue, they went out together."

"Someone is framing Hedy," I said. Even the most incompetent murderer could figure out how not to be the last person seen with three victims.

"And doing a damn good job of it. When can you come back here?"

I had Tinkie's car. I glanced at Graf, who watched me with no expression whatsoever. "Can you ride to Greenwood with me?" I asked him. "I have to return Tinkie's car."

"And dig into this case a little deeper," he said in a flat tone.

"Another contestant has been injured," I admitted.

"Don't you think this killer means business? I don't want you to be next."

I understood his fear. I did. But I also knew I couldn't be ruled by it. "Graf, please don't. You knew I was a private investigator when we met."

"But I didn't realize I was going to love you so much. I didn't know you'd be hurt so badly you'd lose our baby and almost die. I didn't know any of this when we met."

I pushed my anger aside and found the compassion just beneath it. I knew what it was like to fear losing a loved one. "What Tinkie and I are doing isn't dangerous. I promise."

He went to the sink. I waited a full minute.

"Tinkie, I'll be there as soon as I can," I said into the phone before I hung up. "Graf, I have to get her car back to her. How long can you stay?"

"My flight leaves Memphis at noon," he said. "Go on to Greenwood. It's almost time for me to leave for the airport, anyway. My rental car is hidden in the barn. I'll drop Sweetie off at Oscar's on the way."

The trip back to Greenwood was much longer than the drive home had been last night. My heart was heavy and my thoughts turned to a silky Delta night and another vehicle traveling through the cotton fields spread on either side of the road. If I could go back in time and order my parents never to leave the property, I would willingly make them prisoners at Dahlia House to prevent the pain of their loss. I understood Graf's desire to protect his heart. I also knew I'd grow to hate and resent him if he persisted in trying to keep me swaddled in a protective cocoon. How to balance Graf's needs against my own?

The jangle of silver bracelets warned me that Jitty was about to make an appearance. Arriving in a moving vehicle was another neat trick from the Great Beyond I had a hankering to learn.

Instead of her latest chef outfit, Jitty arrived in full-blown glam: red evening gown that revealed perfect décolletage, dangling diamond earrings, and long, curling blond tresses. "What? Couldn't take the heat, so you got out of the kitchen?"

"Very clever," she said, "for a woman who's leavin' hot action and a good man behind."

I didn't need Jitty to harangue me. I chanced a long look at her. "You remind me of someone . . . a television interviewer for one of the celebrity gossip shows."

"And also a former star of the Canadian television show *Cooking with Love*."

"Good lord."

"Three contestants cook for a mystery date. The guy picks one of the three dishes, the one he likes the best, and he dates the gal who cooked it."

"If you quote Aunt Loulane and say the way to a man's heart is through his stomach, I'm going to stop the car and kick some noncorporeal butt."

"You shoulda served that man lasagna. It's a manly dish. French toast is a Tinkie dish. Lady food don't meet the needs of a hungry man, and I sure think Graf had to be hungry after last night. He musta worked up an appetite."

"Stop it!" I couldn't even entertain the idea that Jitty was spying on me. "I do not want to think of you as a voyeur. I'll never have sex again if I think you're watching."

Her laughter was rich and musical. "I don't have to watch. All I had to do was look at your face when you got up this morning. It was like the dark cloud of Mordor had lifted and the sun was shining at last. Graf worked a knot in your spine and then jerked it loose, didn't he?"

"That is none of your business."

"Don't ask, don't tell. Is that your policy?"

"Jitty, I'm removing the televisions from Dahlia House. You have way too much time on your hands if you're digging up Canadian television shows and military slogans. Now why are you deviling me today of all days? I've got a comatose contestant in Greenwood and an angry fiancé in Zinnia. I don't need your bitching in between."

"I've come to help you with this problem."

For a moment, I almost believed her. Then I remembered she was Jitty. "And how will you do this?"

"History, Sarah Booth. I'm here to remind you of history."

Protesting would do no good. Jitty would have her say. "Okay, is there a specific period we're going to examine? Marie Antoinette? Anne Boleyn? Mary, Queen of Scots? Oops, didn't they all lose their heads over what boiled down to a romantic interest?"

"Just go right on sassin' and prancin'. Life's gonna slap you upside the head with the facts if you don't listen to me. And it was a power issue with those ladies, not romance."

I'd really gotten under Jitty's skin. Her accent was thickening like lumpy gravy. "Okay, say what you came to say." We were on the outskirts of Greenwood. In another twenty minutes I'd be pulling into the Alluvian parking lot. Technically, I supposed Jitty could follow me into the hotel, but she wasn't that kind of ghost. She was more subtle and had more class.

"When Coker and your great-great-grandpa

went off to war, Miss Alice and I were devastated. Maybe your great-great-grandpa had to go. He was a landowner, a man folks in the region looked up to. He felt it was his duty to fight for his state. But Coker? My husband was a slave, like me. If he was gonna fight, he mighta thought about joinin' the other side."

I took a right off the highway. Traffic had picked up, and while I paid attention to my driving, I also listened to Jitty.

"When he tole me he was goin' off to the war, he might as well have taken a knife and stabbed me in the heart. The pain. I thought I would die right there. He'd chosen his master over his wife, and it was a choice he didn't have to make."

"Why did he?" I knew the outcome of this story. Both men died. Alice and Jitty struggled to feed themselves and cling to the Delaney property. They'd lived hard lives filled with loss and sacrifice. And as Jitty pointed out, neither man *had* to go to war. Both had chosen. One for his ideals, and one out of loyalty to a man he loved.

Jitty's frown softened as the memory grabbed hold of her. Not even the dead were immune to the power of the past, it seemed. "I remember to this day what Coker told me. He said stayin' with me was what his body told him to do. But going with Mr. Delaney was what his spirit said was

216

right. Both men expected to come home. You know how young men are, never thinkin' fate has anything in store except life and work and pleasure. Had they known the outcome, they woulda chose different. I know that."

"How long did you hate Coker?"

Jitty laughed. "A while. Grubbin' for potatoes in the dead neighbor's garden or tryin' to catch a near-starved chicken to pen it up for eggs. At times, despair slipped under my skin and bitterness tainted my blood. But underneath the pain was the fact I loved Coker because of the man he was. And that man followed Mr. Delaney off to war to help protect him. Coker thought Alice and I were safe. He never thought Union troops would get this far or the Yanks would try to starve us to death. I guess he never thought about what war really is. 'Til he got in the thick of it, and by then it was too late to get out."

"So are you saying Graf will forgive me if I pursue this case?"

Jitty pushed back her blond curls. "If he understands the reasons why you have to do it, I think he will."

That was the most straightforward answer I'd ever gotten from Jitty. Surprisingly enough, it made me feel better. "Thanks, Jitty."

"Cook him up a big pan of lasagna, just to be on the safe side. Never hurts to have a carb blackout on your side when it comes down to the wire."

I turned to thank her, but the front seat was empty. The smallest wisp of vapor disappeared into the air-conditioning vent. She was getting better and better at these show-stopping disappearing acts.

Tinkie sat in an overstuffed chair in our room at the Alluvian. She'd thrown over our morning cooking class, too worried about Babs to concentrate on the difference between coddle and poach. "Babs hasn't regained consciousness, so Chief Jansen can't question her. He suspects she's been poisoned." Worry etched lines in her forehead. "He's called in Doc Sawyer."

Doc was Sunflower County's emergency room physician. For a country doctor who'd tended my family—and most of the county—he'd developed a highly respected reputation for diagnosing strange maladies and poisons. Babs had to be very sick to call him in.

"Is Babs going to make it?" I'd taken a liking to the tall redhead.

"No one can say, but the chief thinks she was meant to die. He thinks we have a serial killer on the loose. I'm afraid he thinks it's Hedy. He just doesn't have enough evidence to make a charge stick. Yet."

Easing onto the arm of Tinkie's chair, I gave her shoulder a squeeze. "Where is Hedy now?"

"In her room. She's taking this hard."

"Last night she and Babs went out together?"

"They went to a blues club in Clarksdale. Hedy said they had a few drinks, listened to the band, and came home. She left Babs in the car in the hotel parking lot listening to the end of a song. She said Babs was fine, a little tipsy. She wanted to smoke a cigarette and finish her song."

"Do you believe Hedy?"

"Of course." She stood up. "You don't?"

"I do, but it's strange that whenever something bad happens, Hedy is right on the scene."

Tinkie put her hands on her hips. "That's not true. Brook Oniada. Everyone saw her. She was on a stage with *all* the finalists."

Once Tinkie believed in a person, she stuck through thick and thin.

"How do you account for the fact that Hedy was the last person to see Janet Menton alive and Babs in good health?" I asked.

"It's Marcus. He's engineering this. He has the money and the resources to make this happen. All Hedy wants is a chance to know her daughter. Marcus took advantage of her—twice! Once to get her pregnant, and then to get her to sign away her rights to Vivian. He used the most low-down tactics. Who can say he won't kill to get what he wants? Maybe he planned the whole thing. Maybe he deliberately got Hedy pregnant. Now he has a child and no wife to tie him down." Her hands clenched into fists. "Hedy has been sitting outside his home for two years, Sarah Booth. Whenever she gets off work for two days in a row, she comes up here and prays to get one tiny glimpse of her baby. Marcus won't even give her a picture of Vivian."

Tinkie's scenario was possible, but I couldn't buy into it totally, despite her passion. I didn't doubt Marcus was a bastard through and through. Spoiled, undisciplined, lazy—those attributes applied. Murderer? I didn't know him well enough.

"Clive and Marcus are good friends. Dawn told you so," Tinkie said. "Clive could be helping Marcus. Why is Clive even a judge? For the past ten years women have been trying to get him off a horse and in the sack, but he'd rather ride than date. Why now, suddenly, is he judging a beauty contest?"

"You should go to law school." I tossed her a pair of jeans. She was still in a silk pajama set. "Get dressed. We need to get busy."

As she pulled on her pants, I continued. "Is the killer deliberately framing Hedy, and if so, how does he or she know Hedy will be the last one to see them? Are the girls dying to frame Hedy specifically, or is she just the most unlucky person I've ever run across?"

"That's a flaw in my theory." Tinkie went to the chest of drawers to find a top.

"If he called Hedy the night Janet died, he

could have lured her out of the room. Once she was gone, he could have sneaked the poison to Janet in the pastries," I said. It was possible. As far as I knew, Jansen had been unable to trace the pastries to any of the contestants. Maybe because they were baked in the Wellington kitchen.

"Marcus would have to tail Hedy. He'd have to be right on top of her. Remember the picture with Marcus lurking in the background. He's been here since the contest started. If he isn't doing it personally, he has resources to hire someone."

"If you're right, Tinkie, we have to do everything possible to get that child from his care." The idea that Marcus was a cold-blooded killer made me want to jump into action.

Tinkie nodded. "Based on what he did to Hedy, Marcus is capable of anything."

"But what if it is a serial killer who targets only beauty contestants?" I asked. Experience had taught me not to jump on one solution and push all others aside.

"Yeah, someone born so ugly, he or she hates pretty women." Tinkie barely suppressed her sarcasm.

"I'm serious," I said. "There are serial killers who kill hookers or soccer moms or . . . clowns. Why couldn't one have a death wish for beauty pageant contestants?"

Tinkie's head popped through the pullover. "You're right. I stand corrected. We can't settle on a single theory yet. We don't have enough evidence." She pulled on socks and boots. "Maybe the killer really is one of the contestants murdering off the other competitors."

We looked at each other. "Karrie Kompton," we said together.

"But it's almost too obvious—one contestant killing off her competition. Surely Chief Jansen is all over that."

"There are other possible motives," I conceded. "We're going to have to pick a theory and go with it." That was the hard part. If we started down the wrong path, we'd waste precious time, and possibly precious lives.

"We need to find more evidence, before he or she kills again," Tinkie added.

15

When Tinkie was dressed and groomed, we called Hedy's room and got no answer. If she'd been hauled off to jail, she would have called us. If she wasn't in jail, where was she?

Tinkie tried her cell phone. Again, no answer.

"What's on the agenda today for the contestants?" I thought maybe Hedy had early preparation for cooking or rehearsing.

Tinkie consulted the program she'd picked up at one of the events. "There's nothing scheduled for today, which is a relief. Those girls have been put through their paces. The day is free, but tonight is 'Taste and Copy.' "

"Which entails what?"

"Dishes are prepared by visiting chefs at the Viking Cooking School, and the pageant contestants taste the dishes and figure out the ingredients. This is an easy one to judge, I suppose. Either the girls get it right or not."

"It sounds hard to me."

"A good cook should be able to determine the elements in a recipe and re-create it perfectly at home, or at least that's the assumption behind this part of the competition."

"That's like playing the piano by ear—fine if you've got a good ear. Not so great if you don't."

Tinkie shrugged. I could see the whole cooking thing was wearing thin with her. It had been a long week filled with lots of whipping, chopping, sautéing, and killing. "Should we find Jansen? Talk to him about Babs?"

I couldn't see what good it would do to talk with the chief. He viewed us with suspicion and some degree of animosity. Then, on the other hand, where else could we go?

We found Jansen in the police department behind his impressive desk. He'd removed his jacket and rolled up his shirtsleeves. With his mustache and suspenders, he looked a bit out of time, but there was nothing antique about his attitude toward private investigators.

"You two scram," he said. "We've got this under control. Your client—"

"Is innocent. Where is Hedy?" I asked.

"I was going to ask you that same question. She's not supposed to leave Leflore County, but she's not in her hotel room. I sent a couple of officers to pick her up, but she wasn't there."

"She's probably getting a facial or massage," Tinkie supplied with ease. "Big night tonight. 'Taste and Copy.' Things are drawing to a close, and the pressure is on. Nothing like a good massage to work out the tension, Chief Jansen. You should try it sometime."

"What's drawing to a close, Mrs. Richmond, are the lives of the contestants. Ten came to town; two have left in coffins, and one in an ambulance. That's not good statistics, if you ask me. Losing a beauty contest is one thing. Losing your life is another."

"Truer words were never spoken." Tinkie sat on the edge of Jansen's desk. He frowned, but didn't shoo her off.

"Was Babs poisoned with ricin?" I asked.

Jansen shuffled his papers. "The lab results aren't confirmed yet."

I was about to ask another question when he held up his hand. "But it wasn't ricin. Doc Sawyer, who I think you know, believes it's a poison from a common plant."

"And that would be?" Tinkie said.

"Best I understand, it's a flowering plant. Folks can have it in their petunia beds and not even know how dangerous it is. Your Doc Sawyer says the flowers are beautiful. Makes a powerful drug. Digitalis."

I'd read about this plant. "Foxglove, isn't it?" There were certain things I didn't want around Dahlia House just on the off chance Reveler might get out of his pasture and taste them, so I'd learned a few basics on toxic flowers.

"Correct. Doc Sawyer quickly recognized Miss Lafitte's symptoms—fact is, he likely saved her life. We have to wait until the lab confirms it, but right now, that's the assumption we're operating under."

"Could this have been an accident? Digitalis is a legitimate drug. Did Babs have a heart condition?" I asked.

"She was healthy as a horse, according to her pageant records." His neck reddened as his anger mounted. "This damn beauty contest should be stopped now! If I have my way, it will be halted before anyone else gets hurt."

"I see the wisdom in that, Chief." Jansen had a good point.

"How was the poison delivered to Babs?" Tinkie asked.

Jansen reined in his temper. "Doc thinks someone put it in her smokes. The leaves of the foxglove are the deadliest part. They could be dried, chopped, and mixed with tobacco."

"Pretty devious. Someone really thought this through. Have you questioned anyone except Hedy?" I asked.

Jansen gave me a go-to-hell look. "I've questioned every living contestant and the judges and the pageant officials and most of the town. I have ten police officers and they haven't been home at night to sleep since this pageant started. We've fingerprinted half the surfaces in the Alluvian and the auditorium, and all I can say is, those girls touch everything. They use each other's cosmetics and cooking ingredients."

"What about prints in the room Hedy shared with Janet Menton? Anyone unusual show up?"

"The only prints we found belonged to Hedy, Janet, and the hotel cleaning staff, and before you asked, I checked the cleaning and room service staff thoroughly. They've all been working at the Alluvian for at least two years and have spotless records."

"Were there prints on the gris-gris bag under Janet's bed?"

"How did you know about that?" Jansen asked, instantly alert.

"Harley Pitts told me. Janet had confided to him. He told her it was most likely a prank. I gather Janet brought it to you?"

"No. We found it in her room. Had she told me, I would have said the same thing. That it was a prank," Jansen said. "At first. But to answer your question, the leather bag was wiped clean. So was the pastry box."

Jansen's cooperation meter was clicking on high. "Could you tell us what was in the gris-gris bag?" I asked.

"A dried chicken foot, some mummified tissue the state lab identified as a lizard heart, some red lace belonging to a pair of Janet's panties, a page torn from the play she performed."

"The contents were gathered specifically for Janet," Tinkie mused. "And no gris-gris bag was found in Brook's room or in Babs's?"

Jansen compressed his lips. He was deciding whether to tell us the truth or not.

"You found gris-gris, didn't you?" I said.

"We found a similar bag in Brook's vanity."

"And Babs?" I pressed.

"On the front seat of the car."

"What was in it?" Tinkie asked.

Jansen picked up a pen and twirled it with impressive dexterity. "A dried chicken foot, some red hair we think may have been picked up the night she had the reaction to the pepper and tore her own hair out, a small picture of Robert Johnson—"

"The legendary bluesman who was poisoned," I said. The connection was obvious. Babs was a blues singer. Johnson hadn't survived the poison given him. I could only hope Babs would get a better break.

"That's right. And a few small cubic zirconia, the kind used in crowns or tiaras." Jansen observed us closely.

"No prints?" I asked.

He shook his head. "None. Brook's bag contained similar things, including a butane cigarette lighter and a book of matches."

"The bastard planned this very carefully," Tinkie said. "Each girl is profiled, something special to her included. The killer knows these girls and what's important to each of them."

"And the killer knows enough about voodoo to put together the ingredients for a curse." Jansen pulled at his mustache. "The other girls say Hedy has connections to voodoo, a family history."

"What other girls? Karrie Kompton? It clearly serves her purposes to eliminate Hedy," I said.

"You shouldn't put any stock in malicious rumors," Tinkie chimed in. "Marcus Wellington is behind that talk. He's—"

I signaled her to cut it off. "Why is the killer

using different poisons?" I asked. "Why make it so complicated?"

"I think the killer hoped to confound us for a couple of days—likely until the competition was over," Tinkie answered. "It's sheer luck Doc is so knowledgeable about poisons."

"I agree with you, Mrs. Richmond. Doc Sawyer identified the digitalis pretty quick."

"What's next?" I asked.

Jansen pushed back from his desk. "We're hoping Miss Lafitte regains consciousness soon and can give details about what happened. Right now, I'm waiting on a call from Mrs. Phelps about shutting down the pageant. I won't have another girl killed or hurt because of some silly beauty title."

"Closing down the competition could mean a huge loss for the town," Tinkie said. She wasn't being argumentative, only factual. Jansen was so tired, he didn't bristle at her comment.

"Better to have the merchants and the citizens pissed at me than see another young woman leave here in a body bag." The burden of the deaths showed clearly in his face.

"Can we help you?" I asked.

Jansen gave me the evil eye. "You work for Miss Blackledge. I'd say our goals are about as far apart as they could get."

"Not true," I said, "if Hedy is innocent, as we contend, then finding the true killer would clear our client. That's all we want—to find the truth that clears Hedy."

Jansen leaned his elbow on the chair arm and gave it some thought. "Okay, I won't say we'll work together on this, but I will say I won't impede your investigation if you don't hide things from me."

"Not a problem," Tinkie said. She was always more upfront than me. I wisely held back. "So who are your suspects? Surely you're considering someone other than Hedy."

"This isn't a gossip circle." Jansen grew stern. "You two aren't part of my investigation and I'm under no compunction to tell you anything. Unless, of course, you have something you want to share with me."

Tinkie leaned across the desk. "So, it's going to be tit for tat," she said.

I put a hand on her shoulder. "We're happy to share whatever we find, Chief, as long as it doesn't incriminate our client."

Even though he was tired, he gave us a smile. "I expected nothing less. Miss Lafitte was last seen at a blues club in Clarksdale with your client. They had several drinks, danced, and talked with some men. The women were seen getting in a car together and driving away."

"What time?" I asked.

"About midnight, which is pretty late for girls hoping to look their best the next day." His look said they had to be up to no good.

"They had a morning to sleep in," I told him. "Midnight, one o'clock isn't late for young people."

He snorted. "If you'd quit interrupting me, I'm trying to tell you something."

"What?" Tinkie asked softly.

"The witness, one of the band members, saw them leave together in the same car. Another car pulled out and followed them. Joey, Joey Mott, that's the singer, said he thought it was strange."

"What's so unusual about two cars leaving a parking lot at the same time?" I asked.

"Joey was on the porch smoking a cigarette. He spoke to them when they walked by and they seemed perfectly fine. Neither appeared inebriated. They were laughing at something when they got in the car and drove off. The other car followed right away, as if someone was sitting there, watching and waiting. He didn't see anyone else leave the club."

"If that's the case, why isn't Hedy dead, too?" Tinkie asked.

"Could be the person following was Hedy's accomplice," Jansen said.

"Or it could be that Hedy went straight up to her room and Babs lingered outside to talk to the person who'd followed them," Tinkie pointed out.

I could tell by Jansen's expression that Tinkie

had scored a home run. "Was Babs found in Hedy's car?" I asked.

"Beside the car. We think she tried to make it inside, but she never got out of the parking lot. The vehicle's impounded and a forensics team is going over it."

"When you questioned Hedy, what did she say?" We could get the same info from Hedy—when we found her—but I wanted to know how Jansen had processed it.

"Hedy said they ordered a pitcher of margaritas at the club. Babs wanted to stay out, to keep drinking, but Hedy said she was tired. Hedy left Babs sitting in the passenger seat listening to music. She also left the keys, and they were still in the ignition and the battery was dead when Babs was discovered by a hotel staffer this morning."

The dead battery supported the fact that Babs had been listening to the radio or CD player. "Did anyone see Hedy enter the hotel?" Confirmation of an alibi might not help in this instance, but it couldn't hurt. Truth was like mortar between bricks. It allowed us to stack one fact on top of another until we had a solid wall.

"No one was at the desk, and Hedy said she didn't see another soul on the way to her room. She was asleep in her bed when we went looking for her."

His phone rang, and he gave us a nod of apology

as he picked it up. "Yes, Cheryl, I'll speak with the mayor."

I couldn't hear the mayor's words but I caught his tone. He wasn't happy and he had no intention of shutting down the pageant. When Jansen hung up the phone, he sighed. "Direct orders from the mayor not to stop the pageant."

I felt for Jansen. He was squeezed between a rock and a hard place. If he was correct, the killer had easy access and the spree would continue.

"There are only a couple of events left," Tinkie said.

"Hell, the killer may start knocking them off two or three at a time." Jansen was angry and frustrated, but not at us. "There's something else you should know. Had Miss Oniada not caught on fire, she would have died of poisoning."

Tinkie glanced at me. The news was shocking, and we saw no reason to pretend it wasn't. "What kind of poison?"

"Belladonna, or deadly nightshade. We missed it completely at first. It was clear she'd died of burns sustained in the fire. The reason she didn't react or try to save herself is because she was heavily dosed with the poison."

"Holy cow," Tinkie said.

I would have used stronger language, but then Tinkie is a lady and I am not. "Did she drink something or eat something? How does deadly nightshade work?"

"Doc Sawyer is going over the evidence. He ordered more testing on some of her cosmetics. He believes she absorbed the poison through her skin. Apparently there's some history of contact poisoning with belladonna."

"We're dealing with someone who knows a lot about plants and poisons." I regretted those words the instant they were out of my mouth.

"And no one fits that bill better than Hedy Blackledge. She comes from a long line of conjure women, or *traiteurs*, as they're called in Louisiana. Poison, gris-gris—the evidence tells me Hedy Blackledge is in this up to her eyeballs."

"Right, the entire Saulnier family works for a dead voodoo queen, Marie Laveau." I hoped to make him see how foolish all of that gossip was.

"Don't laugh, Miss Delaney. Those conjure women have a lot of knowledge. Don't ever think they're harmless."

"Are you superstitious, Chief?"

The shadow of a smile tugged at his mouth. "Oh, I'm a lot of things that might surprise you, Miss Delaney."

"Did you hear this malicious gossip about Hedy from Marcus Wellington?" I asked.

"I did. He's afraid of Hedy and her family. He said she tried to poison him several times."

"Did he also tell you that Hedy is the mother of his child? Vivian is Hedy's daughter," I said. Marcus had slandered Hedy in the worst way, and Jansen deserved the truth.

Jansen grew completely still. "No. He did not. I've seen him with the little girl. He dotes on her."

"When you're looking for motives, you might examine his. He convinced Hedy to sign away her rights to Vivian. She's been trying to gain partial custody, and he's fighting it with everything he has," Tinkie said.

The telephone rang again. He listened a moment. "No sign of Miss Blackledge anywhere? Well, her private investigators are standing right here. Sounds like a good job for them—to track her down. Thanks."

He replaced the phone. "We need Hedy in here. Now."

"We don't—" Tinkie started.

"We'll find her and send her over," I said, drowning Tinkie out.

"See that you do."

I motioned to the door, and Tinkie and I decamped. When we were outside, she whispered, "We don't know where Hedy is."

"She'll turn up. Her car is impounded. The pageant is tonight. She knows we're working in her behalf."

"She'd better be in town."

"My gut tells me she's in Panther Holler trying to see her kid."

"If she gets caught . . ."

Tinkie didn't have to finish the statement. We both knew Marcus Wellington wanted nothing more than to put her behind bars. Trespassing would work as well as any other charge.

"What are we going to do?" Tinkie asked.

"Make a swing through Panther Holler on our way to or from Clarksdale. We have a witness at the blues club. Joey Mott. Maybe he saw more than he told Jansen."

We stopped by the room to grab the camera. While Tinkie was in the bathroom, I tried to call Graf. He was in the Memphis airport by now, but he shouldn't have boarded his plane already. Wherever he was, he wasn't answering his phone. I called Oscar to check on Sweetie Pie.

"Graf dropped her off," Oscar said. "She's tired but seems fine."

"Dr. Leonard said she would be tired for a couple of days. Let's hope she's too worn out to find more trouble."

Oscar cleared his throat. "She seems a little . . . depressed."

Great. "She's pining for that harrier hound."

"Danny and Bobbie left this morning to return to New York. Do you think Sweetie will be okay?"

Heartbreak was no fun matter, but my hound would recover. "Just give her lots of pats. And thank you, Oscar. I'm sorry she caused so much trouble."

"I'm just glad she's back. Chablis is asleep right beside her."

"There's no comfort like that of a good friend," I said.

Tinkie came out of the bathroom and I signaled to ask if she wanted to talk to Oscar, but she shook her head. I said my good-byes and hung up.

"Oscar's mad because I'm paying for Hedy's lawyer. Russell Dean's already turned in a bill for a thousand dollars."

"For what?" I asked.

"Fees, retainer, something. Oscar wasn't exactly thrilled, but he paid it. I just don't want to talk to him right now. In a day or so, he'll cool off and forget it."

I didn't laugh, because I'd come to admire Tinkie's efficient handling of the men in her life. "We have two options," I said. "We can find Doc and see what he has to say about deadly night-shade, ricin, and foxglove. Or we can hunt down Joey Mott."

"Let's see, a morning of death and poison or tracking a blues musician." Tinkie pretended it was a tough choice.

"Get in the car," I said, tossing her the keys to

the Caddy. "Clarksdale isn't that far away. Joey Mott should be home since he played last night. Maybe we can find him before he takes off for the morning."

Ground Zero Blues Club, so named because Clarksdale and the surrounding area are ground zero for the Mississippi Delta blues, wasn't open, but the Blues Museum was. A renovated train depot housed the museum, and the staff knew Joey Mott. He had a reputation for playing his guitar fast and hard and fighting any comers while reciting Bible verses. The combination wasn't that odd for a bluesman in the Delta.

We located his third-floor apartment without trouble. He'd obviously been sound asleep when we knocked. He opened the door in jeans and a T-shirt advertising the merits of Howling Wolf, a famous bluesman.

"Ladies," he said, rubbing his stubble-covered face, "what can I do for you?"

Tinkie told him who we were and stepped past him into the apartment, which was surprisingly neat. "We need to talk to you about last night."

"May I put on a pot of coffee before the interrogation?" he asked. The man had a certain level of charm.

"Coffee would be lovely," Tinkie said.

While the pot brewed, we sat around a table in his small kitchen and explained why we needed to talk to him. He was happy to cooperate.

"I saw the dark-haired woman right away," he said. "You couldn't miss her. But she wasn't the friendly type. The redhead, though, she was a pistol. She knew how to have a good time. It's a shame what happened to her."

"Do you remember anyone talking with them?" I asked.

"Guys were hitting on them all over the place, but what would you expect? At first, the two of them were having a serious talk. After they relaxed, the redhead danced a few times with some of the guys."

"Names?" I asked.

He shook his head. "Lots of tourists in the club. I don't know them. If I saw them again, I might be able to identify them, but I don't have any particulars."

"Did you notice if anyone took them drinks?"

He shook his head. "I think they had margaritas. Like a pitcher. The redhead could drink. The brunette was nursing hers. Someone could have bought them a round."

"Can you identify the vehicle that left when they did?"

"It was a big car. An SUV. Wide headlights. That's what I remember. Couldn't see the color, but it was maybe blue or black or dark green."

He poured three cups of coffee and set one in front of each of us. "I wasn't paying much attention. You know how it is when something is just a little off and you think, 'Now that's odd,' but you don't really register why."

I knew exactly. "Was there anyone who seemed out of place in the club? Someone maybe in the background. Watching the girls."

He gave it some consideration and a connection came through. "You know, there was someone."

"Tall man, dark wavy hair?" Talk about leading a witness, Tinkie had handed him Marcus Wellington on a platter.

He looked at me blankly. "Naw. It was a woman. Well turned out, dark hair, short. Maybe a decade older than you. She just sat back and held a drink. Never took a sip of it that I saw. I couldn't say for certain she was watching the two beauty pageant girls, but it seemed that way to me."

"I don't know anyone who looks like that," Tinkie said.

Neither did I. But then I wasn't familiar with the female side of the Wellington clan. It would be just like Marcus to get a sister or girlfriend to do his dirty surveillance work.

"Is there anything distinctive that you remember about her?"

He shook his head. "She left before the girls. That's what I remember. But hell, it's not even ten o'clock. My brain doesn't work until after lunch. Leave me a card and if I think of anything, I'll give you a call."

16

Panther Holler, a small community where the Wellingtons had built their dynasty, was our next stop. Always one to taunt the devil, Tinkie suggested that we drive up to the front door and ask to see Marcus.

We had nothing to lose, so we drove between the rows of beautiful oaks that lined the twisting shell driveway canopied by trees and up to the house that looked like a wedding cake confection. Wide double stairs swept up to the second-floor landing to an oak door so massive that a "fee-fie-foe-fum" was probably required to charm it open. Since we didn't have any magic beans, we merely knocked.

Marcus opened the door, his face bloated and his shirt buttoned wrong. Whatever he'd done the night before, he was still suffering the consequences.

"You have three minutes to clear the property," he said, "before I call the sheriff. Cameras at the gate will tell me when you've left."

"We have questions." Tinkie was never intimidated by money or bad manners. Since she had the first, she didn't have to tolerate the second.

"Take your questions and shove them—"

"Daddy?" A young girl with raven hair and eyes so blue they mesmerized toddled up to the door. I'd never been one to melt in the presence of babies, but Vivian, a miniature of Hedy, touched me.

"Vivian, we don't talk to strangers, remember, honey." He swept the child into his arms, shielding her face so she couldn't see us. Fear was plain on his face. "Please leave," he said to us. "My daughter needs me."

I'd doubted Marcus loved his daughter. I'd thought he wanted her only because he could take her. I knew better now. He loved this child. Vivian was perhaps the only weakness his heart had ever known.

"We must speak with you." Tinkie held her ground.

Marcus ignored her, focusing on his daughter. "Vivian, Anna has new paints for you." His hand caressed her dark hair.

Vivian's face lit up. "Paints!"

"Anna!" Marcus called out. "Anna!"

Vivian must have sensed his worry because her smile evaporated and she burrowed her face in his shoulder.

"It's okay," he soothed her. "Daddy's here. Everything is jim-dandy." Still shielding her, he glared at us. "I've asked you nicely to go. You've already upset Vivian, and I want you to vacate the premises."

"We aren't leaving until you talk to us," Tinkie said. "Count on it, Marcus. We don't want to make trouble, but we will."

"Just a moment." He stepped into a beautifully decorated foyer. "Let me find Anna or my parents to watch Vivian." He closed the door behind him.

In a moment he returned without the child. "What in the hell do you want?"

"You're playing with fire, Marcus, deliberately withholding Vivian from her mother. She's two now, but the minute she's around other children, she's going to start asking questions."

"I'll deal with that when I have to."

"Lovely," I said. "Especially since looking at Hedy will be like looking into a future mirror. She will find out, Marcus, and when she discovers you've lied to her and kept her away from the woman who gave her life, you'll pay a harsh price."

"You tell Hedy if she continues to come here and park at the end of the driveway, I'll have her put in jail. I mean it. She can't do that." Fear of the consequences of Hedy's presence showed on his face. I realized then the brilliance of Hedy's vigil. If Vivian so much as caught a glimpse of her, the child would know. She'd know, and Marcus's house of cards would come tumbling about his ears.

"Oh, but Hedy can sit at the end of your drive,"

I said. "As long as she isn't on your property, she can park on the verge all she wants." The Wellingtons owned a lot of property, but they didn't own the roadsides.

"Don't you think it would be better for the child to know her mother?" This was a sore subject for Tinkie, and she had strong opinions.

"Maybe if Hedy wasn't a Saulnier. Maybe if she didn't come from a voodoo family. Maybe if she wasn't murdering the competition in this beauty contest. I don't want Vivian to grow up in that atmosphere. Can't you see I'm only protecting my daughter?"

Tinkie frowned. "You honestly believe Hedy murdered those girls?"

Marcus motioned to some rattan chairs on the porch. "Sit down. I'm about to collapse."

"So I noticed. Rough work deflowering another young girl." I couldn't help it. Marcus annoyed me. What I wanted to accuse him of was poisoning Babs, but if he was guilty, why alert him?

He ignored my jab and eased into a chair. "Let me give you the story in a nutshell. I fell deeply in love with Hedy when I met her. We were at the beach. Those eyes. I looked into them once, and that was it for me. She bewitched me. I couldn't get enough of her, and I asked her to marry me."

So far, his facts parallelled what Hedy had told us. "And?"

"She got pregnant. I don't know how. I used protection, and she was on the pill. Instead of being angry, I was ecstatic. Until the pregnancy, Hedy wouldn't consider marriage. She wouldn't even talk about it. When she found out she was expecting, she relented."

Marcus was giving us the same facts but a different spin. "Why didn't you marry her?"

"I brought her home to meet my parents. I knew they'd dislike her, but I didn't care. I loved her so much, I was willing to defy them. For once in my life . . ."

He turned away, and against my better judgment, I felt a stab of pity for him. A silver spoon could sometimes gag more than nourish.

He continued. "They wanted me to marry money, to solidify the assets of two 'like' families. I'm not defending it, but that's how they think. I hadn't given them cause to trust my decisions on any fronts. They honestly believe the best unions are based on common cause, not love. They thought I was acting like a romantic fool."

"I'm familiar with those thoughts," Tinkie said. "Did you win them over?"

"I never got a chance. Mother was incredibly rude to Hedy. I know it hurt her, and she left. When I went back to the coast to talk to her, she wouldn't see me. Hedy's mother, Clara, told me to leave or I'd regret it. It was clear they intended to cut me out of Hedy's and my baby's life."

"Just as you've done to Hedy," I pointed out.

"But I've done it *for* Vivian."

"Sure." Marcus wasn't the altruistic type. Not even for the daughter he clearly loved.

"Believe what you want. I hired a private investigator to check into Hedy and her family. My intention was to bolster my parental claim when the baby was born. I wanted to be a part of the child's life, even if not a full-time father. When I found out about the Saulniers, I realized I had to save Vivian from them."

"And that's when you coerced a new mother with no resources to sign away the rights to her child." Tinkie barely kept her tone civil.

"They're voodoo practitioners. In each generation, the first daughter serves the queen, Marie Laveau. That would be Vivian's role. She would grow up with those beliefs. It would cripple her for life."

I couldn't stop the laughter. "You are kidding, right?"

"I'm deadly serious." The pallor of his skin proved it. "Vivian would be taught the voodoo ways if she stayed with Hedy. You don't know the truth about those people. I couldn't let that happen to my child."

I couldn't discern if Marcus believed this or if he'd figured out how to lie convincingly. Still, his passion gave me a tiny chill.

"Marcus, tell me you don't really believe in voodoo," Tinkie persisted. "If Hedy had these strange powers, don't you think you'd be dead by now?"

Score one for the Tink. "Yeah," I threw in.

"Mock me if it makes you feel better, but I'm telling you, that family has long links to practices I don't want my daughter to know about. I don't want her dabbling in the dark arts or thinking the way to achieve something is to call on dark forces."

"Certainly not when she can simply use the Wellington fortune to buy it or bully it into submission," I said.

"The Saulniers are dangerous." He wiped a sheen of sweat from his forehead.

"You are superstitious." I was surprised. A lot of wealthy people have no beliefs, except for the power of money.

"Not superstitious. Realistic. Whether Hedy can conjure demons or call on the dark side to help her, I don't know. That's not even the point. It's a mentality, a view of life I don't want Vivian exposed to. Not ever. So I did what I had to do to protect her."

"You sent a nanny to show Hedy how inadequate she was and then you browbeat a vulnerable young woman into giving up her child."

Marcus lifted his chin in a gesture of defiance.

"I did. It may be the only unselfish thing Hedy ever did, giving up Vivian. The nanny I found is wonderful. My two-year-old daughter is already reading simple stories and playing the piano. She's a brilliant child, and with me she'll have every opportunity. Private lessons, the best schools, connections in any world she wants to pursue. Unless Hedy ruins it."

"And Vivian will never know her mother." Tinkie hadn't softened a whit.

"She thinks her mother is happy and busy. That's the best thing for her."

"Maybe not," Tinkie said. "A child needs a maternal connection. It's the strongest bond formed for most women. A surrogate or hired employee can never fulfill that role."

"No matter how fabulous this Anna may be, she isn't Vivian's mother," I said.

"No, she isn't," Marcus said. "She's better for Vivian than Hedy could ever be." Marcus eased from his chair and opened the front door. "Anna! Could you come here a moment!"

She must have been close, because she came out the door in under thirty seconds. She was a short woman, small-framed and elegantly dressed. Her stylishly short haircut was shot through with slivers of gray.

"This is Anna Lock," Marcus said, "Vivian's nanny."

Joey Mott's description of the strange woman

in the blues club stood before me in the flesh.

Tinkie gave me a nod, acknowledging that she saw the same thing.

"Ask her whatever you want," Marcus said impatiently.

"Does Vivian ask for her mother?" Tinkie asked.

Anna hesitated, her gaze on Marcus. "She's an unusual child," she said. "Mature beyond her years and easily influenced."

"You didn't answer the question," I pointed out.

"She does quite well without her mother." Anna went to Marcus and put her hand on his arm in a maternal way. She was in her forties and though she was attractive, there wasn't a smidgen of sexual energy about her. She was all business and all Vivian. "She's extremely intelligent and deserves the opportunities Marcus can provide for her. I supervise her lessons, her meals, her play associates. I treat her as my own child and will continue to do so until she requires more advanced stimulation."

"But she isn't your child." Tinkie rose as she spoke. "And she isn't a brain waiting to be loaded with 'stimulation.' She's a child and she needs her mother."

Anna didn't hesitate. "Marcus and I agree she should have no contact with the mother. Absolutely none."

Marcus had surprised me with his honesty, but he'd also troubled me. The things he'd done in the name of love would result in heartache down the road. Whatever kind of nanny Anna Lock might be, she was off.

"Consider allowing Hedy visitation. For your sake, Marcus, as well as Vivian's. When your daughter realizes what you've done, she'll never forgive you."

"That'll never happen. Hedy is going to jail. How good would that be for Vivian to meet her mother only to have the woman dragged out of her life and put behind bars?" Marcus nodded at the door, and Anna responded instantly by stepping into the house and closing the door.

Marcus confronted us. "You've met Anna. She's responsible, older, well educated. Hedy should stop worrying about Vivian and leave her future to me."

"When pigs fly," Tinkie said under her breath.

"Ladies, I have business to attend to. Tell your client to say away from my driveway or she'll regret it." He slammed the front door as he left us on the porch.

We settled into the Cadillac with the air conditioner roaring. Tinkie looked back at the porch. "Anna could be the woman from the bar."

"I know."

"She's a strange one, isn't she?"

"Strange and creepy."

"She's pretty. Or she could be if she wasn't such a dour old bat. Lessons, intellect . . ." Tinkie mimicked her priggish tone. "Do you think Anna would kill three women to put the blame on Hedy?"

"If it meant keeping Vivian, I'd say yes, it's a distinct possibility."

By the time we got back to the Alluvian, it was lunchtime. Tinkie and I decided to try the Crystal Grill, a locally famous eatery near the railroad tracks. When we entered, the delicious smells made my mouth water.

We ordered burgers, fries, and lemon meringue pie. The place was hopping. Locals chatted at every table. We'd picked this restaurant so we could talk, reasoning that none of the contestants would risk the calories of delicious Southern food.

I read the menu, about to drool on the table with the possibilities we hadn't ordered, when I felt Tinkie's foot nudge mine under the table. She nodded to a secluded corner where Belinda Buck, one of the judges, sat with Voncil Payne. They'd taken a table in an alcove and hadn't noticed us arrive. Belinda was eating, and Voncil was talking. With great animation.

"That Voncil never gives up, does she?" Tinkie said. I'd told her about the encounter in the hall with Harley Pitts and the petit fours.

"Gotta love a mother who stage-manages her daughter and pushes all competition into the ditch."

"Amanda's performance at the barbecue was stupendous. Seeing her in action, working the crowd, managing the entertainment aspect, as well as cooking, I think she's a contender." Tinkie had an eye for such things.

"If that's the case, Amanda may be the next victim."

"Or the killer," Tinkie pointed out.

"I just don't see that." Amanda weighed maybe ninety pounds soaking wet and she was quiet as a church mouse. She wouldn't fit any profiler's outline of a killer. "Voncil is more likely. She's the grease that skids Amanda down the tracks."

"She'll ram Amanda through anyone who gets in the way."

"True, but my thoughts on the killer have changed drastically since meeting Anna Lock. We can't discount Marcus or one of the contestants, but I think we should take a close look at the nanny."

"Me too. She's . . . not right." Tinkie peeled a packet of crackers and munched one. "If it is one of the contestants, though, my vote still goes to Karrie Kompton."

Speak of the devil and she arrives. Karrie strolled into the café just as the waitress put our food in front of us. The whole place fell silent as everyone took note of her arrival. She was hard to miss in a minidress that showed a mile of leg, high-heel sandals, a huge sun hat, and sunglasses.

She walked straight to the table where Voncil and Belinda were confabbing and stuck a finger in Voncil's face. "Everyone knows you're trying to bribe the judges. You're probably killing off the contestants, but I'm onto you."

Tinkie was on her feet and across the room, her digital camera out and snapping. Belinda tried to hide behind a menu as Tinkie captured the moment. Joy would reign in the halls of the *Dispatch*.

"Give me that camera!" Karrie grabbed a fistful of Tinkie's hair. I was on my feet in a flash. Without a second thought, I karate-chopped Karrie. I'd never had a martial arts lesson, but I hit her hard enough to make up in pain what I lacked in technique. She let go of my partner.

"You two have been the bane of my existence since I got here," Karrie said. "You're going to pay." She stalked out of the restaurant to a long, sharp wolf whistle from a table full of young men.

Voncil was in tears, and dismay showed on Belinda Buck's face. "This isn't what it appears to be," Belinda said.

"Looks to me like a judge having lunch with a contestant's mother," Tinkie said. "Can you spell 'compromised'?" Leave it to my partner to call a spade a spade. And I was the ornery one.

"We didn't plan this lunch. I came to eat, saw Belinda was sitting alone." She gasped for breath. "We have other business, non-pageant business. We were discussing . . ." Voncil wiped a tear from her cheek. "We're working together on a fund-raiser for diabetes in Gainesville, Florida. We've both had sad experiences with the disease, and I asked Belinda to headline an event. Please don't ruin Belinda because I did something stupid."

Tinkie wasn't buying it. Her nose for news was itching.

"It's true," Belinda said. "Check with the Florida Diabetes Association. This is perfectly innocent, even though I did ask Voncil to leave as soon as she sat down."

"I'll check it out," Tinkie said.

"Instead of picking on Miss Buck, maybe you ought to run the photo of Karrie showing her true colors as a pit bull," Voncil said. "She's a bitch, and she deserves to be shown as one in print."

"But it would taint the Miss Viking Contest," Belinda said. "Even if *we* know this lunch is aboveboard, other folks won't. One thing I've learned from working in Hollywood: Perception is everything."

Her observation was dead-on, and this gave

Tinkie and me a perfect opportunity. "Miss Buck, Tinkie and I have some questions, when you have time."

"I have a full afternoon," she said. "I'll have my assistant call you and set an appointment."

"Perfect." I too had a busy afternoon planned.

17

Hedy was still MIA when we returned to the hotel. A police officer stood in the lobby, no doubt waiting to snatch her up and take her to Jansen when she finally put in an appearance. Thinking I might find a clue to her whereabouts in her room, I used the key card she'd given Tinkie to trigger the lock.

The door swung wide without a sound. The room was a disaster. And empty. The suite she'd shared with Janet Menton was cluttered—and sealed off. Hedy's new room was wrecked. With a sense of dread, I realized it wasn't merely messy. It had been tossed. By someone either in a hurry or intent on destroying as much as possible.

This put Hedy's continued absence in a new light.

I called Chief Jansen. Though livid at Hedy's

behavior, he calmed down when I told him about the condition of her room and my fears someone had abducted Hedy.

"Don't touch anything," he said. "I'll send forensics."

"I've touched the doorknob and I'm leaving the room."

"Wait for me—"

But I didn't. I had no time to get hornswaggled into Jansen's investigative clutches. If Hedy was in danger, I needed to get on the trail. I called Tinkie from the lobby, and she agreed I should pursue Hedy while she found out all she could about Anna Lock, the amazingly competent nanny for little Vivian. *And* the woman who fit the description of what I'd come to call Hedy's "stalker" at Ground Zero Blues Club.

At the hotel's front desk, I talked with two hotel staffers, Samuel and Lonnie. Neither had seen Hedy. When I explained she was missing and I was concerned someone had "taken" her, Samuel sang a different tune.

He signaled me to follow him out to the court-yard, away from the coming and going of the lobby traffic. He stuffed his hands in his pockets, withdrew them, then stuffed them in again. "Nobody took Miss Hedy except for me."

"What do you mean?" I have to admit, relief was sweet. I'd convinced myself Hedy had been kidnapped. Right off the bat I knew Samuel hadn't done anything bad to her.

"She was so upset by what happened to Babs. She said she'd be blamed. She needed to hide somewhere and asked if I could help her." Samuel almost trembled. He wasn't the best accomplice for nefarious deeds or avoiding the law. He was flawed by honesty.

"Where is she?" I asked.

He looked at the ground and mumbled, "At my place."

"Did you trash her room to make it look like an abduction?"

His head snapped up. "No, ma'am. I couldn't do that. The hotel would fire me for tearing up a customer's things."

I didn't have the grit to tell him lying to the police and helping a person avoid the law weren't pluses with an employer. But his heart was in the right place. Hedy had a way of winning people over, of convincing them to help her. I was a prime example of that.

"I need to speak with her. Where is she?"

He gave me the address, which wasn't far. "Since you're a hotel guest, I can drive you," he offered.

That would leave the Caddy at Tinkie's disposal. He went to retrieve the van key, and I waited in the courtyard. The day had grown hot, and I wished for shorts rather than long pants, but I had no time to change. The luxury of spring's cool breezes had fled. Heat and humidity lay over the land, bringing the cotton on strong. Mississippi's climate took a certain amount of fortitude.

Laughter drifted around the corner of the courtyard, and Voncil and Amanda Payne walked up carrying shopping bags jammed with cooking supplies and clothes. They'd had a real spree in a very short time.

"Sarah Booth," Amanda said, "please thank Mrs. Richmond for the wonderful newspaper photo of me singing. And your friend, Miss Cece, was so kind reviewing my songs."

"You did a marvelous job. Cece never gives praise unless it's due."

"I need to have a word with Miss Delaney," Voncil said. "Amanda, would you take these things to the room?"

Amanda gathered up the bags, disappearing among the purchases. I held the door as she struggled to the elevator.

"I have some information about your client," Voncil said quietly. She looked around as if she expected Big Brother behind a palm. "I saw her last night."

Samuel was taking his sweet time, so I motioned her to a courtyard table. "Where?"

"Hedy and Babs pulled up in the parking lot here at the Alluvian between one thirty and two a.m. They talked a minute, and I heard them laughing. Hedy got out of the car, and Babs remained."

This corroborated what Hedy had told the police chief. "Babs was in the car with the door shut? You saw her?"

"Yes. Babs had some music turned up really loud, and she was rocking down. You know, sort of dancing in the car. I'd guess she was high and not ready to call it a night."

"What were you doing in the parking lot so late?"

She rubbed the tendons at the back of her neck. "This contest is killing me. I can't sleep. The pressure is incredible. When I get this tense, it affects Amanda. I took a drive over to Greenville to see the Mississippi River in the moonlight. I figured it would be my last chance, before we go home. I had to get out of the room or Amanda wouldn't have gotten any rest."

"You'll tell Chief Jansen this?" Voncil's eye-witness account didn't clear Hedy, but it supported her story.

"I'm happy to speak to the chief in Hedy's behalf." She smiled. "On one condition."

I'd figured Voncil for a barracuda. Nothing came for free. "What?"

"Make sure your friend doesn't use the photo of me and Belinda. The implications could ruin Ms. Buck's reputation as a judge. If that happens, Belinda will never forgive me. Worse, she won't help Amanda with the Hollywood contacts she can give us, if she wants to." She took a deep breath. "Besides, we weren't doing anything wrong. It really was innocent. And if there is fault, it should go on me. Belinda did ask me to leave."

"It sure looked wrong."

"That's why I want your word you'll delete the photo in Mrs. Richmond's camera. I can't take a chance it'll get out and be misconstrued."

"You have my word. Now call Jansen and tell him."

Samuel came out the door and stopped, lingering in the background. Voncil rose to her feet, assessing Samuel and then me, putting together god knew what scenario in her head.

"I'll do it now," she said. "Will you be at the cooking event this evening?"

"Tinkie and I both will. It's a difficult task for the girls."

"Amanda can sniff out the most subtle smidgen of a spice. She has a nose for seasonings and blends. That's one of the benefits of the kind of authentic cooking she specializes in. She's going to win this and take the title."

If Voncil had snapped her jaws like a wolverine, I wouldn't have been surprised. "How nice," I said. "I'll see you tonight."

When she was gone, Samuel dangled the key. "I have to be back in twenty minutes."

"Then let's make tracks."

● ● ●

Samuel dropped me in front of a quadriplex on an old street lined with oaks. It was a beautiful neighborhood of homes built in the 40s and 50s on acre-lots designed to accommodate football and games of hide-and-seek. He didn't have time to wait and drove off as I knocked on the door. There was no answer.

I knocked again. "Hedy, it's me, Sarah Booth. Open up. I need to talk to you."

She came to the door, looking out left and right. "Come on in." She almost snatched me into the apartment, then slammed the door. "How's Babs? Is she going to be okay? What are you doing here?"

"Whoa!" I held up a hand to slow the onslaught of questions. "Babs is still in a coma, but she has the best doctor in the state helping her. I'm here because Jansen is on the warpath and looking for you."

"I had to think. I needed a place where no one could find me." Hedy looked pathetic.

"Voncil Payne will tell Jansen she saw you leave Babs, very much alive and well, in your vehicle."

Instead of the relief I expected, Hedy's face showed doubt. "Why is Voncil doing that?"

"Because it's true, isn't it?" I was a tad impatient.

"Of course, but why would Voncil help me?

261

She wants Amanda to win, and even if I'm only disqualified and not charged with murder, it would be to her advantage."

Hedy was nobody's fool. "She worked a bargain with Tinkie about a photo." I didn't need to go into details. While I wasn't certain the Buck-Payne lunch was totally innocent, I also didn't want to tarnish Belinda Buck's reputation without hard evidence.

"What am I going to do?" Hedy asked. She crossed the room, which I noted was neat and orderly, and lifted the window shades. Hundred-year-old white oaks surrounded the apartment. Beyond them, the street was quiet.

"Chief Jansen needs to see you," I said. "Go before he finds you and drags you there. He doesn't have enough to hold you, but if you show up voluntarily, it'll defuse his anger and suspicion."

She nodded her willingness to comply.

"What do you know about Vivian's nanny, Anna Lock?" I asked.

"She would do anything Marcus told her to do. Anything." Bitterness flooded her tone. "If Marcus told her to walk through fire, she'd give it a try. Remember the nanny in *The Omen*? Well, that creature has nothing on Anna. Perfect Anna. Educated, refined, well traveled. So much better to raise my child than I am."

"How tall would you say she is?"

Hedy gave me a long look. "Maybe five-two. Max. Why?"

"She's in her early forties, right?" I had a lot of ground to cover, and my staccato questions made Hedy frown.

"I guess. What's the sixty questions about Anna?"

"Bear with me, I'm following a hunch. Is she married?"

"I wasn't around her long, but she showed no interest in men, in that way. Nothing will interfere with her living in the Wellington home and devoting her life to raising Vivian. She's the perfect nanny." Defeat settled into her features.

"Do you know anything else about her?"

She considered. "She lived in New Orleans and worked for a family there, the Bronsills. Marcus was all over the fact she'd been a governess to Latham Bronsill, heir of the highly prominent Bronsill family. Latham, at twenty-six, was a contender for an ambassadorship to France. Or so Marcus said."

"Marcus is eaten up with such rarified connections, isn't he? It's the pond he swims in." The New Orleans connection with Anna Lock and the whole Saulnier/Marie Laveau hogwash came to mind, but I didn't mention it. Anna could be responsible for Marcus's distorted view of Hedy.

There was something else I needed to bring

up. "I went in your room. It's a huge mess. So much so that I feared you'd been kidnapped. Did you leave it that way?"

"No, Janet was messy. I hated that. I keep things neat. Who would have torn up my room?"

"A better question is what were they looking for? When you get back there, check everything and see if anything is missing. I hope Jansen finds some fingerprints in your room other than the hotel cleaning staff's. That your room was tossed is good evidence we can use to support your innocence." Now was the moment to clear the air about some things. "You haven't been truthful with me, Hedy."

She didn't deny it, she just looked down at the floor.

"You didn't tell me Marcus called you the night Janet died."

"How did you find out?" She looked scared.

"The switchboard has a record of all calls. Tinkie called Marcus, so he knows we know."

"You shouldn't have done that."

"Why?"

"He said I could see Vivian. He said if I stood outside the hotel, down at the end of the block, and wore a scarf or hat to conceal my face, he would drive by with her in the car." Her voice was strained.

"Did he?"

"No. I stood there for over an hour and he

never came. I just wanted to look at her."

I swallowed the lump in my throat. That one glimpse of her daughter would have sustained her for months. It made me want to kick the snot out of Marcus. While he might be able to better educate, clothe, and open doors for Vivian, he could not love her more than Hedy did. His actions were wrong.

"To get you out of your room, Marcus set you up with the only bait he knew you couldn't turn down: Vivian. Why did you lie and tell me you went to play your violin?"

"It wasn't a lie. I did. When he failed to show, I played for an hour or so. I write melodies for Vivian. In case I never see her, one day she'll know I loved her."

Now I really wanted to stomp him. "Do you know anything about a gris-gris bag under Janet's bed? A dead chicken claw?"

She laughed, a reaction that surprised me. "Now I'm accused of mutilating a chicken?"

"Jansen is taking the gris-gris seriously. Marcus has done a good job of brainwashing the chief and some of the judges that you're a practitioner."

That wiped the smile from her face. "What are you saying?"

"I'm not sure. But someone is doing a damn fine job of planting evidence they hope incriminates you. Be very careful what you do and who you hang around with. Do not be alone with any of the contestants. One more coincidental connection to a tragedy, and Jansen will be forced to arrest you."

"Okay." She was more than contrite. She was worried.

"Come on. I'll call a cab and share the ride back to town with you. The sooner you check in with Jansen, the quicker it'll be over with. You have to get ready for the 'Taste and Copy' competition."

I dropped Hedy off at the police department, but I didn't go in. I called Tinkie, who'd assembled a dossier on Anna Lock. We met in the courtyard of the hotel and ordered iced tea.

An afternoon lethargy had settled over the hotel, but not my partner. Tinkie practically sizzled with an electric charge. She was excited. "I found out a lot. Anna worked as a governess for the Bronsills for five years while Latham was a high school student. Thanks to her tutoring, Latham spoke flawless French, won national recognition with his math abilities, and snared half a dozen national and international essay competitions on the economy, the U.S. Constitution, foreign affairs, and the tax structure. Latham was a certified prodigy. According to Melissa, Anna's next act would be to raise the dead."

"How did you get all this information?" I asked.

"I know Melissa Bronsill," Tinkie said. "We worked a charity event in New Orleans two years ago. Lovely woman. Why she married into that family, I'll never know."

Oh, I knew. Old New Orleans money. Power. Prestige. Sugarcane plantation. Did I say money? Lots of women, and men, put up with connubial hell to be attached to financial security. According to Jitty, I should be so smart. My haint's priorities were womb first, 401(k) second, but a man who could tend both areas was certainly preferred.

"What else did she say?"

"She sang Anna's praises to the moon, and was forthcoming"—Tinkie was about to pop—"until I said I needed to find a governess and asked how to get in touch with Anna. Then she clammed up."

"Why?" Tinkie's energy was contagious. My partner may have stumbled on to the mother lode of information that would solve this case.

"It was odd. She was all about praising Anna, then she went cold. Said she had to get off the phone."

Tinkie was killing me with anticipation. "But you pressed her."

Tinkie rattled the ice in her glass. "I did. I wouldn't hang up, and she's too polite to slam the phone down. I kept talking. Finally, I got back to Anna Lock."

"And?"

"She said she thought Anna had gone back to the Northeast, her home."

"Surely she knows Anna is working for the Wellingtons. Marcus told Hedy that he'd gotten references from the Bronsills."

"He didn't and she didn't. She was shocked to find it out. She never gave Marcus a reference for Anna Lock."

"Then how did Marcus find out . . ." I saw it clearly: Anna. Anna had manipulated Marcus. "What else did she say?"

"After Latham went off to school, Anna left the Bronsills' employ. She moved to the French Quarter and taught piano lessons. Melissa said about nine years ago something happened to Anna. Like a nervous breakdown of some kind. She was in a botanica and went nuts. She was hospitalized for a while, and that's when she moved back to the Northeast. As far as Melissa knew, Anna had never returned South."

"What caused the breakdown?" The hairs on my arms stood in a slight breeze.

"This is where it gets really good. Anna was interested in the occult. Melissa said Anna had lost someone very dear to her, someone she grieved for. She never said who, but Melissa assumed it was a child, because she was so good with kids, so patient."

"This isn't good." I had an image of little Vivian

in Anna's arms—and Anna thinking she'd somehow found her own dead child. "Surely Marcus can't be that stupid. . . ." But he could. He was besotted with Anna's teaching abilities, her sophistication and education. She'd worked for one of Louisiana's most prominent families. I doubted he'd checked further than that.

"We have to figure this out. Was she institutionalized?"

"I've tried to find out, but so far, no results. Medical records are private. There's no way we can get our hands on Anna's file. She's a nonentity on the Internet. Other than Melissa, I can't find anyone who knows Anna Lock."

"Maybe Doc can help us."

"Good idea," Tinkie said. She used her cell phone to call him. When he didn't answer, she left a message on his voice mail.

When I checked my messages, I found one from Belinda Buck saying she was riding at Clive Gladstone's plantation. She didn't have time to talk to Tinkie and me today.

The thing Belinda didn't understand was time was running out.

Tinkie drove the thirty miles to Clive's manicured estate. Horses grazed and frolicked in lush pastures bordered by white fences. Even from a distance I recognized the graceful movements of Clive's Thoroughbreds and the power and strength of what appeared to be warmblood crosses.

"Clive may make it to the Olympic team in cross-country eventing," Tinkie informed me. "He's a fine rider."

"And Belinda?"

"I have no idea what kind of horsewoman she is."

"Didn't she guest once on a Western where she had a great chase scene on horseback?"

Tinkie pushed my shoulder. "Strut your Hollywood trivia knowledge. I'm just a country girl with no connections to the celluloid world of the gods."

Before she could duck, I thumped her head. "Let's not mention my movie career," I said. "It seems like another lifetime."

The Gladstone house, where Clive lived alone, bore a striking resemblance to the fictional Tara. An older butler answered our knock, and I thought of Jitty's insistence that I hire a butler when I first got home. Finances dictated otherwise. If I had money to hire personal staff, I needed a fence builder, not someone to answer a door I was perfectly capable of opening.

"Mr. Clive is out in the barn," the butler informed us.

I was eager to see Clive's barn and horses. Tinkie, who had on stiletto heels, was not so enthused. The barn was a good three hundred yards from the house and we were halfway there when Tinkie stopped, huffing.

"Wait here," I said. "I'll talk to Clive and Belinda."

"Just run off and leave me." She hobbled down the gravel path. She was stuck between a rock and a hard place. Her heels slipped on the rocks and sank in the lush grass.

"You could take off your shoes and go barefoot." The day was hot. "The cool grass would feel lovely."

"My foot is a size five, triple A, because I never went barefoot." She was cranky as a cat in a kennel. "A *lady* knows gamboling around without shoes makes the feet widen. Going barefoot is why you wear a size nine."

We made it past a ring set up with stadium jumps that looked Olympic level. Off in the distance a rider took a horse over a cross-country jump. I couldn't identify the rider, but I watched in awe as the horse cleared what appeared to be a huge table.

"If that's Clive, he sure can ride," I said.

"If that's Clive, he doesn't have the sense God gave a flea," Tinkie said. "That's a quick way to a broken neck. The jump is bigger than the horse."

The horse and rider took a water jump with perfect ease.

"The only way you'd get me to jump a horse would be if Satan was chasing me and Trigger was the only means of escape." Tinkie had worked up a sweat on her forehead. I stopped in the shade of a mimosa tree to let her catch her breath. Hobbling did not become her.

"Before you go any farther, let me see if Clive is in the barn, okay?" We were only fifty yards away, but it could be a painful distance for Tinkie.

"I'll wait here," she conceded. "Signal me if he's in there."

I trotted down the gravel path, glad comfort ruled my wardrobe choices. At the barn, I slowed. Horses can be excitable. It's never good to run or yell around them.

After the bright sun, it took my eyes a moment to adjust to the barn's darkness. Forty stalls, twenty on each side of the wide aisle, contained a number of snuffling horses. Soft whinnies greeted me, and large bodies shifted as the equine population registered my arrival.

Far in the distance was the soft murmur of voices.

I eased forward.

A man and a woman talked in hushed, secretive tones. It drew me like honey lures a fly. The noises of intimate communication were undeniable. Belinda had come out for a ride, but it wasn't on a horse. Was she in there with Clive?

I'm generally not a sneak or voyeur, but Clive and Belinda could determine who won the title of Miss Viking Range. And Clive was Marcus's best friend. It could be another deck stacked against Hedy.

At the door of a tack room, I smelled fresh coffee and heard the murmur of a television in the background. My ears were turned to something else, though. A male voice.

"Oh, baby, that's the way."

I had no visual, but my brain supplied several. The ring of iron hooves on the cement aisle of the barn sent me scurrying away from the door.

"Sarah Booth?" Clive called out to me as he led a magnificent bay toward me. "What are you doing here?"

I looked from Clive to the tack room. Who the hell was in the tack room? "I came to talk to you and Belinda." The sounds had stopped in the tack room. Obviously, whoever was in there had heard us.

"She's around here somewhere," he said. "What did you want to talk about?"

"About . . . about the competition."

"You know the judges can't discuss this matter."

"You do whatever you like, Clive. That's the motto you and Marcus live by."

At the mention of Marcus's name, Clive's gaze shot to the tack room. I knew then who was in there, but I didn't know the woman's identity.

Clive had no intention of letting me find out.

He cupped my elbow in a gentlemanly grip. "Let's go up to the house and get Paul to make us some lemonade. Or maybe something a little stronger."

He handed off the horse to a groom, and Clive ushered me out of the barn. When we stepped into the bright sunshine, I shielded my eyes and searched for Tinkie.

She was nowhere to be seen.

18

"Is something wrong, Sarah Booth?" Clive asked as he led me like an errant puppy up to the big house.

"No." I wasn't about to tell him that Tinkie, in a pair of stilettos that could aerate his lawn, had disappeared. I didn't suspect foul play, except on Tinkie's part. What had possessed her and what was she up to?

"You're distracted," he said as he assisted me into the house and took me into a sunroom that framed the beauty of well-tended pastures stretching to the horizon. Horses grazed peacefully in a scene that could have been the subject of a master painter. Indicating a comfy chair, he sat across from me.

The butler appeared with a silver tray, pitcher, and two glasses filled with icy Lynchburg Lemonade. Clive handed me a glass. I inhaled half of it. I was hot and nervous, never a good combo when mixed with potent beverages. If I didn't slow down, I'd be crocked.

Clive arched his eyebrows, inviting me to explain.

"Why are you involved in this contest?" I asked.

"I don't know. Marcus asked me to do it." A furrow etched its way between his eyebrows. "That's been one of the downfalls of my life, going along with Marcus. I wish I hadn't gotten involved. These young girls dying . . . it bothers me."

Ya think? I wanted to say but didn't. Clive struck me as someone unfamiliar with feelings, his or anyone else's. "It is terrible. What do you think is going on?"

He swirled the liquid in his glass and gazed out at his estate. "Marcus wants me to believe Hedy Blackledge is a killer."

The phrasing gave me hope. "But you don't believe it?"

"No." He sighed. "I've tried to, for the sake of my friendship with Marcus. He has a real burn on for that young woman and for the life of me, I can't figure why. He wants her behind bars."

Okay, Clive was handsome, wealthy, and a

talented equestrian. So he wasn't bright enough to put two and two together and get "former relationship." "Marcus has never said why he dislik . . . suspects her?"

"No, he hasn't." Something outdoors caught his attention. If Tinkie showed up now, he'd wonder why I hadn't mentioned her presence. Instead of my partner, a pair of peacocks crossed the lawn, their iridescent "eyes" fanned out behind them.

"Why so interested in my thoughts all of a sudden?" Clive asked.

"Because my client is one of the participants in the beauty contest. If the judges think she's a murderess, it might hurt her chances of getting the title. Miss Viking Range wearing black and white ringarounds in Parchman prison wouldn't be much good to the sponsoring company."

"I don't think Hedy is guilty." He offered to refill my glass, but I waved him away.

"So who do you think is?"

"Isn't that your job? To find the bad guy?"

"Or gal." I let that float for a moment. "But maybe you've seen something I missed. Your opinion might enlighten me."

He only smiled.

I tried a change of subject. "Where did you say Ms. Buck had gone?"

"I don't recall saying."

I was weary of Clive's reticence. "I'd like to

speak with her before I leave. Where is she?"

"She took Rowdy out for a ride." He checked his watch. "She'll be back soon. The judges have a meeting here shortly."

It was time to cut to the chase. "Is it possible someone is leaking information to a contestant? Or to someone else affiliated with the pageant who has a vested interest in the outcome?"

"Anything is possible, Sarah Booth. You might even get married one day. Some stranger, unaware of your reputation, could come to Zinnia and you could snare him before he wises up."

Instead of stinging me, Clive only made me tired. "Ha, ha. Clever, Clive. Your repartee is as sparkling as I remember. But I'm serious. If the murderer is a contestant bumping off the competition, it might be wise to figure this out—and fast!"

He lifted a shoulder. "I haven't talked to any of the contestants. If there's a leak, it isn't me."

"Have you talked to Marcus?"

He started to rise, but sank back into the chair. "He's in love with one of the girls, but he wouldn't harm the other contestants. Ever since Vivian came into his life, he's changed. She's softened him, made him mature."

"Actions speak louder than words, and he's done everything in his power to harm my client."

"I don't understand why he dislikes Miss

Blackledge so much, but I haven't revealed any confidential discussions with him."

"Who's rated the highest, as of tonight?"

He gave a weary sigh. "I gather you aren't leaving until you know this."

"A young woman's life may be at stake. If this is the motive for the murders, at least give me a chance to protect her. Tinkie and I believe the top-rated girl is the killer's target."

"You're serious?"

"I am. There are seven girls left. Someone else will die tonight if I'm correct."

The fake weariness dropped away and left a seriousness that heightened his good looks. "Brook Oniada had moved into the top position the night she died. The chicken kebabs and pineapple daiquiris had sealed the deal for her. Janet Menton was in second place. Each of those girls stepped out from the crowd by their own efforts."

"And Babs?"

"Her 'the show must go on' attitude had swayed us in her direction. I mean, she lost her hair, but she didn't stop trying. That's the attitude of a competitor. The judges agreed she'd moved into the lead position."

Clive had just bolstered my theory. "So who's the likely winner now?"

"I shouldn't tell you this." He topped off my glass, and I didn't stop him.

"Hedy is my client. I'm hired to prove her innocence. Of course Tinkie and I want her to win, but that isn't our focus. What you tell me will be used only to assist in protecting the next potential victim."

"The judges' opinions change after almost every single event, and sometimes in between. We confer often. Our thinking shifts."

"Just tell me." I had to find Tinkie and get out of there before the other judges arrived. While Tinkie and I were legitimately working, it could seem we were pleading Hedy's case to Clive.

"Amanda Payne," he said. "When she sang at the barbecue, she got our attention. She's a package of dynamite, and her songs are chart worthy."

I put down my glass. "Thank you, Clive. For the record, you're an exceptional horseman."

"I have a wonderful horse. Bellacanter deserves all the credit."

I was surprised by his modesty, which wasn't false. At last I'd found an area where Clive and I could meet halfway.

I suspected Tinkie had made it to the barn. If she insisted on walking in those idiotic shoes, there she'd remain until I showed up with a horse, a wheelbarrow, or a tractor to haul her back to the big house.

I carefully drove her Caddy down the gravel

path to the barn. If someone stopped me, I'd plead ignorance, since I was pretty sure Clive would not appreciate tread marks on his manicured property.

The barn's interior was dark and cool, and the groom who'd taken Bellacanter had put him away and disappeared.

"Tinkie!" I stage-whispered. "Tinkie! If you're in here, come out now. We need to beat a retreat."

Blond hair, coiffed and glitzed, rose from behind a stack of hay. She hobbled toward me with as much dignity as she could muster. "Did you talk to Clive?"

"I did. Belinda Buck may be here any minute. We need to leave before she returns from her ride. Clive doesn't know you're with me."

We hurried to the barn door, peeped around the corner, and, with the coast clear, jumped into the Caddy with me behind the wheel.

"Guess who was having a tête-à-tête in the tack room?"

"Who?" I had the car started and the air blowing hard and cold.

"Marcus and Karrie. My lord a'mighty, Sarah Booth, I didn't think Marcus broke a sweat at anything, but that man has some hip action. He had Karrie squalling like a hungry cat in a fish market. And the only thing I can say about her is, she's no lady."

In the tragedy of the deaths of two young women and the poisoning of a third, I'd almost forgotten my dislike for Karrie Kompton. It all came flooding back. "Surely there must be something in the rule book about screwing a judge's best friend."

"Doubtful. And she didn't just screw him, she turned him inside out." Tinkie motioned to someone on horseback riding our way. "Is that Ms. Buck?" If Belinda saw us, she'd definitely mention Tinkie to Clive.

I pushed Tinkie down in the seat, put the car in reverse, and started a slow crawl along the gravel back to the circular drive. I didn't relax until the rubber met the asphalt driveway and the car was nosed north toward home. Clive's lovely horse ranch disappeared in the rearview mirror.

I found Karrie and Marcus's actions confusing. "Why would Karrie and Marcus meet here? This compromises Clive, which could greatly work against Karrie."

"Why meet in a tack room, no matter how nice it is, when you could have the Wellington staff of servants at your beck and call? I mean, Marcus's house has at least fifteen bedrooms. Surely he could find an empty one for his trysts."

"Perhaps Mommy and Daddy don't approve of Marcus bringing his punches home." The entire

Wellington family had slithered in my craw and stuck. I had a kinder thought. "Maybe he doesn't want to fool around in front of Vivian."

"Or else Marcus is deliberately putting his friend's judging credentials on the line."

"That's interesting, Tinkie." It could be a fallback position if Karrie didn't win. "Is Marcus that smart?"

"No, but Karrie is."

Touché! "Brilliant deduction, Tink."

"If this contest doesn't go Karrie's way, she'll have grounds to threaten a lawsuit. She's the poor little wronged contestant who was taken to Clive Gladstone's barn to service his friend—and then didn't get what she was promised."

Tinkie's superior understanding of the baser feminine nature wasn't from personal experience but from years of dealing with that type of society female. There was no world more competitive, and the women trapped there had honed the limited skills allowed them in a social structure where men controlled the power.

We were twenty minutes from town. The day, while profitable, was slipping away from us fast. The evening pageant event would begin soon. Tick tock. I heard it clearly, and it wasn't my uterus making the noise. "I learned something interesting from Clive."

"I saw him march you off like a trespasser."

"Amanda Payne is the top contender for the

title. If our theory is correct, she should be the next victim."

"Amanda?" Tinkie looked genuinely distressed. "She's so innocent. She won't stand a chance against this killer."

"But she has us to protect her. And we're forewarned."

"How can we keep her safe?" Tinkie asked.

"What if we don't need to watch over her?" My thoughts had turned in another direction.

"You mean if she's the killer?"

"Or Voncil."

Tinkie digested the possibility as we drew close to Greenwood. "We still have to warn them."

"I agree. We'll tell Voncil, first off. And then we need to figure out who's leaking the judges' deliberations to the killer. Someone in the know is talking. Clive assured me it wasn't him, and strangely enough, I believe him. He may have piss-poor taste in friends, but I don't think he's involved in these murders, and I actually think he's trying to do a good job of judging."

Tinkie settled back in the seat, one foot in her lap as she rubbed her sore tootsies. We entered the Greenwood city limits. "Chief Jansen is right. This contest should be stopped."

"If I were a contestant, I'd quit. No title is worth my life."

"Assuming Amanda is innocent, how can we

keep her from eating poison if sampling the dishes is required?"

"I don't know, Tinkie. That does present a problem."

Time was running out, so Tinkie and I split up. She volunteered to talk to Evangeline Phelps, the pageant coordinator, while I rounded up Voncil Payne. Someone had to guard Amanda and make sure she didn't ingest, touch, inhale, or otherwise poison herself.

From the house phone in the lobby I called the room Voncil and Amanda shared. "I need to speak with you," I told her. "May I come up?"

"You'll come even if you aren't invited, won't you? Every time I turn around, you and your partner are in my face." She wasn't exactly gracious, but I wasn't running for Miss Popularity.

"I have information you may want to hear. I'm doing you a favor," I pointed out. Voncil got on my last nerve, but my concern was Amanda. I'd endure Voncil to stop another girl from dying.

She let me in with a sour expression. "Amanda is on pins and needles. She went for a walk. You need to be gone before she gets back. I can't have you upsetting her even more."

I took a seat in an overstuffed chair. A bottle of open champagne chilled in a bucket beside me.

"Are you celebrating?" I asked.

"Amanda is going to win this. I feel it in my gut, and I always honor my feelings."

"How can you be certain?"

"She's scored high in everything, and the judges had a chance to see her work the crowd at the barbecue. She's everything necessary to uphold the title of Miss Viking Range." She selected a clean glass and poured champagne for me. "I'm sorry I was rude. The tension is making me act like a bitch." She held up her glass. "To success for my baby girl. She's worked hard and long and she deserves to win."

"And to the other contestants." I clinked her glass. One drink would be wonderful. Two would be a headache. Drinking champagne in the afternoon was never a good idea for a private investigator.

Sunlight through the hotel window fell fully on her blond hair, which shimmered in a myriad of golden shades. Her hairdresser had done a stupendous job. "There's no easy way to say this, Voncil: I have reason to believe Amanda is in danger tonight."

"Why?" She was more puzzled than alarmed.

"Tinkie and I have a theory. Each girl who's been murdered was the top contender for the title. We have it on reasonable authority this is true."

Her eyebrows rose, and a gleam of satisfaction

twinkled in her eyes. "So, my baby is the top contender."

"I'm not positive, but that's the best information Tinkie and I have been able to gather."

"So you think she's the target of the killer now?" Satisfaction fled and panic raced across her features. "She can't participate tonight. If you're right . . . the title isn't worth risking my only child."

Ambition had been replaced by primal motherhood. "I can't prove this, Voncil. It's only a theory. But I felt I owed it to you and Amanda to tell you."

"Amanda's been studying recipes all day. She's going to be bitterly disappointed. If she doesn't participate tonight, she won't stand a chance at the title."

"That's unfortunate." I drained my glass and put it down. I'd accomplished my mission—time to move along.

"Who's doing this?" she asked. "Hedy hired you, but if she's killing contestants, you wouldn't shield her"—her eyes narrowed—"would you?"

"Hedy isn't the killer."

"Then who is? Why can't you stop this so the pageant can continue?" Her questions came rapid-fire. "What's that worthless police chief doing? If you know someone is killing the highest rated girl in the competition, why can't you catch the murderer?"

"We're doing our best, and I told you this is only a theory."

Voncil rose suddenly. "Is this a trick? It just occurred to me Hedy would benefit greatly if Amanda dropped out of the running." The more she talked, the closer she inched toward my face. "The title has to be between Hedy, Amanda, and that bitch Karrie. If Amanda is disqualified because she's afraid to eat tonight, your client would be in a very good position."

When she invaded my personal space too far, I stood and forced her back. "Voncil, I like Amanda. She doesn't take after you in the least. And yes, I do hope Hedy wins. But I wouldn't hand her the title by deception. I'm trying to safeguard your daughter and prevent another death. If I'm right about the killer's M.O., then Amanda is the next target."

"Maybe Chief Jansen should be telling me this."

"A very good point," I said. "I'll inform Chief Jansen and if he decides to repeat it to you, then perhaps you'll do what's necessary to protect Amanda's life." I'd gone from amused to angry in ten seconds. Voncil was the worst stage mother on the planet. Amanda's success was what mattered to her. But I'd also thought she loved her daughter and would take the necessary steps to keep her safe.

Wrong.

I strode across the room before I smacked her. "If Amanda is hurt tonight, remember you had a chance to protect her."

"I'm onto you now," she said. "You come here all worried about my daughter. But Hedy will compete, won't she? She isn't about to drop out."

"Hedy isn't the top contender." I couldn't drive it into her head with a ten-pound hammer.

"Which is exactly why you're doing this." She slammed the door without another word.

19

By the time I got to Hedy's room, I'd calmed down. Our client was in the throes of hairstyling. I didn't want to upset her before the competition, but I had questions. She had some, too.

"Chief Jansen grilled me about Babs. Why didn't he arrest me? He made it clear he thought I was a murderer."

"If he had enough hard evidence, you'd be behind bars. You're on his list, but he probably has other suspects."

Hedy dropped her hairbrush on the bed. "I don't think I can do this tonight. I called the hospital. Babs isn't doing well. I want to visit her. Will you go with me?"

"Not a good idea." If Hedy entered ICU and something untoward happened to Babs, Jansen would be forced to jail her. "I'll go by there tomorrow and see her." My promise was reluctant—I detested hospitals.

"Why was she hurt and I wasn't?" Frustration colored Hedy's tone. "Babs should be at the competition tonight. Talent, personality, cooking skills—she had it all. She was going to win, I think."

My radar tripped. Did Hedy have information on the contestant rankings? "Why would you say that?"

"She *should* win. If she survives, they should award her the title." Hedy retrieved a fine-toothed comb from the bathroom. She bent over and began teasing her long hair.

"You really mean that, don't you?"

"Marcus never intends to let me be part of Vivian's life. I have to accept it. Winning this title won't do me any good. It was a harebrained scheme to begin with." Her face was concealed, but her voice choked with tears. "I want to go home, but I can't walk away from Vivian. I don't know what to do."

Tinkie was the comfort-giver and soother. My nurturing skills rated in the inadequate zone, but I'd try. "You've gone this far, Hedy. You might as well take it to the end. Quitting now accomplishes nothing."

"I can't stand it if someone else is injured or . . . killed. I like Babs, and Brook seemed nice. Janet was sloppy, but she was okay. None of them deserved the terrible things that happened."

I put a hand on her back, and she straightened up and turned into my shoulder for a good cry. "This is the last night," I said, rubbing her back. "Hang in there."

"You and Tinkie are the only people who've ever really stood up for me," she sobbed.

And we were paid to do it—a fact I didn't mention. "Why don't you contact your mother?"

"No." She eased away, struggling for composure. "We're estranged."

"Hedy, I'm sure by now she's forgiven you for getting pregnant. Mothers have a hard time seeing their children suffer hardships, but they get over it in the end."

"Let me get a tissue." When she came out of the bathroom, she'd washed her face. "Mother wasn't upset when I told her I was pregnant. She thought I was a fool to sign the papers giving Marcus custody, but she became angry when I decided to fight for Vivian."

"How peculiar."

"Tell me about it." She was calmer, and I couldn't help but smile at her hair, which was a giant ball of teased black frizz.

"I need to talk to you about the nanny Marcus hired."

"Anna Lock." Hedy put ice in two glasses and poured us both a diet cola. "Marcus was so proud of her. The best nanny to be had. Marcus only wants the best."

"She was with you two weeks before Vivian went with Marcus?"

She sank onto a bed, her shoulders slumped and her hair a dark nimbus around her head. "I was a terrible mother. I couldn't even change Vivian's diaper properly. After three days she got an awful rash. I was inept."

"You were young and inexperienced and you had no one to turn to." I felt my ire rising at Marcus. He'd mined Hedy's fears like a mother lode.

"Anna was a godsend. She could do everything, and she never got flustered or upset. The minute she picked Vivian up, she'd stop crying and laugh. When I touched her, she screamed."

"People tell me babies sense when a person is uncertain. It upsets them. Anna had more confidence than you, that's all."

She blew out a breath. "I was scared and exhausted and worried that I'd harm my baby. I had to work, there was no choice. Once Anna arrived, I could go to work knowing Vivian would have better care than I could give her. When Marcus said he wanted Vivian and Anna would continue to care for her, I resisted at first. Vivian would have the best of everything, she'd lack for nothing, she'd have family and love and opportunities—he made me feel that I had nothing to offer my daughter. In contrast, keeping her with me was dooming her to a life of deprivation. I caved."

I didn't want to be cruel, but to do my job, I had to ask some hard questions. "Did you accept any money to sign the papers?"

"No!" She jumped to her feet. "How could you—"

"I have to ask. Settle down." When she was seated, I continued. "Tell me about Anna. Anything and everything. She's the key to a lot of things, I think."

"She's well educated, smart, calm. She loves babies. She cooks healthy."

I was looking for something else. "What about her family? Did she ever mention them?"

"No. I never thought anything about it. She made herself part of our family so easily."

"She's from the Northeast, I think."

"Maybe. Her pronunciation was off a little. Things like 'roof.' Could be."

"She never revealed anything about herself? You never saw a photograph or anything?"

Hedy's head moved slowly from side to side. "I never even thought it strange. I was so caught up in my worries and concerns, I never realized how odd she was."

"Keep thinking about it. If something comes up, call me immediately. Tinkie and I are on the case."

Tinkie might have been on the case, but she wasn't in our room. She hadn't returned from her appointment with Evangeline Phelps. I decided to grab a glass of the peach tea the Alluvian served in the lobby. I'd give Oscar a call to make sure Sweetie Pie was behaving and rehydrate simultaneously.

The sweating tea glass in my hand, I did a double take as I headed for the elevators. Across the courtyard, Marcus Wellington sat at a table in the hotel restaurant—and he wasn't alone. Belinda Buck sat opposite him.

Marcus picked up the check, rose, and slid Belinda's chair away from the table—a perfect gentleman. They were laughing as they disappeared from sight. I waited, downing one glass of tea and pouring a second. They didn't come through the lobby.

My discovery wasn't ground shattering, just another little fact to add to the pile.

As soon as I was in the room I kicked my shoes off and dialed Oscar.

"Sweetie's depressed," he said. I could visualize his eyes narrowing as he decided how much to tell me. "I didn't want to worry you, but ever since that Danny dog went back to New York, Sweetie has been in a terrible slump. She turned down chunks of steak this morning. I swear, Sarah Booth, I'm worried about her. She hasn't swallowed a morsel since Graf dropped her off."

"Try some buttermilk and corn bread. Nothin' like a little home cooking."

It wasn't Oscar who spoke but a silver-haired woman wearing a long red tunic top and white pants. This stranger had invaded my privacy. It took me a moment to realize Jitty had transformed herself into a Southern cooking icon— Paula Deen.

Waving Jitty away with one hand, I took the telephone and hid in the bathroom. Of course Jitty could float through a wall, but she might allow me to finish my conversation with Oscar. Or she might not. It depended on how determined she was to make me miserable.

"For Sweetie to turn down steak, she must be in a real slump. I have to attend an event right now, Oscar, but I'll come home tonight. If nothing else, I can bring Sweetie Pie here with me. Dogs aren't allowed in the hotel, but I'll work something out."

"That might be for the best," he agreed. "It hurts me to see her like this. Not even Chablis can perk her up. I'm simply at a loss. I've tried every treat I know and she refuses to eat."

"Who would have thought Sweetie could fall so hard for a dog she'd known for just two days?" It sounded like a perfect case of Delaney womb taking total control, but I wasn't about to admit that to Oscar.

"Love is strange, Sarah Booth." He cleared his throat. "Will Tinkie accompany you home?"

Sweetie wasn't the only one at Hilltop feeling blue and lonely. "I'll bet wild horses couldn't keep her away." I had a sudden inspiration. "Or you could come to Greenwood and have a romantic evening with your wife. I'll watch Chablis and Sweetie Pie in Zinnia while you entertain Tinkie in Alluvian bliss."

"It's a deal." Oscar jumped on that like a hungry rooster pecking a doodlebug.

"I'll call you when we're done with the pageant event." I smiled at playing the matchmaker for Tinkie. She missed Oscar, though she would never complain. A surprise "date night" was just what the doctor ordered.

Speaking of doctors, I needed to float my theory of "top dog gets killed" by Doc Sawyer. He might be able to tell me more about the poisons used so far—they seemed so disparate. Tinkie and I had come up with two different motives: for the killer to control the outcome of the competition, or for the killer to frame Hedy for murder. My suspicions about Marcus had me leaning toward the latter.

Hedy, if she were truly a practitioner of the dark arts, would know plants and poisons. But a load of information was available on the Internet. Anyone with reasonable smarts could learn about a poison and how to administer it. Anna Lock had a lot more than reasonable smarts. She was highly educated.

"Sarah Booth Delaney, come out here and see what I've got cookin'." Jitty's voice carried clearly into the bathroom.

I had plenty to do, but first I had to see what Jitty was whipping up in her latest emulative incarnation of a master chef.

I opened the door a crack. At first the room appeared empty and I thought maybe she'd returned to Zinnia. No such luck. She was sitting on the end of my bed, waiting.

"Come out, Sarah Booth." Her voice had a long drawl, only slightly different from her normal cadence, but she had the Paula Deen haircut down to a T. Were it not for her lovely mocha skin and dark eyes, she could have passed for the cooking queen.

"What now?" I asked. Though she was pretending to be a chef, Jitty was clearly on a mission directed only at me.

"I just found a recipe for Paula Deen's fried chicken, and it's exactly the way Miss Alice and I made it. Fancy that. Just goes to show good things don't change. 'Course we didn't have 'lectric or gas stoves. We did it all on the woodstove. 'Moderate heat' was a little harder to judge back them."

"You didn't cook. And neither did Alice. Who

really cooked before the war?" I was certain I'd heard talk, but I couldn't remember.

"Lena was the head cook, back when the plantation was runnin'. Now that woman could spread a table. We had fresh vegetables, grown right there in the Dahlia House gardens, most all year round. Lots of weeks we did fine without meat of any kind. Just those tender greens and tomatoes so full of flavor you could almost taste 'em when Lena sliced 'em up."

Jitty's face softened, and for a moment I saw the loneliness of the passage of time. It occurred to me that perhaps Jitty had sacrificed the chance to be with Coker, her husband, in the Great Beyond so she could stay and look out for me. The thought was humbling. "Who grew the vegetables?" I asked.

"Coker did that. He had a talent for makin' the land give up bounty. It gave him real pleasure to watch the process, to go from puttin' a seed in rich dirt and watchin' it grow into somethin' to put on the table. Cotton was the money crop, but Coker's garden kept everyone fat and full. I can almost hear him callin' me outside to see an especially fine stand of beans or lacy mustard greens."

For a moment both of us were pulled into the past. Jitty went to a place I'd never been, and I was at the dinner table with my parents as they chatted about their day. My mother loved working in her vegetable garden, and she too had been a talented farmer. In my memory movie, my mother served my father's plate with fresh vegetables she'd grown, picked, and cooked. Her hand brushed across his. The look they shared was filled with happy secrets.

"Talkin' 'bout Coker and the garden won't solve what's gnawin' at you." Jitty drew me back to the present.

"What's wrong?" Jitty wouldn't leave until she'd had her say.

"You are." Jitty put it on the line, no apologies.

"What have I done now?"

"You're stirrin' ever' pot in Mississippi 'cept the one that's burnin'."

I didn't follow her. "I'm setting up dates for Tinkie, tending my lovelorn hound, chasing down a serial murderer, and trying to keep a young beauty contestant alive. What else do you want me to take on?" No matter what I did, Jitty was never satisfied.

"I can't believe I'm gonna say this."

I saw it coming then like a big train with a cowcatcher rushing down the tracks at me. "You had better not!" I pointed a finger at her. "You had better not tell me to go to Hollywood. You had better not say those words to me after all the guilt I had to carry about leaving Zinnia."

Jitty stood. "Bubble, bubble, toil and trouble.

You'd best tend to your bubblin' pot, girlie. That's what I'm telling you."

"A watched pot never boils." I could throw around a few famous axioms. "Graf doesn't need me to watch him make a movie. He needs me to be who I am, Sarah Booth Delaney, private investigator. That's the woman he fell in love with, not some unemployed female who could follow him around and be his shadow." I was panting with emotion by the time I finished.

"I'm not here to devil you, I'm here to help." Jitty reclined on my bed. "Graf loves you, Sarah Booth, but if you think he's gonna sit on hold in a place like Los Angeles, you're mighty wrong."

"What are you saying, exactly?" A sick feeling stabbed my gut.

"A man needs a certain amount of your focus. Even your mama, hardheaded as she was, understood this. She didn't leave James Franklin runnin' loose in places like Hollywood or even Memphis. *Think, girl.*"

The possibility of Graf being unfaithful had never crossed my mind. I felt like a fool. But the idea I had to nursemaid him every second to keep his attention focused on me didn't sit well, either. "If he's so damn fickle he can't understand what I'm going through, then—"

"Hold on there, Missy, I'm servin' you up some good advice, not aggravation. Could be Graf sees you've made a choice to investigate cases and risk your life rather than be at his side. You might try walkin' a few steps in his shoes."

I sank into the plush chair. "And he might try walking in mine. I can't go back to Hollywood and act right now. I'm too raw. I'm doing what I need to do to heal."

"I'm not tryin' to put a scare into you or make you worry or fuss at you. But Graf lost something in that cotton field, too. You weren't the only one got hurt. And it seems to me he's way down your priority list. Chances are, it might seem that way to him, too."

Never in a million years would I have figured Jitty would counsel me to go to Hollywood. Never. That she did scared me badly. "Do you know something I don't?"

"I know phone calls ain't no substitute for a tender touch or a moment of holdin' someone. I know the comfort two people can give each other is maybe the only thing that eases the pain of this world a tiny bit. I know if you leave that man out there too long, hurtin' like he is, chances are good he's gonna find comfort somewhere."

"Is Graf . . . interested in someone else?"

"I don't know and I wouldn't say if I did. But he's a man with a clear path to stardom. How many women you think want a piece of that action, even if he wasn't handsome and well mannered. You could go a far piece and do a lot worse."

Aunt Loulane's words haunted me when they fell from Jitty's lips. "I have to finish this case. I can't just walk off and leave Tinkie with a client who may or may not end up in jail, and seven contestants, six of whom may be dead by the end of the competition. And Sweetie Pie is having some kind of crisis." The man and the dog I loved the most were suffering and I wasn't there for them.

Jitty shook her head. "Wrong choice."

"I have an obligation to Tinkie. And to Hedy. And to Sweetie."

Jitty's lips were a thin line. "Then I'd be on the horn telling him that. I'd try a little harder to make it sound like it's a choice you regret." Jitty's form vanished before the last words were spoken. Normally she did a slow fade, but this time there was a loud popping sound, and the only thing left was the smell of ozone.

Once Jitty was out of the way, I got Chief Jansen on the phone. Doc Sawyer had returned to Zinnia. Not a problem. I'd see him when I was home with Sweetie and Chablis. The thought of my loyal hound, so willing to accept me the way I was without judging me and finding me short, made me want to skip the cooking event and head to Dahlia House right now.

Not possible. I had a client to clear and a partner to back up.

Hedy had allayed some of Jansen's suspicions, but she was still "a person of interest." I had another couple to add to his list.

"Could you check into Anna Lock?" I asked.

"Why should I look into her?"

Coleman would have asked the same question. "She's a person of interest for me. She's the nanny Marcus hired to care for Hedy's daughter."

"The child also belongs to Marcus," Jansen said.

"Anna Lock is a professional nanny. She worked for a prominent New Orleans famly, the Bronsills, moved to the French Quarter, had some kind of breakdown, then disappeared for several years. Now she's back in the nanny business. If you could do a background check on her, it would save me a lot of time."

"I'm not making any promises."

"I didn't expect you would." But I also thought if Jansen caught a whiff of anything rotten, he'd pursue it. I only had to put him downwind of Anna Lock.

"What makes you interested in this nanny?" he asked.

"She fits the description of a woman who followed Hedy and Babs from the blues club."

"It's your job to prove Miss Blackledge innocent, but why would a nanny for the Wellington family kill pageant contenders?"

"Hedy has a right to see her child. She signed

the papers giving Marcus total custody under duress. A sure way to keep Hedy from Vivian would be to frame her for murder and put her behind bars." I wished Jansen and I were speaking in person. "Anna Lock has some tentative connections to a New Orleans botanica and she's loyal to Marcus."

"That's a long stretch, even for a private investigator."

"No longer than thinking Hedy would kill pageant contestants for a title and crown."

"If you want to do Miss Blackledge a favor, tell her to stay with someone at all times. If there's any more trouble, she'd better have an airtight alibi."

That wasn't bad advice. "Thanks, Chief."

"Yeah, thank me when we have a killer behind bars."

Tinkie wore a bejeweled slack suit and killer heels. Her feet had recovered from her walk to the barn, and while she'd bemoan her fashion choices, she wasn't about to change her ways. As we sauntered across the street to the cooking school, where top chefs from across the nation had gathered to prepare their special dishes, I couldn't help but admire my partner. I was tempted to tell her Oscar would soon be at her side, or even better, in her bed, but I kept mum.

She'd purchased additional lenses for her

camera and was fast becoming a damn good news photographer. At the door of the cooking school, she slowed me with a hand on my forearm. "It's hard to believe one of these young women would murder to get a title."

Several of the participants, visible through the front window, mingled in the lobby of the school. Karrie Kompton hung on Clive's arm, batting her eyelashes at him. To his credit, he kept as much distance as he could between them. Crystal Belle Wadell, Karrie's former roommate, chatted with Belinda Buck. Mrs. Phelps, the pageant coordinator, flitted from one side of the room to the next, tending to last-minute details.

"Where's Amanda?" Tinkie entered and scanned the room. "I don't see her."

"Hedy isn't here, either." Not a good thing.

Guest chefs stood behind a counter loaded with food set up in a buffet. The wonderful smells made my mouth water. Each contestant would taste a particular dish and write down the recipe deduced by taste.

"Contestants! Contestants!" Evangeline called out. "Come and draw a number for your first assigned chef. You'll rotate clockwise and have fifteen minutes to ascertain the ingredients and cooking methods of each dish. Write them down and move on along the line. Our chefs have prepared a special treat for you."

When the small audience applauded, Evangeline

signaled for silence. "Due to the unfortunate deaths of two of our wonderful contestants and the serious illness of a third, we've decided to conclude the competition tomorrow evening. There will be a final event, the dessert finale, at seven o'clock. After that, the judges will retire to deliberate and the votes will be tallied. Miss Viking Range will be crowned tomorrow at nine p.m."

I shifted at the outskirts of the crowd. Hedy was nowhere in sight, and I was worried.

Mrs. Phelps cleared her throat. "We can't undo what's occurred, but Chief Jansen and the Greenwood officials assure us the person responsible will be captured and punished. For the families of Brook Oniada, Janet Menton, and Babs Lafitte, we offer our deepest regrets."

Sadness and dismay touched every face—except for that of Hedy, who was notably absent. I tugged at Tinkie's arm to tell her I'd return to the hotel to search for Hedy when our client emerged from a door in the back to an audible "ah."

Even I inhaled. She cut a striking figure in black, her pale skin luminous, her lips red and glossy. She'd applied heavy eyeliner and teased her dark hair into a bouffant that would have done the sixties proud. Her look was almost, but not quite, goth. John Waters would cast her immediately.

"Holy shit," Tinkie said, a smidgen of admiration in her voice at Hedy's chutzpah. "Why didn't she just bring her broomstick and a cauldron?"

Her remark was a little too close to the conversation I'd had earlier with Jitty. "She demands attention. You have to give her that. But I'd like to stand her in a corner. This won't help her cause."

Hedy took her place in front of judge three, a portly Frenchman with a handlebar mustache that made Chief Jansen's look anemic. His dish looked to be something with lean beef and mushrooms, but I wasn't close enough to be certain.

"What did Mrs. Phelps say about a plan to protect the contestants tonight?" I asked Tinkie in a whisper.

"Every ingredient was purchased and brought in by Mrs. Phelps this morning. She and her staff remained in the kitchen with the chefs at all times, and she tasted every dish. She said if anything was wrong with the food, she'd get sick first."

"That's dedication to a pageant," I said.

"Some would call it foolish. Mrs. Phelps could die."

"Which may be preferable to having another contestant killed, if you're the sponsor of this event."

Tinkie elbowed me in the ribs. "Hush. She's

done everything possible to make this safe for everyone. She doesn't believe the title is the motive. I talked to her about it, and she simply won't entertain the thought. Pageant girls are not killers, is what she told me."

"Chief Jansen is still suspicious of Hedy." He stood in the back of the room watching Hedy's every move. Police officers were stationed around the area, all on alert.

A silver bell chimed. Each contestant handed her written recipe to the chef and changed position.

Tinkie and I were members of an exclusive group allowed to witness the competition. Mrs. Phelps had decided to close the event to the general public. The fewer people attending, the easier it would be to keep control of things.

As the bell rang several more times, I stifled a yawn. I'd had little sleep the night before—and I certainly wasn't complaining, because I'd enjoyed every second of Graf's attention—and a very busy day. I also had a drive ahead of me. As much as I wanted to skip the remainder of the event, I couldn't.

While most of the pageant competitions had been festive, this was subdued. Tinkie snapped her photos. The contestants were quiet and studious as they tasted and wrote. To my relief, Mrs. Phelps rang the silver bell loudly to announce the conclusion of the evening.

"The judges and chefs will now analyze the written recipes. Thank you all." The tension showed on her face, but she mustered a huge smile and waved everyone out the door.

I fell in step beside Hedy, and Tinkie caught up with us as we walked across the street to the hotel. "How'd you do?" I asked.

"I nailed it," she said. "Easy as pie."

"I want you to go to your room and order something from room service so you can verify your whereabouts. Then lock the door and stay there," I told her.

Before she could answer, someone cleared a throat behind me. Chief Jansen had joined us. "No need for all of that, Miss Delaney. I'm stationing a police officer outside Miss Blackledge's door. She'll have an official escort at all times."

"I think that's a wonderful idea, Chief. Hedy is innocent, and this will prove it."

"We could sit with her," Tinkie offered.

I shook my head. "No, I don't think so."

"Well, we could," Tinkie insisted. "In fact, we need to be with her every moment. We know she's innocent—"

"Not tonight," I said through gritted teeth.

"Why not?" She stopped at the hotel's entrance and forced me to face her.

"Because," I said in a huff, "I need to talk to Doc in Zinnia, and Oscar is coming here to spend some time with his wife."

Tinkie's eyes widened, and a classic sorority girl squeal erupted as she jumped up and down. "Oscar is coming here? Tonight? You're taking care of Sweetie and my precious Chablis?" She retrieved her spare car keys from her purse and pressed them into my hand. "You're such a good friend!"

My surprise was ruined, but it didn't matter to Tinkie. Oscar was in her immediate future. And now I understood exactly what Jitty was trying to get me to comprehend.

I pulled out my cell phone and dialed. "I'm on my way home. Tinkie is all yours," I said to Oscar.

When I hung up, I gave Tinkie a big hug. "See you tomorrow." I jangled the keys to the Caddy. On the way home, I had a phone call to make, too. One I hoped would convey the true depth of my feelings for my fiancé.

20

The night, a soft black tunnel, glittered with stars as I drove north. Beside me, a bag of prime burgers from the Alluvian kitchen tantalized my olfactory sensors. I'd picked up a treat sure to tempt my hound's depressed appetite. It was midnight in the Delta land, but my mind churned with much to do in so little time. The place to start was with my man.

Though it was two hours earlier in the land of celluloid dreams, Graf was obviously asleep when I called. His groggy voice gave me a mental image of him, shirtless, his wonderful hair tousled and a stubble of beard on his handsome face.

"I love you," I said. "Don't talk. Just listen. I've been wrong." I imagined my fingers on his lips—those sexy lips that could make me weak with pleasure. "Not about what I've done, but the way I've gone about it. Graf, there is nothing more important to me than you."

He tried to interrupt. "No, let me finish. What happened to me in that cotton field isn't my pain alone. This is where I made a terrible mistake. I let the loss and sorrow isolate me from you, from the one person who was suffering as much as I was. I'm sorry. I'm so sorry I walled you out when we both needed each other so much."

"I love you, Sarah Booth," he said, and his voice was wide awake. "I love you exactly the way you are."

"The pageant concludes tomorrow. Once your movie is done, can we make that trip to Ireland?"

"Only if you want to make me the happiest man alive."

"Oh, I think I could enjoy doing that."

"Can I ask where this revelation came from?"

Crediting Jitty was out of the question—at least for now. Maybe one day I could tell him about the Ghost of Delaney Women Past. "A good friend turned on a lightbulb for me."

"Thank her, for you and for me, because this conversation also points out some things I need to consider. I thought I knew what you needed, because it's what I need. My focus was on my needs, not yours. While I might not fully understand your needs, I should honor them."

What planet had this man dropped from? "Go back to sleep," I said. "We'll talk soon, when it isn't late and we both have time to really dig in."

"Where are you, Sarah Booth?"

I'd driven halfway home. On either side of the road spread the vast fields of cotton. "Right where I need to be," I said, almost laughing. "I'm in the middle of a cotton field."

"Now I have an image I can take into my dreams."

"Good night." I blew him a kiss and closed the phone with a smile. In another five minutes I'd be home, where Chablis and Sweetie Pie waited for me. Oscar had dropped them off and headed toward Greenwood even as I drove north toward home.

When I turned down the drive, I saw the lights

of Dahlia House blazing a welcome. Oscar had turned on every bulb in the house, but despite the waste of energy, I was glad. The sight of my ancestral home, lit with a warm glow, was exactly what I needed.

Add to that the wagging tails of one dustmop and one hound, and it was as close to bliss as I was going to come for a while. Sweetie Pie's mournful bay rang through the night as I stopped the Caddy in front of the house and got out.

There is no joy like that with which a dog greets her human. Whatever bad decisions I'd made in the past weeks, coming home was a good one.

Sweetie and Chablis snoozed beside my bed. Outside the window, moonlight touched the cotton fields. The trees that shaded the family cemetery at Dahlia House swayed in a light breeze. In the stillness of the night, time seemed to have slowed, but it was an illusion. Events were moving forward at a fast and furious pace. While I should be sleeping, my mind wouldn't rest.

Graf's words whirled in my head, and there was a truth there that refracted on the murder of two girls and attempted murder of a third. He'd said he recognized my needs were different from his. Somehow, I knew this was the key to finding the beauty pageant killer. It all had to do with motive. Every criminal investigation looks at three principal elements: means, motive, and opportunity.

The means was poison, which could be purchased via the Internet. It was almost impossible to narrow a field of suspects by this criteria.

Motive was equally nonspecific. Getting rid of pageant competitors was a motive Tinkie and I had settled on. But we also considered Marcus Wellington's potential desire to frame Hedy and remove her from registering a claim on Vivian by plunking her behind bars. But Graf's simple statement—that he'd wanted to give me what he needed, not what I needed—was the thing that kept me awake. Somewhere in those words was the nugget of truth I sought. In assigning motives to these murders, Tinkie and I—and even Chief Jansen—had assumed the killer would want what we might want.

That was not necessarily true.

Amanda Payne had been the top contestant at the "Taste and Copy" competition. Which by my theory would make her the next victim—unless she, or Voncil—was the killer. Yet no one had been poisoned or harmed.

Had our extra security measures been successful? Had we foiled the killer with our precautions? Or had there been no murder because Amanda, as the potential winner, had no need to kill the woman who stood ahead of her in line for the title? If Amanda, or Voncil, was the killer, why would she go to such trouble to frame Hedy?

Perhaps the poisonings weren't related to the competition at all but to something from the past. So far, our research had found nothing in common amongst the girls. They'd never met until the competition.

I wanted to throw the keyboard across the room. I didn't have enough evidence to settle on a single motive, and I couldn't trust my gut. The attack on me at the Carlisle plantation had deeply shaken my faith in my instincts. Self-doubt gnawed at me.

I stood up and stretched. Sweetie Pie and Chablis had eaten the deluxe hamburgers and now slept in the bliss of a doggie coma. Dr. Leonard, Sweetie's vet, would be on my case if she knew I'd treated my hound to such a fatty meal, but Sweetie had scarfed it down. Whether it was the food or my return, it didn't matter. Her hunger strike was over—she was full and content, as was Chablis.

I considered the third arm of an investigator's approach to crime. Opportunity. Because of the extra security at the "Taste and Copy," the killer might have been thwarted. "Might have been," like any other qualifying phrase, was the opposite of fact. Supposition didn't make for a strong case.

Because the public had been excluded from the "Taste and Copy" event, Marcus Wellington had not been on the premises. Was the lack of a murder due to lack of opportunity? Again, it was impossible to say.

The things linking the poisonings were location, occupation of the three victims, means of death or injury, and timing. The poisonings all occurred in less than a week. Any logical person would assume they were somehow connected to the pageant. Yet a "logical" person would not harm three young women in such gruesome ways.

The use of different poisons was another clue to the killer's mindset. The total lack of forensic evidence told me this person knew something about sophisticated detection. He, or she, was showing off. Unless, of course, there were multiple killers. My head hurt with the possibilities.

I leaned my arms down on my desk and lowered my head. My temples throbbed, and I needed to get up and run. Just run. Without destination or reason. Frustration made me feel this way.

When I woke up, my back and neck were stiff. Sweetie was licking my face while Chablis teethed on my right ankle. I looked around, confused for a moment about where I was. I didn't normally sleep on my desk in the Delaney Detective Agency, a room that had once been a grand parlor and now contained desks, filing cabinets, and the putty gray furniture of an inexpensive office. One day, when Tinkie and I were fabulously wealthy, we'd spring for mahogany credenzas and wall-to-wall framed accounts of our successful cases.

Dawn was just breaking over the pasture, which was empty because Reveler and his buddy Miss Scrapiron were vacationing at my friend Lee McBride's. I trudged upstairs to shower and prepare for the day. I wanted to be back in Greenwood early, but first I had to see Doc.

I left the dogs at Dahlia House. Dew sparkling on the cotton plants and the tree leaves, a billion diamonds glittering in the first shafts of sunlight. My favorite time of day.

Doc was, as I anticipated, in his office. The smell of coffee snaked down the hallway to alert the innocent he was brewing up a witch's pot of strong caffeine. I'd attempted to drink his brew a few times. Never again.

When I tapped on his door and entered at his invitation, I was greeted with a smile. "Sarah Booth," he said as he came around the desk to hug me. "You look healthy. A bit thin for my taste, but your color is good."

"I'm fine," I assured him. "Thanks to you."

He waved my gratitude away. "You're here about those Greenwood murders, aren't you?"

I nodded. "Ricin, digitalis, belladonna—those

316

are unusual poisons." My impulse was to pace, but I didn't. "I know my client, Hedy Blackledge, didn't poison anyone. But I have to find out who did."

Doc settled in the chair behind his desk and motioned me toward another. I moved a stack of documents to the floor. The place looked like a recycling center.

"Coffee?" he asked.

I eyed the pot in the corner. I thought a bubble rose from the primordial goo. "No thanks. I like having enamel on my teeth."

Doc chuckled. "I'm glad to see you up and sassy. You had me worried, Sarah Booth."

"I know." It wasn't a kidding matter. I'd come close to dying. "I'm fine, Doc. But I need some help with those poor dead girls."

"Strange case. No doubt they were poisoned, but the delivery is interesting. More toxicology reports were faxed in this morning."

"What did you find?"

"Because Brook was terribly burned, the cause of death was obvious, or so it seemed. The initial tests revealed her body had been rubbed with ambergris, which is flammable. What they failed to detect was the belladonna in her body lotion. It was masked by the ambergris."

I knew a bit about the plant. "Women used it to make their eyes bright because it dilates the pupils. It translates to 'beautiful lady.' "

"It's the source of atropine, which ophthalmologists use to dilate eyes for an exam. When a cornea has a minor scratch, it can alleviate the pain." He gave me a chance to interrupt, but when I didn't, he went on. "It's also called deadly nightshade and a host of other names like Devil's Elixir. Used topically, it's a critical numbing agent. In an overdose, it can also lead to cardiac arrest and asphyxiation by shutting down the respiratory system."

"Brook would have died even if she hadn't caught on fire."

"She was likely dying as she burned." He took a deep breath. "I don't think the killer meant for her to burn. I think the action of the poison took longer to kick in than expected. The killer meant for Brook to die during her performance. Not of fire but of asphyxia."

"Where does belladonna come from?"

"The plant isn't really native to these parts, but it could be cultivated here. Hell, by manipulating temperature, soil, and water in a controlled or even hydroponic situation, folks can grow just about anything. It isn't a difficult plant, is what I'm saying. You know, deadly nightshade is strongly associated with witchcraft. It's a topical anesthetic and also a hallucinogen. Not a reliable one, because it can kill quickly, but it is potent. That's how it came to be associated with witches and flying."

He rubbed the corners of his mouth. He looked like he'd been up all night. "During the witch trials, possession of belladonna was a hanging offense. A lot of healers who used the plant for good were accused of practicing witchcraft."

"And that gave the real killer a perfect setup to frame Hedy as a 'conjure woman,' " I noted. "The ricin comes from the castor plant, which grows wild here, correct?"

He nodded. "Especially down along the Gulf Coast. The castor plant also has medicinal uses. I doubt Libby ever dosed you with castor oil, but it was used a lot during my sprout days when a young-un looked a might pea-ked."

"Pea-ked?"

"Pale or jaundiced, usually from eating too much junk food or simply having a case of the pouts. Folks my mother's age would get out the bottle of castor oil and give a young-un a table-spoon full." Even the passage of six decades hadn't dimmed the bitter taste. Doc's face com-pressed. "Nasty stuff that cramped your stomach and made staying close to the bathroom a good idea."

"Sounds unpleasant, but isn't it deadly?"

"Not the oil used in the laxative form. Ricin, made from the castor bean, is one of the deadliest poisons around." He picked up a notepad and studied it. "Foxglove, which is the plant that produces digitalis, is also easy to grow in this area. A lot of people are unaware of the medicinal value of the plant and cultivate it for the beautiful blooms. The interesting element with Babs Lafitte is incorporating the poison in a cigarette. She's lucky to be alive."

"Do you think she'll regain consciousness?"

"She has. Early this morning."

"Thank heavens." I checked my watch. It was going on seven o'clock. I needed to get back to Greenwood to interview Babs. She might hold the clue to finding the real killer. "Doc, no one was murdered last night. There were extra precautions in place. The final event is today. I wish they'd cancel the whole thing."

"This may or may not be helpful, but I suspect your killer grows these plants. They can be ordered over the Internet, but with heightened national security, it might set off alarms."

"That will narrow it down."

"Look for someone who has a green thumb and has some knowledge of the occult."

"I'm more certain now that Hedy is being framed. All of these poisons could have come from her backyard. She's admitted she has an interest in botany and marine biology. The killer left gris-gris bags with each girl who was poisoned. This is a complicated setup."

Doc got up and poured another cup of coffee.

I couldn't swear, but I thought I heard a splat, as if a blob of semisolid coffee had splashed into his cup. The idea was disturbing in more ways than one. "Gotta hit the road."

"I shouldn't need to caution you to be careful," Doc said. "Poison is one of the easiest ways to kill someone. Medical science can detect it now and trace it back, as we've done with these young women. But, sometimes, if the poison is metabolized, there's no trace. And no antidote. If you ingest the wrong stuff, Sarah Booth, you'll be dead. Finding the killer doesn't bring the dead back to life."

"Have you spoken with Graf?" I didn't mean to sound suspicious, but it seemed everyone and his brother was trying to protect me.

"No, I've talked with the young coroner, the one better suited to preaching than searching out the motives for murder." Doc came over to me, his coffee cup in one hand. He put a palm on my forehead to take my temperature and then kissed my cheek. "You be careful, Sarah Booth. I mean it."

"Thanks, Doc. If you find anything else, call me."

"I'll do better than that. I've discussed this with Coleman, and he's offered to help Jansen. Things are calm here in Sunflower County, thank goodness."

The thought of Coleman butting heads with Jansen made me smile. "Good idea. Did he say he'd be in Greenwood?"

"Didn't say, but it wouldn't surprise me to see him there." He patted my shoulder. "You're too thin. When you and Tinkie solve this case, I'll treat you to a tray of bear claws from the bakery."

I had one more stop to make before I left Zinnia. I called Tink to tell her the good news about Babs.

"Can we talk with her?" Tinkie was raring to go. Oscar had recharged her batteries.

"We'll give it a try. Ask Jansen if he's interviewed her yet." The Greenwood chief would not appreciate us preempting him.

"Will do. I'll wait in the room. We can visit Babs together."

"I'll be there as quick as I can." I disconnected as I pulled under the big shade tree in Tammy's, aka Madame Tomeeka's, front yard.

Our psychic friend had been strangely silent in the last few days. It wasn't uncommon for me to hear from Tammy at least once a week. Sometimes I played a big role in her dreams and visions, and she always alerted me to danger when she sensed it. After the tragedy of Brook Oniada's death, I hadn't heard a peep from Madame Tomeeka.

I was relieved no other car was parked there. Tammy's services were popular with area residents who sought her advice on everything from dating to illnesses.

The screen door wasn't latched, so I went in, calling her name.

"In the kitchen," she yelled back.

No surprise since the smell of bacon and fresh coffee wafted through the house. Tammy, along with her special talents, was an excellent down-home cook.

She indicated a chair at the table, and I sat while she poured me coffee and broke two eggs in the frying pan. "You're here about those pageant girls, aren't you?"

Her tone was neutral, but she didn't face me. Tammy had made it clear she wanted no part of the competition. I'd brought trouble to her doorstep. "Actually, I need to ask you about poisonous plants and voodoo."

She put a plate of eggs, bacon, grits, and biscuits in front of me and prepared one for herself. She'd cooked enough for two people, as if she'd expected me, or someone, to arrive.

"I don't truck with voodoo." She refreshed our coffee.

"Do you believe in it?"

"Why are you asking?"

I told her about the gris-gris bags and the girls who'd been attacked.

"Doesn't matter what you or I believe. Voodoo, charms, the power to harm or heal—that comes from the person. If you believe it, it's real."

I'd learned this lesson from Doreen Mallory

in a previous case. "Do voodoo practitioners use poisonous plants?"

She nodded. "Many groups use drugs in rituals, whether you classify them as religious or spiritual or evil. There's a history of drug use in voodoo. Whether poisonous or not, elements are designed to hurt people. In voodoo, intent is the weapon."

Tammy always told me when she had a vision about me, but since she'd volunteered nothing, I asked. "Have you seen anything happening to me?"

Pushing back her chair, she went to her kitchen window. "Not you."

Her words constricted my chest. "Tinkie?"

"Yes."

"Why didn't you tell us?" Fear made me react poorly.

"I told her, Sarah Booth. It was her vision to know. I urged her to share it with you. Obviously she didn't."

"What did you see?"

She returned to the table and took my hand. "The dream wasn't specific. She was walking in the woods in a white gown. It was a beautiful place, with sunlight and big oaks. Ferns carpeted the ground. Tinkie slowly staggered and fell. She stretched out with the ferns as a cushion, and she went to sleep."

"That doesn't sound so bad."

"When I touched her, she was cold. I couldn't wake her up."

I stood up so fast, my chair slammed to the floor. "Are you saying she died?"

Tammy held tight to my hand. "I don't know."

"What did she say when you told her?" Tinkie hadn't shared this information with me—she meant to spare me worry. Not a good idea.

"She assured me she would be careful. She promised not to eat anything remotely related to the competition." Tammy tried to tug me back into my chair, but I pulled free.

"That's not good enough. I'll make her go home."

Tammy sat up tall and regal. "You can try. I did. But when you fail, stay close to her. If anyone can keep the devil at bay, Sarah Booth, it'll be you."

21

Along with making her man feel like the king of the world, Tinkie had been a busy gal. I opened the door of our hotel room to find her at the window with some high-powered binoculars watching the front of the Viking Cooking School.

We had a pretty good view, unassisted, of the building, but the binoculars snapped everything into sharp focus—including the expression on Karrie Kompton's face as she lurked outside the building.

"Jansen said we could speak with Babs at ten." She kept her binoculars glued to Karrie.

"What's the bitch queen up to?" I asked, fighting to keep my voice neutral. Confronting Tinkie about Tammy's dream would accomplish nothing. She was, indeed, as hardheaded as I ever dared to be.

"Her attitude says no good." Tinkie reached over and pinched me hard on the waist.

"Ow! What's that for?"

"Leaving me alone with Oscar."

"He's your husband," I protested loudly. "I thought the two of you would work out a few kinks, have some yucks, and he'd be in a better mood."

Tinkie lowered the field glasses. "His intent was to convince me to drop this case and go home."

Now I wished he'd succeeded. "That rascal. And I thought I was doing a nice turn by clearing out of the room and taking care of the pups so you two could have a romp."

"Oh, you did. It took me all of two minutes to divert his attention from the case. By the time he left this morning, he'd forgotten why he came here." She bit her bottom lip and let it slowly pop from her mouth. Oscar, even after years of marriage, was not immune to her wiles.

"I wish I'd learned guerrilla tactics in man management," I said. I made a choice right there: I wouldn't tell Tinkie I knew about the dream. I would watch her like a hawk.

"My strategies are time-tested and true," she conceded with a smile. "As your aunt Loulane tried to tell you, Sarah Booth, you can catch more flies with sugar than vinegar."

I only rolled my eyes. It seemed everyone in my life felt free to quote my dead relatives to me—even my dead relatives, since I counted Jitty as family.

"What's Karrie up to now?"

"The cooking school isn't open, so she's beating on the window. The person inside is pointing down the street."

Karrie walked away, her hips swaying in a motion that was all sex. "Let's check out her room."

"Even though it's a hotel, it's still breaking and entering."

"Only if we're caught," I pointed out.

"Let's go."

We sauntered around the lobby until we found Samuel, Hedy's friend, alone. We twisted his arm—only a little—to get a copy of Karrie's room key. Samuel wasn't thrilled with helping us, but he knew we were working to save Hedy from false accusations.

"If she doesn't get her baby back, I don't know what she'll do," he said glumly. "You think she has a chance?"

"The whole idea of winning a beauty pageant to save her child is far-fetched, if you ask me." Tinkie slipped the key card into her pocket.

"Haven't you ever been so far down that a long shot seemed like the only chance you'd ever have at a dream?" Samuel's tone held disapproval. "Hedy's never had anybody on her side. She's never had anyone to talk her up or tell her she could do things. Sure, her mama loves her, but Miss Clara doesn't see who Hedy really is. All she sees is a teenage girl got herself in trouble and lost her baby to a rich family. In Miss Clara's book, there's no point fighting the rich. She already had a heap of public spotlight on her life when her husband disappeared in the swamp, and she doesn't want any more of that. To Hedy, this contest looked like it might be a ticket to a new life."

"Even if she wins it, Samuel, they'll take the title from her when they realize she has a child." Hedy wasn't dumb; she couldn't believe they'd let her keep the title. Something else occurred to me. "How do you know so much about Hedy's family situation?"

" 'Cause I listen to what she says." The angle of

his chin told me he knew a lot but he wouldn't spill it voluntarily.

"How do you know Hedy?" I should have asked this question long before. He'd offered Hedy a refuge in his apartment. He was not merely a casual acquaintance, someone she'd spoken to in passing.

"We went to high school together." He struck a pose of defiance. "She's a good person. All she wants is her baby girl."

Tinkie touched my arm. "If we're going to scope out Karrie's room, we have to do it now. She won't be gone forever."

True enough. We had to get busy. "We'll talk later," I promised Samuel as Tinkie and I hustled to the elevator.

"What are we looking for specifically?" Tinkie asked.

"Poisons. Confessions. Hell, I'll know it when I see it."

"That's comforting."

Tinkie was sleep deprived from her wild night with Oscar and it made her snippy. I ignored her sarcasm and led the way into the lioness's den.

We stopped in the doorway. The room looked as if a professional staging crew had entered and cleaned up. Fresh flowers and a fruit basket adorned the table beside a reading chair where a comfy throw lay bunched on top of *The New York Times*. I'd expected Karrie's reading material to reflect her attitude. Maybe the collected works of Miss Snark.

The place smelled like heaven, and I realized the floral arrangement contained stargazer lilies, one of my favorites.

"Take the bathroom and I'll take the dresser drawers. Check out her prescriptions. Maybe we should even take a sample of each one—to have it analyzed."

"Got it." Tinkie pulled on latex gloves. My hands were already protected by the icky things. I hated the feel, and smell, of them, but they were a P.I. necessity. I'd brought a box from the office at Dahlia House.

Tinkie disappeared into the bathroom and I heard rustling noises. I opened the top dresser drawer. Karrie's things were folded so neatly, I hesitated to touch them. There was no way I could put them back exactly right. I looked, anyway. Other than a fetish for leopard-print thongs, I found nothing.

I went through all three drawers, then hit the closet. Her clothes, hung in groups by color, were pressed to a fare-thee-well, as if they'd just come from the cleaners. Amazing. I hadn't figured Karrie for a neatnik.

On the floor beneath her clothes were four empty suitcases. I examined her shoes, hoping to find god knows what. They were polished, and the soles looked as if they'd been pressure washed. This wasn't extraordinary neatness—it was either obsessive-compulsive or criminal.

"Nothing." Tinkie exited the bathroom. "It's like a pod person lives here. The only thing in there other than cosmetics and toothpaste is a bottle of aspirin, and I checked each tablet. They're all aspirin. She has cotton balls, swabs, cosmetics—a really wonderful brand I've never tried—and personal items. I examined everything. What isn't sealed is exactly what it appears. Even the shampoo."

"There's nothing here, either," I admitted.

"This is one of the scariest things I've seen." Tinkie's arm swept the room. "Who did this, because I know Karrie didn't? And why?"

"There's not a cookbook or recipe or secret ingredient anywhere in this room." All of the other girls brought vials and condiments to spice up their special recipes. I'd seen them in Hedy's and Amanda's rooms. Even my limited cooking experience involved a couple of "secret" ingredients, like the fresh horseradish in the Jezebel sauce Aunt Loulane taught me to prepare.

"Maybe Karrie's stuff is at Marcus's house." Tinkie peered under the inset television.

It would allow Marcus to use Karrie, whether she knew it or not. If he was the killer, he could be contaminating her condiments.

Under the bed was the last place I'd been taught to look before I left a hotel room. That was where stray books, a sandal, a sock, or underwear went to hide. I knelt down on the soft carpet and scanned. Only one item, something dark and shapeless, blighted the pristine condition of the room.

I reached. My fingertips caught the edge of what felt like leather. I pulled it toward me, realizing it was a bag with a drawstring. My first thought was jewelry. Tinkie's too, if I correctly read her expression. Holding the black bag, I sat up.

The ties were knotted, but I unlaced them and dumped the contents on the carpet.

"Holy crap!" Tinkie stepped back from the curled, shriveled chicken claw that tumbled onto the carpet amidst leaves, small bones, a die, a toy figurine of a beautiful girl, and an earring. "It's a curse."

"Or a charm." Though my knowledge of voodoo or witchcraft was limited, Tammy had confirmed that charms could be either light or dark. I stared at the things scattered across the eggplant-colored carpet. "Do you think Karrie's the next victim?"

"Or the killer." Tinkie nudged the chicken foot with the toe of her shoe. "Sure hope the chicken wasn't alive. We need to report this to Chief Jansen."

I gathered the contents and returned them to the bag, which I stuffed back under the bed. "We need to get out of here."

Putting words into action, we hauled it out the door, down the hallway, and to the bank of elevators. "Do we tell Karrie about that thing?" Tinkie asked as we waited for our ride.

"I think—"

The bell *dinged*. The elevator door opened, and Karrie stepped out. She carried several packages, which she tried to hide. "What are you doing on my floor?" she demanded.

"I didn't realize you owned Park Place, Boardwalk, and an entire floor of the Alluvian," Tinkie said. "What's in the bags?"

"Nothing you would be interested in." Karrie brushed past us.

Tinkie stumbled, lurched forward, and caromed off Karrie. The sacks tore, and grocery items spilled across the floor.

"You careless oaf!" Karrie regained her balance but not her temper. "You did that on purpose."

"No, I didn't." Tinkie was so busy documenting the contents of Karrie's purchases, she didn't even bother to look up. She grabbed a bag of hazelnuts. Beside her knee were macadamia nuts, a fresh coconut, and a specialty brand of dark chocolate. "So, we're making something chocolate with fresh nuts and coconut. Yum."

"You *can't tell* anyone," Karrie sounded like a petulant five-year-old. "You cheated. You'd better not tell anyone what I'm making."

"Or what?" Tinkie asked.

"The rules state each contestant's dessert is a surprise. If you tell Hedy, it wouldn't be fair."

I offered Tinkie a hand up. "We don't care what you're baking," I said. "And you have our word we won't tell the other contestants the ingredients we saw." I wanted to ask her who'd cleaned and ordered her room—or, better yet, who'd left a dead chicken claw under her bed—but that would give away the fact I'd been snooping there.

Smugness crept over Karrie's face. "I made the highest score on the 'Taste and Copy' last night. That puts me in the top position. I told you I'd win, and after tonight, the vote in my favor will be unanimous."

She had no idea what "top spot" really meant in this contest. It could be a death sentence instead of a crown. "How do you know you won last night?"

"A little bird told me." She was so confident, she didn't even feel the need to invent a creative lie.

"A bird named Clive?"

"Tweedle-dee-dee." She snatched up her ingredients. "What I can't weasel out of Clive, Marcus can charm out of someone else."

So that was Marcus's early meeting with Belinda Buck. She likely had no idea she'd been pumped for vital information.

Karrie smiled her photo-op smile. "See you tonight. Bring that camera, Mrs. Richmond. I want a front-page banner when they put the crown on my head."

"Karrie, if you're the front-runner, you need to know Tinkie and I believe someone may try to kill you."

"You are desperate, aren't you? Two sad old ladies trying to influence a pageant. Can't you see how pathetic that is?"

What I could see was the toe of my shoe planted in her butt. "We're trying to warn you. You're in danger, *if* you truly are the front-runner."

"Amanda Payne was in the lead before last night and she's just fine. No one tried to poison her."

"The circumstances last night were controlled. Tonight, they won't be. You girls are cooking, all at the same time. If one of you is the killer—"

"Voncil told me how you two tried to keep Amanda from participating last night." She shrugged a shoulder. "Nothing you say or do will stop me from finishing this competition."

Tinkie listened with a stony face. "Then I wish you luck, Karrie. Give it your best shot."

"I don't need luck, I have talent." Karrie shifted her purchases and marched down the hallway.

"Do you think she's in the lead?" Tinkie asked.

I shook my head. "I don't know. The chicken claw under her bed . . . now it concerns me even more. The killer may have marked Karrie for death. We need to deliver the gris-gris bag to Jansen. There might be evidence in it."

"We should have snatched it when we had the chance," Tinkie said.

I followed her into the elevator. "We still have an hour before we can talk to Babs."

"Do you think Hedy's mother could be behind this?" Tinkie hesitated to express the thought.

"Her mother is killing girls and framing Hedy?" That angle would never have occurred to me, but Tinkie had a point. Hedy was estranged. A definite past existed, and if Clara Saulnier Blackledge was as nutty as Marcus made her sound . . .

"She's the swamp woman, not Hedy. It sort of fits."

"It does."

"I'll work on the Saulnier family," Tinkie said. "I have a sorority sister who lives in the Pearl River area. I'll call her and see what the score is."

"We have something better than that. Find Samuel. Hem him up in a corner and make him talk. He knows more about Hedy than he's let on."

It wasn't the best investigative technique, but we didn't have time to drive to the southwest portion of the state and track down Clara Saulnier Blackledge.

"I can do that." Tinkie put her arm around my waist and gave me a quick hug. "I know you didn't want to work this case to begin with, but this is what we're meant to do, Sarah Booth. Maybe not all the time, but at least part of the time. Think how we're helping Hedy. Without us, she'd likely be in jail by now and would never see her daughter again."

I fought the fear that threatened to take me under. "We haven't solved this thing yet. There's a killer loose," I reminded her. "Hedy could be in danger. Or you could." I stopped to swallow a lump of emotion. "Graf is right about one thing. This work can be dangerous, and we have to take every precaution."

We parted ways at the lobby. Tinkie went to stalk Samuel, and I went out to the courtyard to call Coleman. Lucky for me he was in his office at the Sunflower County courthouse. I needed a favor.

"You need to report the gris-gris to Jansen," he said after listening to my account of finding the leather bag.

"I'd have to admit to breaking and entering. Jansen might put me in jail." That was true. "He doesn't value me as an investigator."

"His taste is questionable," Coleman said, "but I understand where he's coming from. Did you touch anything?"

"You know me better than that." I wasn't

insulted. "I hoped you might tell him about the chicken foot. Anonymous tip and all."

Paper ripped and there was the noise of a printer chewing away in the background. "You want me to tell Jansen I got an anonymous tip about a case in Leflore County."

"Your reputation as an excellent lawman permeates the entire Delta." I groped for the right words. "Tinkie may be in danger. I can't afford to end up in jail, even for a few hours."

Coleman could do what I couldn't. While I had charm and sass, he had a badge. There was a definite "brothers in blue—or brown or black—mentality" amongst law enforcement types. A mere private investigator garnered no respect. "If he arrests me, I'll have to give you up."

"Not likely to happen." I almost sighed with relief. "Thanks, Coleman."

"I'm glad you're back in Mississippi working cases, Sarah Booth."

"Me too."

He must have heard the melancholy in my voice, because he asked, "Everything okay?"

"Yeah. Things are fine. It's just been a long week, and I'm worried about tonight. It's the final event."

"Maybe I'll come watch."

The thought of Coleman there, keeping an eye on things, made me feel much better. "That would be a good thing." It wasn't that I didn't trust

Jansen to do his job, but one man and a small police department couldn't cover everything. And Coleman would be, essentially, undercover. No one participating in the competition would know he was a lawman from an adjacent county.

Except Clive and Marcus.

They would know. But it would only matter to them if they were involved in the killings.

22

When I hung up from my call with Coleman and went back inside, there was a note at the desk from Tinkie.

"Meet me in the room," she wrote. "Hurry."

I did just that and once the elevator released me, I sprinted down the hall. I rushed inside to Tinkie and a worried Samuel.

"Tell her what you told me," Tinkie ordered Samuel.

Brow furrowed, elegant fingers twining, Samuel began. "You know the story about Hedy's daddy, how he disappeared in the swamps and nothing was ever found of him except his boat, which was spinning in circles."

I nodded. Whatever Samuel knew weighed heavily on him.

"Kids in school teased Hedy all her life. Her mama's people were from New Orleans. There was always talk about a Creole background, but that never meant much to Hedy or me. It was the Marie Laveau tales that tormented Hedy. Folks saying her mama was a conjure woman who killed her daddy."

"Some members of the Saulnier family may have been involved with Marie Laveau, at least in some limited way," I said.

"That was back before the Civil War. Close on to two hundred years have gone by, but folks won't let it rest," he said. "Miss Clara, Hedy's mama, made some healing potions and sold a few charms, but she never consorted with the devil."

"Now is a fine time to come clean with all of this." I was aggravated.

"Hedy swore me to secrecy. Miss Tinkie here made me realize I had to speak up or someone else might die."

Thank goodness for Tinkie's persuasive talents, but I was still annoyed at Samuel's and Hedy's stonewalling.

"Hush up your fussing, Sarah Booth, and let the young man talk." Tinkie pushed me into a chair beside Samuel.

"Miss Clara was so hurt by what happened after her husband disappeared in the swamps, it changed her, and it impacted Hedy. You know

340

how cruel people in small towns can be. Well, Hedy never had a chance. Especially not the way she looked. I think most of the ugly talk had to do with jealousy. Those teenage girls, they were awful. If Hedy had to give a speech in school or had a date, they wrote things on the blackboard or on her locker." Samuel shook his head. "I did what I could, but it wasn't a lot."

"Okay, I feel sorry for Hedy. What does this have to do with anything?"

"Hedy's father, Larry Blackledge, was a good man, from what Miss Clara told me. He was from up North, from a very educated family. When he met Miss Clara, it was love at first sight. He decided to stay in Mississippi with her, because she wouldn't leave."

There were overtones here of the Rubella and James Gramacy romance. Several articles portrayed the first Saulnier daughter in service to the voodoo queen. Rather than help, this information could hurt Hedy if she was charged with anything.

"The Blackledge family was very upset," Samuel said. "Mr. Larry was the favored child, a brilliant scholar, an architect whose designs as a young adult attracted attention around the world. Miss Clara said his family had great expectations for him. But Mr. Larry didn't care. He wanted Miss Clara, and he was determined to be with her, no matter what."

"Did she bewitch him?" I asked. I thought with a chill of Marcus's claim that Hedy had glamoured him.

Samuel's face eased into a smile. "I didn't think you'd be superstitious."

"Okay, so what happened?"

"The way Miss Clara told me was that she had Hedy, and the three of them were happy. They were isolated, but privacy was what they wanted. Mr. Larry built them a wonderful house. It's unique, high up in the trees so when the river floods, they're snug and safe. But it wasn't a typical house, and that's hard on a kid."

"I get the picture. Poor Hedy, surrounded by brilliant and kind eccentrics." I checked my watch. "What does this have to do with anything?"

"When Mr. Larry disappeared, his family tried to have Miss Clara charged with murder. They all came down to Mississippi with high-powered lawyers and the newspapers in their pocket and they destroyed her. She was never charged with murder, but everyone believed she killed Mr. Larry because he was going to leave her and take Hedy."

Despite myself, I was riveted. I didn't believe Hedy or her mother practiced voodoo, but the repetitive patterns in their lives were enough to make me consider some higher intervention. Hedy and Vivian were reliving the hell that Clara and Hedy must have confronted.

"Did Mr. Blackledge plan to leave Clara?"

Samuel shrugged. "I wouldn't think so. Miss Clara always talked like Mr. Larry was the best thing that ever happened to her except for Hedy. She took it hard when Hedy got pregnant with Marcus Wellington's child. They had a big fight and Hedy left. She was alone and scared when she gave Vivian up. When Hedy went home to get Miss Clara to help her fight for the baby, it was awful."

Hedy had resurrected Clara's nightmare.

"Miss Clara told Hedy to give up, said she couldn't fight money and power."

"Your story is interesting, but we know most of this." I looked at Tinkie, who tick-a-locked her lips. I was getting a little weary of being told to shut up.

Tinkie stepped in front of me. "I was down in the hotel computer room borrowing the printer—"

"And that's when I saw her," Samuel interrupted.

"Saw who?" I asked.

"Larry Blackledge's sister, Anna."

Confusion made me look from one to the other. "Who?"

"Anna Blackledge is Anna Lock," Tinkie said. "I looked up the Bronsill family and went through newspaper clippings. There was a photo of Latham Bronsill receiving an award and a woman identified as Anna Lock is standing with him."

"But it's really Anna Blackledge," Samuel said.

"But why didn't Hedy recognize her?" I asked. "She lived with Hedy for two weeks as a nanny before Marcus took Vivian."

"The past was painful for Hedy. Especially the Blackledge family angle. Mr. Larry had old photos of his relatives, but Hedy avoided all things connected to people who thought her mother had killed her father. I was over there one afternoon and found the photo albums in the trash. I flipped through them out of curiosity. Miss Clara came out the back door and caught me. She wanted to talk. Even the strongest people need to unburden sometimes."

Tinkie went to a folder on the bed and brought out a somewhat blurred copy of a newspaper picture. A younger version of Anna Lock stood proudly beside a young man who wore a huge medallion. "Are you sure about this, Samuel?"

He nodded. "I'm sure. She's older, but it's the lady from the photographs at the Saulnier house."

When I met Tinkie's gaze, I could see she was thinking exactly what I was thinking. Anna Lock or Anna Blackledge had a lot of reasons to hate Hedy, not because of anything Hedy had done, but because of old history. Raising and alienating Vivian would be sweet revenge—the Saulnier family had taken her brother, so she would take the daughter. Framing Hedy for murder would be even sweeter, and Anna knew the weaknesses of the Saulnier family.

"What are you going to do?" Samuel asked. "If Hedy gets wind of this, she's liable to head over to Panther Holler with a gun and a box of ammunition. She'd do anything to protect Vivian."

"We have no proof of anything," I pointed out.

"When has that ever stopped us?" Tinkie asked.

"Good point." My first thought was for the safety of the child. Anna had raised the little girl, but that didn't mean she wouldn't harm her. "We have to get Vivian away from the household."

Samuel nodded. "I was hoping you'd say that. I want to help."

"Do you think we can convince Jansen to take legal steps to remove her from the house?" I checked my watch. We didn't have time to waste persuading him.

Tinkie hesitated. "There's another way. Let me call Marcus, get a feel for Vivian's schedule."

"He won't give us the time of day." Tinkie must have forgotten we'd been a thorn in Marcus's side.

"Maybe he won't, but Clive might."

"Good idea." I handed her the phone book from the bedside table.

She dialed and held up a hand for silence.

After a few opening gambits, she went after pay dirt. "I'm concerned for Vivian's safety," she said. "It's long and complicated, Clive, but you have to trust me. Vivian is in danger. We can't be certain Marcus isn't involved. My guess is that he's been used, but it doesn't matter right now. Vivian's safety is my concern. Will you help us make certain she's safe, until things are resolved?"

Tinkie blanched, and I knew the news was bad. "Thanks. Can you find out if the nanny went with them?"

She replaced the phone and turned to us. "Vivian has gone with Gilliard and Frances to Memphis for a weekend at the Peabody Hotel. Marcus told Clive they might take a vacation to Europe."

"This is awfully sudden. Is Anna with them?" I asked. The upside of Anna's disappearance would be Tinkie's safety.

"Clive's trying to find out. In the meantime, I'll call Oscar. He's friends with the owners of the Peabody. If Oscar asks, the hotel security can arrange to keep an eye on Vivian and her grand-parents." She had her phone out and was dialing.

"Excellent plan, Tink." Vivian was out of our reach, but Anna was unaccounted for. If she was crazy enough to frame her own niece, no telling what she might do to keep control of her great-niece.

"This isn't good," Samuel said. "If Anna wants to hurt Hedy, Vivian is the way to do it."

Tinkie relayed the situation to Oscar, who assured her he would handle it. She'd just hung up when the phone rang. Tinkie nodded. "Clive, did Marcus say where Anna had gone?" Her grip on the phone whitened her knuckles as she listened for several moments. "Thank you, Clive," she said before lowering the phone.

"Did he know where Anna is?" I asked.

"Anna and Marcus had an argument yesterday. About Hedy." Tinkie didn't try to hide her worry. "Anna threatened to quit and Marcus told her to take a week off. He made arrangements for his parents to take Vivian on a trip."

"What did they argue about?" Was it two murderers at odds with each other, or an innocent man who'd awakened to the possibility of a viper in his home?

"Clive didn't know."

"The upshot is Anna's whereabouts are unaccounted for. If she is the killer, she's on the loose."

The hospital room was bright and sunny. Babs reclined against several pillows, the TV remote in her hand. She greeted us with a wan smile. "What's shaking?" she asked.

I admired her spunk. "You're lucky to be alive."

347

"Tell me. It should come as no surprise I've given up smoking."

Smiling, I patted her ankle. "Do you know who did this?"

"Chief Jansen asked the same thing. I don't. I guess it's the same person who killed the other girls."

Tinkie slipped to the other side of the bed and took Babs's hand. "We're worried the killer will strike tonight. Can you help us?"

"I'll try." Babs eased forward and I plumped her pillows. Her skin was a pasty gray and her red hair sprouted in clumps.

"Did you notice anyone around your cigarettes?" I asked.

She punched off the television and sank back with a sigh. "Dr. Sawyer said the poison was in a cigarette. It could have been inserted into my pack at any time."

"At the blues club did anyone get close enough to your stuff to slip a poison cigarette in with your regular brand?" Tinkie got a glass of water and held it for Babs to sip.

"There was a woman . . . Hedy and I went to the bathroom. We had a pitcher of margaritas and a couple of guys at our table." She thought a moment. "I left my cigarettes. When I sat down, one of the guys said a woman had bummed a cigarette. He pointed at her, but she was going out the door."

"What did she look like?" Tinkie and I were in symphonic mode again.

"Short, dark hair. Didn't see much else. She was out the door and gone."

"Did Doc Sawyer give a prognosis?" I asked.

"He said I was lucky to be alive. They're monitoring my heart. He's ordered tests to see if permanent damage was done. He seemed hopeful."

"Doc's a good guy." I had to get to Jansen. "We'll bring some real food when we come back," I told her. "We've got to dash."

"Pull up a chair." Chief Jansen motioned to two wooden armchairs. "I had a call from Sheriff Peters, and he urged me to hear you out. He sets quite a store by the two of you."

"He told you about the gris-gris?" Jansen made me feel like I'd been sent to the principal's office.

"I should arrest both of you."

Tinkie and I scooted our chairs closer to Jansen's desk. "That's not necessary," Tinkie said. "We're here to tell you everything we discovered."

"Spill it," Jansen said.

"Marcus's nanny, Anna Lock, is really Hedy's aunt, Anna Blackledge. She fits the description Joey Mott gave of the woman who followed Hedy and Babs from Ground Zero. We believe

349

she bummed a cigarette from Babs's pack, which gave her opportunity to slip the poison to Babs."

"All very interesting, but why would Hedy's aunt want to frame her for multiple murders?"

This was going to take a while.

We continued with the revelation of Anna Lock/Anna Blackledge and her reasons for potentially being angry with Hedy.

To his credit, Jansen listened and made notes. When we finished, he leaned on his elbows. "You think Anna Lock is seeking revenge for the death of her brother two decades ago?"

"We think it's possible," I said. "We have no solid evidence. But we felt compelled to tell you what we'd discovered. We gave you our word."

He nodded.

"Anna knew Hedy's background. She knew how to implicate Hedy. Planting gris-gris bags, using poisons that can be grown locally. It's possible Anna influenced Marcus against Hedy for the past two years," Tinkie said. "Our client has been framed. My fear is that someone else will die tonight. Karrie Kompton told us she's the top candidate to win. She may be the next target."

"But to kill innocent people for something that occurred so long ago just to frame a young woman who is technically her niece." Jansen adjusted his suspenders. "Why now?"

"Opportunity and the child. If it's the child Anna wants, this is the perfect chance to get her." I could see he wasn't convinced, and I didn't blame him. Tinkie and I had woven a lot of stray threads into a tapestry that vindicated our client. "You have to take this seriously."

"One thing I promise. Anna Lock or Anna Blackledge won't come near any contestants or their desserts tonight."

I nodded. "Thank you."

"Now, since Mrs. Richmond here is a shutter-bug for the papers, do you have any photos that show Anna in attendance at the pageant events?"

"I never noticed her, but isn't that the point?" Tinkie asked. "I mean, if she were intent on murdering the girls, she'd be subtle."

"Except for Brook, none of the girls were killed at an event. The killer works behind the scenes," I said.

"That's true," Jansen said. "Janet Menton was poisoned in pastries and Babs Lafitte was in a parking lot. We found the cigarette butt with traces of the poison."

"This last event is a dessert competition," Tinkie said. "The contestants will be allowed into the Viking kitchen at two o'clock. Dessert will be served at a final gathering tonight at seven. Karrie Kompton may be the next victim. Mrs. Phelps asked me to help watch over the final event. I told her I would."

"It's going to be a long day," Jansen said.

23

The deputy guarding Hedy's hotel door was young, handsome, and smitten with my client. When I said her name, his face lit up.

"Go get some coffee," I told him. "I'll be with Hedy until you return."

"The chief told me not to leave this post."

"Up to you." I shrugged. "It's in Hedy's best interest to have someone monitor her every move. Seriously, she's innocent, and her best defense, if anything else happens, will be your alibi. I have no intention of allowing her to leave this room, so if you need a bathroom break or coffee, I'll stay with her until you return."

Apparently I was unconvincing. He called Jansen and got his boss's okay before he nodded his thanks and trotted down the hall for a ten-minute break. Jansen might play favorites with the rich and powerful, but he also inspired loyalty in his men.

I tapped on the door and Hedy opened it. "Where's Eddie?"

"Coffee." My task was to tell Hedy about Anna Blackledge without sending her into a panic. Oscar had found the senior Wellingtons and

Vivian at the Peabody Hotel, and hotel security was watching over them. For the moment, Vivian was safe.

"Eddie's a good guy," she said.

In contrast to the last time I saw her room, it was neat and orderly—except for the cooking supplies piled on the bed. I took note of the ingredients. "What are you baking for this evening?"

"A chocolate Dobostorta."

"Which is?" Tinkie and I never made it to the dessert phase of our cooking lessons, and I had a moment of regret. I loved desserts. Especially chocolate. To be able to build something chocolate and dense and rich—that might have been worth learning.

"A six-layer sponge cake invented by and named for a Hungarian baker, Jozsef C. Dobos. It's rich and moist and one of the best chocolate cakes I've ever tasted. For all its elegance, it's plain. I'm hoping the other contestants create ornate desserts and my Dobostorta will stand out."

"A fine strategy." The chocolate she intended to use was a brand I'd never heard of.

"Imported," she said. "Holland. The art of this cake is in the chocolate. I want it to be dark and lush."

Just to be on the safe side I checked to be sure no one had tampered with the chocolate package. It was sealed.

"So eggs, milk, flour—all provided at the cooking school?" Unless Evangeline Phelps stood guard over the larders, those ingredients were vulnerable.

Hedy nodded. "I turned in my ingredient list and they'll have everything there, except for specialty items, which must be brought into the school sealed." She waved at supplies on the bed. "I'm going over at two and start cooking. I want the cake to cool and chill in the refrigerator. It's better that way."

She slumped down on the bed. "Actually, I just want this to be over. I don't even care about winning anymore. The title won't make a difference. Marcus will never allow me to see Vivian, much less gain partial custody of her. Maybe he's right. Maybe I should walk away and let her have the privileged life he can give her."

I almost gave her the "buck up" speech, but instead I sat down beside her. Tinkie was the gentle, nurturing partner; I was the kick-ass and complain side of the equation. But Hedy didn't need anyone to fuss at her. I suspected she did a better than average job of doing that to herself.

"You can't give up on Vivian," I said. "Samuel told me a little about your background, Hedy. You can't see this as a repetition of what your mother went through."

She didn't bother to deny it. "Maybe we are cursed. Maybe there's something to the Marie

354

Laveau thing that Marcus accuses me of. He would do anything to keep me away from my baby girl."

"It may not be Marcus. At least not totally." Now was the moment to tell her the hard news. "Hedy, this is going to upset you, but you need to know. Anna Lock, the nanny taking care of Vivian, is really Anna Blackledge, your aunt."

Her head tilted slightly as if the words were rolling around in her head. "My aunt? That's crazy."

"Perhaps, but it's true nonetheless."

"My father's sister is a nanny for the Wellingtons? Why? The Blackledge family has tons of money."

I swallowed. "To keep Vivian away from you." I felt like I'd punched her a few times with a nail gun. I doubt it would have hurt her worse. I gave her the last of it. "It's possible she's influencing Marcus to keep Vivian from you."

"Why would she do such a thing? I've never done anything to her." Instead of getting angry, she was hurt. "I don't even know her."

"I don't have answers, Hedy, but I intend to find them. Vivian is with her grandparents in Memphis. Anna isn't with them. Someone Tinkie knows is watching over Vivian to be sure she's safe. I'll find Anna and see what she has to say."

"My aunt wants to take the thing I love most

away from me. For what? For revenge? To get even with me because my father died?"

I could only shake my head.

"This is sick." She staggered as if her legs were failing. "I don't understand a person who would do such a thing."

"The question is, is she vengeful enough to poison three young women just to frame you?"

"I can grasp Marcus doing something to have his own way. I know him, and I know how ruthless his family can be. But Anna Blackledge is my blood. She's Vivian's great-aunt. I can't . . ." She wiped away her tears. "If this is true, Anna is evil."

"I agree." I spoke calmly, hoping to settle her down.

"The Saulnier family is cursed. My mother warned me. She told me if I pursued custody of Vivian, terrible things would happen. Those girls are dead because of me."

This had to stop. "You don't truly believe your mother serves Marie Laveau or that she'd sacrifice you to that kind of life." I was stern.

She thought about it. "The mother I have now isn't the woman who gave birth to me."

"What do you mean?" The confession creeped me out, just a little.

"When my father was alive, Mom was always laughing. She planned picnics and adventures. She and Dad loved those swamps. They knew

356

the dangers with the snakes and alligators, but there was a wealth of healing plants and herbs there. My mother was highly regarded in the community as a healer. People came from as far away as Baton Rouge. And my dad, well, his designs were so different, so earth-friendly. Several movie stars hired him to design their homes. They had a wonderful life, and I can remember feeling wrapped in their love. That's what I want for Vivian. To feel that love."

Her voice faded and she stared down at her hands. The energy seeped from her leaving dismay.

"And then your father went into the swamp one day and . . ."

"And never came back," she whispered. "My mother was wild with worry. I was very young. She put me in our second boat, and we went looking for him. We hunted for a long time until she went back and called for help to search. Of course, delaying while we hunted for him alone went against my mother. Folks said she wanted Dad to die, that she'd killed him and put his body in the swamp for the alligators to eat."

That was an image no child should have in her head. "But you knew it wasn't true."

"And Mom did, too. My parents loved each other. When the search and rescue found his boat and declared Dad dead, it was the end of my mom. She started to believe those crazy things she heard—that she'd killed him. She'd taken him from a safe, cultured environment and pulled him deep into the dangerous swamp. Folks believed she served the darkness and said Dad was some kind of sacrifice. From the first grade at school, the other kids were afraid of me. I was that Saulnier girl, daughter of a hoodoo woman, daughter of a murderess. The other kids wouldn't play with me, except for Samuel."

"He's a good friend."

"Yes, he is. Daddy's family, the Blackledges, tried to get custody of me, but somehow Mom managed to hold them off. Fighting for me kept her from killing herself. She said Dad had been unhappy as a child and he wouldn't want the same fate for me. So she fought. She fought hard. And ultimately we stayed in the swamps by ourselves. I went to school, but almost no one talked to me. I made good grades, did the work, and dreamed about getting out of that place and going somewhere built on solid ground with people who laughed and had fun."

She took a deep breath, her blue eyes wide and honest. "I grew ashamed of my mother and the way she behaved. I only wanted to be normal."

The fantasy of normalcy wasn't such a huge dream. By most standards it was modest. "You were working on your college degree. You were finding those things."

"I made some friends who didn't know or care

about my childhood. My professors said I was smart and talented. I had scholarships. I was about to climb out of that place."

"And then you got pregnant." The story was as old as humanity.

"I never realized how lonely I'd been until I found out I was pregnant. I was consumed with love for my child. My entire world shifted focus, just in that instant. And when Vivian was born, Sarah Booth, there is nothing like that feeling. Nothing in the world."

Now it was my turn to pull back from the conversation. I'd never held my child, but I felt the loss nonetheless. I went to the window while I sought composure. "You have every right to share custody of your daughter."

"I've begun to question what's right for Vivian," she admitted. "I don't want her growing up ashamed of me or my family, suffering the whispers and innuendos."

"You don't have to stay in the swamps, Hedy, but if you want to earn a living for your child, you need a better plan than vying for a pageant title."

"I know that. But why should I worry about any of this when I'm likely going to prison for murder."

She sounded so hopeless. "You haven't even been charged and I don't think you will be. Jansen is smart. He'll follow the evidence, and it doesn't lead to you." I was surprised that she was ready to throw in the towel.

"I'm not a fool, Sarah Booth. Chief Jansen has delayed doing anything because he's under pressure from the mayor and town not to destroy the pageant. When it's over, Karrie will be crowned, and I'll be taken away in cuffs."

"It won't play out that way. Have some faith in me and Tinkie." She'd raised an interesting point. "So you think Karrie is the top dog?"

"I hear she aced the 'Taste and Copy.' " Hedy joined me at the window. Her room also gave a view of the cooking school across the street. "She got every component exactly right. Almost as if—"

"Almost as if someone fed her the ingredients?" I finished.

"Exactly." Hedy shrugged. "But what does it matter? Maybe the true test of any competition is who is willing to do whatever is necessary. Based on business models these days, Karrie has exactly what it takes to be a winner. She's ruthless, greedy, willing to stomp anyone in her path. Maybe those are the qualities necessary to be the best."

"Not true. Integrity, honesty, and fairness matter. Even when it seems they don't."

"That hasn't been my experience." She gathered up her recipe purchases and put them in a reusable shopping bag. "I should start baking."

"I don't think the cooking school is open until two."

"Then why is Karrie Kompton going inside?"

I glanced back out the window and caught Karrie's backside disappearing into the building. "That's not right," I said.

"And you were just giving me the speech on honesty and integrity. Life isn't fair, Sarah Booth. No matter how much we wish it were."

Tinkie was at the cooking school, and I needed to back her should Karrie break bad. "Don't give up, Hedy. You aren't a quitter," I reminded her as I opened the door.

Eddie was back at his post, a half-finished coffee in one hand and a newspaper in the other. "Keep her safe," I told him.

"Yes, ma'am." He was so eager to fulfill his job I felt a twinge of pity for him. Hedy was a sweet and basically kind woman, but with her plate overflowing, she might not notice what an admirer she had in the young cop.

As soon as I cleared Eddie's sight, I took off at a run. Karrie's presence at the cooking school could be innocent. Or not. But Tinkie was there, and Tammy's haunting vision motivated me to keep an eye on my partner.

The day had grown hot and humid when I crossed the street and hurried to the cooking school. Mrs. Phelps was in the lobby and unlocked the door. "Sarah Booth, what can I do for you?"

"I saw Karrie Kompton come in." I glanced behind her. "Where's Tinkie?"

"That's what I'd like to know. Where is Mrs. Richmond?" Evangeline Phelps was a tad hostile. "She promised to help me but she hasn't shown up. Karrie was gracious enough to run an errand for me because I can't leave my post here. Since Mrs. Richmond didn't show up, there was no one else to help me."

"Tinkie didn't show up here? She left half an hour ago to come over."

My panic finally touched Evangeline. "Where could she be?"

"That's what I need to find out." I sprinted back to the Alluvian. When I entered our room, I knew Tinkie wasn't there. The sizzle was gone. A pale sheet of hotel stationery centered my bed.

"Gone to Panther Holler to check for Anna. Tinkie."

I dialed her cell phone—which rang on the bedside table beside her camera. Tinkie had launched a frontal attack on Anna and didn't even have a way to contact me or call for help.

Something was very wrong. Tinkie was in trouble. I felt it. She'd never abandon her obligation to Evangeline Phelps, nor would she take off on a dangerous assignment without telling me —and without her phone.

She'd also taken the Caddy, which left me with no wheels. Never again would I ride with someone else. Not even for cooking lessons.

I went downstairs, wondering if I could talk police officer Eddie out of his patrol car. Not likely. Samuel was my best bet. I found him getting ready to leave for the day, but he turned over the key to his pickup truck without question.

"Drop it off at Buster's Bluetop when you finish. You can leave the key with the bartender," Samuel said.

"Thanks."

"Make sure Hedy doesn't go to jail for something she didn't do."

"I'll do my best."

The old Ford had seen better years, but it started with a roar. As I circled the hotel, I saw the Caddy parked where we'd left it. I felt like someone had whacked me in the stomach with a sledgehammer.

I killed the engine, jumped out of the truck, and ran back into the hotel. Samuel was chatting with Betty, the concierge, and a couple of clerks.

"Did you see Tinkie leave?" I asked. Everyone in the hotel knew her by now.

Samuel shook his head, but Betty spoke up. "She left about an hour ago."

"Was she alone?"

Betty thought about it. "She walked out the

door by herself, but there was a woman close behind her."

"Can you describe the woman?" I wanted to tear my hair and scream.

"Petite, good figure, a bit older than you, and short, black hair. Oh, and she was wearing dark sunglasses."

"Did Tinkie say anything?" Surely she'd tried to leave a clue. Even a small one.

Betty frowned. "She's always so friendly, but she walked out like the Queen of Sheba. I thought she was rude, which wasn't like her."

"Betty, call Chief Jansen," I said. "I think Tinkie's been abducted. She left a note in our room, which may have fingerprints on it."

Betty whipped into action.

I retrieved my cell phone from my pocket and dialed Coleman. When I heard his voice, my control crumbled. "Can you come to Greenwood now?"

"What's wrong?"

"Tinkie has been taken by someone."

"I'm on the way," Coleman said.

As I closed the phone, it rang. Hoping it was Tinkie, I answered quickly.

"We're wrapping the shoot today." Graf's voice was filled with sunshine and glamour. "I can catch a late flight to Memphis or the first one in the morning. What's your preference, my love?"

"Tonight." I managed to say it without crying

"Sarah Booth, is something wrong?" Graf asked.

There was no simple way to tell him how awfully wrong things were.

24

"Sarah Booth, what's happened?" Graf asked for the third time.

I wanted to answer him, but I was struggling to maintain control. "It's Tinkie. I think she's been abducted. By someone bad." I moved from the front desk reception into the plushly carpeted lounge area. The sounds of the hotel were instantly muffled. I was alone with Graf. "Madame Tomeeka warned me, and I failed to protect her."

"I'll catch the next flight to Memphis, rent a car, and be there as soon as I can."

Graf wasn't angry, he was worried. I had an overwhelming desire to feel his arms around me. "I can't call Oscar." Coward that I was. No way in hell was I going to phone Tinkie's husband and tell him I'd let Tinkie fall into danger.

"Don' worry about Oscar now. You'll do what's necessary," Graf said. "Who has her?"

"I'm not certain. Tinkie left a note saying she was headed to the Wellington home, but her car is in the parking lot. The hotel receptionist said a woman left right behind Tinkie."

"The killer?" Graf sounded as if he were feeling his way through a minefield.

"Maybe."

"And maybe not. You don't have enough evidence to jump to conclusions. Don't call Oscar until you know something. There's no point scaring him into a coronary if Tinkie caught a ride with someone and went off on a lead."

Bless Graf for his sensible approach. "Thank you. Please hurry home, okay?"

"I'll make them fly the plane as fast as it'll go."

I hung up and found myself facing Franz Jansen. He stood in the doorway, eavesdropping without a smidgen of apology. Tension radiated from him. "Are you certain Mrs. Richmond is missing?" he asked. "This isn't some ploy to distract me while your client takes a runner?"

"Tinkie isn't in the hotel, but her car is parked in the lot." I kept it calm and factual. More than anything I wanted Jansen to laugh and call me a fool. "She left a note. In the room."

Jansen took my elbow and led me to the elevator. It wasn't until the doors closed behind us that he loosened his grip. "Are you okay? You're not going to faint or do something embarrassing, are you?"

I shook my head. "I have to find her."

"We will," he said. "I don't want Oscar Richmond or worse, Avery Bellcase, riding my ass 'cause Mrs. Richmond got hurt in my town." Beneath his gruffness was something else.

As we exited the elevator I said, "You've got the good ole boy shuffle down pretty good, but I sense money isn't the driving factor here." I stopped at the door. He was the head lawman in charge of the search for my partner. His agenda had suddenly become vitally important. "What is?"

"Let's take a look at that room." He edged me aside with his body and took the key card from my hand.

We entered and Jansen scanned the interior, from the cell phone and camera on the table to the white stationery and the clothes scattered around. The room exuded emptiness, and he picked up on it, as I had.

"Money and power control a lot," he said. "Like it or not, the wealthy expect preferential treatment. I don't mind going a little extra in some cases, as long as justice is served." He twitched his mustache. "My motto is 'whatever it takes.'"

"My friend's life may be in danger. I have to know you'll run over anyone blocking the path. Even the Wellingtons."

"I should be insulted, Miss Delaney, but instead I admire your directness. I'll return the favor. If

Marcus is involved in these murders, or the abduction of Mrs. Richmond, or illegal means of gaining custody of his child, he'll be arrested. I can't guarantee he'll be punished, because money has a way of tipping the scales of justice. But he will be arrested and charged."

"It's possible Marcus is a dupe of Anna Lock."

"I'm having a hard time justifying why Anna Lock would poison three people to frame her own niece."

"Are the actions of any killer reasonable?"

"Some more than others," he said. "But I agree with your assessment that Miss Kompton is our next target."

"Damn!" I'd forgotten all about Karrie. "She's over at the school. She was helping Mrs. Phelps, which may or may not be dangerous. If Karrie is the killer—"

Jansen slapped the microphone hooked to his shirt. "Timothy, get Linda and head over to the cooking school. Pick up Miss Kompton and hold her."

"On what charge, Chief?"

Jansen thought a moment. "Book her for prostitution. That'll cook her bacon and get her all churned up. Tell her if she cooperates, we won't put the charges on the books, but if she stirs up a stink, we'll book her and call Cece Dee Falcon."

"Yes, sir." There was doubt in the young officer's voice, but he didn't question his boss.

"Your men are well trained and loyal," I said. "Even when asked to step all over the law."

"The women, too." For the first time I saw a glint of humor. "Now let's get to work. Time's a'wasting."

"What do you know about Anna Lock?"

"A whole lot more than I did this morning." He pulled a latex glove from his pocket, picked up the note, and bagged it. "I want this finger-printed and the room, too. Did you check the cell phone for messages?"

I could have slapped my own forehead. "No."

He did that and frowned. "You recognize these numbers?"

I took a look. "Her husband or me or Cece at the newspaper."

"No strange numbers, at least on the cell phone. I'll check at the front desk for a record of calls to the room. Come on."

"Where are we going?"

"To pay a visit on the Wellingtons of Panther Holler."

"You're taking me with you?" I was surprised.

"You'd be more dangerous running around here on the loose."

I left a message at the reception desk for Coleman and got in the patrol car with Jansen. The chief made the necessary radio calls to the sheriff's office.

"I don't have authority outside the city of Greenwood," he said. "We play this like a social call. We're there for a chat about Hedy."

I nodded. I didn't care if we had to wear cow costumes and dance the polka as long as we got in the gate and I could search for Tink. We'd just cleared the city limits when Jansen's car radio crackled.

"Chief, Miss Kompton isn't at the cooking school. Mrs. Phelps said she left half an hour ago."

"Find her," Jansen said into the radio.

He was about to put the radio away when it squawked again.

"Chief, this is Eddie." He sounded like a kicked dog.

"Go ahead," Jansen said.

"Miss Blackledge got away from me."

I thought Jansen's grip would crush the microphone. "She did *what?*"

"She put something in my coffee. She said it was a vanilla flavoring. I passed out and she's gone."

"I'll deal with you when I return. Find her. Find her and arrest her for assaulting an officer, suspicion of homicide—anything you can think of. Put her in jail and swallow the key if that's the only way you can keep her there."

"Yes, sir."

Jansen flipped on the lights and siren and

stepped on the gas. The patrol car jumped forward.

"Hedy wouldn't run without good cause."

Jansen only tightened his grip on the steering wheel. His hands were massive. "Hedy left under her own power, according to Eddie. She drugged him somehow. Something fast acting. Mrs. Richmond left a note. She walked out seemingly of her own volition, except for being followed."

"And Karrie left on her own, too. But that doesn't mean they weren't coerced in some fashion."

"My men will have more facts shortly."

The cotton fields were a blur as we whizzed down the highway. Tinkie was a fast driver, but Jansen was no holds barred. We hit a bump and only my seat belt kept me from striking the roof of the car.

"Tinkie discovered something." I wracked my brain trying to think who or what it could be.

"Maybe she's at Panther Holler right now, one step ahead of us."

"Let it be true," I whispered under my breath. "Chief, there weren't any unusual calls on Tinkie's cell phone, but could you check and see if Hedy received any calls?"

He radioed a female officer in the hotel lobby. In a moment I heard her report back. "There was one call from Mrs. Richmond's room to Hedy's room thirty minutes before Hedy left, and another call to the room shared by Voncil and Amanda Payne."

"Thanks." Jansen cast a swift glance at me but never slowed. "You're really convinced someone forced your partner into persuading Hedy to slip protective custody."

I nodded, knowing that only something vile could have made Tinkie put Hedy's future, if not her life, on the line.

"You look a little green around the gills," Jansen said. "Want me to pull over?"

"No. The sudden stop from light speed might be my undoing." I pointed to the wrought iron gate of the Wellington home. "Besides, we're here."

"And not a moment too soon," Jansen said. His hand went to his holster to check his gun as we drove slowly down the shell drive to the big house.

The front door stood wide open. The senior Wellingtons were out of town, but Marcus could be home. Or Anna.

Jansen inched forward, finally coasting to a stop at the sweeping steps that led to the shady gallery. "This doesn't look good."

I reached for the door handle but he stopped me. "Stay in the car."

"Give me a gun." Firearms weren't my thing, but I was determined to protect myself.

"Do you have training?"

I shook my head. "I can use a gun, though."

"Not today. Stay in the car." He got a spare gun out of his glove box and tucked it into his belt.

As soon as Tinkie was safe and I was back at Dahlia House, I was signing up for the weapon classes Tinkie had begged me to take. And she was, too. She always protested, saying the ear protectors would mess up her hair. Too bad.

Jansen glided up the steps to the door like a big cat. He had become adept at concealing so much about himself that I wondered if the people of Greenwood knew anything about their police chief. I'd vastly underestimated him.

When he disappeared inside, I got out of the car and followed him. There was no way I intended to sit patiently while Tinkie might be in danger.

I made it in the door before Jansen grabbed me and snatched me inside. "I told you to stay in the car."

"I have to find Tinkie."

He roughly pulled me behind him. "Act like a fool and I'll put you in the back of the car," he warned me.

Gun moving slowly from left to right, he stepped into the empty parlor.

"Marcus!" he called. "It's Franz." His footsteps were silent as he moved deeper into the house. I followed, stepping into his tracks.

"Marcus!" Only the whir of the air conditioner answered his call.

We checked the downstairs room by room, and Jansen motioned upstairs. He headed up with me right on his heels. There had been no sign of Tinkie—or anyone else—in any of the downstairs rooms.

We found Vivian's bedroom, a paradise of stuffed animals and bright colors. "The child and the grandparents are in Memphis," I reminded Jansen.

He nodded. "Marcus?"

I shook my head.

He headed down the carpeted hall, opening doors swiftly and entering fast. When we were certain no one was home, Jansen waved me into the nanny's room. "See what you can unearth," he said. "I'll take Marcus's room."

I expected to find a closet full of black dresses with sensible shoes, but that wasn't the case. Anna-the-nanny dressed expensively, if blandly. The most impressive feature of the room was a wall of books, her personal library. She was a student of American literature and had a fine collection of first editions.

Tucked beneath her undies I found a photo album. I put it on the bed to examine later, but the slick leather slid to the floor. Photos spilled across the carpet. Some were old family pictures, but most documented the childhood and adolescence of a blue-eyed, dark-haired boy named Larry Blackledge, Anna's brother. Hedy's father.

From young boy to teenager to college student, Larry's life was recorded by a loving hand. The last photo was of the young man standing beside packed bags. The note under it said, "Destination Pearl River swamps." That was when the Blackledge family lost their young man to a Saulnier woman.

There were also pictures of Hedy. They were infrequent and taken at a distance, but they covered the years of her childhood and adolescence.

Dozens and dozens of photographs showed Hedy pregnant. Anna's obsession was clear to see. I gathered them up to show Jansen. The snapshots weren't concrete evidence that Anna was behind the poisonings or anything else, but they clearly showed her compulsion where Hedy was involved.

The rest of the room yielded no secrets. While I'd expected to find resource material on poisons in the bookcase, there was none. Jansen's luck was no better. If Anna or Anna and Marcus were poisoning the pageant gals, they weren't keeping the how-to manuals or ingredients in the house.

"I'll check the grounds," Jansen said when I joined him in the hallway. "I've put out a call for Marcus. No one has seen him lately, which worries me."

"He might be at Clive's horse ranch," I said. If Anna had lost her mind completely, it was possible she'd harmed Marcus. Jansen was right to be concerned.

"I'll have an officer check. Let's hope he's there. We could stand some positive news."

When we arrived back at the hotel, Coleman was waiting in the Alluvian lobby. He shook hands with Jansen, who wasted no time listing the pertinent facts. Marcus, he'd learned, was not at Clive's and hadn't been seen all day.

"So the facts are, Tinkie left the Alluvian and a woman resembling Anna Lock followed her," Coleman said. "Except for the note, there was no indication where she might be headed?"

"None. But she wasn't at the Wellingtons' and there was no sign she'd ever been there. She forgot her phone. And her camera, which has virtually grown to her hand in the last week. She never goes anywhere without it." The same thought struck Coleman and me.

"The camera," we said.

"She might have recorded a picture." Jansen made the leap with us.

We all three hustled to the room.

Holding the camera where we could see it, I played back the images. In the last shot, Voncil Payne stood in the bedroom doorway wearing a wide smile.

"Crap. I was certain Tink had left us a clue," I said.

"Maybe it is." Coleman put a warm hand on my shoulder. "We should check it out. Maybe Voncil saw something."

"You two go ahead," Jansen said. "I'll check at the cooking school to see what I can find. It's almost time for the contestants to begin preparing their dishes. Perhaps Hedy will put in an appearance."

"She'd be in her room if she could," I said. "Someone forced her to drug Eddie and leave."

"Your partner was the last person she spoke to. If they're together, you'd tell me, right?" Jansen asked.

"Let me just say if the two of them have run off together and didn't bother to tell me, you won't have to arrest them. I'll kick their butts into a cell."

"She means it," Coleman said.

A smile lifted one corner of Jansen's mouth. "Yeah, I think she does."

While Jansen took an elevator down, Coleman and I walked to Voncil and Amanda's room. I'd known all along this case was trouble. I'd let Tinkie talk me into it, even when my gut screamed something awful was brewing.

"Tinkie is okay," Coleman said, as if he could read my mind. We'd always had a connection when it came to danger.

"Graf and Oscar want us to dissolve the agency. They say it's too dangerous, and maybe they're right." I could be honest with Coleman in a way I couldn't with anyone else. "I didn't want to take this case. Tinkie pushed it. If we closed the agency, Tinkie could become a photojournalist."

"And that's safer?" Coleman asked. "Some people fear exposure in the newspaper far more than jail."

"Good point."

"And what would you do, Sarah Booth?" He wasn't asking as if I had no options.

"I could focus on my acting career."

We turned the corner and were almost at the door of the Paynes' room. "Funny how a dream isn't ever what we think it is," he said.

I couldn't look at him. It wasn't that acting wasn't satisfying. It was. But in coming home to Zinnia from New York as a failure and reinventing myself as a private investigator, I'd found something of value in myself and my heritage. It wasn't that I wanted to act less, but I needed to hold on to the me I'd discovered in Zinnia.

Coleman read it all over me. "You've never done the expected."

"Maybe I'm just hardheaded," I said. "Maybe I fought too hard to make Delaney Detective Agency a success."

"Maybe you love the work and helping people," Coleman said.

We stopped in the empty hallway and stared at each other. We'd been high school crushes and antagonists, newfound friends when I returned from New York, and in love and almost lovers for most of a year. Now we were . . . more than friends. Coleman knew me in a way no one else ever would.

"If Tinkie has gotten hurt because of—" I stopped.

"Because of you?" He shook his head. "Give her credit for being smart and capable, Sarah Booth. She makes her own decisions. As do you. While others may hurt *for* us when we're injured, no one bears the blame but us."

I couldn't speak around the lump in my throat. I nodded and Coleman brought his fist against the wooded door.

"Mrs. Payne, it's Sheriff Coleman Peters, from Sunflower County. I'd like a word with you."

25

"Sheriff who?" Amanda Payne opened the door wearing cut-off shorts and a stained T-shirt. She wiped her hands on her shorts. A bowl of carrots and a small grater were on the bed. "Sarah Booth, what's wrong?"

"Is your mother here?" I asked.

"She went out about an hour ago." She frowned. "Why is the sheriff of another county here?"

"We're concerned about some Sunflower County residents," Coleman said smoothly. "We're hoping your mother saw something when she went to Tinkie Richmond's room."

Amanda waved us into the room. "Please don't tell anyone what I'm making," she said. "The girls are so competitive. Surprise is one of the big elements in this last part of the contest."

"Amanda is highly ranked in the competition," I told Coleman. "Along with cooking, she writes and performs great songs."

Amanda blushed. If she wasn't shy and modest, she was damned good at faking it. "Thank you, Sarah Booth. I don't know where Mother is. She gets so uptight about these contests. She makes me more nervous than I already am. When I told her that, she got angry. She left without saying where she was headed."

"She spoke with Tinkie at eleven forty-five this morning." The photo in the camera was time-stamped.

"I haven't seen her since about eleven, maybe eleven thirty." Amanda sank onto the bed. "She was pretty upset with me, said I was ungrateful . . ." She clamped a hand over her mouth. "More than you wanted to know, I'm sure. She's probably shopping. She likes to hit the stores when she's emotional."

"Any idea why she might visit Mrs. Richmond?" Coleman asked.

Amanda bit her bottom lip. When Tinkie did it, she was sexy. Amanda reminded me of a lost child. "Mrs. Richmond called Mom, and Mom was eager to talk to her. I don't know what Mrs. Richmond wanted, but Mom's plan was to convince her to include pictures of me in the paper. Mother is obsessed with publicity. She's always aggravating the media. She doesn't understand people think she's half a bubble off plumb when she keeps on and on. In the world of celebrity news, I'm a nobody. She just can't accept that."

To think I'd envied Amanda the presence of her mother to help support and encourage her. Voncil was directing her daughter's life, and down a path that Amanda found stony and hard.

"Do you want this title?" I asked her.

She shrugged. "I need the money. *We* need it. But I'd just as soon stay home and write my songs. I like that, and I could support myself while I finished my college degree." Her cheeks flushed as she straightened her shoulders. "This pageant stuff . . . it's always been Mother's dream, not mine."

"Why don't you tell Voncil?" I asked.

"This is the last contest. I'm twenty-three. If I don't win this, I'm too old. It'll be over without a confrontation. My mother doesn't handle resistance well, especially from me."

"And if you win?" Coleman asked.

"It's only a year. I'll do everything the Viking people want, and I'll do a good job. After that, I can pay off our debts, settle down to write songs, finish college, and live my life."

"Voncil will accept that?" My take on Voncil was that as soon as Amanda wasn't pageant material, Voncil would push her to marry well and have a baby. Amanda was the main course meal ticket, even if the menu changed drastically.

Amanda's smile was tender. "Mom gets desperate sometimes. We've had some rough times, especially when I was younger. But she wants what's best for me. She pushes too hard, but only because she wants me to have the security she never had."

"It's hard for a single mother with a child," Coleman said. "Are your parents divorced?"

"No. My dad died when I was fourteen. Heart attack. He was only thirty-nine. Mom used to say they were lucky they got an early start and had me because his days were numbered."

Coleman put a hand on her shoulder. "When your mother comes in, tell her to contact us," he said. "Amanda, maybe I'll ask Chief Jansen to put an officer on you, just to keep you safe."

"That isn't necessary. Karrie's going to win. If not her, then Hedy."

"But it would make me feel better to know you're safe."

"Okay. Now I have to get back to my preparations."

We stood up to leave when her cell phone rang. She held up a finger as she checked the caller I.D. "It's Mother," she said.

She started to say something several times but stopped short. Her expression shifted from concern to worry to outright horror. "Sarah Booth Delaney and the Sunflower County Sheriff are here right now. I'll tell them. They'll help." She reached out a hand to us.

"What's wrong?" I asked.

"Mrs. Richmond has been taken hostage by a woman in a blue SUV. Mother's tailing them."

Coleman took the phone from her hand. "Mrs. Payne, Sheriff Peters here. Where are you?"

He took the pen and paper I offered and made quick notes. "Stay with them. I'll call you from my cell phone as soon as we're on the way."

He gave Amanda back her phone after he'd programmed her mother's number into his.

"What should I do?" Amanda asked. "Is Mom in danger?"

"I think your mom is safe. Get ready for the cooking event," I told her. I wasn't clear on what was happening, but Coleman was ready to bolt from the room. "Finish the pageant. We'll call when we know more," I assured her.

. . .

When Amanda's room door snicked shut behind us, I grasped Coleman's arm. "Where is Tinkie?"

"Cottondale Plantation, a B&B on the Tallahatchie River just out of town."

"Are we going there?"

Coleman tucked my hand through his arm as if he meant to escort me, while what he really intended was to frog-march me down the hall as fast as he could go. "Chief Jansen, his men, and I will handle this. You'll stay in the hotel where you're safe."

"Coleman, that is not—"

"You're not going. End of story."

Red swam behind my eyes—and no doubt shot from them. "You can't stop me. You have no jurisdiction here. Jansen is police chief of Greenwood, not the outlying county."

Coleman sighed as he hustled me into the elevator. "After what happened at the Carlisle plantation, I won't let you walk into danger." When I started to interrupt him, he grasped my shoulders and gave me a light rattle. "Listen to me, Sarah Booth. My heart can't take it." His blue eyes snapped with frustration and hurt as he forced me to look into his gaze.

The elevator door opened to reveal Chief Jansen, his mustache twitching as he stared at the two of us, caught in such an emotional clinch.

"Some women just can't keep their hands off a

man in uniform." He motioned for us to follow him. "Back in my younger days, the women were on me like flies on a . . . never mind." His mustache almost hid his smile.

No matter what Coleman said, I would defend my partner. They'd have to handcuff me to a wall to keep me away. Tinkie was in danger. I had to be there.

The chief and several of his best officers were gathered in the hotel's office. Coleman relayed Voncil Payne's message. Jansen took charge instantly. "I'll coordinate with the Leflore County Sheriff. We'll have units all over Cottondale. They won't get away from us."

Coleman tried Voncil's number. No answer. He dialed again, and the call went straight to voice mail. "This isn't good," he said.

"We'll go in quietly," Jansen said. "No grand-standing. A plainclothes officer can check in, scope it out. The B&B is spread out with cottages tucked among twenty acres of gardens. When we locate the women, we'll move in with a team. We don't want a hostage situation if we can avoid it."

I sat quietly, hoping in the rush of strategic planning, Coleman would forget about me. I was not that lucky.

As the officers filed out, Coleman confronted me. "I'll bring Tinkie back safely. I want your word that you won't sneak out there." He put a hand on my shoulder. "Give me your word."

385

This was not a moment to hedge or prevaricate. If I promised, I was honor bound to uphold it. "I can't."

Jansen and his men stood at the ready. All eyes were on Coleman and me. "Sarah Booth, Tinkie's life hangs in the balance. This is a serial killer who has already murdered two women and almost killed a third. If you won't give me your word, I'll cuff you to something."

He would, too. "This is wrong. Tinkie is my partner."

"Your word."

I could be killing my own partner with my unwillingness to yield. "You have it."

They were gone within seconds.

Fifteen long minutes passed where I devoted myself to fretting. Betty brought me a steaming cup of fresh coffee. "The sheriff sure cut you off at the knees," she said, "but he's concerned for your safety."

I couldn't muster an argument, but I also couldn't sit on my hands and wait. I realized there was a course of action I could pursue. I could search for Hedy. In the rush of concern for Tinkie, everyone had forgotten two pageant competitors were missing.

The top two candidates. And the Wellington heir.

My promise not to go to the B&B to search

for Tinkie didn't include hunting for Hedy or Karrie.

I jumped to my feet. I wasn't going to wait at the Alluvian like I'd been gut shot.

"Well, you just came back to life. Where are you off to?" Betty asked.

"I'm going to find Hedy and Karrie." I pushed through the Alluvian's revolving door and into the midday heat of downtown Greenwood. When I checked my watch, it showed one o'clock. An hour to go until the contestants began cooking.

I went to the school and peered through the front windows. When someone in the back walked by, I waved frantically. Evangeline Phelps came with a key.

"Did you find Mrs. Richmond?" she asked.

"No. Do you know where Karrie Kompton went when she left?"

Evangeline grasped my shoulders. "What in the world is going on? The police asked me the same question. Karrie was only here for a few minutes. She never left my sight."

Right now the pageant outcome wasn't my top priority. "Do you have any idea where Karrie went? Did she say anything?"

Her mouth made a small O. "No, not again. Has something happened to her?"

"Please, work with me. There's not much time."

"She got a call. I don't know who it was, but she left in a hurry."

"Do you remember anything she said?"

She rubbed her temples as if she might massage the information out. "She said something about how much she hated the smell of horses. She jabbered on in that smug tone of hers, and I was busy, so I didn't pay a lot of attention."

"Any idea who she was talking to?"

"She was excited. That's all I know."

"Thanks." Before I pushed into the street, I stopped. "Mrs. Phelps, have you seen Hedy?"

"No. Is she—" She couldn't bring herself to ask.

"I'm sure she's fine. She's just out of pocket."

"This pageant was supposed to give a young woman an opportunity to build a career while exposing nine others to internationally famous chefs, photographers, actresses, and media attention. It was meant to bring tourism to Greenwood, but it's been a nightmare."

She was about to snap and I didn't have time to console her. "This is no one's fault but the killer," I said. "You did a good thing. Someone else forced the pageant into tragedy. And we'll catch that someone and see that justice is served."

It wasn't much of a speech in the grand scheme of Lincoln or Kennedy, but it would have to suffice.

The Alluvian's lobby was quiet, and I ducked into the office. If Coleman returned with Tinkie,

I wanted to be there. Betty looked up from a stack of pages and signaled me over.

"Find anything?"

"No." I collapsed into a chair and Betty returned to her work.

I was missing something. I had to think clearly and piece the clues together. Both Hedy and Karrie left after receiving phone calls. Tinkie left after talking with Voncil. All three women had disappeared around the same time from within fifty yards of each other.

It stood to reason that somehow, their disappearances were linked. And somehow Marcus was involved. Was he missing or part of the whole Anna scheme?

The sound of rustling made me glance over at Betty. She held a small box of pastries. "Care for a fresh peach tart?"

The plain white box stopped me. Janet Menton had died from poisoned pastries in a similar box. "Where'd you get those?"

"From the cooking school. They had a class yesterday and Mrs. Payne picked them up for me. She's so thoughtful, and a fine baker."

I slowly brought out my phone and called Amanda's room. When she answered, I spoke calmly. "You said your father died of a heart attack?"

"Yes, why? What's wrong, Sarah Booth? You sound strange."

"Was an autopsy performed?"

"No. There was no need. He had a heart attack." Her voice started to rise. "What's this about?"

"Just one more question. Does your mother garden?"

"Why are you asking me this?"

Voncil was the killer. Tinkie had been trying to tell me with the photo in the camera. "I need you to answer the question. Does Voncil grow flowers?"

"Yes, she has a green thumb. So what?"

"Thank you, Amanda." I hung up. "Betty, please call Coleman and Jansen. Voncil Payne is the killer. Tinkie found out and must have confronted her. The B&B is a diversion. Tinkie isn't there and neither is Anna Lock."

"Where are they?" Betty asked as if I were Carnac the Magnificent.

"I don't know."

"What do I tell Chief Jansen?"

Inspiration struck. Babs might know something. The boldness of Voncil's scheme almost took my breath away. She'd deliberately changed her appearance to resemble Anna Lock, and then she'd stood in the parking lot talking to Babs while Babs smoked the cigarettes she'd poisoned.

Betty had the chief on the phone and she tried to hand it to me. I backed away. "Tell them I

390

believe Voncil has Karrie and Hedy as well as Tinkie. She's taking out the competition to clear the path for Amanda. She'll kill anyone she perceives as standing in her way."

"You tell him," Betty said.

But I was sprinting to the Caddy. The hospital was only minutes away, and I wanted to speak to Babs face-to-face.

The redhead was much improved. She was applying mascara when I burst into her room.

"You've come to tell me I'm wanted at the pageant," she said, fluffling one of her sad tufts of hair. "I knew they couldn't go on without me."

"Do you remember talking to Voncil the night you were poisoned?" I asked.

"Sure. I was in the car listening to Big Mama Thornton. The song was almost over when Voncil came up and tapped on the window. Made me jump. She wanted to know if I'd go for a drink with her, but it was time for me to turn in."

"That's it?"

Babs shrugged a shoulder. "I smoked a cigarette while we talked. My last one. I've quit."

"What did Voncil say?"

"That Amanda was going to win." She touched the mascara wand to the tips of her lashes. "She was so smug about it. When I mentioned Hedy was the front-runner, in my opinion, she laughed.

She said Hedy had a date with destiny and her aunt would put her behind bars."

"You're certain she said her aunt?"

"Positive. I remember because it sounded kind of crazy, but I'd been drinking and then I got sick."

The only way Voncil could have known about Anna was from either Marcus, if he knew the whole story, or Anna herself. I had to go back to the Wellington estate. I had to find Anna, or at least a clue to where she'd gone.

Jansen and I had shut the Wellingtons' front door, but it stood wide open once again. Marcus's car was parked askew at the front steps. Uncertain of Marcus's role, I stopped fifty yards down the driveway and got out of Tinkie's car. This time I didn't have a lawman with me, so I chose stealth as my partner.

I zigzagged through the thick trees and shrubs until I was at the house. Moving along the foundation, I found several windows to spy in. The house looked strangely empty. The temptation to call Coleman or Jansen was strong, but I resisted. I had nothing to report. Yet.

A side staircase led to a second-story door. The private entrance to Anna's room. I took the stairs quickly and quietly and peered into Anna's bedroom through a window.

My heart almost stopped. Marcus Wellington

sprawled across the floor, a pool of blood beside his head. Inches away was a chartreuse stiletto that belonged to my partner.

"Shit." I fumbled with the phone and punched in 911. That done, I tried the door—locked. "Shit, shit, shit." Panic numbed my fumbling hands. Tinkie's shoe centered the pool of Marcus's blood. Where was she?

Creeping down the stairs, I angled to the front door. I was about to step through when the phone rang.

Coleman was upset and worried. "Where in the hell are you?"

"The Wellington estate. Marcus is injured, maybe dead. He's on the floor of Anna's room. I've called the EMTs, but I'm going in."

"Stay out of that house!" Coleman didn't order, he commanded. "I'll be there in twenty minutes tops."

I didn't want to go in the house, but I had to. Tinkie might be injured. She might need my help. "Good-bye, Coleman." I carefully closed the cell phone and turned the ringer to vibrate.

Looking down the empty entrance hall of the house, I heard a grandfather clock ticking. Time may have run out for me and my partner.

26

All around me the Wellington house creaked and whispered. Perhaps it was my imagination, but it sounded as if someone walked overhead. The hesitant, uneven steps of a drunk or someone injured.

I wished mightily for a gun. Concern for Tinkie and even a little for Marcus pushed me up the stairs. The probability of danger from any direction kept my feet moving slowly.

As I neared the second-floor landing, I thought of Graf. He'd be home tonight. My mind grasped that image, Graf so handsome on the front porch of Dahlia House, Sweetie Pie at his side, smiling as he welcomed me home. That would be my reality in a few short hours, as soon as Tinkie was safe.

Jansen, his men, and Coleman were on the way but I couldn't wait. I couldn't follow my gut impulse, which was to run out into the sunshine. Someone was shuffling around, and it might be Tinkie, wounded and needing my care.

On the landing I picked up a solid pewter candelabra from a table. A potential weapon. Not as good as a gun, but what the hell.

Irregular footsteps sounded directly behind me.

Whirling, I raised the candelabra and found myself face-to-face with Tinkie. She wore one shoe, and one foot was bare.

Her blue eyes were impossibly wide, the black of her pupils consuming the iris. Her face contained no expression. She came toward me.

"Tinkie?"

She never even blinked.

"Tinkie?" I reached out to her, but she brushed past me toward the second flight of stairs.

"Tinkie!" I grabbed for her, catching the beaded top she wore.

She pulled away, but I knew she wasn't lucid. She was able to walk, but she was in some kind of dream-state. "Tinkie!"

She jerked hard. The stretchy material of her top gave. To my horror, she shrugged free of the sweater. For one split second, she tottered at the top of the stairs before she fell.

"Tinkie!"

She never uttered a sound as her body whumped and slammed against the oak treads.

It seemed I reacted in slow motion. I wheeled, clattering back down the stairs. From the corner of my eye I saw Hedy slumped against the wall in the upstairs hallway. Another foot protruded from a bedroom across the hall. Karrie? I couldn't tell. Tinkie was my priority.

"Tink—!" My voice broke. My lungs squeezed with fear that she was dead.

I was almost to the stairs when someone grabbed me. I wrenched and confronted a petite woman with black hair cut to frame her face. Not Voncil—Anna. Before I could react, she held up a palm and blew something into my face.

Almost instantly my body began to numb. I tried unsuccessfully to blink away the sensation that I'd lost control of everything. I struggled to lift my hand, but it refused to obey.

Anna reached up. In hazy slow motion she drew the black wig from her head revealing the glitzed do of . . . Voncil Payne.

She pushed me toward the stairs. I caught the rail and looked down at Tinkie in a crumpled heap. It didn't matter. Nothing mattered. I just wanted to sleep.

Regaining consciousness, I found myself in the passenger seat of Voncil's SUV. While my brain seemed to be waking, my muscle control was nonexistent.

Cotton fields flashed by the window in the afternoon sun, and I tried to calculate how long I'd been completely out of it by the slant of sunlight and the length of the shadows when we passed trees. I'd say at least five o'clock. What had happened in the three hours that had elapsed? I had no recollection of anything.

Coleman had surely found Tinkie, Hedy, Marcus, and Karrie by now and gotten them help. Surely. While I had the urge to cry, my body was incapable of the follow-through. Good thing, too. I didn't want to draw Voncil's attention. Somehow I had to energize my unresponsive arms and legs and prepare to kick some butt.

"Sarah Booth?" Voncil said.

I pretended to be deaf.

"You can't fool me."

Obviously she was right. She'd caught me off-guard and delivered a coup de grâce of epic proportions with whatever crap she blew in my face. My partner was terribly injured, and I was a captive.

I tried to speak. My vocal cords were as paralyzed as the rest of me.

"Don't worry, Sarah Booth, it's the scopolamine. Another happy benefit of plants in the deadly nightshade family. Belladonna, atropine, scopolamine—so useful in subduing, or killing, those who get in my way. Although digitalis is also useful. Took out my husband like a charm."

Words jammed my throat, but I couldn't force them out. I sat like a wooden dummy staring straight ahead.

"You want to hurt me, don't you?" Voncil asked. "I know. It's a terrible feeling to be so . . . constrained. But I didn't give you a fatal dose. You might be interested to know scopolamine is often known as the zombie drug. Excellent tool when things unravel a bit too fast."

I struggled to speak, to lift a finger.

"Don't get your panties in a knot about your partner. There's nothing you can do. I checked her pulse before we left. She's dead. No need to fret about it."

When the rage and blind fury cleared from my brain, the sun had dipped a little farther in the west. The road surface had changed drastically. The SUV bumped and lurched down a rutted lane that cut through brakes and fields left fallow for too many years. Weeds towered over the SUV.

Voncil was taking me somewhere isolated. Whatever she'd given me had stolen my will. I had to snap out of it.

I shifted slightly. To my surprise, Jitty had managed to squeeze in between Voncil and me. Jitty in a headscarf, a gingham dress, and a white apron. She'd put on at least two hundred pounds, yet she was still able to wedge onto the seat. My brain couldn't grasp it.

"You lookin' like your great-great-uncle Gustave after the mule kicked him in the head." Jitty smiled, and I couldn't believe how fat her cheeks were.

I wanted to shush her, but I couldn't make the sound.

"Don't worry your pretty little head about Voncil hearin' us," Jitty said. "We committin' telepathic communications. Fancy, huh?"

Since I couldn't answer, Jitty had the entire stage. "That's right. For once you can't interrupt what I've got to say and you're gonna have to listen."

Tinkie! I projected the image of my best friend lying broken at the bottom of the stairs. If Jitty could read my mind, she might as well put it to good use.

"I can't be with Tinkie, Sarah Booth. I'm your haint. I can only be with you. Trust that Coleman is doin' ever'thing possible. You have to focus on savin' yourself."

Why are you dressed like Mammy from Gone with the Wind? I squeezed that thought out of my frozen mind.

"Sarah Booth, you are an embarrassment to the world of advertisin'. If you could look at me, you'd see I'm not Mammy. Think syrup or pancakes or grits. Back when you were a baby girl, you used to think I was married to Uncle Ben. Now that was some foolishness. Uh-huh, I see that light dawnin' in your eyes."

Mrs. Butterworth. I shot the name at her knowing it would get her goat.

"I am *not* Mrs. Butterworth, and don't you say that again. You know me. Another great icon of American cooking. My pancake mix was the first ready-made one ever created. And on top of that, Nancy Green portrayed Aunt Jemima, the first living trademark. Now that's some facts to chew on."

I did indeed recognize Aunt Jemima. *Not very PC.*

She laughed. "I'm dead, I'm black, I'm a ghost, and I never age. PC doesn't count much in my world. And I'm honorin' a fellow black woman. Nancy Green was born in Kentucky as a slave. She was fifty-six years old when she went to the World's Fair as Aunt Jemima and served thousands of pancakes while she chatted and told stories with the crowd. She was a huge hit. Ain't that somethin'?"

Why are you doing this now?

"You need some help, and I'm here to give it."

Did you bring the Pillsbury Doughboy for kung fu moves?

"Very funny. Glad to see that even though you've been dosed with a drug that could be fatal, you've kept your sense of humor. I thought maybe you'd appreciate my suggestions. But if you're handlin' this on your own, I'll—"

No. Stay.

While the manifestation of Jitty in a SUV driven by a psychotic serial killer might be a measure of my own insanity, I needed Jitty. She gave me courage, and I surely needed some of that as I tried to figure out how to get myself out of the mess I was in. Tinkie, I could not think about. Coleman was on the case, and I had to trust in him.

Why Aunt Jemima? Jitty operated in strange and unusual ways, but there was generally a method to her madness. Aunt Jemima was symbolic.

Keeping my thoughts going in one direction was a difficult feat. I had a mental image of Aunt Jemima with a platter of pancakes or pouring syrup over said pancakes or holding a bowl of grits, but I couldn't summon up an association of anything except breakfast.

"Aunt Jemima represents somethin'. A good hot breakfast served by somebody who cares. She's the image of motherhood, always there, in the kitchen, smilin' and ready to put that hot breakfast on the table."

Jitty had still not answered my question. I concentrated on filling my lungs with air and feeling my rib cage expand. Sensation was returning.

"Aunt Jemima wasn't selling foodstuffs. She sold home and love and security. Someone who cared." Jitty leaned forward. "Do you get it?"

At last Jitty's point hit home. I cut my eyes to let her know only to discover she was gone. There was only Voncil, gripping the steering wheel as we bumped over the rutted road.

Jitty had reminded me that someone would be waiting at home for me, relying on me to be there. I had to fight. The powerful drug wanted to rob me of my will, but I couldn't let that happen. Once Voncil got within grabbing distance, I was going to clamp hold of her, and like a snapping turtle, I wasn't going to let loose until it thundered.

The SUV hit a pothole and threw me into the door. The impulse to lift my arms and protect myself from further jostling was strong, and I felt a tingle race through my body as it started to come back to life.

Voncil laughed as she hit another hole and I was nearly thrown off the seat.

"Sorry about that," she said. "We're almost there. I'll take care of you and have time to get back to Greenwood, change, and be on hand when Amanda wins the title."

In the distance I saw a building. Not an old barn, but not a house, either. It looked like it had once been a business of some kind. Auto repair. Something with multiple bays. I didn't have a good feeling.

I clenched my fist and my fingers responded, slowly, but they responded. I tried the other hand with the same result. I moved my toes up and down at my command. Could I run? Could I fight? I didn't know.

Voncil stopped. "Time to get out and walk," she said. She picked up my hand to assist me in exiting. I didn't move a muscle.

"Sarah Booth!" she snapped. She got a rope from the back of the vehicle. "Move it."

I didn't dare to breathe. She drew back her fist as if to slug me, but I didn't flinch. Her laughter was deep and rich. "You're still under, aren't you? I thought you were coming out."

She grabbed my arm and tugged and I allowed my body to follow, mimicking the behavior of someone with no will.

I tested the ground beneath my feet, amazed I could walk. It occurred to me I could shamble off into the weeds, but Voncil would smack me in the head with something. I had to hold on to the fact that each passing moment gave me more control over my body.

"Let's go," Voncil ordered. Instead of heading into the building, which I now realized was a defunct boat building facility, we walked through weeds and rubble around it. In the distance I heard something, a soft murmuring.

We trudged along a weed-choked path, Voncil holding my arm. A short distance from the building I realized where we were going and what Voncil intended to do.

In a matter of minutes we were on the banks of the Tallahatchie River. And we were about to have a Billie Joe McAllister moment, except I was what Voncil intended to throw off the bridge.

27

Voncil marched me to the bank of the river. It wasn't a steep drop, and the water was yellow and sluggish. Not exactly what one would call dangerous. But if I couldn't move my arms and swim, I could easily drown in two inches of water.

Voncil stepped toward a goat trail that led down the steep incline.

The buzz of a cell phone stopped her. She pulled my confiscated phone from her pocket and waited for voice mail to kick on. She smiled at me. "Doc Sawyer calling for you, Sarah Booth. Isn't he the older doctor who knew so much about poisons? He almost ruined my plans."

A beep signaled a message had been recorded.

"Just for kicks," she said, retrieving it. She switched the phone to speaker.

"Sarah Booth. Doc here. Call me. I'm at the Greenwood hospital. It's urgent."

Voncil snapped the phone closed. "Nothing you can do or say. Down to the water," she ordered.

I stood like a zombie. If she wanted to drown me, she was going to have to work a little harder.

"Now." She tugged my unresponsive arm. "Get moving, Sarah Booth," she ordered. She gave me a little push. I stumbled and almost fell but recovered before I tumbled down the bank.

"Oh, for heaven's sake," she said. She was panting from exertion. She brought out my phone again and went through the contact list. "Let's see, I recognize Cece Dee Falcon." She placed the call.

The sun was hot on my back, and I caught a whiff of the river smell of leaves and mud.

"Miss Falcon," Voncil said. "I thought you should know I have Sarah Booth as a hostage. I'm going to tie her and leave her in a dangerous place. What I want you to do is call the Leflore County authorities and tell them that Amanda will win the title tonight. If they ever want to see Sarah Booth alive, my daughter will be crowned the winner and receive all of the scholarships and prizes that are her due. If that doesn't happen, Sarah Booth will die a slow and terrible death."

She snapped the phone closed and slid it back in her pocket. "Get down that bank," she ordered.

Or what? The magical thought came to me like a bolt of lightning. Voncil had no weapon that I could see. She had only the zombie-like effects of a drug, which had begun to wear off.

She pushed me and this time I fell to my knees. Both fists clutched dirt. I'd learned a few things from watching bad guys in cowboy movies. I brought the dirt up and threw it in Voncil's eyes.

Blinded, she was an easy target, even for a half zombie. I swung hard with everything I had. My fist connected with her jaw and literally lifted her off the ground. She landed like a sack of disjointed bones.

Though my fingers were clumsy, I managed to tie her sufficiently with the rope she'd brought. She was coming around as I finished.

"You can't leave me here," she said. "What if something wild comes out of the woods? It'll kill me?"

"New dish," I said. "Pate of bitch."

I removed my cell phone from her pocket. There were dozens of calls from Coleman, Jansen, and Graf. I dialed.

"Sarah Booth," Coleman said, relief clear. "Where are you?"

"I'm okay." I gave him my location as best I could and let him know Voncil was subdued. "What about Tinkie?" I couldn't get rid of the image of my partner in a heap at the bottom of the stairs.

"She's still unconscious. She's at the hospital in Greenwood and Doc and Oscar are with her. Nothing was broken, but . . ."

"But what?" If the fall didn't kill her, surely she'd be okay.

"Tinkie was overdosed with scopolamine."

There was no reason to tell Coleman my own experiences with the drug. "But it isn't fatal, right? She'll come out of it?"

He sighed. "It's touch-and-go. It's like she's fallen into a deep sleep and can't wake up."

Madame Tomeeka's vision. Tammy had seen this, but I would not accept it. "She'll be okay. Doc is there. He'll pull her through it."

"No one is giving up."

"Doc will save her."

"He's doing everything possible. Oscar too. Cece and Millie are on the way. Calm down and tell me what happened?" Coleman's voice was a lifeline for me to cling to.

I gave him the details as I limped toward the SUV. "How are Karrie and Hedy?" I asked.

"Both are okay. Karrie is demanding the contest be rescheduled."

"And Amanda?"

"She's at the police department. She voluntarily turned herself in. Jansen doesn't believe she's involved, but she's waiting there."

"And Marcus?"

"Severe concussion. He's in a coma. They've flown him to Memphis. His parents have been alerted and they're with him. Anna Lock is caring for Vivian. She had nothing to do with the murders, except for perhaps inspiring Voncil to pin the murders on Hedy."

"How so?"

"They met last year at a gardening seminar in Jackson, Mississippi. They talked. Anna had pictures of Vivian. She told Voncil about her family. I think the idea for killing the contestants and framing Hedy has been growing for a long time in Voncil. She knew Amanda hated this life. This was her last chance."

"She admitted to me that she killed her husband."

"She has a lot to answer for. Where are you?" he asked.

"I'm on my way." I'd reached the SUV. The hospital in Greenwood was my destination.

I'd come to despise the smell of hospitals. My gut reaction as I hurried into the Greenwood emergency ward was one of fear and anxiety. I rounded the corner to the swinging doors clearly marked for hospital personnel only. I was about to push through when a strong hand clamped my wrist.

"You can't go in there, Sarah Booth."

Coleman held me in place. I was about fed up with people grabbing and tugging on me. "I need to see Tinkie." When I finally looked around, I saw Hedy sitting in a plastic chair in the hallway. Tears dripped from her jaw.

"No, you don't." His tone, the deep lines etched in his face stopped me short.

"I have to see her."

He put his arm around me and pulled me close. "Oscar's with her. Let him have this time. Doc thinks it may be short."

If he'd punched me in the stomach with a blackjack it wouldn't have been more brutal. "That's not possible. If she didn't break anything in the fall, she'll be fine. She was moving. I saw her. Just like Hedy and Karrie and me. And we're over it. We're fine."

Coleman's gaze scanned over me. "Are you sure you aren't injured?"

"As sure as I need to be. It's Tinkie I'm worried about. Let me see her."

He pushed the door open a crack, but he kept his hand on my arm.

Tinkie lay on a stretcher, a white sheet drawn up to her chin. The bright emergency room lights seemed to enclose her in a cone of white, as if the heavens had opened up a path for her to ascend. Oscar sat in a chair beside her, his head bowed as he grasped her hand, clinging to her, holding her to this time and place.

I tried to wrench free of Coleman, but he enfolded me in his arms and held me against his chest, which I pounded with bitter fury. "I have to see her."

"She's Oscar's wife. Let him be with her."

"No!" I struck him repeatedly. "No! No!"

Gentle hands took my shoulders and I turned to find Hedy beside me. Those huge blue eyes, so much like Tinkie's, were filled with tears.

"I'm so sorry. This is all my fault. I never should have involved you."

"Let's get her out of here." Coleman edged me away from the door. "There's nothing you can do, Sarah Booth. A specialist is on the way from Boston, but Doc says there was permanent damage to Tinkie's nervous system."

There was no point arguing, but I would not accept that diagnosis. I'd seen Tinkie. She'd been zombie-like, but no more so than the three of us. "What's wrong with all of you? You're quitting. You've given up. That's Tinkie in there we're talking about. Without her, what's the point of Zinnia or Sunflower County or any of this?" I waved my arm wildly, encompassing the world, the universe.

"Sarah Booth, there's nothing we can do. Doc—"

I shook off their hands. "I have lost too much. Do you hear me? I have lost too much. I will not let Tinkie go."

I brushed past him and stomped out of the hospital. Hedy was right on my heels. When I tried to get in the SUV, she blocked the door. "You shouldn't drive. You're too upset."

That she was right only made me more furious.

"Stop telling me what I can't do. Why don't you tell me what I can?" I glared at her. "I wish you did know the secrets of Marie Laveau. I wish you were a conjure woman who could whip up a spell and save my friend."

Hedy took a deep breath. "I can't, Sarah Booth. But I know someone who can. No promises, but she might be able to help."

"Who?"

"My mother." She reached out her hand, and I put my cell phone in it.

An hour passed while I paced back and forth outside the hospital as night fell around me. Jansen was trying to sweat some answers out of Voncil. The beauty pageant dessert event had been cancelled. Graf had landed in Memphis and was on his way. I welcomed the news, but it brought me no comfort. My focus was Tinkie. Totally.

An old truck careened into the hospital parking lot on two wheels. It halted at the curb near where I stood and Hedy and Samuel scrambled out.

She handed me a small vial. "Mother can't make any promises. I told her about the scopolamine, part of the deadly nightshade family. She knew the properties and effects. She said to try this and she would pray for your friend."

"What is it?" I examined the vial in my hand.

"A lot of things. Samuel helped me find all the ingredients I needed."

"What do I do?"

"Blow it into her mouth and nostrils. She has to inhale it. That's the way Tinkie was originally poisoned, right? The same way as us?"

I didn't know. No one knew except Voncil, and she wasn't talking. Not even when Amanda begged her to help Tinkie. Not even when Cece questioned her. I hadn't heard the details, but I had no reason to believe Cece had been as restrained as law officers.

I looked at the vial. Did I believe this could help Tinkie? I had no other choice. I had to believe, and I had to believe it with every ounce of my heart. Tinkie had taught me that lesson— I couldn't go into something like this half-assed. I had to be in it 100 percent.

Every time I'd checked in the last hour, the medical team was expecting death at any moment.

"How will you get in?" Hedy asked.

"That's where you come in."

"I don't like the sound of this," Samuel said.

"I need a diversion. Start a fight, pretend you were raped, say that the high school or church or something is on fire. Do whatever it takes to get Coleman and the rest of them away from the door."

Hedy nodded. "We can do that." She took

Samuel's hand and they huddled together, plotting, as they approached the ER entrance.

I followed, the vial unnoticeable in my hand. At the door, Hedy and Samuel paused. They nodded to each other, and then burst inside. Hedy was screaming rape and Samuel was grabbing and fake punching her.

All hell broke loose. In the melee, I slipped past Coleman and everyone else and into the room where Tinkie remained unchanged. Oscar faced me, the sorrow and sadness falling away to reveal fury. "Get out!" he demanded.

So this was what Coleman had hoped to spare me from.

"You dragged her into this dangerous job. You made her love it. This rests at your feet, Sarah Booth."

Each word was like the slice of a knife blade. I forced myself into the onslaught. Nothing mattered except that I get to Tinkie.

"Stay away from my wife." Oscar's eyes were crazed with grief and anger. "I'll hurt you if you so much as touch her."

I ignored him. I was only three feet from Tinkie. I felt his hand grip my shoulder, but I shrugged him off. I flipped the top off the vial and dumped the white powder into my palm. With my free hand I opened Tinkie's mouth. I blew the contents of the vial into her face.

Oscar struck me sideways in a tackle, and I

went flying across the room. We tumbled in a heap against the wall as the door burst open and Coleman and Graf rushed in. Coleman restrained Oscar while Graf pulled me into his arms.

"Are you okay? Are you hurt?"

"I'm fine." If my legs had snapped in six places, it wouldn't have stopped me from struggling to my feet. I had to get to Tinkie. It was time for her to wake up.

I pushed Graf aside and hobbled to the stretcher. "Tinkie! Tinkie!" I shook her shoulder.

"Don't touch her!" Oscar thrashed about in Coleman's grip.

"Tinkie." She lay there, pale, barely breathing, unmoving. "Tinkie." Her skin was cool, too cool. There was no response whatsoever. I kissed her cold cheek.

The monitors that registered her fading life force beeped and then screamed as a flat line scored across the screen.

"Damn you, Sarah Booth," Oscar cried out. "Damn you. She's gone, and I wasn't even holding her hand."

28

The vial lay crushed and empty on the floor where I'd dropped it in the struggle with Oscar. I touched Tinkie's cheek. Surely someone could help. Someone had to help. I wasn't strong enough to do this alone.

Doc Sawyer stopped at the door. A doctor and nurse pushed their way through.

"No." It was the only thing I could say.

The doctor checked the machines. "She's gone," he said. He glanced at his watch. "Time of death, nine twenty-eight." He reached for the sheet.

"No!" I struck his hand hard. "Oscar!" I spun, looking for him. "Oscar!"

Oscar's anger was gone, drained. There was nothing left but grief.

"Oscar." I dragged him toward the stretcher. "Kiss her."

Oscar put a hand on my arm, the touch of a dead man. "She's gone, Sarah Booth."

"Kiss her," I commanded.

The room was frozen. No one moved to help me or stop me. The horror of my actions held everyone in place.

I had to believe. To rely on what I knew to do. "Kiss her," I told him. I waved the doctor and nurse out of the way.

There was no fight left in Oscar, and he leaned down and gently kissed her lips.

Without urging, he kissed her again. "Tinkie!" he whispered her name.

The beep of the machine was like an explosion in the room. A tiny green spike blipped across a black screen. Tinkie!

I went to the other side of the stretcher and picked up her hand. "Tinkie. Come back to us."

The numbers on the screen began to climb as the faintest tinge of pink touched her features. When I pressed my lips to her cheek, it was warm with the flush of life. "Tinkie!"

She opened her blue eyes and stared at Oscar and then me. "Hey," she said softly. "I had the weirdest dream."

Sweetie Pie and Chablis cavorted in the front yard of Dahlia House, wiggling and wallowing in the sun-warmed grass. Graf and I had slept in. Though it was near noon, we were on the front porch sipping our first cup of coffee. We'd discussed none of the events of the previous night, and they lay between us like quicksand. For now, we could skirt the edges and take comfort in the joy of each other's company. Tinkie was safe. Voncil was behind bars. Chief

Jansen had obtained an order from the judge for Hedy to see Vivian once the Wellingtons brought her back from Memphis.

Karrie Kompton and Hedy had been disqualified from the competition, and Amanda had withdrawn.

"Do you want to go back to Greenwood to see Crystal Belle Wadell crowned as Miss Viking?" Graf asked.

I shook my head. Tinkie had been transferred to the Sunflower County Hospital, though she was insisting she was well enough to go home. I had no reason to go back to Greenwood.

"Who's that coming up the drive?" Graf asked, rising to his feet.

Coleman's brown patrol unit led several others. It wasn't until the entourage stopped and the passengers climbed out that I recognized Hedy, holding the hand of her beautiful daughter, Vivian. Cece and Oscar joined them.

"I'll put on a fresh pot of coffee," Graf said.

"Let's help him," Coleman said, nudging Cece along clearly against her will.

"We'll all help," Hedy said, following them inside.

Oscar and I were left alone on the porch. "I didn't mean what I said, Sarah Booth. It wasn't your fault."

I could have told him I hadn't wanted to take the case. I'd argued against it. I could have told him Tinkie pressed me into it. None of it was important. "It doesn't matter," I said.

"It does to me, and to Tinkie. In the hospital, when she couldn't move or communicate, she heard everything I said. My wife is highly agitato with me." The tiniest smile flitted across his face. "I love the fact she's pissed off. She can stay mad at me every day for the rest of her life, and it'll be okay. Anything is preferable to her being so . . . sick."

"I know what you mean." I sat down on the steps and patted a place for him beside me. "You don't have to apologize. You were scared."

"I knew Tinkie wanted to keep the agency alive. It wasn't you, but I lashed out, anyway. I owe you my life, Sarah Booth, and the way I treated you shames me."

I put my arm around his shoulders and gave him a squeeze. "Forget it, Oscar. I have."

"You won't close the agency? Tinkie made me promise to ask."

I weighed the truth against what Tinkie needed to hear. "I won't make any decisions until my partner can make them with me."

"Thank you, Sarah Booth. If you quit now, Tinkie will never forgive me."

"Go grab a cup of coffee, Oscar. Ask Hedy to come out here."

In a moment Hedy and Vivian slipped out the heavy front door. Abandoning the adults, Vivian skipped into the yard to play with the dogs. Hedy sat beside me. "What's up?" she asked.

"Are you okay?"

"The best I've been in years. I have my daughter and, thanks to you, I've breached the wall between my mother and myself."

The wind kicked up, ruffling the bright green leaves of the sycamore tree. Aunt Loulane used to say that when the wind rattled the tree branches, a spirit was passing by. "What was in the potion you made for Tinkie?"

Doc Sawyer had analyzed the powder and found nothing except finely ground salt, baking soda, and trace amounts of cocaine.

Hedy put a hand on my back. "What does it matter? It worked."

"But Doc said—"

"Don't question it, Sarah Booth. You believed it would work. You took the risk and administered it. And it worked. Accept the miracle with grace and stop trying to find a reason to disbelieve. The true art of conjure has as much to do with believing as with any medicinal herbs."

She stood up. "Vivian wants to get some of her things at the Wellingtons' and see her grandparents before we leave. Marcus won't be there." A slow smile spread across her face. "He's recuperating in the tender care of Karrie Kompton."

"Good luck with that," I said. "And Anna?"

"Returned to Massachusetts. I don't believe she'll ever be able to forgive Mother for what happened to my father. She's so bitter. Now she's going to lose Vivian, too. But after some time passes, I'm going to try to talk with her. One thing I've learned is that time passes too quickly to hold anger and hard feelings. And Vivian and I have a lot to look forward to."

"Where are you going?" Dynamics had shifted on all fronts in a matter of hours.

"Hollywood, for a short time. Belinda Buck has a guest spot for me and Vivian on a television show she's producing. Your wonderful boyfriend found us a place to stay. Things are working out, thanks to you and Mrs. Richmond."

"For heaven's sake, call her Tinkie."

"Okay." She smiled. "I'll do that. And as soon as I get my first check, I'll pay you what I owe you."

The front door opened and the three most important men in my life came out together, along with one of my very best friends.

"That was some Sleeping Beauty number you conjured up, dahling," Cece said. "The fairy princess deep in the throes of a deathlike sleep. Then the magical kiss. I want an exclusive interview this afternoon."

"You'll have to get it from Tinkie," I told her. "She's the journalist in the detective agency."

Coleman avoided direct eye contact, but he

kissed my cheek. "You had me worried, Sarah Booth. But that's nothing new. When I get used to it, I'll know we're both in trouble."

We settled on the porch to finish our coffee and watch Vivian play with the dogs. She was a fiercely beautiful child, and she had no reserves about expressing her joy with Sweetie and Chablis. I was unprepared for the pounding bolt of loss that shot through me.

"I want a fresh cup." I needed a moment alone. The last week had overwhelmed me emotionally and physically.

In the kitchen I wiped the tears from my eyes. One day Graf and I would have a child to gambol on the front lawn. A child as beautiful as Vivian.

"Tick tock, Sarah Booth." Jitty's soft voice, as rich and black as the Delta soil, came from a spot near the sink.

"For heaven's sake, have a shred of compassion, Jitty. I'm wrung out. Don't start that Delaney womb shit right now."

"Shoo your company off the porch and you and that good-lookin' man get upstairs and set to work on makin' us an heir."

For some reason, Jitty's haranguing made me sadder. I put my hands over my ears. "Stop, just stop," I whispered. "I can't do this. I don't know what to do, but you have to stop pushing me."

To my surprise, when I looked around, Jitty was gone.

The curtains ruffled in a breeze. The kitchen was empty. I went to the window and gazed out upon the Delaney family plot. Jitty, no longer a chef, stood in the cemetery near the life-size headstone of an angel that marked her grave. The full skirts of her tightly bodiced gingham dress blew in the breeze. She was too far away for me to hear her, but I knew what she said.

"Dahlia House is where I heal." I repeated it softly to myself. I didn't have to speak it loud to hear the truth of it.

Center Point Publishing

600 Brooks Road ● PO Box 1
Thorndike ME 04986-0001 USA

(207) 568-3717

US & Canada:
1 800 929-9108

www.centerpointlargeprint.com

ML   1/11